Rowanwood

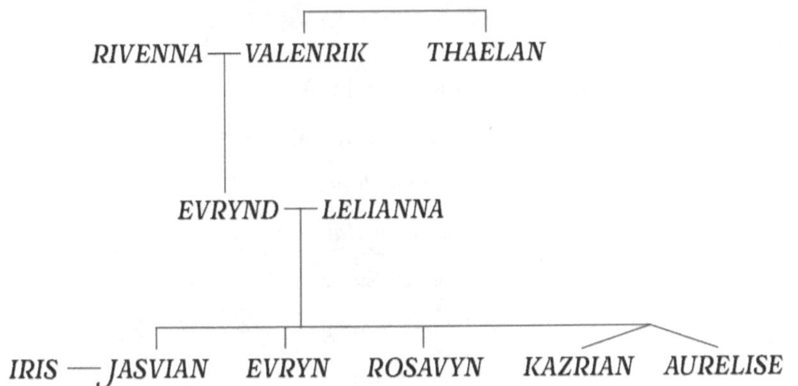
RIVENNA — VALENRIK   THAELAN
EVRYND — LELIANNA
IRIS — JASVIAN   EVRYN   ROSAVYN   KAZRIAN   AURELISE

Brightcrest

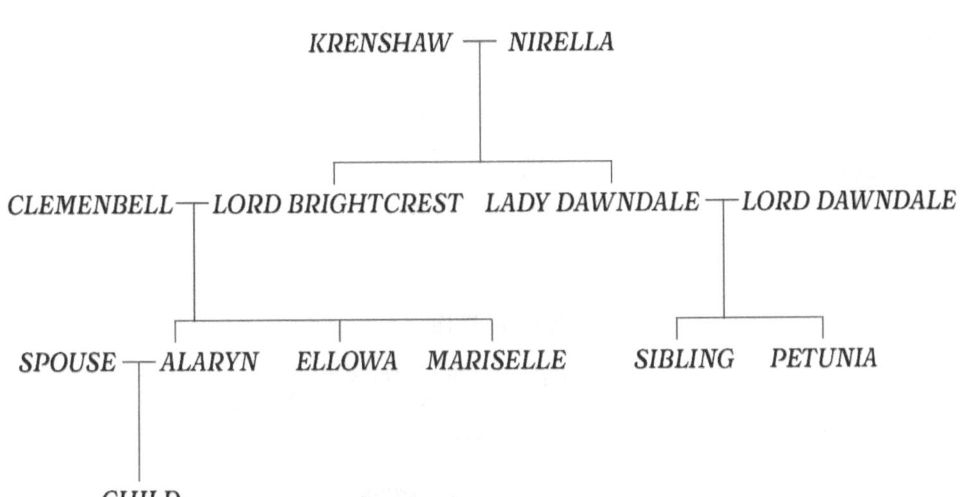
KRENSHAW — NIRELLA
CLEMENBELL — LORD BRIGHTCREST   LADY DAWNDALE — LORD DAWNDALE
SPOUSE — ALARYN   ELLOWA   MARISELLE   SIBLING   PETUNIA
CHILD

ALSO BY RACHEL MORGAN

THE CHARMED LEAF LEGACY

Tempests & Tea Leaves

Deals & Dream Spells

CREEPY HOLLOW

The Faerie Guardian

The Faerie Prince

The Faerie War

A Faerie's Secret

A Faerie's Revenge

A Faerie's Curse

Glass Faerie

Shadow Faerie

Rebel Faerie

CREEPY HOLLOW COMPANION TITLES

Of Kisses & Quests

Scarlett

Raven

RIDLEY KAYNE CHRONICLES

Elemental Thief

Elemental Power

Elemental Heir

CITY OF WISHES

The Complete Cinderella Story

STORMFAE

From Storm and Shadow

Deals & Dream Spells

RACHEL MORGAN

To those who have never felt truly loved.
You are worthy.

Chapter One

THE MOST AGGRAVATING QUALITY OF BRIGHTCRESTS, EVRYN Rowanwood decided as he urged his pegasus to impossibly greater speeds, was their persistent talent for ruining perfectly good evenings.

This particular evening had begun with such promise. Slipping away from the tedium of the Season's Opening Ball, enjoying the exhilarating rush of midnight wind against his face, and basking in the satisfaction of thwarting his mother's matrimonial machinations. Now, however, that same evening threatened to culminate in the one outcome Evryn found utterly intolerable: finishing second to a Brightcrest in a race he should rightfully win.

He'd left the other riders far behind by now, including his friend Crispin, whose shouts of protest had faded into the night leagues ago. Fin had assumed the role of this evening's designated judge, thus abstaining from the race, while Ryden was unable to participate in the night's contest. Unlike the rest of them, he couldn't escape the Opening Ball's suffocating formalities quite so easily.

Cobalt's midnight-blue wings cut through the night, leaving trails of silver sparks that faded into darkness as he and Evryn strained to close the narrowing gap. "Faster!" Evryn called out to Cobalt between gritted teeth. "We cannot lose *again!*"

But the rider ahead remained maddeningly out of reach. Their pegasus—a sleek beast with a burnished copper coat and flame-tipped wings—navigated the unofficial 'course' with infuriating skill. Each time Evryn thought he'd found an advantage, the rider pulled ahead yet again, tilting into a turn or diving around the trees that Fin had enchanted to stretch or shrink without warning, an added challenge for this evening's race.

Evryn leaned forward over Cobalt's neck as new determination surged through him. He simply could not lose this race. The thought of the inevitable gloating was entirely unbearable. Of course, there would be other consequences beyond wounded pride. The evening's unauthorized adventure had already ensured that regardless of whether he finished first or second, a reckoning awaited him at home. His mother would undoubtedly be upset. Not about the race itself; Lady Lelianna would never learn of his nighttime exploits if he could help it. It was his conspicuous absence from the Bloom Season's Opening Ball that would earn her disappointment.

It was precisely the sort of behavior she had warned Evryn against—again—but after five previous Seasons spent watching newly manifested fae preen and posture before the High Lady, Evryn would rather brave his mother's disappointment than endure another evening of tedious formality. The thrill of racing through moonlit skies proved infinitely preferable to exchanging proper pleasantries with ambitious young ladies who viewed him merely as a convenient stepping stone to the Rowanwood fortune.

Well. It was preferable when he wasn't about to lose to a Brightcrest.

Cobalt swerved suddenly to avoid a sudden updraft of wild magic, likely released from the converging ley lines beneath Bloomhaven that gave the town its potent magical energy. Evryn gripped the reins tighter with one hand while adjusting his goggles with the other. He should have noticed the spinning swirls of magic—the lenses of his goggles were enchanted with night-vision enhancement—but he'd been too distracted by that infernal Brightcrest who seemed determined to humiliate him.

Drawing a steadying breath, he swept his gaze across his surroundings. Below, Bloomhaven glittered like scattered gems on black velvet, blissfully unaware of the ancient rivalry playing out in the skies above. Faelights illuminated the winding paths that connected elegant manor houses and shops nestled between flowering archways. A vast shadow interrupted the twinkling lights—the sprawling expanse of Elderbloom Park with its ancient trees and secret grottos—while beyond it, a barely visible ribbon of enchanted road curved toward the grand hill where Solstice Hall presided in all its glory.

Light poured from every window of the High Lady's summer palace, and even from this height, Evryn could make out the enchanted cherry trees lining the approach. Solstice Hall bustled with the cream of fae society, gathered for this most significant evening. The night when young fae who had manifested their magical abilities during the previous year would be formally presented to society.

It was a ritual that had remained unchanged for centuries. Families from across the United Fae Isles converged on Bloomhaven after the start of spring so that their newly manifested sons and daughters, typically eighteen or nineteen years of age, could demonstrate their magical powers before the assembled elite at the Bloom Season's Opening Ball. The remainder of the Season would be spent strengthening their newfound magical abilities while navigating the intricate dance of courtship, all building toward the Summer Solstice Ball when the most fortunate would announce their engagements.

Evryn had little interest in participating in any of it. He'd manifested at eighteen, like most respectable fae, but his lumyrite-shaping abilities—while impressive enough to earn him the coveted 'Lord' title—lacked the practical utility of his older brother's magic. Not that it mattered. Evryn was merely the second son, perpetually in Jasvian's shadow, expected to ornament family gatherings rather than contribute anything of substance to the Rowanwood lumyrite empire. His ability to physically manipulate lumyrite like a sculptor, reshaping solid crystal as if it were clay, could perhaps be considered impressive. But it was hardly essential when compared to Jasvian's life-saving ability to sense and calm the tempests that formed around raw lumyrite deposits in the mines.

Evryn clenched his jaw and returned his focus to the Brightcrest rider who maintained the lead as they soared over the dense copse of singing willows that marked the approach to their improvised finish line. Ahead, Evryn could make out Fin, a lone figure stationed at the base of an ancient, lightning-struck oak—the designated endpoint for tonight's unsanctioned race. Frustration mounted as he urged Cobalt into a steeper dive, the wind howling past his ears despite the leather cap secured beneath his chin.

Cobalt surged forward with a final burst of speed, wings straining against the night air. For a split second, Evryn's heart leaped as Cobalt gained precious inches. Almost … almost … *almost …*

But it was the Brightcrest rider and pegasus who shot across the invisible threshold first.

A bellow of frustration escaped Evryn's lips as the copper pegasus ahead of him began a spiraling descent toward the clearing just beyond the lightning-struck oak. He directed Cobalt to follow.

"Second again?" Fin shouted up to Evryn, and Evryn caught a glimpse of the impish grin on his friend's face. He ignored Fin, who was well aware of the decades-old Rowanwood-Brightcrest family feud and would no doubt enjoy teasing Evryn about this most recent loss. Instead, he guided Cobalt in tight circles toward the ground.

The moment they touched down, he leaped from Cobalt's back, tearing off his leather riding gloves and flinging them to the ground in frustration. His goggles and leather cap followed swiftly.

"Brightcrest!" he called, striding toward the victor who had already dismounted.

Behind him, the remaining racers began to descend, their pegasi's wings stirring the night air as they landed at various points around the clearing. Voices called out, some congratulatory, others commiserating, but Evryn didn't spare them a glance.

His competitor turned, and with one fluid motion, removed the riding cap that had been secured tightly throughout the race. A cascade of golden hair tumbled free, spilling down in a messy braid over one shoulder. She removed her goggles and tossed her head. In the moonlight, her blue eyes gleamed with triumph.

"It seems I've bested you again, Rowanwood," said Lady Mariselle Brightcrest, her voice musical with taunt.

Evryn's jaw tightened. "A favorable wind and dubious shortcut hardly constitute superior skill."

"Excuses become tiresome after the third defeat." She tapped one gloved finger against her chin, frowning. "Or is it the fourth?"

"Third," Evryn ground out. For someone celebrated throughout Bloomhaven for his effortless charm and unflappable demeanor, it was remarkable how quickly a Brightcrest victory could transform him into a tightly wound coil of indignation.

"Three losses in a row suggests a pattern rather than luck, wouldn't you agree?" Mariselle's smile was glacial. "Perhaps Brightcrests are simply superior riders."

"Superior cheats, more like," Evryn retorted, straightening the cuffs of his midnight-blue riding jacket. "It must be exhausting, constantly finding new ways to bend rules that were clearly established at the outset."

"I have never once cheated, nor even bent a rule," Mariselle replied, her jaw tightening. "Unlike your little masquerade at the races last year when you took someone's place in the professional circuit. You think I did not recognize your riding style? The race officials might have been fooled, but I wasn't."

Evryn's retort died on his lips. He gritted his teeth, anger flaring hot beneath his collar. "Shouldn't you be at Solstice Hall preening for potential suitors? Or has your second Season begun with the eligible lords of Bloomhaven maintaining a safe distance?"

"I'm surprised *you* did not remain at the ball to support your family," Mariselle countered. "Your sister Rosavyn looked positively bereft without her gallant brother's support. Rather inconsiderate of you, considering her precarious situation. She turned nineteen some months ago, did she not? And still no signs of manifesting?" Mariselle's expression shifted to one of exaggerated sympathy. "How mortifying for your family."

The barb struck home. Evryn had promised Rosavyn he would attend, knowing the pressure she faced to manifest soon. It was too late for her to be presented this Season, but surely she would manifest before turning twenty—an age where failure would transform concern into scandal. He tamped down a flicker of guilt.

"How touching that you monitor my family's activities so closely. One might almost suspect envy."

Mariselle's laugh grated on his nerves. "Envy? Of *your* family? My family cultivates dreams, Rowanwood. Yours merely digs in dirt."

"At least we build something tangible," Evryn replied, "rather than peddling illusions and addiction disguised as dream magic."

"That is a *lie*," Mariselle snapped. "A lie spread by Rowanwoods. Dream-Bright Elixir does not cause—"

"So defensive," Evryn drawled, a hint of a smile tugging at his lips as he settled back into his natural rhythm of practiced nonchalance. "I merely referenced what everyone across the United Fae Isles whispers behind closed doors."

Mariselle inhaled deeply, eyes narrowing, before she spun around and headed toward her pegasus. A surge of satisfaction warmed Evryn's chest as he watched her retreat, smug in his victory. He'd successfully provoked her into abandoning their verbal sparring match—a rare triumph worth savoring.

But instead of mounting her copper steed, Mariselle reached into the saddlebag and withdrew something with a dramatic flourish. Her pegasus unfurled its flame-tipped wings and took flight with a powerful downdraft. Evryn was vaguely aware of Cobalt similarly retreating, but his attention remained fixed on the papers Mariselle now held aloft. His heart stuttered to a halt as recognition dawned. The familiar pages with their distinctive penmanship—*his* penmanship—fluttered slightly in the night breeze.

"I must say," Mariselle continued, her voice dropping to a silken murmur, "I never expected to discover literary ambitions among your otherwise unremarkable pursuits. How bold of you to publish such scathing satires. That caricature of the High Lady in last week's Gazette—which perfectly matches the handwritten version in these pages—was particularly audacious."

A cold sweat broke out across Evryn's forehead. "Where did you get that?"

"Does it matter?" She ran one gloved finger along the edge of the manuscript. "I'm sure the High Lady will find this particularly damning." Her eyes lifted to his, glittering with malice. "E. S. Twist."

The blood drained from Evryn's face as though someone had pulled a stopper, leaving him lightheaded and strangely hollow. His carefully constructed world of deflection and charm seemed to crumble beneath his feet, leaving only the horrifying certainty that his secret—the one thing that was truly his own—now rested in the hands of a Brightcrest.

Rage and panic surged through him in equal measure. Without conscious thought, he lunged forward, reaching for the damning evidence that could destroy not just his reputation but potentially his entire family's standing.

Mariselle shrieked, spun around, and darted away between the trees.

Mariselle rushed headlong into the forest, clutching the stolen manuscript tightly to her chest with one hand and ducking beneath low-hanging branches dripping with luminous sap. One caught her shoulder, the magical substance momentarily splattering across her racing jacket with a bright green glow before fading back to dormancy.

"Come back here, Brightcrest!" Evryn shouted behind her.

Mariselle, of course, did not obey.

Her parents would be livid when they discovered her absence from the Opening Ball. Her mother had spent an entire ten minutes selecting the 'perfect' (hideous) gown for her, in a shade of yellow-green that clashed magnificently with her coloring. Lady Clemenbell had even exerted herself to the apparently exhausting extent of arranging two potential introductions with lords whose conversational skills rivaled those of particularly dull garden statues.

But the look of panic on Evryn Rowanwood's face was worth whatever punishment awaited Mariselle at Brightcrest Manor. Though perhaps her parents would be pleased when they learned what she had stolen from him.

The thrill of discovery still hummed through her veins. To think that carefree, irreverent Evryn Rowanwood was secretly publishing scathing social satire as thinly veiled allegorical tales under a pseudonym! This could be precisely the leverage her family needed to finally humble the insufferable Rowanwoods.

Mariselle wove between the ancient trees, grateful for the racing attire her mother would have deemed scandalously masculine. The fitted breeches and short-waisted jacket afforded her a freedom of movement that would have been impossible in proper ladies' attire—one of many reasons she secretly cherished these forbidden nighttime races.

"Return my property!" Evryn called, his voice closer than she'd expected.

"Property?" she tossed over her shoulder without slowing. "Or evidence?"

Her lungs burned pleasantly with exertion, the night air crisp in her chest. Despite his longer stride, he hadn't caught her yet. The trees were her ally, forcing Evryn to navigate obstacles that she, smaller and lighter, could slip past with ease.

She heard a satisfying thud and muffled curse as Evryn collided with something solid behind her, followed by the unmistakable sound of a body hitting the forest floor. A triumphant smile curved her lips—until her own footing suddenly betrayed her. She'd been distracted just enough that she missed seeing the exposed root in her path. It flared with amber light as her boot caught against it, sending her pitching forward with a startled cry.

She threw one arm out instinctively to break her fall, her hand landing on something wickedly sharp that sliced clean through her riding glove. White-hot pain blazed across her palm, drawing a hiss through her clenched teeth as something—Evryn's hand?—wrapped around her ankle and tugged. She kicked hard with her free leg, her boot connecting with something solid, and was rewarded with the satisfying sound of Evryn's pained yelp. His grip slackened just enough, and she wrenched her ankle free, scrambling back to her feet as pain pulsed across her lacerated palm.

She took off again, blood warming her hand within the confines of her torn glove as she pushed herself harder, unwilling to surrender her advantage. Her legs burned as she dashed between the trees. Branches whipped past her face.

Then she burst from the forest into a familiar moonlit clearing. The ruins of Dreamland spread before her, hauntingly beautiful in the silvery light. She'd visited this place dozens of times during her solitary rides, drawn by the tales of what had once been her family's crowning achievement.

Well, to be entirely accurate, it had been a joint venture between the Brightcrests and Rowanwoods, before the Rowanwoods had ruined it with their selfishness and greed. But Mariselle preferred to think of it as a magnificent creation belonging solely to the Brightcrests. It was called *Dream*land, after all.

The skeletal pavilion frame rose against the night sky like the ribcage of some enormous magical beast, dull lumyrite still embedded in the structure. Luminous moss covered the crumbling columns, and nightveil orchids unfurled slowly, petals transforming from near-black to intricate silvery patterns wherever the moonlight touched them.

With no clear plan beyond escape, Mariselle sprinted toward Windsong Cottage, the mysteriously preserved building that stood a short distance away from the ruins. Unlike the rest of Dreamland, the cottage remained pristine behind its shimmering veil of preservation spells, impossible to enter yet perfectly maintained. If her grandmother's tales were to be believed, this cottage was where the very first plans for Dreamland had been conceived. Mariselle had tried countless times to find a way inside, hoping to discover the forgotten secrets of Dreamland that no one from her grandmother's generation was willing to share. But it had always remained firmly beyond reach, wrapped in enchantments that refused to yield to even her most determined attempts.

Mariselle planned to dart around the cottage's eastern side, where the wild briars grew less densely, but skidded to a halt when she spotted the echo-bark that must have fallen during last week's spring storm. The cottage itself remained undamaged, protected by its enchantments, but the massive trunk and tangle of branches completely blocked Mariselle's escape route.

Panic fluttered in her chest as she glanced frantically for another path, finding none. With Evryn's footsteps crashing through the underbrush behind her, she had no choice but to dash straight for the cottage's front door, though she knew perfectly well that no one had breached those preservation spells in decades. For the first time that night, genuine fear replaced her triumphant excitement.

The sound of Evryn's footsteps pounded closer as she reached the cottage door. She spun to face him, tightly clutching the manuscript pages behind her and pressing her back against the weathered wood. Her injured palm throbbed in protest.

"Will you truly take it by force?" she demanded, struggling to catch her breath. "How very gentlemanly of you."

Evryn came to a halt before her, his chest heaving. His previously immaculate riding jacket was now smeared with mud along one sleeve and half of his chest, while dirt streaked the left side of his face. Even in the moonlight, she could see the storm-gray of his eyes had darkened with anger. "When have Brightcrests ever concerned themselves with respectable behavior?" he said, his own breathing ragged. "I'll tear those papers from your hands if necessary."

"You'll have to catch me first," she taunted, knowing he would advance and planning to duck beneath his arm and race away.

"Consider it done." He stepped forward, and Mariselle attempted to slip beneath his outstretched arm. But his reflexes proved quicker than she'd anticipated. His fingers snatched her wrist, tugging her back and trapping her against the cottage door as she shrieked in outrage. She kicked at his shin, vaguely aware of how utterly horrified her mother would be at such unlady-like behavior. The manuscript crumpled between them as Evryn crowded her against the door, one hand planted firmly on the weathered wood beside her head while he grabbed for the papers.

"I won't—let you—have them," she insisted through gritted teeth, stuffing the crumpled papers behind her back once more. She pressed her injured palm against the door for support as she attempted to sidestep him.

"They are *mine*," he countered, his eyes ablaze with fury and desperation. "You cannot—"

"I will ensure that all of Bloomhaven knows of E. S. Twist's true identity before sunrise," she hissed, meeting his gaze defiantly. "I swear it. You—"

"And *I* swear that you shall never—"

Searing light erupted from the door. Pain lanced through Mariselle's palm, white-hot and electric, racing up her arm in pulsing waves. She jerked away with a startled cry, echoed by Evryn's gasp as he likewise recoiled.

The light vanished as abruptly as it had appeared, leaving behind an unsettling tingle that crept beneath Mariselle's skin. She hastily shoved the manuscript beneath her left arm, clamping it tightly against her ribs and twisting her body to shield it from Evryn's reach before yanking off her torn glove with her teeth. (Her mother would have collapsed into a well-timed swoon at this point.)

She stared at her bloodied palm with its clean slice across the center, dread pooling in the pit of her stomach as she slowly turned her hand. A silvery pattern had appeared on her skin. An intricate, swirling design that curled from the edges of her palm, across her hand, and up around her wrist, gleaming faintly. She looked over her shoulder at Evryn, who was staring at his own hand where an identical mark emblazoned his skin.

And it was at precisely that moment that the front door of Windsong Cottage, which had remained magically sealed for over fifty years, quietly swung open.

Chapter Two

THE DOOR THAT HAD DEFIED ENTRY FOR MORE THAN HALF A CENTURY now stood ajar, and for a moment, Mariselle could not move, could not breathe, could not fully comprehend what her eyes beheld. And then, in the quiet stillness of her shocked mind, an idea that should have been obvious far sooner suddenly presented itself.

With a steadying breath, she reached for that elusive boundary she had spent years exploring, the veil that separated the waking world from the dream realm. Most fae had no hope of consciously accessing it, but the Brightcrests were not most fae. Without another moment's hesitation, she slid the crumpled manuscript from beneath her arm and slipped it straight into the air in front of it—directly into the dream realm.

A small, satisfied smile curved her lips at Evryn's stunned exclamation behind her. "What … what did you just do?" he demanded.

"I've hidden it in the dream realm," she replied, as though she had merely tucked it into a pocket. She glanced over her shoulder and met his disbelieving expression.

"That's—that's not possible," he stammered.

She arched a brow. "And you know so much about dream magic?"

"I know your manifestation of it is weak at best," he countered. "I saw your display last year when you were presented at the Opening Ball. I almost fell asleep."

The barb stung more than it should have, considering she had deliberately performed below her capabilities during her debut. Her presentation had shown only the most basic extraction of dream essence, the same power almost all Brightcrests manifested, a decision that had been calculated.

Her true abilities would have immediately made her valuable to her family but in ways that would strip her of autonomy rather than grant her the validation she so desperately craved. She needed to reveal her true powers on her own terms and in her own time, when she could present them as an achievement rather than a resource to be exploited. After more than a year since her manifestation, she was still awaiting the perfect opportunity.

"Be that as it may," she said, eyes narrowing. "It does not change the fact that I've hidden your manuscript in the dream realm. You have no hope of retrieving it."

Evryn spluttered with fury and indignation, but Mariselle's attention had already returned to the cottage doorway. Windsong Cottage was open. *Open!* After decades of standing impervious to all attempts at entry, its preservation spells seemingly unbreakable, it now appeared ready to welcome her inside.

Without waiting for Evryn's next protest, she stepped over the threshold, her heart thundering. The interior, illuminated by warm faelight emanating from some inexplicable source, was pristine, as though time had never touched it. Not a speck of dust marred the elegantly carved cherrywood sideboard, nor the polished oak table that dominated the main room. Chairs stood neatly arranged around it, cushions still plumped as if expecting guests.

She took another few steps inside. Beyond the formal dining arrangement was a wide window offering a view of the moonlit cottage garden, its upper frame softened by vines that trailed along the top and curled down one side. Their green leaves were edged with gold that seemed to shimmer faintly. To the left lay a cozy sitting area. Several plush armchairs flanked a small sofa, their emerald upholstery barely faded despite the decades. Against the wall behind the sofa stood a charmingly haphazard bookshelf crowded with mismatched volumes, curling scrolls, and leather-bound journals.

As Mariselle drew closer, she could make out the delicate, hand-etched titles on some of the spines, dulled by age but still legible: *Dreamland Architect Notes. The Chronicle of Dreamland: Volume III. Dreamland: Opera-*

tions & Oversight. One labeled simply *DL – Ideas.* A soft, wondering exhale escaped her lips.

She turned and peered through a doorway into a small kitchen area, where copper kettles and pots gleamed from hooks above a tidily swept hearth, and logs that had never been lit lay stacked in readiness. Strangest of all was the air itself, not stale as abandoned places tended to be, but somehow alive, the faintest scent of cinnamon pastries and freshly brewed tea still lingering.

Mariselle heard Evryn enter behind her, his footsteps hesitant. "How is this possible? This place has been sealed for years."

"Decades," Mariselle murmured, her instinct to argue with a Rowanwood reflexive and immediate, almost like breathing. She looked around, her attention caught by a solitary page resting in the center of the otherwise empty oak table. She approached it cautiously, then reached out with slightly trembling fingers to lift the parchment.

Her brow furrowed as she scanned the elegant script. "It appears to be a contract of some sort," she said, half to herself. Her eyes jumped to the bottom, and her heart squeezed strangely when she recognized her grandmother's name beneath one of the signatures. Nirella Brightcrest. And beside it ... Valenrik Rowanwood. Was that Evryn's grandfather? The one who had passed some years ago?

Mariselle's eyes scanned the document, her lips moving as she murmured the words. "'... wherein the signatories do hereby agree that the attraction known as Dreamland shall remain sealed from public access until such time as heirs of both Brightcrest and Rowanwood bloodlines willingly consent to its restoration.'" Her breath began to grow shallow as her heart pounded faster. "'The terms of this binding agreement shall lie dormant until activated by the blood of both families freely given and accompanied by a sworn ...'" She trailed off, swallowed hard, and reread the line before whispering, "'A sworn oath.'"

A chill raced through her as she lowered the page. Slowly, she turned to look back past Evryn at the open doorway where two bloody smudges stained the weathered wood. Her injured palm throbbed in accusatory rhythm. "Did you cut your hand when you fell in the forest?" she asked faintly.

"What?" Evryn asked, irritation obvious in his tone. But he glanced down nonetheless. "Yes. Merely a scrape."

What was it she had said to him in the moments before that blinding flash of light? Something about telling all of Bloomhaven of E. S. Twist's true identity? Something about … *I swear it.*

She stared at the parchment again, her eyes picking out individual phrases. *The heirs bound by this mark shall combine their magics to restore Dreamland to its former glory. … Neither shall sabotage the other's efforts, and both shall work in honest partnership until restoration meets the criteria detailed herein. … The binding mark shall remain until such time as Dreamland stands ready to welcome visitors once more, whereupon either party may voluntarily relinquish their claim to the other, but no coercion or force shall compel such surrender.*

"Rowanwood," Mariselle whispered, horror dawning. "I do believe we have unwittingly agreed to a magically binding contract."

"What?" he demanded, marching over to snatch the contract from her hands. His eyes darted across the page, brow deepening into a scowl with each passing second. "Preposterous," he muttered. "You and I have agreed to nothing. There must be a way to undo this."

But Mariselle barely heard him. Her gaze had drifted beyond the open doorway to where moonlight illuminated the remains of what had once been Dreamland's grand entrance arch. The lumyrite embedded within the structure still pulsed with faint, residual magic, echoes of what had once been the United Fae Isles' most extraordinary attraction.

She had spent countless nights secretly visiting these ruins, imagining what it might have been like in its heyday. A place where visitors could experience the wonder of genuine dream reality while fully awake. She had grown up hearing tales of its former splendor, longing to be able to see this magnificent creation with her own eyes.

Now, standing within the cottage where the very concept of Dreamland had first been conceived and nurtured, a new possibility unfurled before her. She possessed most of the dream-related magical powers necessary for such an undertaking—powers she had carefully hidden from her family—but had always lacked the complementary lumyrite magic required to stabilize dream reality in the physical world. Based on the story fragments she had heard from her grandmother, this was why the realization of Dreamland had required a partnership with the Rowanwoods in the first place. A Brightcrest could not manage it alone.

But Evryn Rowanwood possessed a lumyrite-shaping ability. And now a magically binding contract effectively forced him to work with her.

This situation she had inadvertently landed herself in was actually rather … perfect.

Mariselle could do this. She could restore Dreamland to its former glory. Create something magnificent that was truly her own. Finally prove to her family that she was worth something. The Brightcrests could once again possess an achievement of such magnitude that it would rival the considerable influence the Rowanwoods wielded through Lady Rivenna's enchanted tea house. Perhaps even surpass it. Surely the sophisticated society of the United Fae Isles would prefer experiencing the wonders of an enchanted dream realm to taking tea in a stuffy establishment that had remained unchanged for decades.

Mariselle turned to face Evryn, heart still pounding beneath her restrictive riding attire. "Help me restore Dreamland."

Evryn stared at her as though she had suggested they sprout wings and fly to the moon. "What?"

"Do as the contract says," she said, her voice growing stronger with each word. "It isn't as though we have a choice."

"Of course we have a choice," he scoffed, tossing the contract back onto the table and striding past her toward the door. "I don't have to do a damn thing that old piece of paper says."

"And be bound to me forever by that mark on your wrist?" she called after him.

He paused, then turned back to face her, a flicker of hesitation crossing his face. "I'm sure that can be dealt with. I'll speak to my family's solicitor. He'll know of magic that can break this ridiculous enchantment."

"Do that," Mariselle said, her voice hardening, "and I will reveal your secret pseudonym to the whole of Bloomhaven."

Evryn's eyes narrowed dangerously. He drew himself up to his full height, inhaling deeply as his eyes traveled over her with deliberate assessment. "Am I to understand that you are attempting to employ blackmail against me, Lady Brightcrest?"

"You understand perfectly," she confirmed. "I have dream magic, you possess power that allows you to shape lumyrite, and all the plans and details necessary to restore Dreamland are in this very cottage. You and I will rebuild

Dreamland, and we will not tell a soul. I don't want anyone knowing of this until we are finished. If you do not agree, I will tell everyone your secret."

"Lady Mariselle," Evryn said, his voice taking on a patronizing tone that set her teeth on edge, "you cannot do this. You don't possess the necessary magic, the skill, the business acumen. You are a mere ..." He seemed to struggle for a moment as he searched for an appropriate insult. "Girl," he finished. "This is the most ridiculous idea I've ever—"

"Do not presume to tell me what I can and cannot do," she interrupted fiercely, her composure close to cracking. "You have no comprehension of the power I possess."

Something flickered in his eyes then. A brief recalibration, as though he were seeing her anew. For a moment, she thought he might actually have recognized the truth in her words, but instead, he merely gestured to his marked wrist. "And what of this? Do you think people will not notice?"

Mariselle frowned. She had been so caught up in the possibility of resurrecting Dreamland that she'd neglected to consider the implications of the visible mark they now shared. Her mind raced again. The challenge was considerable. She was absolutely determined that no one should discover their undertaking before its completion—her family would put an end to it if they discovered her working with a Rowanwood—yet the mark they now shared would inevitably draw attention and speculation.

And then, as her eyes traced the pattern that now marked her skin, an idea took form in her mind. "We ... we shall announce that we are engaged."

Evryn made a choking sound that culminated in actual coughing, his face a mask of abject horror. When he finally recovered enough to speak, he managed, "I had no idea a Brightcrest was capable of such droll witticisms."

"This is no jest," she insisted. "The mark—"

"There is not a person in Bloomhaven—in the entire United Fae Isles— who will believe that a Rowanwood and a Brightcrest have agreed to marry," he interrupted. "There is simply no way."

"If you would let me finish," she ground out, frustration mounting. "As I was saying, the mark looks almost precisely like a soulbond. We can pretend that it is, in which case no one can argue with us."

"A soulbond?" he repeated incredulously.

Mariselle released an exasperated sigh. "Surely you know of a soulbond, Rowanwood."

"I am aware of their mention in overwrought romantic novels that cause ladies to swoon and gentlemen to roll their eyes. A convenient plot device for authors to force reluctant characters together, I believe."

"They are not mere fiction," Mariselle said, crossing her arms. "Soulbonds are rare, but documented cases exist throughout fae history."

"And you would know this from your extensive reading of romantic novels, I presume?" A familiar smirk returned to his face. "I can only imagine the content of such literature would make one blush right up to the roots of one's hair."

Mariselle maintained an impeccably composed expression, not a hint of warmth rising to her cheeks as she replied, "I would rather acquaint myself with the most blush-inducing of romantic literature than the thinly veiled allegorical drivel penned by E. S. Twist. And no, my knowledge comes from my leisurely perusal of the Historical Archives of Magical Phenomena. Believe it or not, Rowanwood, some of us take pleasure in reading materials of academic substance rather than merely whatever reinforces our presumptions about the world."

Before he could retort, she plunged ahead, outlining her plan in detail. "Now. Tomorrow we shall announce to our families, independently, that the soulbond appeared and we have fallen inexplicably in love overnight."

Evryn made an exaggerated retching sound, miming the act of vomiting. Mariselle rolled her eyes. "Don't be such a child," she said before continuing. "The news will spread through Bloomhaven like wildfire. I'm sure the gossip birds will feast upon such deliciously scandalous tidings. At night, instead of racing, we will come to the cottage and secretly work on Dreamland together.

"When Dreamland is complete to the satisfaction of the contract, the magical binding mark will disappear. You will then relinquish control of your half to me, we'll tell our families that—oh look!—the soulbond has mysteriously dissolved, and we need not marry after all." She gestured expansively, warming to her scheme. "You can then return to your merry pseudonymous way, and I shall reveal Dreamland to my family."

Evryn regarded her with profound skepticism. "Why not simply tell our families the truth? They would be as horrified as we are that you and I have magically bound ourselves together. They would do whatever necessary to break the agreement. This entire charade will be unnecessary."

"Because I want this," she said simply, her voice suddenly quiet but intense.

"Dreamland?" he asked, studying her with apparent confusion. "You want Dreamland?"

"Yes."

"Why?"

"That is no concern of yours," she replied coolly, swearing to herself right then and there that he would never know the true reason. Never know the years of yearning for her family's approval, the desperate hope that creating something magnificent might finally make them look at her with pride instead of disappointment.

"I shall be frank, Rowanwood. Either you agree to the arrangement I have proposed, or I shall ensure that by teatime tomorrow, every soul in Bloomhaven knows the true identity of E. S. Twist."

A tense silence stretched between them, broken only by the distant call of a night bird. Evryn ran a hand through his already disheveled hair, his expression cycling through frustration, calculation, and finally, reluctant capitulation.

"Very well," he said at last, his voice tight with suppressed anger. "I agree to your terms."

"Good." She leaned against the table and folded her arms across her chest. "Now, we should agree upon our story. How we discovered the bond, how we … realized our feelings." The last words emerged strangled, as though her throat rebelled against them.

"Perhaps we might claim temporary insanity," Evryn suggested dryly. "It would be the most believable explanation."

Mariselle shot him a withering glance. "Be serious for once in your life. If we are to convince anyone—particularly our families—we must present a unified narrative."

"Very well," he sighed. "What do you suggest?"

"We shall say we encountered each other on a terrace outside the ballroom at Solstice Hall," she began, the fabrication taking shape in her mind. "Our families will undoubtedly have noted our respective absences from the ball, so this much, at least, cannot be contested. We argued, as we always do, and during the course of our disagreement, our hands accidentally touched. The mark appeared instantly, accompanied by the sensation of …"

She faltered, uncertain how to describe something she had never experienced.

"A sensation like lightning beneath the skin," Evryn supplied. When she glanced at him in surprise, he shrugged. "Is that not what it felt like to you?"

"I meant the sensation of *falling in love*, Rowanwood," she said tartly. "Not the sensation of the mark itself."

"Ah. Well I don't believe we need to get into the specifics of that. We can say we were both overcome with … with … inexplicable attraction," he finished, his expression pained. "Despite our better judgment and the lifetime of animosity between our families."

"Yes." Mariselle nodded, relieved that he was finally participating constructively. "We were as shocked as anyone would be, but the soulbond cannot be denied, and nor can our …" Despite her earlier admonishment that he not behave like a child, she couldn't suppress a shudder of revulsion. "And nor can our feelings," she finished in a rush. "We decided to retire home early and share the news with our families in the morning."

"That should suffice, I suppose," Evryn said with resignation. "Though you must realize our families will not simply accept this preposterous revelation. My grandmother will be suspicious, my mother will faint, Jasvian will question my sanity, and Rosavyn will laugh until she cannot breathe." He expelled a weary breath. "Then they will all attempt to break the bond by any means necessary."

Mariselle refrained from pointing out that he was fortunate to have at least one family member who might find humor in the situation. There would be no such levity in Brightcrest Manor when she delivered this news.

"We cannot allow them to break the bond," she reminded him. "We must insist that we …" She shivered again. "Care for each other," she forced herself to say, "and wish to honor the bond."

Evryn straightened his riding jacket with an impatient gesture, his expression making it clear he wished to be anywhere but in her presence. "Very well. As you wish. Consider me your devoted suitor from this moment forward. But know this, *Lady* Brightcrest. When this charade is through, I shall take immense pleasure in never having to pretend to like you ever again."

"I can assure you, *Lord* Rowanwood," Mariselle said with a brittle smile, "the sentiment is entirely mutual."

Chapter Three

Mariselle kissed Cinder's soft nose, relieved to have successfully returned to Brightcrest Manor without detection. They had followed their familiar route through the property, keeping to the shadows and skirting the meticulously maintained gardens with their distinctive cerulean roses. She was grateful as always that the copper mare's wings only blazed with golden fire during flight. Their secret nocturnal escapades wouldn't be possible otherwise.

"Tomorrow we begin something extraordinary," Mariselle whispered, having carefully unbuckled and removed the riding saddle from Cinder's back. Her injured palm throbbed beneath the makeshift bandage she'd fashioned from her riding scarf, the pain flaring with each movement. "All those nights we spent circling the ruins, imagining what it might have been …" She ran her fingers through Cinder's silken mane. "Soon it will be real again."

After ensuring Cinder had fresh water and a measure of oats, Mariselle pressed a final kiss to the pegasus's soft nose. "Rest well," she murmured, then slipped out of the stable, carefully securing the door behind her.

The gardens stood between her and the manor house, with flowerbeds laid out in ornate patterns, bordered by clipped hedges and pale gravel paths that gleamed beneath the drifting faelights—any one of which might betray her presence if she wasn't careful. Fortunately, Mariselle knew exactly which paths remained unlit, having mapped them meticulously over years of clandestine excursions.

She skirted the luminous fountain and darted behind a hedge sculptured to resemble a prancing unicorn. Another quick dash brought her beneath the shadow of the western wing, where her bedchamber awaited two stories above. A soft whistle, pitched just high enough to be heard by its intended recipient, summoned a flickering light from her window. Moments later, a slender rope ladder unfurled down the wall. Mariselle grinned. Tilly, her lady's maid, had received her signal.

Ignoring the persistent ache in her palm, Mariselle began the familiar climb, grateful that her unseemly attire afforded the freedom of movement such ascents required. Near the top, a pale face peered out from between the drawn curtains. "You're earlier than I expected," Tilly said as she helped Mariselle through the window. "The rest of your family is still at Solstice Hall."

"Thank the stars." Mariselle slipped out of her jacket and handed it to Tilly, who gasped when she caught sight of Mariselle's bandaged hand. "My lady! Whatever happened?"

"A slight mishap during my ride," Mariselle replied. "Could you perhaps draw a bath? I need to wash away the dirt and blood before anyone sees me."

Tilly nodded. "I'll prepare the enchantment. It won't take long."

Though Tilly was human and lacked the innate magical abilities of the fae, she had mastered the simple enchantments accessible to her kind. Like most servants in noble fae houses, she knew the precise incantations to activate the household's magical conveniences. In the case of bathtubs, specifically, this meant applying the correct enchantment to the layer of ever-warm stones that sat beneath the copper tub in order to warm the water to the perfect temperature.

While Tilly busied herself with the tub tucked behind a painted screen in the corner, Mariselle sank onto the edge of her bed, allowing herself a moment of pure, unbridled excitement. Dreamland. She was going to restore *Dreamland!* The thought sent a shiver of anticipation down her spine.

Of course, the price for this opportunity was steep: pretending to be in love with Evryn Rowanwood, of all people. The very idea made her stomach churn with distaste. But it was a price she would gladly pay. The restoration of Dreamland would finally prove her worth to her family. She would transform from the disappointing youngest daughter into the architect of the Brightcrests' greatest achievement in generations. And she would have Dreamland too! She couldn't wait to see it in all its glory.

Tilly stepped back around the screen, interrupting Mariselle's reverie. "For your hand, my lady," she said, offering a small jar with a green-glazed lid. The familiar scent of Mariselle's favorite variety of healing salve—peppermint and comfrey with an undertone of something distinctly magical—wafted from it as she removed the lid.

Her maid disappeared behind the screen again, and Mariselle unwrapped the blood-stained scarf from her palm. The angry red slice looked worse now than when she'd hastily bandaged it earlier, but she was distracted once more by the silvery mark starting at the edges of her palm, looping around her fingers and over her hand in an intricate, swirling pattern. Another painful throb forced her attention back to the cut.

She scooped a dollop of the cool salve onto her fingers and spread it carefully across the wound, breathing a sigh of relief as the herbs and minor enchantments began their work, instantly soothing the pain and beginning the healing process. By the time Tilly appeared from behind the screen once more and announced, "Your bath is ready, my lady," the cut was little more than a faint pink line across Mariselle's palm. She hastily lowered her hand and tugged her sleeve downward, concealing the mark. The last thing she needed was Tilly noticing the strange pattern and asking questions Mariselle wasn't yet ready to answer.

She rose and moved behind the screen, where steam rose invitingly from the copper tub. "Thank you, Tilly. I believe that will be all for tonight."

"Are you sure, my lady? Perhaps you require—"

"No, no. I shall be quite all right." Mariselle had informed Tilly years ago that she was perfectly capable of removing her riding garments herself, but her maid always offered assistance regardless.

Tilly inclined her head in a polite nod. "Sleep well, my lady. Shall I wake you at the usual hour tomorrow?"

"Yes, thank you," Mariselle replied, already anticipating the confrontation that awaited her come morning. "I have a feeling I'll need all my wits about me."

Tilly departed, and Mariselle removed the remainder of her garments— which Tilly would discreetly launder the next day—before stepping into the bath and lowering herself with a sigh. The warm water, scented with wild jasmine and enchanted twilight herb, soothed her aching muscles and washed away the evidence of her evening's adventure.

Though she was tempted to linger, anticipation bubbled through her veins. She couldn't possibly luxuriate when Petunia remained unaware of the night's extraordinary developments. With quick motions, she worked vanilla-scented soap through her hair and scrubbed away every trace of soil and blood.

After drying herself with swift pats of a plush towel, Mariselle slipped into her nightgown and robe, then hurried to her bedside table. From the drawer, she withdrew a small hand mirror framed in delicate silver filigree, one of a pair she and her cousin Petunia—the only person she truly trusted—had discovered in an oddities shop years ago. The mirrors were enchanted to allow communication between their bearers.

"Petunia," Mariselle whispered urgently, pressing her palm flat against the glass before peering into its surface. "Petunia, are you there?" The mirror's surface darkened, then return to his previously glassy reflection. She set it down on the bedside table and leaned over it as she pulled her damp hair over one shoulder and began braiding it.

For another few moments, the mirror reflected only Mariselle's own face, cheeks flushed from her warm bath. Then the surface rippled like disturbed water, and Petunia's face appeared, auburn hair falling in loose waves around her shoulders.

"Where in all the realms have you been?" Petunia demanded without preamble. "Did you go off on one of your nighttime rides? On the night of the Opening Ball? I was sooooo bored without you. Mother paraded me before every eligible bachelor with a pulse, and I had to feign interest in the most tedious conversations imaginable. Fortunately she developed a convenient headache and insisted we return home early, so now—"

"Petunia, you'll never guess what happened," Mariselle interrupted. "I raced Evryn Rowanwood again, and I won, naturally, but then we—"

A sudden commotion from elsewhere in the house cut her off mid-sentence. A familiar voice—her mother's—rose in a piercing call. "Mariselle! Mariselle, where are you?"

Panic fluttered in Mariselle's chest. "Oh no!" she hissed. "I have to go!" In her haste to scramble off the bed, the mirror slipped from her grasp and hit the floor with a dreadful crack. The glass splintered into a dozen glittering shards that scattered across the floorboards.

"No, no, no," Mariselle moaned, dropping to her knees and frantically attempting to gather the pieces. The swift sound of approaching footsteps sent her into a fresh panic. With no time to properly clean up the mess, she hastily swept the fragments beneath her bed with one slippered foot mere moments before her chamber door flew open without so much as a courtesy knock.

"There you are," Lady Clemenbell declared, her voice as cold and cutting as the night air above Bloomhaven. She stood framed in the doorway, her copper-toned hair still arranged in an immaculate coronet of braids, not a single strand daring to stray from its appointed place. "Would you care to explain why you departed Solstice Hall without a word to anyone?"

Mariselle smoothed her nightgown with hands that threatened to tremble. She had hoped for the remainder of the night to carefully consider how best to present her news, to rehearse her words until they sounded convincing, but it seemed the revelation couldn't wait. "I—yes. Something has happened, Mother. Something … entirely unexpected."

"Indeed?" Her mother stepped into the room, sharp eyes taking in Mariselle's freshly bathed appearance. "Curious, that this 'unexpected' event allowed you sufficient time for a bath but not the courtesy of informing your family of your whereabouts."

"I … I needed to think. It all happened so quickly."

Lady Clemenbell groaned, her eyes rolling skyward as though seeking divine patience. "For stars' sake, Mariselle, if you're referring to Lord Bridgemere requesting your hand for the first dance before the presentations began, then yes, we were all rather surprised." She adjusted the folds of her evening gown with a dismissive flick of her wrist. "It was indeed unexpected that someone of his station would show interest in you, with your limited magic. But it signifies nothing of consequence. He likely acted on some wager or momentary whim. Nothing will come of it, so there's hardly anything to contemplate. You should have remained focused on prospects that might actually materialize into something."

"Actually, Mother, that wasn't quite—"

"You have embarrassed us, Mariselle," her mother continued. "The elder Lady Titterleaf inquired after you specifically, and I was forced to fabricate an excuse for your absence. Do you have any idea how that reflects upon our family? Upon your sister?"

"I—"

"Your actions have consequences beyond yourself. Ellowa is working tirelessly to secure an advantageous match, and your behavior reflects upon her prospects."

As if summoned by the mention of her name, Ellowa appeared in the doorway, making no attempt to disguise her irritation. Her golden hair—so similar to Mariselle's—had been styled in an elaborate arrangement of curls and pearl pins that must have taken her lady's maid an hour to perfect.

"Have you been *here* the entire time?" Ellowa demanded. "Do you have any idea how difficult it was to explain your sudden departure? Lady Fawnwood asked me directly if you were unwell, and when I said I wasn't certain, she looked at me as though I were the most negligent sister imaginable!"

Mariselle swallowed the urge to point out that Ellowa was, in fact, a rather negligent sister.

"I told you we were to remain at the ball until its conclusion," Lady Clemenbell continued. "This sort of behavior is precisely why we've struggled to find suitable prospects for you. Your sister, despite being only one year older, conducts herself with appropriate decorum at all times. She understands her obligations to this family."

"Yes, Mother," Mariselle replied automatically, the words worn smooth from years of repetition.

"Last Season was a disappointment," her mother pressed on. "Your magical demonstration was adequate at best, and your subsequent behavior did little to recommend you to potential suitors. This Season represents an opportunity to rectify those impressions, yet already you seem determined to sabotage yourself, and by extension, this family."

Ellowa folded her arms over her chest. "Lord Titterleaf was asking for you specifically," she added, her tone suggesting this was a great honor rather than a source of dread. "Mother and Father have gone to considerable trouble to arrange potential matches for you, despite your limitations."

"I appreciate the efforts made on my behalf," Mariselle said carefully, knowing any hint of defiance would not be well-received. "You will be relieved to know that such efforts are no longer necessary."

Lady Clemenbell narrowed her eyes further. "And why is that?"

Mariselle's heart hammered against her ribs. She swallowed before continuing. "I was not referring to the dance with Lord Bridgemere when I said that something unexpected has occurred."

"Well," Ellowa demanded when Mariselle didn't immediately continue. "What is it?"

Mariselle's gaze shifted from her mother to her sister and back again. "When I stepped out onto one of the terraces at Solstice Hall for fresh air, I … I encountered Lord Evryn Rowanwood."

The temperature in the room seemed to drop several degrees. Lady Clemenbell's expression hardened to granite, while Ellowa's eyes widened with scandalized interest.

"You spoke with a Rowanwood?" her mother asked, each word precisely enunciated.

"We argued," Mariselle hastened to clarify. "But something happened during our disagreement. Our hands accidentally touched, and …" She extended her right arm and pushed up the sleeve of her robe, displaying the silvery mark that encircled her wrist. "This appeared."

For a moment, neither her mother nor sister spoke. They stared at the mark as though Mariselle had presented them with a poisonous serpent. Then Lady Clemenbell stepped forward and seized Mariselle's wrist in a grip far too tight to be comfortable, examining the pattern with naked horror.

"What is this?" she demanded, her nails digging into Mariselle's skin.

"I believe it's a soulbond mark," Mariselle replied, resisting the urge to wince.

"Impossible," Lady Clemenbell breathed, dropping Mariselle's hand as though it had burned her. "A soulbond? With a Rowanwood? I have never heard such absolute nonsense."

"It's not nonsense," Mariselle insisted, summoning the conviction she would need to convince her family. "Lord Evryn bears an identical mark. It appeared simultaneously when our hands touched. We were both equally startled by the development."

"Startled?" Ellowa repeated incredulously. "One doesn't simply become 'startled' by a soulbond with a member of the family our own has despised for generations!"

"I know it seems impossible," Mariselle continued, "but neither of us can deny what happened. The mark appeared, accompanied by a sensation like lightning beneath the skin, and with it came … feelings … that neither of us expected."

"Feelings?" her mother echoed in a sharp voice.

Heavy footsteps out in the corridor and a bellowed "Mariselle!" announced her father's arrival. He appeared in the doorway, his eyes landing on Mariselle with obvious displeasure. "I demand to know what calamity required you to abandon tonight's gathering without so much as a word of explanation."

"Oh, there is an explanation," her mother said faintly, "though it is far from good. Your daughter," she continued, gesturing toward Mariselle with a hand that trembled slightly, "appears to have magically bound herself to a Rowanwood."

Lord Brightcrest's expression shifted from irritation to stunned disbelief. "What did you say?"

Mariselle took a steadying breath and repeated her carefully constructed tale, extending her marked hand for her father's inspection. With each word, his complexion grew more ashen, his shoulders more rigid. When she finished, silence descended upon the room.

"What have you done to us?" her father finally asked, his voice barely above a whisper. "Betraying the family name like this? *Family comes first, Mariselle!* Have you learned nothing from us?" He released an exasperated breath. "I thought you were an embarrassment before, with your lackluster magic, but this? This is beyond anything I ever feared."

Mariselle pressed her shaking lips together. Years of disappointment and disapproval should have prepared her for the raw contempt in her father's voice, yet somehow his words still sliced through her.

"Father, I … I didn't choose this. It simply happened. I can't help that I …" She gulped and prepared herself to force the lie out. "I love—"

Her father was across the room in two quick strides, his hand gripping her jaw before she could finish the sentence. "Do not ever utter those words again," he hissed. "Your grandfather lay in an enchanted sleep for almost a *decade* after the closure of Dreamland before death finally took him, precisely because of what a Rowanwood did to him. That family almost tore ours apart. You will never *love* one of them. You will never be *bound* to one of them. And I do not want to see you again until you rid yourself of that abominable mark."

He released her with a dismissive shove that sent her staggering backward several paces. She caught herself against the edge of the bed as a thought struck her: *This isn't worth it.*

The desperate need for her family's approval—the approval she'd spent her entire life chasing—clawed at her chest. She wanted to use Dreamland to prove herself to them, but not if it meant alienating herself entirely in the process. She opened her mouth, ready to confess everything, to beg forgiveness, to promise she would find a way to remove the mark.

"This is precisely what I expected," her father spat before she could speak. "You've always been incapable of managing anything on your own. The moment you're left to your own devices, you create catastrophes that our family must clean up. Without our guidance, you are utterly useless."

The words struck like daggers, but instead of drawing blood, they hardened something within her. Mariselle clamped her mouth shut, her jaw tightening. She was *not* useless on her own. She was not some helpless, empty-headed girl who needed constant supervision. She was, however, smart enough to lower her gaze to the floor. Meeting her father's eyes with defiance would only anger him further.

Without another word, he turned and strode from the room.

"Well," Lady Clemenbell said quietly. Mariselle looked up to find her mother's eyes trailing up and down her form with disgust. "I find I have nothing more to say to you." And with that, she turned and followed her husband.

Ellowa lingered a moment longer, her expression a curious mixture of disgust and fascination. "A soulbond," she murmured, shaking her head. "With Evryn Rowanwood. Wait until everyone hears about this." And then she, too, left, closing the door firmly behind her.

Mariselle remained rooted to the spot, the full weight of what she had set in motion crashing over her. She had anticipated her family's disapproval, even anger, but the reality of their reaction left her feeling hollow. With shaking fingers, she touched her jaw where her father's grip had left a lingering ache, then lowered her hand and glanced down at the silvery mark encircling her wrist.

She felt more distanced from her family than ever before, but this was a necessary step toward her ultimate goal. This was her chance to prove herself not merely another daughter to be married off, but a worthy heir to the Brightcrest name and all its illustrious history.

She moved slowly to the side of her bed, extinguished the faelights with a half-hearted wave, checked that the dream-chime hanging above her bed was humming faintly, and climbed beneath the covers. Pulling them up to her chin, she sought solace in the knowledge that soon sleep would claim her, carrying her to the dreamscape that had always been her sanctuary. The secret space she had crafted for herself where reality's sharp edges couldn't reach her.

But a single tear escaped, tracing a hot path down her cheek before soaking into her pillow. She blinked rapidly, refusing to allow more to follow. She had not betrayed her family; she would prove that when the time came. When Dreamland stood restored to its former glory, when the Brightcrests once again possessed an achievement to rival the Rowanwoods' influence, her family would understand that she had done all of this for them.

She shifted restlessly beneath the covers, trying to recapture the exhilaration she had felt upon realizing she could restore Dreamland. It would be worth it, she assured herself. It would all be worth it in the end.

Chapter Four

The plan was utterly preposterous and doomed to unravel at the slightest scrutiny, but Evryn had committed himself to this charade for as long as necessary. His reputation—and by extension, his family's standing—depended upon it. Mariselle Brightcrest held his secret in her delicate, dangerous hands, and until he could reclaim it, he would play whatever part required.

Which meant that he now paced the main floor of the Charmed Leaf Tea House rehearsing an announcement he had never anticipated making before the age of thirty, if at all: that he had found himself a wife.

Well. A pretend wife, at least. And thank the stars above for that. Nineteen-year-old Mariselle Brightcrest was possibly the most unpleasant young woman he'd ever had the misfortune of crossing paths with, with the sole exception of her dreadful mother and sister. Not to mention she appeared to be delusional as well. Did she truly believe herself capable of resurrecting Dreamland? The very notion was absurd. She was little more than a *child*. A disgustingly pampered one at that. She hadn't the faintest inkling of the complexities involved in such an undertaking.

And now he must pretend to be besotted with her. Evryn halted mid-stride and physically shuddered at the reminder.

But it would be worth it if he could hold onto the one thing that felt as though it were truly his. His writing, his stories, his careful construction of satirical tales that held up a mirror to elite fae society. It had begun on a whim as simple journaling, an attempt to process his frustrations at being perpetually overshadowed by Jasvian's far more important magic. But the daily observations had quickly transformed into something more, characters emerging from the people around him, fictional scenarios that sometimes felt more real than his actual life.

He'd spent months during the quiet season working up the courage to submit his first story to the literary section of the The Gilded Gazette, a publication magically distributed weekly across the United Fae Isles. He couldn't publish under his own name, of course, so he'd settled on the pseudonym E. S. Twist. To his great delight, it had been accepted! Three published stories later, he'd finally found something that was entirely his own achievement.

And now Mariselle Brightcrest had her wretched hands on one of his manuscripts. He still couldn't fathom how she'd managed it. It was the original draft of his latest published story, written in a moment of midnight inspiration a few weeks before arriving in Bloomhaven for the Season. He'd been enjoying a solitary evening ride with Cobalt, and had tucked the pages safely into the saddlebag when he was done. He'd then crafted a second version, slightly different, after another late night ride. He'd submitted that revised manuscript to the Gazette and promptly forgotten the original was still in Cobalt's saddlebag.

Had part of it been sticking out? Had Mariselle seen it while Evryn had been distracted by discussing Fin's modifications to the course obstacles? Either she'd noticed the pages peeking from beneath the flap, or—more likely, given her character—she'd deliberately rifled through his belongings the moment his back was turned. The audacity of it shocked him. Though he supposed it shouldn't. Not when a *Brightcrest* was concerned.

For a moment, he considered whether it might be worth sacrificing his secret pseudonym to avoid this ridiculous charade. But then he remembered the more scathing passages he'd written—the fictional queen who bore a striking resemblance to the High Lady, portrayed as vain and disconnected from her subjects' concerns, and the manipulative matriarch who seemed suspiciously similar to his own grandmother, weaving social webs for her own entertainment. No, he simply could not allow anyone to know that *he* had penned those words. Even the great Rowanwood family might not survive such a scandal.

Which led him right back to the inescapable fact that he must lie to his family about a fake soulbond with a woman from a family whose very name had been treated like a curse word amongst the Rowanwoods for as long as he could remember.

He'd decided it would be best to announce the news to them all at once, but logistics had complicated matters. Jasvian no longer lived at Rowanwood House since his marriage to Iris; they maintained their own residence in Bloomhaven now, visiting frequently even during the quiet season due to Iris's ongoing apprenticeship at The Charmed Leaf. And his grandmother habitually departed for the tea house before breakfast during the Bloom Season, her presence required to oversee preparations for each day. So Evryn had asked everyone to meet at the tea house instead, not long before it was due to open for the day.

The Charmed Leaf looked particularly fine in the early morning light, golden beams streaming through the large windows to cast warm dappled patterns across the polished wooden floor. The tables were neatly arranged, each draped with freshly pressed cloths of pale cream and adorned with delicate vases holding sprigs of freshly cut flowers from the tea house garden. From the kitchen came the mouth-watering aroma of Orrit's legendary scones, along with the clatter of kitchen pixies preparing for the day ahead.

Evryn continued his restless pacing, pausing occasionally to adjust his cravat in one of the tea house's ornamental mirrors. He looked respectable enough in his dark gray morning coat and neatly pressed trousers, having taken extra care with his appearance. If one was going to announce a scandalous engagement, one might as well look dapper while doing so.

The floor creaked suddenly beneath his feet, and a sound like an impatient sigh issued from the whispering leaves of the foliage that adorned the walls. A nearby vine suddenly shot out with alarming speed and wound itself swiftly around Evryn's wrist before giving a decisive tug. The unexpected force sent him stumbling sideways until he landed with an undignified thump in the nearest chair.

"I beg your pardon!" Evryn sputtered, attempting to yank his wrist free. "Is manhandling guests now part of the—"

But before he could finish, the door to the kitchen swung open. The offending vine retreated immediately, slithering back to its place on the wall with the guilty haste of a child caught stealing sweets from the pantry just as Evryn's grandmother emerged. Despite her simple morning gown, Lady Rivenna looked every inch the formidable matriarch with her no-nonsense stride and her chin held high. She carried a small stack of ledgers tucked beneath one arm and a plate bearing two scones in her other hand.

"I trust this summons involves something more substantial than your usual dramatics," she said, settling into a nearby chair. "It's the first week of the Season, and I have no less than fourteen different crises to address before we open." She gestured toward the plate of scones. "And do excuse me for eating while we speak. I left home in such haste that I haven't had a bite."

"I wouldn't dream of coming between you and Orrit's scones, Grandmother," Evryn replied, attempting a light tone that fell somewhat short of convincing, while his fingers tapped a soundless rhythm against his knee.

Lady Rivenna narrowed her eyes. "You're fidgeting worse than Rosavyn at a formal event. What exactly is this about?"

"I'd prefer to wait until the rest of the family arrives, Grandmother," Evryn said, glancing toward the door with undisguised hope for immediate rescue. When none came, his gaze darted back to his grandmother, who was now eyeing him with a great deal of suspicion, eyes narrowed even further.

"Interesting," she murmured, taking a delicate bite of one of her scones without breaking her gaze.

Evryn was saved from having to reply by the cheerful tinkling of the bell above the front door. He stood as his mother swept inside, followed by Evryn's younger brother and sister, Kazrian and Aurelise.

"… should work much better now," Kazrian was saying to Aurelise as he held the door open for her.

"But I liked it the way it was," Aurelise said, her features pulling into a frown.

"Why?" Kazrian's answering frown almost perfectly matched his twin's. "It was broken."

"It wasn't broken!" Aurelise insisted. "It was *supposed* to sound like that."

"Like a dying gossip bird?" Kazrian asked dryly.

Aurelise sighed. "It was atmospheric. The dissonance created emotional complexity."

"The only emotion it created was confusion," Kazrian said, looking around. "Oh, Grandmother, did you enchant that hanging teapot to display the time? How clever!"

Evryn glanced up, only now noticing the silver numbers glowing like moonlight along the curve of the large silver teapot suspended from the ceiling.

"Confusion?" Aurelise demanded. "Are you completely incapable of appreciating artistic nuance?"

Kazrian folded his arms over his chest as he faced his sister. "Are you completely incapable of—"

"Please, my dears," Lady Lelianna interrupted as she crossed the room toward Evryn. "Let us not begin the day this way."

"It is indeed a new enchantment," Lady Rivenna confirmed. "It was Lucie's idea."

"Ah, is Lucie here?" Kazrian asked, his face brightening. "I don't believe I've seen her yet this Season, and I wanted to ask her about—"

"That's 'Miss Fields' to you, young man," his grandmother said sternly. "And yes, she is here, attending to important tea house matters. Please do not distract her."

"Has anyone seen Rosavyn?" Evryn asked, feeling rather like a condemned man hoping to expedite his own execution before he lost his nerve entirely.

"Evryn, darling," his mother said, reaching his side and pressing a kiss to his cheek. "How mysterious of you to summon us all. Does this have something to do with your disappearance from the ball last night? In case you thought I hadn't noticed," she added with a raised eyebrow, her attempt at maternal disapproval undermined by the fond warmth that always softened her gaze when looking at any of her children.

"If you don't mind, Mother, I'd rather share my news just once," Evryn said, glancing anxiously at the front door again. "I thought Rosavyn would be with you."

"Oh, she was." Lady Lelianna turned back toward the door. "I wonder where she—"

"And what about Jasvian? He's usually—"

"Share what news?" came Jasvian's voice, though not from the front entrance as Evryn had expected. He turned to find his older brother descending the staircase from the tea house's upper study, looking every bit as composed and serious as ever.

Of course Jasvian would already be here, probably since dawn, being industrious and responsible as always. The man practically exuded duty from his pores. The upper study had been his sanctuary until their grandmother had forced him to share it with her new apprentice the previous Season. If Evryn recalled correctly, that enforced proximity was how Jasvian and Iris had begun their unlikely romance. His brother scowling over ledgers while Iris carefully documented tea leaf readings or whatever it was apprentices did. How very *Jasvian* to turn shared workspace into matrimony.

As if prompted by Evryn's thoughts, Iris hurried into the main room of the tea house from the direction of the kitchen, tucking stray wisps of hair behind one ear and clutching a notebook beneath her arm. Her presence was still sometimes surprising to Evryn—this half-human woman who had captured first his grandmother's attention and then his serious brother's heart. "Forgive me," she said, directing a sheepish smile in Evryn's direction as she stopped at Jasvian's side. "I know you said this was important. I was making a few notes—" she waved the notebook before placing it on the nearest table "—and lost track of time."

"Oh, that's—quite all right." Evryn couldn't help but feel a flicker of kinship with Iris in that moment. He understood all too well how words could capture one's attention so completely that time itself seemed to bend around the page. Though in his case, the compulsion to write usually struck in the darkest hours of night rather than with the morning sun.

The front door swung open once more, and Rosavyn strode in. "Apologies for my tardiness," she said, dusting what appeared to be dirt off the front of her skirt. "I saw Lucie on the side path trying to wrangle a pair of garden pixies who were engaged in mortal combat over a single hyacinth. I thought I should help. You wouldn't think such tiny creatures could be so—Oh. Why do you all look so serious?" She paused as she glanced around at the assembled family. "Has someone died?"

"Not yet," Evryn muttered under his breath.

"Rosavyn, dear, do sit down," Lady Lelianna said, taking a seat and patting the empty chair beside her. "Your brother has news to share."

"News?" Rosavyn's eyes widened with interest as she slipped into the seat. "Is it scandalous? Please tell me it's scandalous. The ball was dreadfully dull last night after you left."

"Rosavyn!" their mother admonished.

"Oh I can't wait until I'm allowed to attend the Opening Ball," Aurelise said wistfully. "Please can I go next year, Mother? Even if I haven't manifested yet? Rosavyn first attended when she was eighteen, and she hadn't yet …"

Her voice trailed off as she no doubt realized what she'd said. An uncomfortable silence descended upon the group as everyone except Evryn studiously avoided looking at Rosavyn, whose expression had frozen into careful neutrality.

"Well," Evryn began, deciding that if he was going to detonate a family crisis, this awkward moment was as good a time as any to light the fuse, especially if it would spare his favorite sibling further discomfort. "I've gathered you all here because I have an announcement of … significant personal import."

"Oh, for stars' sake," Lady Rivenna said, setting down her half-eaten scone. "Out with it, boy. Some of us have establishments to run."

Evryn straightened his shoulders. "Very well." He swallowed. "I am to be married."

His mother's expression transformed instantly into one of delighted surprise. "Married? Oh, Evryn! To whom? Do we know her family? When did this happen?"

"*How* did this happen?" Jasvian asked with a frown. "Were you caught in a compromising position? Please tell me you haven't created yet another scandal requiring hasty resolution. The Season has barely begun."

"Well, this is rather boring," Rosavyn said, slumping a little in her chair. "And here I thought you'd done something truly outrageous. Marriage is perfectly respectable. Disappointing, really."

"Oh, nonsense," their mother scolded. "Do ignore her, Evryn dear. Now tell us. Who is this young lady?"

Evryn's throat felt remarkably dry. He took a deep breath, savoring what would likely be the last peaceful moment in this room for some time to come. "The young lady in question," he began, then paused, steeling himself for his family's inevitable outrage, "is Mariselle Brightcrest."

The silence that followed was so profound that even the sounds from the kitchen seemed to fade. Lady Rivenna, who had been raising her scone for another bite, froze mid-motion. The scone slipped from her fingers and landed on the floor with a dull thud, her hand remaining suspended in the air as though her body had forgotten how to complete the motion. Evryn's mother released a pained gasp, pressing her hand to her chest.

"Mariselle Brightcrest?" Iris repeated, seemingly the only one among them whose vocal cords hadn't been paralyzed by shock.

"Yes," Evryn confirmed, his voice sounding oddly hoarse.

Iris's head snapped toward Lady Rivenna, and Evryn watched as his grandmother's sharp eyes immediately found Iris's face. They exchanged a look so loaded with meaning that Evryn wished desperately he could interpret it.

But before he could open his mouth to question this strange look, his grandmother's hard gaze swept back to him. "No," she said, her voice dangerously quiet. "You'll see me buried before that happens."

More likely I'll be the one in the ground, Evryn thought grimly. It wouldn't surprise him if Mariselle was indeed the death of him before this charade concluded.

"A Brightcrest?" Jasvian's voice had dropped to a horrified whisper. "Have you taken complete leave of your senses?"

"I assure you, I am perfectly sound of mind," Evryn replied with as much dignity as he could muster.

"You will not marry a Brightcrest," his grandmother said.

"I'm afraid it's not exactly a matter of choice, Grandmother," Evryn answered as calmly as possible, extending his right arm to display the silvery mark that curled around his hand and wrist. "We appear to have formed a soulbond."

Another sound escaped his mother, this one a pained whimper that she quickly stifled behind trembling fingers.

"It, ah, appeared quite unexpectedly," Evryn continued, pushing his sleeve up to reveal the rest of the mark, "while the two of us were arguing on one of the terraces outside the ballroom at Solstice Hall last night."

"No," Lady Rivenna repeated. "What absolute nonsense. I refuse to acknowledge it."

The notebook Iris had placed on one of the tables somehow slipped off the edge and landed on the floor with a loud slap. She retrieved it hastily and tucked it beneath her arm after directing a furious whisper at … the notebook itself?

Evryn shook his head before returning his gaze to Lady Rivenna. "Grandmother, you cannot *will* this out of—"

"I said no."

"Evryn." Rosavyn leaned forward, her expression uncharacteristically grave as she searched his face. "You cannot possibly go through with this. I admit I delight in the occasional impropriety, but even I must protest. Have you forgotten how Mariselle and her sister treated Iris last Season? We cannot permit a *Brightcrest* to infiltrate our family circle."

"I … yes, I am aware of what happened." In all honesty, Evryn retained only the haziest recollection of some incident in a garden maze that Rosavyn had recounted with theatrical indignation while he'd nodded at appropriate intervals, his mind wandering to other matters. "Lady Mariselle feels truly dreadful about it." He had no doubt that Mariselle possessed not a single crumb of remorse over whatever had transpired, but she would need to manufacture a convincing apology if they had any hope of maintaining this farce.

"Perhaps the soulbond can be broken?" Lady Lelianna suggested, her voice thin with desperate optimism. "Or simply refused?"

"I have no desire to break the bond," Evryn declared, surprising himself with how convincing he sounded. "I know it defies all logic and reason, but I have feelings for her."

Rosavyn physically shuddered. It was taking every ounce of Evryn's self-control not to mirror the gesture with twice the intensity.

"Feelings?" Lady Rivenna repeated in a tone that suggested Evryn had just announced he'd developed an affinity for eating garden soil. "You most certainly do not. You have been ensnared by a cheaply constructed spell straight from the pages of nonsense fiction peddled to impressionable young ladies. This 'soulbond' is nothing but magical trickery designed to manipulate your emotions. We shall see to it that this enchantment is undone as soon as possible."

"Um, I don't believe it quite works that way, Grandmother," Aurelise offered hesitantly. "And it isn't nonsense fiction. I read about it in—"

A small commotion erupted at the kitchen door as three garden pixies, their gossamer wings glittering in the morning light, dashed across the main floor carrying armfuls of freshly cut blossoms twice their size. Lady Rivenna immediately straightened in her chair.

"Out!" she shouted, waving a hand imperiously. "Now is *not* the time!"

The pixies skidded to a halt, pausing before exchanging glances of collective confusion. One of them had the audacity to stick out its tongue at Lady Rivenna before the trio retreated in a flurry of petals and indignant chatter.

Iris, who had maintained a curious silence throughout most of the exchange, finally spoke. "I believe I have as much cause as anyone to harbor ill feelings toward the Brightcrests," she said in a measured tone. "But perhaps we might all benefit from a moment's reflection. What if—and I realize this seems improbable—what if Evryn truly has developed an attachment to Lady Mariselle? Would we deny him the chance at happiness that I've found with Jasvian, simply because of a family name?"

"We most certainly would," Lady Rivenna declared. "Evryn will not find happiness with a Brightcrest."

On this particular point, Evryn couldn't help but silently agree with his grandmother—a rare occurrence that would have been worth savoring had it not been entirely irrelevant to his current predicament.

"With all due respect, Grandmother," Evryn replied, his voice tight, "I don't believe that decision falls to you. The soulbond has formed. Lady Mariselle and I are connected by forces beyond our control. I wish to marry her, and I will be doing so with or without your support."

The indignation in his voice surprised him with its genuine heat. How dare they dismiss his happiness so readily? What if he truly did wish to marry Mariselle? His entire family stood prepared to deny him without a moment's consideration. When Jasvian had fallen for Iris—a match that had raised its own share of eyebrows due to her mixed heritage—his grandmother had not given it a second thought before accepting it. In fact, she'd practically orchestrated the relationship, placing Iris directly in Jasvian's path as her apprentice. But for Evryn, the redundant second son with his 'useless' magic? No, there would apparently be no such accommodation.

"Goodness," Kazrian murmured, his expression slowly turning to one of horrified realization. "Does this mean Lady Mariselle will be coming to family gatherings? Will she be sitting at our dinner table? What if she poisons the soup?"

"Kazrian!" Lady Lelianna scolded. "The Brightcrests may have actively worked against our interests for generations, but they are not murderers."

"Though Grandmother did once say she'd sooner drink poison than accept hospitality from any of them," Aurelise murmured.

"The point remains," Jasvian said firmly, "that this union poses significant complications for both families. The Brightcrests have made no secret of their animosity toward us. How do you propose to navigate that, Evryn? Have you given any thought to the practical realities?"

In truth, Evryn had given precisely no thought to the practical realities, having been far too preoccupied with the immediate crisis of his exposed pseudonym and the ludicrous scheme that had followed. "Love … finds a way," he offered lamely.

"This is not *love!*" his grandmother exclaimed, slapping her hand down on the table. The vines adorning the walls shivered. Lady Rivenna rose to her feet in one fluid motion, and though she stood a full head shorter than Evryn, something in her bearing made him feel as though she were looking down at him. "You will not *love* a Brightcrest! Your grandfather's brother is *dead* because of that family!"

The silence that followed was absolute. Even the vines ceased their shivering. Evryn's heart hammered in his chest. His great-uncle had *died* because of the Brightcrests? From the collective shock rippling across his siblings' faces, this piece of family history was as new to them as it was to him.

It was Jasvian who finally broke the silence. "Do you mean Great-Uncle Thaelan?" he asked slowly. "But his death was an accident, was it not? No one ever mentioned the Brightcrests being involved in any way."

Lady Rivenna's lips pressed into a thin line, but she offered no further explanation.

"What do you mean, Grandmother?" Rosavyn pressed. "You cannot make a statement like that and then refuse to explain it."

"That family was directly and entirely responsible for Thaelan's death. That is all you need to know."

Evryn cleared his throat, his mind reeling. Was his grandmother really speaking of *murder?* Surely she was exaggerating, transmuting an ancient disagreement into something more sinister through decades of resentment. But even if it were true … "Grandmother, that was generations ago. Lady Mariselle cannot be held responsible for what happened in the past."

"No, but the fact remains that we will not be tied to that family."

"Perhaps, Lady Rivenna," Iris said gently, "this could be a first step toward reconciliation. After all, feuds cannot persist indefinitely."

"This one certainly can," Lady Rivenna said darkly. She gathered her pile of ledgers and the plate with its remaining scone before fixing Evryn with a glacial look. "You and I will discuss this later. In private."

"There is nothing more to discuss," Evryn replied with a defiance he would never have dared display under ordinary circumstances. His grandmother, who had already half turned away with the imperious air of someone accustomed to having the final word before making a grand exit, froze. "I intend to wed Lady Mariselle Brightcrest. The soulbond has sealed our fate."

And with that, Evryn tugged sharply at the hem of his jacket, squared his shoulders, and strode past his stunned family. He pushed through the tea house door and out into the morning air before anyone could utter another syllable—and, more importantly, before his grandmother could attempt to transform him into something small and slimy that might be found beneath a garden stone.

Outside, he exhaled a shuddering breath, disturbed to find his hands trembling slightly. Had he truly just defied Lady Rivenna Rowanwood to her face? Not in his usual manner of playful insolence that they both understood as merely the expected role of the family troublemaker, but with genuine opposition? He had. And now he felt … what, precisely?

Terrified? Absolutely. There would be consequences later, likely severe ones. And yet beneath the terror lurked something unexpectedly intoxicating —the first heady taste of true rebellion rather than merely sanctioned mischief.

The moment of triumph deflated swiftly when reality settled back in. This grand stand wasn't truly about asserting his worth or demanding the same consideration afforded to Jasvian. It was about Mariselle Brightcrest and a ridiculous charade he'd been blackmailed into performing. When this farce eventually concluded, he would feign heartbreak, and his grandmother would enjoy the vindication of having been right all along. The family hierarchy would reestablish itself with Evryn firmly in his assigned place—the charming but ultimately inconsequential second son.

The bitter disappointment that washed over him at this thought caught him entirely off guard. Why should he care? This was merely an unfortunate situation to be endured until he could reclaim his manuscript and return to his life of comfortable insignificance.

He cleared his throat and straightened his cravat with a resolute tug. Best get on with the performance. The sooner this particular play began, the sooner he could reach its final act.

Chapter Five

"Stand still, Ellowa. How can Madame Spindriel properly measure you if you persist in fidgeting like a restless sprite?" Lady Clemenbell's voice cut through the hushed atmosphere of the dressmaker's shop with all the delicacy of a butcher's cleaver.

Mariselle observed the scene from her perch on a velvet settee, savoring the rare moment when her mother's exasperation was directed at her sister rather than herself. Ellowa stood upon a raised platform, arms extended as Madame Spindriel's enchanted measuring tape flitted around her like a restless snake.

But her attention soon returned to her hands and the silver pattern that marked her skin, mostly concealed beneath lace-trimmed gloves. The events of the previous night still hung heavily in her thoughts. Her father's rage. Her mother's disgust. The bitter disappointment that had settled over the household.

And then this morning at breakfast—where her father had been conspicuously absent—her mother had casually broken the uncomfortable silence as she selected a piece of toast. "There have been some developments regarding this absurd situation with the Rowanwood boy." Then, with the precision of a master torturer, she had smiled thinly and added, "We shall discuss it later," before returning to the far more pressing matter of buttering her toast to perfection.

Later, apparently, meant after forcing Mariselle to endure a carriage ride of excruciating silence, followed by what felt like half a lifetime watching Ellowa being fitted for yet another gown she scarcely needed.

"I cannot help it, Mother," Ellowa complained, shifting her weight again. "My feet are growing numb. How much longer must I endure this torture?"

"Beauty demands sacrifice," Lady Clemenbell replied with the weary air of someone who had repeated this maxim countless times. "Mariselle, do stop slouching. You're not at home."

Mariselle straightened instinctively, years of conditioning making her body respond before her mind could form a protest. "Yes, Mother," she replied automatically, then cleared her throat as her mother's attention returned to Ellowa. "I wondered if we might perhaps discuss the matter you mentioned this morning," Mariselle ventured, her voice carefully modulated to hide the anxiety churning beneath her composed exterior.

"Not yet," her mother replied with a dismissive wave. "Ellowa's gown takes precedence."

Mariselle pressed her lips together to keep from scoffing aloud. That was an outright lie and both she and her mother knew it. If her parents' reactions last night were anything to judge by, *nothing* should be more pressing than severing Mariselle's connection to their sworn enemy, and yet now her mother pretended a dress fitting demanded greater urgency.

Mariselle forced a slow breath through her nose, recognizing the familiar pattern. This calculated indifference was merely another weapon in her mother's considerable arsenal. Mariselle would be forced to wait until her mother was willing to unveil the machinations she had been orchestrating behind the scenes.

Lady Clemenbell held up a sample of shimmering fabric that shifted between pale gold and the faintest blush pink as it caught the light. "This one, I think. It will complement your coloring beautifully, my dear."

Ellowa tilted her head as she admired her reflection in the trio of ornate mirrors strategically positioned to capture her from every angle. "Do you think it will make a sufficient impression at the Emberdales' Spring Gala? I should so hate to be merely one among many in a sea of pastel silks and predictable lace."

"Undoubtedly," Lady Clemenbell assured her. "Though perhaps with a touch more gold embroidery than we initially discussed. Nothing ostentatious, of course, but enough to ensure you'll be remembered."

The measuring tape, seemingly satisfied with its assessment of Ellowa's proportions, coiled itself neatly on Madame Spindriel's workbench. The dressmaker—a slender fae woman with moss-green hair twisted into a severe knot—muttered an incantation under her breath. The air shimmered momentarily before a ghostly outline of a gown appeared, draped over Ellowa's figure like a gauzy specter.

"What do you think of this silhouette, Lady Brightcrest?" Madame Spindriel asked, her tone professionally deferential as she circled Ellowa, occasionally pinching the magical projection to adjust a sleeve or neckline. The ethereal fabric rippled and reformed with each touch. "I've taken the liberty of incorporating some of this season's newest innovations while maintaining the classic elegance your family prefers."

Lady Clemenbell scrutinized the ghostly gown with narrowed eyes. "The bodice seems rather plain. I was thinking something with more detail. Perhaps a cascading pattern of small blooms that appear to be growing naturally along the neckline?"

"Of course, my lady," Madame Spindriel replied, though Mariselle detected the faintest tightening around the dressmaker's mouth. With a flick of her fingers, the projection shimmered and transformed, ethereal flowers now blossoming along the neckline in an elaborate pattern. "Something like this, perhaps?"

"Better," Lady Clemenbell said, her frown still in place. "Though the flowers should be smaller toward the shoulders and gradually increase in size as they approach the center."

Madame Spindriel's nostrils flared, but she made the requested adjustment without comment. The magical projection flickered again as the flowers rearranged themselves according to Lady Clemenbell's specifications. "And what of the neckline, my lady?" she asked. "The current fashion favors a modest scoop, but I've noticed that among the younger set, a slightly deeper décolletage has become quite popular."

Ellowa immediately brightened. "Oh, Mother, I should like that very much!"

Lady Clemenbell hesitated, her lips pursing as she considered this suggestion. Mariselle knew her mother was calculating the precise balance between modesty and allure, between traditional propriety and fashionable appeal.

"I suppose," Lady Clemenbell conceded finally, "a slight modification in that direction might be acceptable. But nothing too daring, Madame Spindriel. This is not the Fields establishment, catering to those of … less discerning tastes."

Despite herself, Mariselle felt a flicker of indignation on behalf of the human dressmaker whose establishment was favored by many of Bloomhaven's elite families. She had admired several of Mrs Fields's creations from a distance. The woman created gowns of extraordinary beauty without the benefit of innate fae magic. Though it was clear she sometimes employed the enchantments accessible to skilled humans, it seemed to Mariselle that her true gift lay elsewhere: in the perfect drape of fabric, the intuitive understanding of how color and texture might complement a wearer's natural attributes, and a level of craftsmanship that Madame Spindriel had always lacked.

But the Brightcrests had never frequented Mrs Fields's shop, not merely because the woman was human, but because, as Lady Clemenbell had once sniffed, "the Rowanwoods endorsed her first, and thus made the choice for us."

"What about that new glimmer-lace I heard several ladies discussing at the Opening Ball?" Ellowa asked, pivoting gracefully on her platform. "They said it catches the light in the most becoming way."

Madame Spindriel's eyes lit with professional enthusiasm. "Indeed, I received a shipment a few days ago. We can certainly incorporate that." She nodded. "This gown will be my finest creation this Season. Is this to celebrate your engagement, Lady Ellowa? I can add traditional betrothal symbols into the—"

"Engagement?" Lady Clemenbell interrupted sharply, just as Mariselle's head snapped up with renewed interest. "What nonsense are you speaking, Madame?"

The dressmaker blinked in evident surprise. "Why, the gossip birds have been squawking about it all morning, my lady. Something about a 'Rowanwood-Brightcrest union.' I assumed …" Her voice trailed off as she noted Lady Clemenbell's darkening expression. "Have I spoken out of turn?"

Mariselle sank deeper into the settee, wishing the cushions might swallow her entirely. So it had begun already. The gossip birds had taken flight with her juicy secret clutched in their beaks, just as she'd predicted. After last night, she'd foolishly hoped for a brief reprieve, perhaps a day or two to navigate the treacherous waters of her family's reaction before the tide of public opinion crashed upon them.

But the birds had acted with their usual efficiency, and now all of Bloomhaven would be abuzz. She wondered where they had overheard the news first. Had one of them perched outside her bedroom window last night, drinking in every heated word of her father's tirade? Or perhaps they'd descended upon the Rowanwood household just as Evryn made his own revelation?

Oh, stars—Petunia! The realization struck Mariselle with sudden force. Her cousin remained completely unaware of what had actually transpired last night. The shattered mirror had severed their usual means of communication, and by now, Petunia would surely have heard the news of Mariselle's soulbond and consequent engagement to Evryn Rowanwood.

She had originally planned to send a discreet note this morning via messenger pixie and then slip away to meet Petunia at their secret sanctuary —the forgotten greenhouse that stood precisely between their family properties. But after her mother's breakfast announcement of their immediate departure for the dressmaker, there had been no opportunity. Mariselle would have to try visiting their meeting place this afternoon, to explain everything properly.

"Those wretched creatures," Lady Clemenbell muttered. "Utterly lacking in discretion or decorum. And why must it always be 'Rowanwood-Brightcrest'? Why should their name invariably precede ours? As though they claim precedence in all things."

"I do apologize if I've overstepped," Madame Spindriel said, though her eyes glittered with barely disguised curiosity. "Then it is true? There is to be a marriage between the families?"

Lady Clemenbell sighed with the weary resignation of one greatly burdened by fate. "My younger daughter," she said, gesturing vaguely toward Mariselle without actually looking at her, "has found herself unexpectedly entangled with one of the Rowanwoods. A *soulbond*, of all things."

"A soulbond?" Madame Spindriel gasped. "But that's extraordinarily rare! Which Rowanwood, if I may ask?"

"The second son," Lady Clemenbell said, her lips curling in distaste. *"Evryn."*

"Oh! The charming one with the handsome—" The dressmaker coughed and broke off at the sight of Lady Clemenbell's darkening expression. "That is —I simply meant—how … unexpected."

"Indeed," Lady Clemenbell agreed coldly. "Madame, might I examine that new shipment of glimmer-lace you mentioned? I wish to see if it's truly as extraordinary as people claim."

"Of course," the dressmaker replied, clearly relieved to escape the sudden tension. "This way, my lady."

As the two women disappeared into an adjoining room, Ellowa turned to Mariselle, her eyes bright with mischief, the corners crinkling in what might pass for sisterly affection if not for the slight curl of her upper lip that Mariselle had learned from childhood preceded her most cutting remarks. "Did you hear that? She called him *charming*." Ellowa stepped off the fitting platform, the gown projection trailing behind her. "That's what everyone says about him, you know." She leaned into Mariselle's personal space and trailed one finger down the exposed skin at her throat. "What *charms* of his have captivated you so thoroughly, little sister?"

"Stop it," Mariselle muttered, swatting Ellowa's hand away, even as Ellowa laughed. "It only happened last night. There has been little time for me to become acquainted with any of his … charms."

"But you were missing from Solstice Hall for *hours*, sister dear. I'm only curious about what transpired between you and Lord Evryn after this soul-bond mysteriously appeared. Or perhaps,"she added with a delicate arch of her eyebrow, "it wasn't the soulbond that came first. Perhaps the marking formed in response to more … intimate activities?"

"I would *never*—"

"Oh, no. Of course not." Ellowa's laugh tinkled. "I jest, of course. The virtuous, obedient Mariselle would never behave with such impropriety. To engage in such scandalous behavior with *anyone* would be unthinkable, but with a Rowanwood? Why, the betrayal to our family name would eclipse even the indecency of the act itself."

Mariselle bit the inside of her cheek to suppress the unexpected twitch of her lips. If only Ellowa knew what 'indecent acts' had truly transpired. Racing through the night on a pegasus, hurtling wildly through a moonlit forest, kicking Evryn's shins, tugging her own glove off with her teeth. She rather doubted Ellowa's delicate sensibilities could withstand the shock of her younger sister engaging in actual, genuine rebellion.

"Perhaps," she said with a poise she had spent years perfecting, "you should worry less about my activities and more about securing your own matrimonial—"

Her retort was interrupted by the shop bell as another customer entered, a young woman with a nervous smile and unfashionably simple attire. Mariselle recognized her as Miss Nerie Skystone—no, she was *Lady* Skystone now—daughter of a modestly successful fae merchant whose recent ventures had elevated the family just enough to participate in society events, especially after Nerie manifested magic that was considered significant enough to be presented at Solstice Hall this Season. Mariselle had watched her magical display the previous night before making her escape from the ballroom.

"Oh, look," Ellowa whispered, her voice dropping to a register Mariselle had come to dread. "If it isn't little Miss Climbing-Above-Her-Station."

Mariselle felt the familiar twist in her stomach, the knowledge that she should defend this innocent girl warring with the certainty that doing so would redirect Ellowa's cruelty toward herself. Years of experience had taught her that joining Ellowa was the safer choice, a way to maintain the fragile illusion that she belonged within her own family.

"Her sleeves are at least a season behind," Mariselle heard herself say, hating the words even as they left her mouth. "And that shade of yellow does nothing for her complexion."

Ellowa smiled—that rare, approving smile that Mariselle still pathetically craved—and leaned closer. "Did you see the hem of her dress last night? An attempt at animated embroidery. Flowers, I think? But they barely fluttered. Like wilted weeds clinging to the edge of her gown," she snickered.

Nerie glanced their way, a hesitant smile forming. Ellowa immediately raised her voice. "I simply cannot comprehend how anyone could appear in public with such inferior magical embellishments. It reflects a fundamental lack of understanding about proper society."

The girl's smile faltered, her cheeks flushing with embarrassment as she turned away to join her mother beside a display of ribbons. Mariselle's stomach clenched with shame.

But before she could decide whether it was worth it to challenge her sister's casual cruelty, Lady Clemenbell returned. "The glimmer-lace will do for the final embellishments," Lady Clemenbell declared. "Now, Ellowa, back on the platform. Madame Spindriel will return shortly."

She turned to Mariselle, her voice dropping to a confidential murmur. "Since we have a moment of relative privacy, regarding those developments I mentioned this morning …"

Mariselle steeled herself, entirely unsure what to expect.

"Your father and I have discussed the situation at length," Lady Clemenbell continued. "While we cannot and will not ever support a marriage to a Rowanwood, we have recognized certain … strategic advantages to this unexpected connection."

"Strategic advantages?" Mariselle repeated, hardly daring to hope.

"Indeed." Her mother's voice dropped further, barely above a whisper. "Your position offers unprecedented access to the Rowanwood family. You will undoubtedly be invited to their gatherings, perhaps even to The Charmed Leaf itself, a place no Brightcrest has ever been permitted to enter."

Understanding dawned, and Mariselle had to suppress a wild urge to laugh. "You want me to spy on them."

"I would never use such a vulgar term," Lady Clemenbell replied with a haughty look. "But information is a valuable currency. Lady Rivenna has maintained her social stranglehold for far too long. There must be something —some method, some secret—that explains her dominance of Bloomhaven society. Your father believes you are now uniquely positioned to discover what that might be, whether it is evidence of how they've manipulated their standing in society, or insights into their business practices. Even something as simple as an embarrassing family secret would suffice."

Oh, the irony. Mariselle already possessed precisely the sort of embarrassing secret her mother sought—Evryn's hidden identity as E. S. Twist, author of thinly veiled satires mocking the High Lady herself. Yet she could not reveal it without destroying her own carefully constructed plan.

But relief flooded through her nonetheless. The charade could continue. Dreamland could be restored. And best of all, her parents no longer viewed her with quite the same disgust.

"I see," she said, keeping her expression neutral. "So … you are not forcing me to end the engagement?" she asked carefully. "You're not going to attempt to break the soulbond?"

"Mariselle, dear, I understand that you *think* you are experiencing certain … *feelings* for this boy," her mother said, each word coated with the same saccharine patience one might use when explaining simple arithmetic to a slow child. "And no doubt you harbor some fantasy that we will eventually embrace this absurdity. But make no mistake—this is merely a temporary arrangement. You will gather what information you can while your father and I locate a means to dissolve this repulsive magical tether. Once free of its influence, you will recognize how thoroughly your emotions have been manipulated, and you will thank us for rescuing you from such an abhorrent fate."

Mariselle carefully arranged her features into an expression of reluctant acceptance, knowing she must appear appropriately lovestruck yet dutiful, a daughter torn between newfound passion and familial obligation. Too much enthusiasm for her parents' plan would seem suspicious when she was supposedly enthralled by her soulbond.

"I … I suppose if that's what you wish, Mother," she said, allowing a tremor to enter her voice. "Though it's difficult to imagine ever feeling differently than I do now. But I trust your judgment in this matter."

"Good," her mother said.

"And I'm pleased to be of service to the family."

"Excellent." Lady Clemenbell patted her hand, a rare physical gesture that Mariselle couldn't help leaning into slightly, despite herself. "We knew you would see reason once you'd had time to reflect. This may well be the most valuable contribution you've ever made to the Brightcrest name."

The backhanded compliment stung, but Mariselle maintained her composed expression. "I'll do my best not to disappoint you."

"Yes, well, even you should find this task manageable," her mother said. "Simply observe everything and report back to me faithfully. I shall be the one to determine what information holds genuine value. You needn't trouble yourself with—"

A sharp rap on the shop window interrupted her mother's instructions. A small figure hovered outside, its wings catching the morning light. Mariselle blinked in surprise. Unlike the plainly dressed messenger pixies typically employed by Bloomhaven's elite, this one wore what appeared to be a miniature palace uniform, complete with the High Lady's insignia prominently embroidered across its chest.

Madame Spindriel hurried to open the door, and the pixie scurried inside, its expression distinctly irritated as it surveyed the room. Upon spotting the three Brightcrest women, it darted toward them, muttering under its breath about "searching half of Bloomhaven" and how someone was "most insistent upon immediate delivery." It produced a small envelope from its delivery pouch and called out, "Lady Brightcrest?"

"Yes, that is I," Mariselle's mother said, extending her hand.

The pixie, however, swooped straight past her outstretched fingers and hovered between the two sisters, its tiny features pinched with concentration. "Lady *Mariselle* Brightcrest?"

Mariselle's mouth formed a small 'o' of surprise as she nodded, acutely aware of her mother's stiffening posture and the sudden frost in her expression. With slightly trembling fingers, Mariselle accepted the envelope, its weight substantial despite its modest size. The parchment was cream-colored and smooth, clearly of the finest quality and sealed with a wax impression of what was unmistakably the royal insignia. She stared at it in bewilderment. Her family rarely received correspondence from Solstice Hall. The Rowanwoods—or Lady Rivenna, at least—seemed to enjoy some level of favor with the High Lady, but the Brightcrests had never been granted similar distinction.

"Well, what is it?" Ellowa demanded, visibly affronted at being excluded from whatever mysterious communication had arrived.

Mariselle broke the seal and unfolded the note. "'Lady Mariselle Brightcrest,'" she read aloud, "'Her Grace, the High Lady of the United Fae Isles, requests your presence for tea at Solstice Hall this afternoon at precisely three o'clock, along with Lord ...'" She trailed off and swallowed, suddenly realizing precisely what this summons was about. "'... along with Lord Evryn Rowanwood,'" she continued faintly. "'A carriage will arrive at Brightcrest Manor at half past two to convey you to the palace.'"

"Oh, stars above!" Lady Clemenbell exclaimed, her previous frostiness instantly melting into a flurry of excitement. "We must return home at once! What gowns do we have that might be suitable? Oh, this is *such* short notice! But what an extraordinary honor for us to be summoned personally by the High Lady!"

"Mother," Mariselle interjected, "the invitation specifies that I am to attend alone."

Lady Clemenbell paused and blinked. "What? Nonsense! A young unmarried lady cannot possibly—"

"It says so explicitly," Mariselle insisted, turning the note so her mother could see. "Here, at the bottom."

"But you cannot arrive alone in—"

"I'm certain all proprieties will be observed, Mother," Mariselle assured her. "The note mentions a carriage will be sent. The palace will undoubtedly ensure everything is conducted with impeccable decorum."

"Let me see that." Lady Clemenbell snatched the invitation, her eyes narrowing as she scanned the elegant script.

As she muttered something about it being 'highly irregular' and 'most improper,' Mariselle's mind continued to race. This was about the soulbond, of course. The *fake* soulbond that the High Lady herself no doubt wished to examine. Mariselle clasped her shaking hands together. What had begun as a desperate scheme to restore Dreamland and prove herself to her family had somehow escalated into a matter of royal interest. And now she was going to have to deliver the performance of her life.

Chapter Six

Every step Mariselle took through Solstice Hall's glittering corridors felt like approaching the center of a spiderweb, where the High Lady waited like a calculating arachnid, ready to detect the slightest tremor of falsehood in Mariselle's carefully constructed tale.

Breathe, she commanded herself, though her lungs seemed to have forgotten how to function properly. *You are Lady Mariselle Brightcrest, and you are hopelessly, tragically in love with Evryn Rowanwood.*

The very thought made her want to laugh hysterically, which would undoubtedly be the death knell of this already precarious charade. But she could do this. She had spent a lifetime honing the art of calculated performance, and now she simply needed to channel her hard-won skill into this most challenging role: convincingly portraying an emotion she'd never experienced for a man she thoroughly despised.

The palace steward moved silently a few paces ahead of her, his formal white attire bearing the High Lady's insignia embroidered in gold thread. He hadn't spoken a single word since greeting her at the entrance with a perfectly calibrated bow and a murmured, "This way, Lady Brightcrest."

They crossed the expanse of yet another grand hall, their footsteps echoing against the marble as they approached a series of tall archways that opened onto the sunlit gardens beyond. Mariselle had been inside the palace several times before, but never during daylight hours, and never beyond the ballroom where seasonal festivities were held. Without the press of bodies and the distraction of music, the palace seemed impossibly vast, making her feel small and insignificant.

During the carriage ride here, she had briefly considered the unthinkable: confessing everything. Laying bare the falsehood of the soulbond, explaining about the ancient contract, the Dreamland restoration, her deal with Evryn. Such an admission would spare her the anxiety of maintaining this elaborate charade before the High Lady's scrutinizing gaze—and the repercussions should the High Lady discover this lie *without* Mariselle confessing it.

But such a confession would render all her efforts meaningless. She would return to precisely where she had begun—staring wistfully at Dreamland's ruins by moonlight, the perpetually disappointing youngest Brightcrest daughter, destined to be bartered away to whichever stuffy lord her parents could convince to take her. She would exchange one cage for another.

And it wasn't merely about proving herself to her family, nor even about witnessing Dreamland's resurrection. Something deeper burned within her, a conviction that *she* should be the one to do it. It had been less than a day since she had set this plan into motion, and already she felt in the very depths of her being that Dreamland was *meant for her*. And this deal she had struck with Evryn was the only way she was going to manage it.

So she would lie to the High Lady's face. The thought made her stomach clench with anxiety. Lying to her parents, to society, even to herself—these were familiar territories. But to deceive the ruler of the United Fae Isles while seated across from her at tea? It seemed like tempting fate in the most foolhardy manner possible.

I've survived almost twenty years in the Brightcrest household, she reminded herself. *I can survive an afternoon tea with the High Lady.*

The corridor widened, and ahead, Mariselle could see where it opened onto a sunlit terrace. The steward slowed his pace, allowing her a moment to take in the view as they approached. Beyond the elegantly carved archway lay what appeared to be a small, intimate garden. Not the legendary Royal Gardens that surrounded the palace, sprawling for acres. This was something else entirely: a secluded sanctuary, clearly designed for private conversations away from curious ears.

Stone pathways wound their way between beds of flowers, and iridescent butterflies flitted about, their shimmering wings catching the light. A delicate table had been set beneath the dappled shade of a flowering tree, and seated beneath it, already waiting, was the High Lady herself.

Mariselle had seen her before, of course, from a respectful distance at various formal functions, most recently at the Opening Ball. But never this close. Never in such an intimate setting. Her pale blue hair cascaded freely down her back in rippling waves—a style no one else dared copy—and her ink-blue eyes seemed to miss nothing as they swept the garden. She was relatively young compared to previous rulers of the United Fae Isles, somewhere between Mariselle's parents' generation and her grandparents', yet her presence still managed to convey the quiet authority and measured wisdom of someone who had witnessed centuries rather than decades.

Mariselle looked around, but there was still no sign of Evryn. Had he declined the invitation? Unlikely. Even Evryn Rowanwood wouldn't be foolish enough to snub the High Lady herself. Perhaps he had already come and gone? No, the invitation had made it seem as though their presence was requested simultaneously rather than in succession.

The steward paused at the threshold of the garden. "Lady Mariselle Brightcrest," he announced with perfect diction, bowing deeply.

The High Lady inclined her head in acknowledgment, and Mariselle responded with a deep curtsy. As she straightened, she heard footsteps on the pathway to her left and another voice announcing, "Lord Evryn Rowanwood."

So that was it. They had been brought from different entrances, timed to arrive simultaneously. No opportunity to confer beforehand, to align their stories or refresh the details of their fabricated romance. Mariselle suspected the High Lady had orchestrated this deliberately.

She glanced up, her gaze drawn to the sound of approaching footsteps. Evryn stepped into view and executed a flawless bow, somehow managing to look both respectful and utterly unruffled in his impeccably tailored morning coat. It was as if the events of the previous night had been nothing more than a minor social inconvenience rather than a life-altering entanglement.

"Lady Brightcrest. Lord Rowanwood." The High Lady's voice was melodious but carried an undercurrent of authority that demanded immediate attention. "How delightful that you could join me on such short notice. Please, be seated."

She gestured toward two chairs positioned on the same side of the table, but with a respectable distance between them. Close enough to suggest courtship, yet far enough apart to maintain propriety. Mariselle suppressed a sigh. This arrangement would require her to demonstrate affection through adoring glances rather than casual touches. A far more challenging performance.

"Thank you for the invitation, Your Grace," Mariselle said, settling herself into the offered chair. She smoothed her skirts and folded her hands neatly in her lap, the very picture of a well-mannered young lady.

"Indeed, we are honored by your interest," Evryn added, his voice carrying that effortless warmth he bestowed upon everyone except herself. *The charming one*, Madame Spindriel had called him. And indeed, it was infuriating how naturally that charm seemed to flow from Evryn Rowanwood, as though he'd been born knowing precisely how to put others at ease.

The High Lady waved a hand, and a palace attendant materialized from the shadows of a nearby flowering archway. The woman lifted an ornate silver teapot and began pouring fragrant amber liquid into delicate porcelain cups.

"News of your unexpected connection has reached my ears," the High Lady said, the faintest hint of amusement coloring her tone. "I confess, my curiosity was piqued. A soulbond between a Brightcrest and a Rowanwood? One might as well announce that water has begun flowing uphill."

Mariselle allowed herself a small laugh. "Indeed, Your Grace. We were equally surprised."

"May I?" the High Lady asked, extending her hand toward Mariselle's wrist. "I should like to examine this mark that is already causing such a stir among the gossip birds."

Mariselle swallowed hard as she removed her glove to reveal the silvery pattern that curled around her wrist and palm. She extended her arm and tried not to shiver as the High Lady took her hand. Her touch was cool and light as she turned Mariselle's forearm this way and that, studying the intricate design with undisguised fascination while the attendant finished pouring the tea, setting each cup on its saucer with a barely audible clink before dissolving back into the garden's periphery.

"Extraordinary," the High Lady murmured. "And yours matches exactly?" she asked, looking to Evryn.

He nodded and presented his own marked hand for inspection. The High

Lady studied them side by side, her expression unreadable. "In all my years, I have encountered only one other couple bearing such a mark," she said finally. "It is exceedingly rare."

Mariselle's heart skipped a beat. If the High Lady had seen a genuine soulbond before, would she detect differences between it and their counterfeit version? She glanced at Evryn, forcing her features into an expression she hoped resembled lovesick adoration in the hopes of masking the anxiety that was building in her chest.

"How curious that it should form between members of families with such a contentious history," the High Lady continued, releasing their hands and sitting back. She lifted her teacup and brought it toward her lips. "Tell me," she said, before taking a sip, "how exactly did this occur? The gossip birds have been most unreliable on the details."

Mariselle caught Evryn's eye, a silent question in her gaze. He responded with the slightest quirk of his eyebrow, a clear message: *Proceed as you will. This elaborate game is all yours to direct.*

"It happened last night at the Opening Ball, Your Grace," Mariselle said to the High Lady, "during a … well, while we were arguing. Our hands accidentally touched as we both reached for the same railing, and there was a flash of light."

"The mark appeared instantly," Evryn continued, "spreading across our hands and wrists."

"Fascinating," the High Lady. "Did you feel anything?"

"It was … somewhat painful," Mariselle admitted. "Like lightning beneath the skin, as my beloved—Lord Rowanwood, I mean—described it."

She glanced at Evryn again, noticing the slight tensing of fingers where they rested upon his knee at her use of the endearment 'my beloved.' Most likely trying to hold back a snort of laughter.

"And beyond the physical sensation?" the High Lady pressed. "Emotionally, I mean."

This was the part Mariselle had dreaded most. Describing fictional feelings for Evryn Rowanwood without dissolving into either laughter or revulsion seemed an impossible feat. Yet she managed to fix her gaze upon him, softening her expression into what she hoped resembled affection.

"It was … confusing at first," she began. "A rush of feelings that made no sense, given our history. But then … it was as though I was seeing him clearly for the first time. All the animosity, all the years of family resentment—they simply fell away." She lowered her lashes, partly for effect and partly to hide the sheer absurdity she feared might be visible in her eyes.

"Yes," Evryn said, his voice unexpectedly soft. "I found myself seeing her anew. As though a veil had been lifted, revealing someone I'd never truly noticed before."

Mariselle blinked, startled by the sincerity in his tone. She looked up to find him gazing at her with an expression of such tender regard that she might have actually believed him if she didn't know the truth. Her heart rate slowed as she relaxed slightly. She'd been concerned he might not be able to act convincingly enough, but it seemed she'd worried for nothing.

She tore her eyes away to address the High Lady once more. "We both tried to resist, of course. It seemed impossible that I could develop such feelings for a Rowanwood, of all people. But the connection was undeniable."

The High Lady observed this exchange with evident pleasure, a smile playing at the corners of her lips. "How romantic," she said. "I confess, I have always harbored a weakness for tales of unexpected love. The notion that magic itself might intervene to bring together those who would otherwise remain apart … it quite captivates the imagination."

Mariselle couldn't quite hide her surprise. The High Lady—a romantic? The woman whose very presence could silence a ballroom, whose decisions shaped the political landscape of the entire realm—this formidable figure admitted to being enchanted by notions of fated love? It seemed incongruous with her cool, composed demeanor.

"Your families must be beside themselves," the High Lady continued, a knowing gleam in her ink-blue eyes. "Lady Rivenna, in particular, has never been one to disguise her feelings regarding the Brightcrests, though she has never elaborated on the precise origins of this feud. I came into power only after it was well established and am still unclear about the precise details."

"Ah, yes. My grandmother has expressed … reservations," Evryn acknowledged diplomatically.

"As have my parents," Mariselle added. "Though they are coming to terms with the situation."

"Delightful," the High Lady said, then glanced past them suddenly, her expression brightening. "Ah, my dear, do come join us." To Mariselle and Evryn, she added, "You know my son, Prince Ryden."

A hard knot formed instantly in Mariselle's stomach, dread washing through her veins like ice water. She did indeed know the prince, though not in the way the High Lady must surely be imagining. She lifted her gaze and saw him approaching from a side path. Tall, with midnight-blue hair and skin several shades darker than his mother's. He moved with the casual grace of someone who had never needed to worry about being judged for their posture or deportment.

"Your Highness," Mariselle said, rising to curtsy while her heart continued racing in her chest. She had nothing to worry about, she assured herself as Evryn bowed beside her. Prince Ryden would reveal nothing. He had as much to lose as she and Evryn did.

"Mother," the prince greeted, dropping into a chair with none of the formality one might expect from a prince. He stretched his long legs before him and suppressed a yawn that seemed deliberately provocative.

"I wonder, my dear," the High Lady said, her serene expression unchanged despite her son's casual disregard for etiquette, "have you met Lord Evryn Rowanwood and Lady Mariselle Brightcrest?"

The prince's gaze swept over them both, and Mariselle held her breath. His eyes—the same ink-blue as his mother's—betrayed not a flicker of recognition.

"No, Mother," he said with an exaggerated sigh. "You keep me caged here like some exotic bird, so of course I've never met these people." He straightened slightly, his posture still relaxed but his attention more focused. "But I'm well aware of the notorious rivalry between these two families, and the fact that two of their offspring now find themselves romantically entangled …" A slow grin spread across his face. "Well, I have to say, it's the most entertaining thing I've heard this Season."

Mariselle worked hard to keep her smile to herself, inwardly acknowledging that Prince Ryden could pull off an act even better than she could. His performance was flawless—the bored royal prince, entirely unacquainted with the wilder elements of Bloomhaven society.

"Ryden," the High Lady muttered, the serene mask of her features slipping just enough to reveal a flash of maternal displeasure. "Your observations, while perhaps accurate, lack the diplomacy one expects from someone of your station."

"Forgive me for speaking plainly in your exalted presence," Prince Ryden replied, not sounding remotely contrite. His mother's lips thinned slightly before her composure returned in full.

"I believe I've kept you both long enough," she said, turning back to Mariselle and Evryn with a gracious smile that made the previous tension seem imagined. "I have matters requiring my attention, and you must have much to discuss regarding your future together." She rose, and Mariselle and Evryn immediately followed suit, Mariselle acutely aware that neither she nor Evryn had taken so much as a sip of the tea that now cooled in their untouched cups. "This has been a most illuminating conversation. Your connection is quite remarkable." A smile curved her lips. "In fact, I believe it deserves proper recognition. I shall host an engagement ball in your honor, here at Solstice Hall."

Mariselle blinked, hoping she had misheard. "An engagement ball, Your Grace?" she repeated faintly.

"Indeed," the High Lady confirmed. "We shall celebrate your newfound love for each other with the entirety of Bloomhaven in attendance." Prince Ryden coughed loudly, pounding his chest with his fist several times before finally clearing his throat with dramatic emphasis. His mother directed a withering glance at him before returning her attention to Mariselle and Evryn. "It will be the event of the Season."

Mariselle fought to keep her dismay from showing on her face. She had anticipated curiosity when news of their engagement spread, but not this level of attention. Not a royal celebration that would make their charade the focal point of the entire Season.

"Your Grace, we are deeply honored," Evryn said, recovering more quickly than Mariselle. "Though we would not wish to impose upon your generosity."

"Nonsense," the High Lady said with a wave of her hand. "We shall celebrate tomorrow night."

"*Tomorrow?*" Mariselle blurted before she could stop herself. "That is … soon, Your Grace."

"Why, of course it must be tomorrow," the High Lady replied with elegant certainty. "I cannot possibly allow your first public appearance as a betrothed couple to take place at some lesser social gathering. No, an event of this significance—a genuine soulbond—must be properly celebrated at

Solstice Hall under my auspices. The herald pixies shall be dispatched at once to inform the elite of Bloomhaven."

"But surely the preparations for such an event would require more time," Mariselle ventured cautiously.

"My dear child," the High Lady said, "when one commands the resources of the Summer Palace, time becomes a rather flexible concept. My staff is exceedingly capable, and with the appropriate application of magic, we shall create an evening worthy of your extraordinary connection." Her eyes softened momentarily as she regarded them both. "And when might we expect the wedding itself? While soulbonded couples traditionally marry with haste, given the intensity of their connection, perhaps your unusual family circumstances warrant a more measured approach?"

"Indeed, Your Grace," Evryn interjected smoothly. "While our feelings for each other are undeniably powerful, we recognize that our families require time to adjust to this unexpected development. We thought perhaps a wedding toward the Season's end would strike the appropriate balance, acknowledging the depth of our connection while allowing our families the courtesy of preparation."

"How sensible," the High Lady observed, though Mariselle detected a hint of disappointment in her tone. "Now," she continued, waving her hand, "Mannings will escort you out. The carriages that brought you here should be waiting to carry you home."

"If I might offer my services instead, Mother," Prince Ryden interjected, pushing himself to his feet with sudden enthusiasm. "I'm sure Mannings has far more important duties than escorting guests through corridors."

The High Lady regarded her son with a long, measuring look. "Very well," she conceded. "You may see Lord Rowanwood and Lady Brightcrest to their carriages."

They departed the intimate garden, leaving the High Lady seated beneath the flowering tree.

Once they had rounded a corner and found themselves in the relative privacy of a deserted corridor, the prince's demeanor transformed. A broad grin spread across his face as he flung one arm around Evryn's shoulders with casual familiarity. "Well, well. A *soulbond*, my friend? With your sworn rival? Of all the preposterous twists of fate!"

"A delightful surprise, indeed," Evryn said between gritted teeth.

Ryden's laughter echoed through the corridor. "So it's true then? This isn't the tragic result of some bet you've lost? You mean to tell me you've *genuinely* fallen for a Brightcrest?"

"It's hard to believe, isn't it?" Mariselle said in her most honeyed voice, followed by a dreamy sigh that suggested profound yearning. "But Lord Evryn and I find ourselves quite besotted with one another."

By now, Prince Ryden's entire frame was shaking with barely contained mirth. "Oh, this is too good." He feigned wiping away tears of laughter from beneath one eye. "Well, one benefit is that I shall easily be able to claim victory in all future races now that the two of you will be exchanging sickening looks of adoration from the backs of your pegasi rather than attempting to knock one another off course."

"Nonsense," Mariselle said serenely, keeping her gaze directed forward and her chin tilted up. "I remain perfectly capable of leaving you *both* in the smoke trail of Cinder's wings, no matter how smitten I may be."

Chapter Seven

Mariselle pushed open the door of the old greenhouse later that afternoon, wincing at the slight squeak of its hinges, and found Petunia already inside, pacing between the rows of potted plants they had cultivated over the years. Mariselle felt a surge of relief—Petunia must have received the hastily scrawled note she'd dispatched with one of the household pixies the moment she'd returned from Solstice Hall.

"Please," Petunia said without preamble, halting her agitated circuit to fix Mariselle with a piercing stare, "tell me that all this nonsense the gossip birds have been shrieking about you and *Evryn Rowanwood* is complete and utter rubbish."

Mariselle closed the door behind her and leaned against it, expelling a breath. "Yes! Well, partly." She pushed away from the door and crossed the space to drop into one of the pair of worn velvet chairs they had pilfered years ago from the Dawndale attic. A small table between the chairs held a wicker picnic basket, Petunia's customary offering whenever they met in the greenhouse. "When did you hear?"

"This morning, around dawn," Petunia replied, abandoning her pacing to take the chair across from her cousin. She swiped in annoyance at the wayward strands of auburn hair that had fallen around her face. "I told you the darned things were building a nest in that tree outside my window. Now I have to endure their rubbish at all hours of the day."

"Those wretched birds," Mariselle muttered. "They work quickly. It would have been barely a few hours since they heard me telling my parents about the soulbond. Could they not rest for at least—"

"Soulbond?" Petunia's eyebrows shot up. "I didn't hear *that* part. They were screeching something about a 'shocking Rowanwood-Brightcrest engagement' and an 'outraged family,' but their vocabulary tends toward the dramatic rather than the specific." She leaned forward, her expression softening with genuine concern. "Mari, what have you done?"

Mariselle took a deep breath before launching into her tale. The midnight race against Evryn, their chase through the forest, the discovery of a secret she could use as leverage against him. She deliberately omitted the precise nature of this secret, having pledged her word not to reveal it—and a promise remained a promise, even when given to a detestable Rowanwood. She continued with their confrontation at Windsong Cottage, the unexpected activation of the magical contract, and finally, the agreement that followed.

"So you see," she concluded, "it isn't actually a soulbond at all. It's a contract mark. But it looks so similar that we've decided to claim it's a soulbond to explain its appearance without revealing our true purpose. Well, *my* true purpose, to be exact." She leaned forward and rested her elbows on her knees, holding her cousin's gaze. "Tunia, I'm going to bring Dreamland back to life. The Brightcrest name will finally be elevated above the Rowanwoods, and my family will be forced to acknowledge me as more than merely the insignificant younger daughter."

Throughout Mariselle's explanation, Petunia had simply stared. Now she sighed and reached into the picnic basket, withdrawing a large slice of cake wrapped in a linen napkin. "Cake?" she asked, breaking it into two pieces.

"Oh, yes, thank you," Mariselle said, gratefully accepting the half Petunia offered to her. She realized suddenly she hadn't eaten much since breakfast, having been too nervous about her audience with the High Lady to manage more than a few bites at luncheon. She tasted the cake. It was delicately spiced with cinnamon and cardamom, exactly the sort of comfort she'd been craving.

"Let me understand this correctly," Petunia said, watching her. "You've magically bound yourself to a Rowanwood, of all people, to restore a failed attraction that destroyed your grandfather's life, all based on magic you've been hiding from the family, and you expect this to somehow win their approval?" She took a bite and chewed before adding, "Your optimism continues to be your most baffling quality."

Mariselle felt a smile pulling her lips up despite the gravity of her situation. This was why she treasured Petunia above all others—her cousin's unflinching honesty, delivered with that perfect blend of exasperation and affection that made even criticism feel like care.

"I know it sounds mad," she admitted, brushing crumbs from her skirt, "but you should have seen the cottage, Tunia. I took a closer look after that Rowanwood idiot left last night. Everything is perfectly preserved, all the Dreamland documentation and blueprints arranged on a bookshelf, as though waiting all these years for someone to return. And the contract wouldn't have activated unless this was meant to happen."

Petunia snorted. "Magical contracts activate because of specific conditions being met, not because of cosmic destiny. You cut your hand, bled on the door, and made an oath. That's not fate—that's unfortunate timing."

"Perhaps," Mariselle conceded, leaning forward to grasp her cousin's hand, "but now I have the chance to turn unfortunate timing into a magnificent opportunity. Don't you remember how we always spoke about returning Dreamland to its former glory?"

Her mind drifted back to those sun-drenched afternoons in the library tower at Foxleigh Hall, during the summers their families had spent there together. She and Petunia had created their own sanctuary, far from the judgmental eyes of their overbearing mamas, lined with pillows and forbidden books. With lemonade in hand and bare feet tucked beneath them, they had spun stories about the legendary Dreamland that neither had ever seen but both had imagined in vivid detail.

"No," Petunia said flatly, interrupting Mariselle's brief reverie. "I remember us *imagining* what it might have been like, but I certainly don't remember any fanciful notions to restore it."

"Well, fine. Perhaps it was only me. But that's beside the point! This is our chance, Tunia!"

"*Our* chance?" Petunia repeated. "I'm certainly not participating in this madness."

"Oh, but I need you, Tunia!" Mariselle said in earnest. "I need your magic. *Dreamland* needs your magic."

"I highly doubt that."

"I mean it," Mariselle insisted. "To be fully operational, Dreamland requires the type of magic that allows visitors to cross from waking reality into dream space while remaining conscious. Otherwise they would simply fall asleep, and then it's almost impossible to wake them on the other side. Didn't you ever pay attention to Grandmother's stories?"

"No," Petunia said, without a shred of remorse.

"Petunia Dawndale!" Mariselle smacked her cousin's knee, but she was laughing now. "Don't tell me you've bought into your parents' nonsense that threshold magic is of no use to anyone."

"You must admit," Petunia replied with an arched brow, "that until this precise moment, when Dreamland has suddenly become a possibility again, there was precious little practical application for dream threshold magic. Who wants to remain conscious within someone else's dream? How terribly awkward."

"Well, I suppose that's true. Dream sharing is far more enjoyable."

"Mariselle!"

"So I've heard!" Mariselle hastened to clarify. "Naturally I've never experienced such a thing myself."

"I should certainly hope not." Petunia's normally composed features betrayed her as a flush of pink swept across her cheeks.

"As I was saying," Mariselle continued, redirecting the conversation, "if Dreamland is to function as it once did, your threshold magic is absolutely essential. My magic, of course, will take care of everything else relating to the dream space, and that insufferable Rowanwood I've now bound myself to will handle the lumyrite networks that stabilize and power everything. When one considers it properly, the arrangement is rather perfect."

Petunia heaved a long-suffering sigh. "Perfect is *not* the word I would use when contemplating becoming entangled with the Rowanwoods."

"Rowan*wood*," Mariselle corrected with a theatrical shudder. "Just one, thankfully. And only temporarily."

"Did you tell him what you can do? The true nature of your manifestation?"

"No. He doesn't need to know that, and I see no reason to share more than necessary. His contribution is limited to the lumyrite networks. Let him focus on that while I manage everything else. He'll find out eventually, along with everyone else."

"You realize you could simply *tell* your family what magic you actually possess instead of going through this elaborate ruse and *then* revealing it?"

"And surrender my future to their designs?" Mariselle shook her head firmly. "If I confessed my abilities now, my magic would become merely another Brightcrest resource to be directed as Father sees fit. He remains convinced that I lack the capacity to manage anything important without supervision. But if I present Dreamland as a completed achievement rather than a mere possibility, then he shall be forced to recognize my worth on my own terms, not as a pawn to be maneuvered but as an equal deserving of respect."

Petunia slowly consumed another bite of cake, her hazel eyes never leaving Mariselle's face. "I don't understand," she said eventually, "why you're still so insistent on earning their approval after all these years. You realize both our families are awful, don't you?"

"They're not that bad," Mariselle protested automatically. "They are merely … misunderstood. Our family's dream magic empire is truly remarkable, yet we're continually overshadowed by the Rowanwoods, constantly at a disadvantage in society, so often left on the periphery of circles we rightfully deserve to—"

"Oh, come now," Petunia interrupted with a snort. "That's hardly an excuse for their behavior. The truth remains, Mari. They're simply dreadful people."

The blunt assessment hung in the air between them, and Mariselle found she couldn't quite summon a convincing argument against it. If she was being honest, most members of her family weren't particularly nice, but it was circumstances beyond their control that had forced them to be that way.

And they weren't *all* dreadful. Mariselle had been close to her grandmother once, when she was a child. But Lady Nirella had withdrawn to one of the more modest Brightcrest properties on the outskirts of Bloomhaven years ago and had grown more distant with each passing Season.

As for Mariselle's brother Alaryn, he'd effectively escaped the worst of their family's dynamics by managing a separate branch of the dream magic business far from the main estate after his marriage several years ago.

"Perhaps you're right about them," Mariselle said quietly, unable to meet Petunia's knowing gaze. "But they're our *family*, Tunia. The only family we get. And I want to feel as though I *belong* in the family I was born into. Don't you?"

Petunia arched a brow. "Even if belonging means joining Ellowa when she tears others to shreds?"

Mariselle felt that familiar twist of shame. This well-worn argument had passed between them countless times before—Petunia's steadfast disapproval of the cold, cutting persona Mariselle adopted in her sister's presence. But Petunia had never fully understood the delicate balance Mariselle maintained. When Ellowa set her sights on a target, there were only ever two options: join in, or pay the price later.

But if Mariselle could prove her worth to her family, everything would change. Ellowa wouldn't dare treat her as a disposable pawn any longer. She'd finally be free of her sister's cruel games.

Mariselle squared her shoulder and quietly asked, "Will you help me?"

Petunia sighed, her expression softening almost imperceptibly. "Of course I will."

Mariselle launched herself from her chair and threw her arms around her cousin, nearly knocking them both over in her enthusiasm. "Thank you, thank you!"

Petunia returned the embrace, her arms tightening briefly around Mariselle's shoulders. "I can't exactly refuse and leave you working alone in that cottage with Evryn Rowanwood. The impropriety is staggering. If someone discovered the two of you alone there, your reputation would be utterly ruined."

Mariselle couldn't help her snort of laughter as she released her cousin and settled back in her chair. "As if I don't already commit reputation-ruining acts on a regular basis. Imagine if someone discovered me racing a pegasus through the night."

"I imagine it regularly, and I still maintain that your enthusiasm for plummeting through the darkness astride a temperamental magical beast is evidence of a deeply concerning absence of self-preservation instinct."

Mariselle sighed happily, imagining the intoxicating freedom of soaring above the sleeping town, that delicious shiver of exhilaration racing down her spine with each swift dive and turn. "It is truly marvelous."

Petunia groaned and rolled her eyes.

"And you'll need to set aside your own self-preservation instinct, dear cousin," Mariselle continued, refocusing on Petunia, "because you shall soon be joining me for nocturnal pegasus flights to the cottage."

"No thank you. I shall walk."

A bubble of laughter burst from Mariselle's lips. "Through town? In the middle of the night? A young lady of quality, unescorted? And you say I'm the reckless one."

"At least on the ground, the worst that can happen is a twisted ankle or a damaged reputation," Petunia countered. "Not plummeting to one's death."

"Cinder has never dropped anyone," Mariselle insisted, reaching across to grab Petunia's hand. "It will be fun, I promise."

"Very well," Petunia conceded with exaggerated resignation. "I shall ride the beast if I must, but I categorically refuse to enjoy it."

"How perfectly in character," Mariselle replied with a teasing smile. "Your determined commitment to misery is truly admirable."

Petunia stuck her tongue out in a rare display of childishness. Both cousins dissolved into laughter then, the tension of their earlier conversation melting away.

"I suppose we could steal one of my family's enchanted carriages," Mariselle said once their mirth had subsided. "There's a cloaking spell I've been wanting to try out. I think with a few adjustments, I could extend it to cover an entire carriage."

"Oh, that's a *much* better idea! I approve."

Mariselle smiled. "It's settled then. We'll take a carriage to Windsong Cottage. Tonight, if you can sneak out. Just the two of us. I'd like to examine all the documents before involving that Rowanwood further. The less time spent in his company, the better. And you'll *love* the cottage, Tunia. It's simply delightful. So cozy. Oh, and I found a whole collection of journals belonging to the woman who originally owned the cottage before my grandfather ended up with it as part of the land acquisition for Dreamland. Lady Eugenia something-or-other. She was a renowned botanist. The journals are quite fascinating—though nothing to do with Dreamland of course."

Petunia wrinkled her nose. "Mm, yes. Nothing says thrilling like centuries-old notes on root systems."

"Petunia! They're not *centuries* old."

"Let me guess—volume seven is titled 'The Thrilling Adventures of Lady Eugenia and her Pet Dandelions.'"

"Tunia."

"And I was just lamenting the lack of bedtime reading about chlorophyll."

"Oh, stop it."

"Truly, Mari, I can't imagine why you didn't open with this. Plant journals are the very height of intrigue."

With a sigh, Mariselle stood, recognizing that her cousin was in full flow with her jests and deciding it was best to leave before becoming thoroughly entangled in an endless thicket of botanical witticisms.

"I should return before anyone notices my absence," she announced.

Petunia released her own sigh before standing as well. "Yes, I suppose I should too."

The two embraced once more. Petunia lifted the basket, slipping it deftly onto her arm through the woven handle so it rested in the crook of her elbow, before they walked to the greenhouse door.

"You'll have to send a note with one of the pixies if we need to change our plans," Mariselle said. "We can't speak via the mirrors at the moment. Mine broke last night in my hasty attempt to hide it when my mother returned home unexpectedly."

"Oh, that explains why you weren't answering me all day. I've been calling your name into my mirror every chance I could get. But how are we supposed to coordinate our plans now?"

"I collected all the shards this morning," Mariselle assured her. "They're fairly large pieces, not too small. I'm planning to try a restoration spell. I would have attempted it already if not for the High Lady's tea this afternoon."

Petunia blinked. "The High Lady's what?"

"Oh, goodness, I haven't told you about that yet!" Mariselle exclaimed. "Nor about the engagement ball she's hosting in our honor *tomorrow night.*"

"She's—*what?*" Petunia looked horrified.

"Turn right around, cousin dear," Mariselle said, looping her arm through Petunia's and directing her back inside the greenhouse. "This visit will have to last a little longer. You simply cannot leave until I've recounted every mortifying detail of this latest development."

Chapter Eight

Evryn stood before the unassuming door of Cromwell's Antiquities that evening, his fingers clutching the obsidian token in his pocket. The evening air carried the faint scent of honeysuckle from the flowering vines that climbed the walls of Sweetbriar Confectionery nearby, and the subdued glow of faelights illuminated the cobblestone street with a gentle amber hue.

He'd almost turned back three times on his journey here. Once at the threshold of Rowanwood House, where he'd lingered in the shadow of the grand entryway, second-guessing his decision to maintain his usual social engagements when everything else about his life had been thrown into disarray. Again as the enchanted carriage had slid to a stop at the corner of this very street. And finally, mere moments ago, standing at the door of Cromwell's Antiquities, where he'd actually pivoted on his heel before forcing himself to turn back toward the entrance.

The thought of facing his friends after the day's events made his stomach churn with dread. It had been difficult enough to fabricate a romance with Mariselle Brightcrest for his family, but his friends knew him in ways the Rowanwoods did not. Well, aside from Rosavyn, perhaps, but she'd been too overwhelmed by shock this morning to notice anything strange. His friends, however, were more likely to perceive the subtle inconsistencies in his demeanor, the forced nature of his enthusiasm. Particularly Fin, who had known him the longest.

Perhaps he should simply tell them the truth. The Obsidian Circle maintained powerful enchantments of discretion that prevented its members from discussing certain matters beyond its walls. He could invoke these protections, ensuring his confession remained secure.

But even as the thought formed, he dismissed it. Such enchantments might seal his friends' lips, but they couldn't erase their knowledge. If he revealed the charade, he would need to explain why he had agreed to Mariselle's absurd scheme in the first place. The truth would necessitate confessing his secret identity as E. S. Twist, exposing the very thing he was desperate to conceal.

No, he couldn't risk it—especially not with Ryden present. How could he admit to penning satires that mocked his friend's own mother? Despite the prince's carefully cultivated facade of indifference, Evryn knew Ryden harbored a fierce loyalty to his mother.

No, honesty was not an option tonight. The performance must continue.

With a resigned sigh, Evryn approached the shop door and inserted his token into a small, nearly invisible aperture beside the handle. The token vanished with a soft click, absorbed into the mechanism.

The door swung inward without a sound, revealing not the cluttered interior of an antiquities shop but a narrow staircase descending into velvety darkness. Evryn stepped inside, and the door closed behind him with a whisper of magic. The staircase illuminated itself as he descended, each step lighting with a soft golden glow that faded once he passed.

At the bottom of the stairs Evryn passed beneath an archway of polished mahogany, intricate carvings of mythical creatures dancing along its curved surface. The Obsidian Circle unfolded before him as he stepped through. The main chamber formed a perfect circle beneath a dome of midnight blue, where enchanted stars shifted slowly in accurate reflection of the night sky above Bloomhaven. Rich wooden panels lined the walls, punctuated by private alcoves. The club's centerpiece—a circular bar crafted from a single piece of polished black stone—gleamed in the warm glow of floating amber lights.

Behind the bar, attendants mixed drinks with theatrical flourish. The air carried notes of cedar, aged spirits, and a hint of smoldering driftshade leaf.

Leather armchairs and intimate conversation nooks invited relaxation, while the ambient hum of magical enchantments preserved the Circle's exclusivity and promised absolute discretion.

As Evryn made his way across the chamber, he noted the usual assortment of elite fae society—lords engaged in quiet business negotiations, young heirs lounging as they debated the latest pegasus racing odds, several of the High Lady's advisors. Unlike most evenings when he moved through the space largely unnoticed, he couldn't help observing a few surreptitious glances and hastily concealed whispers.

So the gossip had preceded him even here. Marvelous.

Evryn wove between clustered seating areas toward the club's eastern alcove—their usual gathering place. The familiar space came into view, his three friends already assembled. The golden-orange glow from a hearth of dancing magical flames illuminated their faces as they gestured energetically in conversation, their movements stilling abruptly when they caught sight of him approaching.

He hesitated once more, gathering his resolve before stepping beyond the invisible magical barrier that ensured conversations within this space remained private.

"The lover arrives at last!" Prince Ryden's voice greeted him immediately, loud enough to make Evryn wince.

The alcove was arranged in its usual configuration—four leather armchairs gathered around a small table, facing a hearth of warm copper that housed flames dancing in shades of amber and gold. The fire crackled pleasantly without producing heat, a sophisticated enchantment that provided all the comfort of a real fire without the sweltering temperature. It was almost summer, after all. On the table sat a decanter of amber liquid alongside four glasses, three of which bore signs of having already been emptied at least once.

Ryden lounged in his customary seat, legs stretched before him in a pose of deliberate casual elegance that only someone of his station could affect without appearing slovenly. His royal features were subtly altered by the complex glamour he always wore within the Circle, his midnight-blue hair a dark brown, his nose more prominent, his jawline slightly softened. The glamour left him with just enough resemblance to Prince Ryden that one might note a passing similarity, but not enough to suspect he might actually be the prince.

Beside him sat Crispin Ironvale, his posture as impeccable as ever, one eyebrow already arched in what Evryn recognized as his expression of profound skepticism. The chair nearest the entrance was occupied by Evryn's oldest friend, Findrin Thornhart. He leaned forward to clap Evryn on the shoulder as Evryn sank into the remaining chair. "You came after all."

"We thought perhaps you'd eloped," Crispin remarked dryly. "Given the extraordinary nature of the gossip flying about town today."

"Or that the lovely Lady Brightcrest had come to her senses and strangled you," Ryden added with a grin.

Evryn forced a smile. "Your concern is touching," he said, reaching for the decanter and pouring himself a generous measure. "Though I'm disappointed no one has offered congratulations on my impending nuptials."

"It's true, then?" Fin asked, his eyes never leaving Evryn's face. "The rumors claim you've somehow formed a *soulbond* with Lady Mariselle Brightcrest, of all people."

Evryn took a slow sip of his drink, allowing the liquid to burn a path down his throat as he considered his response. This was the moment, the first test of his resolve to maintain this charade even with his closest friends. He set down his glass and spread his lips into what he hoped resembled a lovesick grin. "It's true," he confirmed, the words nearly sticking in his throat. "Though I admit it came as quite a shock to us both."

Ryden hooted with laughter. "I told you!" he exclaimed, turning to Crispin with evident delight. "I witnessed it with my own eyes this afternoon, but Ironvale refused to believe me."

"You'll forgive my skepticism," Crispin replied, still staring at Evryn as though he'd sprouted a second head. "I was genuinely hoping it was another of His Royal Abstruseness's ridiculous jests."

Ryden snorted at the latest nickname.

"It does seem rather implausible," Fin observed, his gaze disconcertingly perceptive. "Are you certain this is genuine? Do you actually feel ..." He hesitated, grimacing slightly. *"Love?"*

Evryn's heart stuttered, but he maintained his expression with the ease of long practice. "It's not like falling in love normally, if that's what you mean," he replied. "It's a soulbond—some greater magic beyond my control. One moment we were arguing, and the next I was overcome by ..." His cheeks flushed as he scrambled for words that might sound convincing. Damn Mariselle Brightcrest for putting him in this absurd position. "Feelings," he finished lamely. "I'm still adapting to the sensation of loving a Brightcrest." He emphasized the family name, hoping to deflect their scrutiny toward the obvious source of tension. "My family is … less than pleased."

"I should think not," Crispin said with feeling. "The Rowanwoods and Brightcrests have been at odds since before any of us were born. It's not merely a social preference. There's genuine animosity there, deeply rooted in historical wrongs."

Evryn heard again his grandmother's words from that morning: *Your grandfather's brother is* dead *because of that family!* She had to have been exaggerating, surely? Caught up in the heightened emotions of the moment. That was probably why she had refused to say anything further when pressed for details.

With his friends' gazes still on him, Evryn extended his right arm and pushed back his sleeve to reveal the silvery pattern that curled around his wrist. "Magic, it seems, cares little for family feuds."

Fin leaned forward to examine the mark, his brow furrowed in concentration. "A soulbond," he murmured. "I'd never heard of such a thing before the gossip birds began shrieking the word about town this morning."

"Neither had I," Crispin admitted, leaning forward as well.

"My mother has mentioned them," Ryden confirmed, giving the mark only a passing glance before leaning back in his chair. "Though I admit I'd never given them any thought before today."

"Nor I," Evryn said with a rueful chuckle. "Yet here we are."

"So tell me," Ryden said, crossing his legs at the ankles as he leaned further back in his chair, "how exactly does one transition from 'I loathe everything about you' to 'you're the love of my existence' in the space of a few moments?"

"Magic, of course," Evryn replied dryly, withdrawing his arm as Fin and Crispin sat back.

"Fascinating," Crispin deadpanned as he reached for his half-full glass and brought it toward his lips. "Do elaborate on this sophisticated courtship strategy."

"I believe it went something like: 'Brightcrest, you insufferable menace—oh wait, you have rather lovely eyes—shall we marry?'"

Crispin nearly choked on his drink. "Please tell me you didn't actually say that."

"Of course not. I was far more eloquent."

"He probably quoted terrible poetry," Ryden said.

"I'll have you know my poetry is exceptional," Evryn said.

"Exceptionally awful, I'm sure," Ryden snorted.

Fin caught Evryn's eye but said nothing. He was the only one among them who knew of Evryn's private writings. Not the satirical pieces published under his pseudonym, but some of his other scribblings, as well as the raw verses he occasionally composed. Fin had discovered them purely by accident one evening in Evryn's study at Rowanwood House. He'd called them 'surprisingly insightful' and encouraged Evryn to continue, while Evryn had wished fervently for the floor to swallow him whole.

"And now there's to be an engagement ball tomorrow night?" Fin said, moving the conversation deftly away from Evryn's poetry skills. "Hosted by the High Lady herself? A herald pixie arrived at Thornhart House this afternoon, riding one of those oversized dragonflies they use for formal announcements."

"Ironvale Manor received the same," Crispin confirmed. "I initially dismissed it as an elaborate prank orchestrated by our royal friend here."

Evryn grimaced. "I'm afraid not. Her Grace was most enthusiastic about celebrating our connection."

"You're going to have to actually *dance* with her," Crispin said, one side of his mouth curling in disgust. "Lady Mariselle Brightcrest."

Evryn forced himself to picture every other young lady he'd ever found attractive instead of Mariselle Brightcrest and tried to keep the sarcasm from his voice as he said, "I know. I'm so looking forward to it."

"How does one dance with someone one has publicly despised for years?" Fin asked.

"Carefully," Ryden advised.

"With heavily reinforced footwear," Crispin suggested. "Lady Mariselle strikes me as the type to express her true feelings through strategically placed heel stomps."

"I doubt she would try something like that with the High Lady watching," Fin said.

"True," Ryden agreed. "The real danger will come later, in the gardens, when she lures you behind a topiary and throttles you with her fan ribbon."

Evryn bit down his instinctive response: Yes, it was very likely Mariselle would attempt to throttle him at some point. "You have an unpleasantly vivid imagination," he remarked instead. "And you seem to be forgetting that Lady Mariselle feels the same way about me as I do about her."

"I admit I'm finding that very hard to imagine," Fin said, still watching Evryn with undisguised concern.

"As I mentioned," Evryn offered awkwardly, "it's magic."

"Hmm," Fin murmured, his expression making it clear he remained unconvinced despite choosing not to press further.

"When's the wedding to be?" Crispin asked, swirling the amber liquid in his glass.

"End of the Season," Evryn replied, grateful this farce would be over by then.

"How romantic," Ryden sighed, clutching his heart. "Nothing says true love like 'I'm delaying our union in hopes you might perish naturally before I'm forced to commit.'"

Evryn caught himself before a snort of laughter could escape. He cleared his throat and clarified, "I was thinking more along the lines of giving our families time to adjust. And I'd appreciate it if you could show a little more support," he added, reminding himself that he needed to defend this union as if it were real. "She is to be my … wife." The word felt so wrong in his mouth that he had to grip the arms of his chair to stop himself from performing a full-body shudder.

"Oh but it's far too entertaining teasing you about it!"

Evryn fixed him with a glare.

Ryden leaned forward, his expression softening as he squeezed Evryn's shoulder. "I'm only having a bit of fun, my friend. We may not be fond of Lady Mariselle, but if you're truly determined to marry her, then of course we support you."

"Speak for yourself," Crispin muttered. "Though if you must marry her," he added, "at least try never to fall asleep in her presence."

Evryn arched a brow. "I imagine that will be difficult once we are wed." Which, fortunately, would never happen.

Crispin leaned forward. "The Brightcrests might deny it until their dying breath, but who's to say the rumors about dream influence aren't true?"

"Oh come now," Evryn scoffed. "You saw Lady Mariselle's debut last Season. You've seen other demonstrations from that family. You know the most any of them can do is extract dream essence from …" He waved a hand vaguely, uncertain of the exact terminology. "I don't know, from the general population of all those who are asleep at that precise moment. So they can make their precious Dream-Bright Elixir."

Evryn couldn't help the contempt that crept into his voice at the mention of the Brightcrests' flagship product. The small blue bottles with their signature silver stoppers graced bedside tables in homes throughout the United Fae Isles. A few drops before sleep guaranteed pleasant dreams, banishing nightmares and ensuring restful slumber. Even middle-class families kept a bottle in their medicine cabinets. The Brightcrests had built most of their fortune on that concoction alone.

The Rowanwoods, of course, refused to allow a single drop past their lips. In Evryn's childhood home, merely mentioning Dream-Bright had been enough to earn a stern reprimand. His father had called it 'bottled manipulation,' explaining to his children that anyone who drank too much of it came to develop an unhealthy dependency on it. Evryn wondered, however, if the true objection was simply that it had the name Brightcrest attached to it.

"Perhaps that's all someone like Lady Mariselle is capable of," Crispin continued, "but my uncle swears he once dozed off at a dinner where her aunt was present and woke up with the inexplicable desire to sell his prized racing pegasus to her at half its value."

"That sounds more like your uncle's fondness for expensive wine than dream manipulation," Evryn countered.

"Perhaps," Crispin said, "but the rumors persist for a reason. *Dream invasion*, I've heard some call it. The ability to enter someone else's dream and plant suggestions that linger after waking."

"Do you remember Alaryn Brightcrest speaking of 'dream sharing'?" Ryden asked, frowning. "What was that about?"

"That was something more … intimate, was it not?" Fin said.

"Ah, I see." Ryden's gaze took on a knowing glint.

"An intimacy of the *mind*," Fin hastened to add. "Only possible between two people who trust each other."

"Of course, of course," Ryden said, though his grin suggested he didn't believe Fin for a moment.

"Ah, yes, I believe it was something about trust opening a doorway between two sleeping minds," Crispin said, nodding, "as long as one of them possesses dream magic. But that's entirely different. I'm speaking of an *invasion* of the subconscious mind, and I'm almost certain there are some who are capable of it."

"Your concern is noted," Evryn said, hoping to put an end to this line of conversation. "I shall endeavor to sleep as far away as possible from my beloved after the wedding."

He offered silent thanks to whatever celestial powers might be listening that this charade would end long before he ever found himself in a position where sleep—or anything more intimate—near Mariselle became necessary.

"Nonetheless," Ryden said with a warm smile, "strange sleeping arrangements aside, we stand with you in this unexpected union, my friend. Brightcrest or not, she'll be a Rowanwood soon enough."

Evryn suppressed a grimace. "Thank you."

"And perhaps," Ryden continued with a mischievous glint in his eye, "your legendary charm will eventually rub off on her. What a service to society—one less spiteful Brightcrest to contend with at social gatherings."

"Speaking of social gatherings," Evryn said, his insides tightening with anxiety, "I could do without tomorrow night's engagement ball."

"Ah, yes, on that note," Ryden declared, "you cannot possibly attend without adequate preparation. This soulbond connection may feel genuine to you, but your public expressions of devotion need work." He straightened in his chair. "You require intensive instruction in the art of performing besotted adoration."

Evryn narrowed his eyes, immediately suspicious. "I believe I've observed enough lovesick fools at society functions to manage."

"Oh no, you need to do more than simply manage, my friend," Crispin said, setting his glass down as he warmed up to this idea. "You must convince everyone in that ballroom that you and Lady Mariselle are consumed by passion beyond reason. Mere adequacy will only invite suspicion."

"Agreed," Fin said, apparently enjoying this idea too. "The soulbond story requires nothing less than a performance of legendary proportions."

Evryn groaned inwardly. If only his friends knew how close their games strayed to the truth.

Ryden rose dramatically to his feet. "Allow me to demonstrate proper hand-kissing technique," he announced, bowing with exaggerated formality before an invisible partner, his gaze fixed on empty air with such convincing adoration that one might almost believe a beautiful woman stood before him. He delicately lifted an imaginary hand while Crispin and Fin exchanged amused glances, barely containing their laughter as Ryden proceeded to place the most reverent kiss upon a nonexistent hand.

"You must hold her gaze the entire time," he instructed solemnly. "The effect is utterly ruined if you look away."

"I'll develop a permanent crick in my neck trying to maintain eye contact while kissing her hand," Evryn protested, playing along and demonstrating the awkward angle. "Not to mention looking completely deranged in the process."

"Love is supposed to look deranged!" Ryden insisted, straightening and looking across at Evryn. "That's how everyone knows it's genuine. Not only that, but you must hold the contact for precisely seven seconds."

"Seven seconds?" Evryn couldn't contain his laughter now. "That's an eternity for such a gesture. People will think I'm trying to devour her knuckles."

"Is that not precisely what you desire to do?" Ryden asked, eyes wide with feigned innocence. "Surely your magical connection compels you toward such *passionate* displays of affection?"

Evryn lunged across the space between them to land a solid punch on his friend's shoulder, sending all four of them into peals of laughter at the sheer absurdity of it all.

Eventually, the conversation shifted away from the upcoming ball to their customary pegasus racing schedule, a topic that prompted a fresh wave of anxiety in Evryn's chest. Between his social obligations as a newly engaged man and the secret work to restore Dreamland, he would have precious little time for such pursuits.

"I'm afraid I may need to reduce my participation this Season," he admitted reluctantly. "Given my new circumstances. It would be inappropriate and invite unwanted questions if I were absent from too many society events."

"Disappointing," Crispin declared. "But we shall simply have to continue without you. Thornhart was telling us about his plans for a new course with gravity-defying spiral sections where riders must navigate while completely inverted."

The conversation continued to flow around him, but Evryn found himself withdrawing into his thoughts. The weight of his deception pressed heavier with each passing moment. These were his closest friends, the people with whom he had shared his triumphs and failures for years. Yet here he sat, feeding them elaborate falsehoods simply to protect a secret that suddenly seemed simultaneously vital and trivial.

As Fin continued to detail the intricate challenges of the new racing course, Evryn's thoughts returned to the engagement ball awaiting him tomorrow. Hours of pretending to be enamored with Mariselle Brightcrest while navigating the treacherous waters of high society, all under the High Lady's watchful eye. His stomach clenched at the prospect.

That wretch Mariselle had thrust him into this impossible situation with her blackmail and her grand plans for Dreamland restoration. All because, as she had put it with such entitled certainty, "I want this." As though her desires naturally outweighed all other considerations, like a spoiled child who always got whatever she wanted. Here he was suffering the indignity of fabricating affection for her before his friends and family, while she was likely sleeping peacefully, satisfied with her clever machinations.

A slow smile spread across his face as an idea occurred to him. If he was to suffer through this charade, then by all means, so should she—in equal measure. Ryden's ridiculous instructions for performing convincing displays of affection had planted the seed of a delightful possibility in his mind.

After all, what was more fitting than ensuring that Mariselle Brightcrest received precisely the sort of demonstrative, adoring fiancé she had unwittingly signed up for?

Chapter Nine

Evryn tugged at the sleeves of his formal jacket as he peered through the half-open doors of the antechamber into Solstice Hall's grand ballroom. The cavernous space glittered with floating faelights that cast a golden sheen over the assembled guests, their finery sparkling as they milled about in anticipation.

The High Lady had spared no expense. A string ensemble occupied one corner, light and color shimmering in the air above the musicians as they played. Arrangements of golden blossoms spilled from vases atop every pedestal and alcove. And around the edges of the ballroom, enchanted marble sculptures poured endless streams of wine into crystal basins. A rose-veined maiden with outstretched palms, a stag with honey-colored wine pouring from gilded antlers, an elegant swan whose parted beak released a slow trickle of amber vintage. The scents of fruit and spice mingled on the air.

Evryn exhaled slowly, working to calm the fluttering in his stomach. The entire cream of fae society had turned out for this spectacle—this farce—and soon he would be the center of their attention, alongside Mariselle Brightcrest of all people. Upon his arrival, a palace steward had directed him to this antechamber with instructions that he was to wait here until Lady Brightcrest arrived. "The High Lady wishes for you both to make your entrance together when she signals," the man had explained.

This news might previously have made Evryn squirm with discomfort, but tonight he approached the situation with newfound resolve. He had a plan. One that brought a smile to his lips every time he considered it. If Mariselle Brightcrest wanted him to act besotted, then by all the stars above, he would give her a performance so convincing that she'd regret ever dragging him into this ridiculous charade.

A palace attendant approached with a slight bow. "Lord Rowanwood, Lady Brightcrest has arrived and will join you momentarily."

"Thank you," Evryn replied, straightening his posture and adjusting the silver cravat that matched the embroidery adorning his sapphire-blue formal coat. The silver threads caught the light as he moved, rippling like water across the fabric in a display of last-minute magical tailoring that had cost him a small fortune. But if he was to play the part of besotted fiancé, he would do so in appropriate style.

The soft sound of approaching footsteps drew his attention toward the corridor. He turned, prepared to greet his fake fiancée with practiced cordiality.

And felt his carefully rehearsed greeting die in his throat.

Mariselle Brightcrest stood before him, and Evryn found himself momentarily speechless. Her gown was the color of dawn, pale gold at the bodice melting into the softest blush pink at the hem. The fabric shimmered faintly as she moved, embroidered with delicate threads of gold that caught the light like the first rays of morning. At her throat gleamed a rose-gold pendant set with a single pink opal, and matching drops glinted at her ears. Her golden hair had been swept up into an elegant arrangement of curls, with a few artful strands left to frame her face.

She was beautiful. Like a deadly silksnare lily—mesmerizing until the moment its pollen paralyzed you and its tendrils wrapped around your throat.

She released an impatient sigh as she entered the antechamber. "Have you forgotten how to speak, Rowanwood?"

Evryn recovered his composure with a slight bow. "Not at all, my radiant buttercup. I was merely wondering how I'm to endure an entire evening pretending to be enchanted by someone whose very presence makes me contemplate the appeal of slow strangulation."

"How charming," she replied, looking him over with cold assessment. "I see you've put considerable effort into your appearance tonight. A pity the same cannot be said for your manners." She faced the ballroom. "We have an audience to persuade. Do try to perform convincingly. I realize artifice doesn't come as naturally to you as it does to me."

Evryn pinched the bridge of his nose, exasperation washing over him. "Must *everything* be a competition with you?"

"My treasured love," she replied with saccharine sweetness, "it isn't about competition. It's merely an observable fact that I excel at social performance. As I do in most endeavors."

Evryn leaned closer, as though whispering sweet nothings into her ear. "Your modesty continues to enchant me, my precious sapdrop. Though I look forward to demonstrating my own considerable talents throughout the evening."

"Sapdrop?" she hissed, her smile never faltering.

"Too much?" he asked innocently. "I have an extensive repertoire prepared. Would you prefer 'my blushberry muffin' or perhaps 'my enchanted toadstool'?"

Her eyes narrowed dangerously, but she said nothing as she stepped closer to the half-open doors and peered into the ballroom. Evryn shifted uncomfortably as her shoulder brushed against his chest. He leaned away from her instinctively, the scent of vanilla reaching his nose.

"I can see both our families," she murmured, "positioned at opposite ends of the ballroom as though preparing for battle. Your grandmother looks as though she's contemplating how to dispose of my body without leaving evidence. And your brother looks …"

Evryn straightened to his full height and peered over Mariselle's head until he located Jasvian across the room. "Constipated?" he offered helpfully.

Mariselle snickered. "Indeed."

"That's his natural expression. It's how you know he's still breathing."

"And my father looks—"

"Like he just swallowed something extremely unpleasant."

"That is *his* natural expression," she sighed.

"Well," Evryn said, reaching up to tug slightly at his cravat, "let us hope the evening doesn't conclude with bloodshed and the end of several noble lineages."

Mariselle stepped back from the doorway, turning to face him. Her gaze traveled from his face to his cravat, her brow furrowing slightly. "Stop, you're making a mess of that."

He adjusted the silver fabric. "I'm sure it's perfectly fine."

"It is not. Stop fidgeting—you're only making it worse."

Before he could protest, she smacked his hand away and reached for his cravat herself, her fingers working to straighten the folds. Horrified—the impropriety of the gesture would have raised eyebrows even between genuinely engaged couples—Evryn pulled his head back, trying to avoid contact with her skin.

"Oh, for stars' sake," Mariselle muttered. "Stop being ridiculous. In fact …" She gripped both his shoulders and tugged him closer to the gap in the door, ensuring they were perfectly framed for anyone who might glance toward the antechamber. "Let us give the gossip birds something more to squawk about. By morning they'll be jabbering that the two soulbonded sweethearts can barely keep their hands from one another." A wicked smile curved her lips as she deliberately brushed her fingertips against his jaw. "Which is precisely the impression we wish to convey."

Evryn remained still, though it required considerable effort not to flinch away from her touch. "You're enjoying this far too much."

"Oh, *enjoy* is certainly not the word I'd use," she corrected, maintaining her sweet smile, "but I shall play my part nonetheless." She stepped back to admire her handiwork. "There. Now you look presentable enough to be seen on my arm."

"Your generosity overwhelms me, my shimmering honeycomb."

The palace attendant reappeared behind them. "Her Grace requests your presence," he announced with a bow. "If you would please take your positions."

Mariselle inhaled deeply, squaring her shoulders as though preparing for battle. "Remember," she whispered, "everyone must believe we are genuinely in love."

"Oh, I assure you," Evryn replied, offering his arm with an exaggerated flourish, "no one will doubt the depth of my devotion after tonight."

She eyed him suspiciously but placed her gloved hand on his offered arm. The ballroom fell silent as the grand doors swung fully open. On the other side, a herald stepped forward, his voice ringing clear across the hushed space.

"Lord Evryn Rowanwood and Lady Mariselle Brightcrest!"

Evryn pasted a lovesick smile on his face, one he had practiced diligently before his mirror, and guided Mariselle forward. The assembled crowd parted before them, creating a path toward the High Lady, who sat at the far end of the ballroom upon a throne of woven gold branches that seemed to grow directly from the dais beneath it, blossoms of pale blue crystal adorning its curves.

As they processed through the crowd, whispers followed in their wake. Evryn caught fragments of conversation—'never heard of a soulbond,' 'oh isn't it *romantic*,' 'the families will never allow it'—but kept his gaze trained on the dais ahead.

They reached the High Lady, who stood from her throne and extended her hands in welcome. "Lord Rowanwood, Lady Brightcrest," she greeted. "It brings me great joy to celebrate your extraordinary connection."

They bowed and curtsied in perfect unison.

"The soulbond is among the rarest and most sacred of magical phenomena," the High Lady continued, her voice carrying easily across the ballroom. "It represents the ancient magic that flows through our realm, taking a form beyond our mortal comprehension. Throughout our history, only a handful of such bonds have been recorded. Such a rare and precious connection deserves to be honored by all of us together."

Evryn noticed the High Lady's diplomatic omission of any reference to the families' long-standing feud. A wise choice, he thought, given that acknowledging it might trigger open hostilities from the opposing corners where the Rowanwoods and Brightcrests had established their separate territories. He resisted the urge to glance toward either family.

"To mark this auspicious occasion," the High Lady declared, "I invite our betrothed couple to open the evening with the first dance."

She gestured toward the string ensemble, who immediately readied their instruments. Evryn guided Mariselle toward the center of the ballroom as the crowd retreated to form a wide circle around them. He remembered Crispin's comment from the previous night about reinforced footwear and bit the inside of his cheek to keep from laughing.

As the first notes of a traditional waltz filled the air, Evryn drew Mariselle into the proper position, one hand at her waist, the other clasping her right hand. They began to move in perfect synchronization, gliding across the polished marble floor, eyes locked on each other in perfectly feigned adoration.

"You dance better than I expected," Mariselle murmured after several moments. "For someone who spends far more time on the back of a pegasus than in a ballroom."

"And you move with surprising lightness," he replied with a tender smile, "for someone carrying the weight of such an inflated opinion of herself."

They turned gracefully, their steps perfectly matched as they traversed the ballroom floor. "Your eyes are positively radiant tonight, my sugar-dusted moonbeam," Evryn continued after executing a perfect sequence of steps that brought them close to the edge of the assembled crowd. "Like pools of water in which I could happily drown myself."

Mariselle's smile tightened almost imperceptibly. "How poetic, my love. One wonders why you've never pursued publication given such unique talent."

Evryn tensed momentarily before recovering his composure. He tightened his grip on her waist ever so slightly as they continued their circuit of the dance floor.

"I've been saving all my poetry for you, my precious strawberry tart," he replied, spinning her beneath his arm before drawing her back into a hold. "Every word, every thought, every dreadful metaphor—all for you."

"Your devotion leaves me speechless," she countered, her smile fixed in place.

They lapsed into silence as they continued their circuit of the dance floor. Evryn directed his gaze just over Mariselle's shoulder, finding it impossible to maintain the pretense of adoring eye contact for the entire dance. He carefully avoided looking at his friends, knowing that catching Ryden's eye in particular would surely break his composure.

He watched the assembled crowd as the the two of them turned, his eyes scanning the faces around them—admiring glances from the gentlemen, dreamy sighs from several young ladies who pressed their hands to their hearts, and the inevitable whispering behind fluttering fans and cupped hands that accompanied any significant social event. His grandmother stood rigid as marble, her expression carved from the same unforgiving stone. Beside her, Jasvian watched with a furrowed brow, while Iris whispered something into his ear that softened his expression into a genuinely warm gaze as he looked down at her.

A peculiar tightness gripped Evryn's chest. An unwelcome pang that felt suspiciously like envy. He pushed the feeling away immediately, his gaze swinging across the room toward the Brightcrests. Ellowa Brightcrest's lip curled in evident disgust as she leaned toward another young lady, no doubt sharing some particularly venomous observation, while Mariselle's parents regarded him with such cold hostility that he wouldn't have been surprised if frost started materializing on his formal wear.

The music swelled toward its conclusion, and Evryn made a split-second decision. As the final notes hung in the air, he swept Mariselle into a low dip, supporting her weight effortlessly as he gazed into her startled eyes.

"Rowanwood," she hissed, barely audible. "What are you doing? This isn't part of the—"

"Giving the people what they want, my glittering dewberry," he replied softly, before slowly returning her to an upright position. A stunned silence fell over the assembly. For several heartbeats, not a single sound disturbed the stillness. Then the High Lady began to clap, and as though released from a spell, the entire gathering erupted into enthusiastic applause.

"What a magnificent display," the High Lady called out as the applause subsided. "Please, everyone, join our soulbonded couple for the next dance."

As other couples moved to take their places, Evryn maintained his hold on Mariselle's hand. "Before the next dance begins," he announced, his voice carrying across the ballroom, "I should like to present my betrothed with a small token of my affection."

Mariselle's eyes widened fractionally, a flash of panic crossing her features. "Darling," she said, her voice sweet but her eyes promising retribution, "there's no need for such displays."

"Nonsense, my cinnamon moonflower," he replied warmly. "There is every need."

With a dramatic sweep of his hand through the air, tiny sparkles of magic cascaded to the ballroom floor directly before Mariselle. The marble shimmered and rippled like disturbed water, and suddenly, enchanted red roses began to grow upward at an impossible speed, their stems twisting elegantly, buds unfurling before the astonished eyes of the gathered guests.

With another flourish of his hand, the stems detached from the floor and the bouquet swept itself up into a perfect arrangement, ribbons of silver light binding the stems together before the entire creation floated gently into Mariselle's startled hands.

"Ever-blooming flowers," he proclaimed, bowing deeply, "for you, my sweet pumpkin snowflake."

A collective sigh rose from the surrounding ladies as Mariselle accepted the bouquet, her performance flawless as she summoned a blush to her cheeks. In all honesty, she was horrifyingly good at this. What manner of magic allowed her to call forth a genuine blush on command?

"They're beautiful," she said, her voice carrying just the right note of pleased surprise. "Thank you, my love."

"But wait," Evryn said, raising one finger. "There's more."

Another sweep of his hand, and the floor near Mariselle's feet shimmered again. This time, delicate pink orchids sprouted and grew. Once again, they detached and arranged themselves into a perfect bouquet before floating up to join the roses in Mariselle's arms.

"For my dazzling cloudberry," he declared.

Before she could respond, he produced a third floral display with the same magical flourish, this one comprising exotic purple blooms.

"And these," he added, "for my dearest sugarplum starshine."

Mariselle juggled the growing collection of flowers, an awkward laugh escaping her lips as she glanced around at the rapt audience. "Is that not enough, my love?"

"There will never be enough flowers for you, my spiced nutmeg cookie," Evryn replied earnestly, causing yet another patch of marble floor to ripple and bloom with yellow flowers that hummed a gentle melody.

"How thoughtful," Mariselle managed, her arms now completely full of magical flora. She looked around with increasing desperation, clearly uncertain how to gracefully extricate herself from the mounting foliage.

Taking pity on her—though only slightly—Evryn signaled to a nearby palace attendant, who hurried forward. "Would you be so kind as to assist Lady Brightcrest with her floral tributes?" he asked. "I fear I've overwhelmed her with my enthusiasm."

"Of course, my lord," the attendant replied, carefully relieving Mariselle of her fragrant burden.

"To grace your chambers at Brightcrest Manor," Evryn added, smiling broadly at Mariselle as the attendant carried the flowers away. "So you'll always be able to think of me, even when we're apart."

He was rewarded by the sight of several young ladies nearby pressing hands to their hearts, visibly moved by this display of affection. Even better was the flash of genuine irritation that crossed Mariselle's face before she smoothed it into a loving smile.

"How could I possibly forget you?" she replied sweetly, though her eyes promised revenge.

The string ensemble struck up the introduction to the next dance, and Evryn once again offered his hand to Mariselle. As they resumed their position, she leaned close, her lips nearly brushing his ear.

"You're going too far," she whispered fiercely. "I told you to act convincingly, not to make a spectacle of us both."

"My darling enchanted rosebud," he replied in a low tone, guiding her into the first steps of the dance, "you wanted everyone to believe in our love. I'm simply ensuring that no one harbors the slightest doubt."

They executed a graceful reverse turn, Mariselle's serene smile never wavering. "If you produce one more bouquet," she threatened quietly, "I will find a way to make you eat it."

"Such passion," he sighed dreamily. "It overwhelms me."

As they navigated the complex patterns of the dance, separating briefly to circle other partners before returning to each other, Evryn took a moment to savor how exquisitely vexed she was by his theatrics, mentally reviewing his growing collection of absurd endearments and wondering whether 'my dainty doomblossom' or 'my shimmering snugglewump' might push her further toward delightful exasperation.

The dance ended, and they bowed to each other once more. Before Mariselle could escape, however, Evryn captured her hand and raised it to his lips. Remembering Ryden's ridiculous instructions, he maintained unwavering eye contact as he pressed a lingering kiss to her knuckles, counting slowly in his head.

One ... two ... three ...

Mariselle's eyes narrowed.

Four ... five ... six ...

A subtle flush crept up her neck, and Evryn found himself wondering if it was manufactured or if he might possibly have provoked a genuine reaction from her.

Seven.

He released her hand but maintained his gaze, a slow smile spreading across his face.

Mariselle drew in a delicate breath, her lashes fluttering in a display of demure passion that looked remarkably convincing. "My love," she murmured, just loud enough for those nearby to hear, "do remember we are in public. I know how desperately you yearn for me, but such lingering attentions are hardly proper." Her blush deepened as she added, "Even if I might secretly wish them to continue."

Evryn bit down hard on the cough that threatened to escape his throat. Damn her. Here he was, doing his utmost to discomfit her, and yet she remained utterly unaffected. Maintaining his ridiculously lovesick expression, he leaned closer and muttered through gritted teeth, "Tell me, do you enchant your cheeks to flush on command, or is that another natural talent of yours?"

She smiled sweetly, leaning closer. "A lady possesses many skills, my dearest. The right enchantment can do wonders for one's complexion."

"How impressive. You truly do excel in every realm of deception, my sweet venomous pixie of love."

Her perfect smile wavered almost imperceptibly, the corners of her mouth tightening. "Your endearments grow increasingly nonsensical," she hissed with barely moving lips.

"Nothing about this ridiculous farce makes sense, Lady Brightcrest. Yet here we are." He drew back, his smile in place once more. "Would you care for refreshment, my luminous sunbeam?"

Her jaw tensed slightly, a muscle flickering beneath the smooth skin of her cheek as she fought to maintain her serene expression. "Yes," she replied. "That would be lovely."

Evryn glanced around the ballroom, spotting several attendants in white and gold uniforms circulating with trays of crystal glasses. He caught the attention of the nearest attendant, who glided toward them. With a graceful gesture, he caused two glasses containing a pale blue drink to rise from the tray and hover momentarily in the air before settling into Evryn's waiting hands. He offered one to Mariselle.

"Luminous sunbeam?" she muttered under her breath as she took the glass.

"To match your perpetually sunny disposition, my dearest."

"You need to exercise some restraint."

"I'm merely giving our audience what they expect," Evryn replied innocently. "The High Lady herself seems enchanted by our connection. Would you have me disappoint her?"

"I would have you maintain some semblance of dignity," Mariselle countered as she lifted her glass to her lips.

"But my fluttering nightingale, how can one maintain dignity when swept away by the tides of passion?"

Mariselle took a rather large sip of her drink, her smile now looking decidedly strained. She swallowed and whispered, "You're going to regret this."

"On the contrary, my sparkling raincloud," Evryn replied cheerfully. "I'm rather enjoying myself."

"Rowanwood, Lady Brightcrest," a deep voice interrupted. They turned to find Crispin approaching. "My congratulations on your unexpected union."

"Lord Ironvale," Mariselle acknowledged with a slight nod. "How kind of you to offer your good wishes."

"I would not miss such a historic event," Crispin replied smoothly. "A Rowanwood and a Brightcrest, united by magic itself. Truly unprecedented."

"Quite so," Evryn replied, noting that now would be a good time to slip his arm around Mariselle's waist and draw her a little closer, but finding he simply couldn't bear the thought. His theatrical abilities were already stretched to their absolute limit without introducing unnecessary physical contact. "We are both truly delighted by this unexpected turn of events."

"Indeed," Mariselle agreed. "Though I admit, had anyone suggested such a match a week ago, I would have questioned their sanity."

"And yet here we are," Crispin observed, his gaze flickering between them. "How ... delightful."

"The High Lady certainly thinks so," Evryn said. "Now, if you'll excuse us, my friend," he added. "Lady Mariselle has not yet been formally introduced to my family."

They turned away from Crispin, and Evryn heard the first true hint of alarm in Mariselle's voice when she hissed, "We are not *actually* going to speak with your family now, are we?"

"Of course not, but did you really want to remain in conversation with my deeply suspicious friend?" Evryn asked, his smile never faltering. "He still harbors—Ah, Lady Thornhart, Lady Whispermist!" He stopped abruptly before colliding with two elegant older women, longtime friends of his grandmother.

"Evryn," Lady Amarind Thornhart said in that tone she had perfected over decades, one that managed to convey disappointment even in a simple greeting. Her dark gaze swept over Mariselle, brows drawing together in disapproval. "And Lady Mariselle. What an extraordinary development this is. I must confess, when I first heard the news, I wondered if perhaps the gossip birds had finally lost what little sense they possess."

"I assure you," Evryn said as he bowed respectfully to Fin's grandmother, "the rumors are quite true."

"Hmm. So I see."

Lady Lycilla Whispermist, a short woman with lavender hair, offered a more diplomatic smile. "The High Lady seems quite delighted by your connection. That alone suggests there must be something genuine in this unexpected bond, despite the … historical considerations."

Evryn looked down at Mariselle, and for a moment, he pictured Jasvian gazing at Iris. Though the stab of envy earlier had irritated him, he now did the unthinkable and attempted to channel his older brother, allowing his expression to soften into what he hoped resembled genuine warmth. "Neither of us anticipated such a connection," he said, his voice tender as he gazed into Mariselle's blue eyes. "But magic has a way of revealing truths we never knew existed."

"So lovely," Lady Lycilla said, appearing somewhat more convinced now. "And I do hope," she added with a glance at Mariselle, "that we shall have the pleasure of seeing you at The Charmed Leaf soon, my dear. As Evryn's betrothed, you'll naturally be most welcome there."

Lady Amarind released what sounded like a horrified snort of laughter. "Goodness, in all my days, I never thought I'd live to see a Brightcrest enter The Charmed Leaf! What remarkable times we live in."

"Of course Lady Mariselle will be visiting the tea house," Evryn replied smoothly, even as his stomach dropped with the sudden realization that he hadn't considered this particular social obligation. His grandmother would likely attempt to poison Mariselle's tea. Or possibly strangle her with the vines that adorned the walls. "I look forward to introducing her to all its charms."

Lady Amarind coughed, her eyebrows rising sharply. "Indeed! I highly doubt your grandmother is looking forward to it with quite the same enthusiasm."

Something rebellious flared in Evryn's chest at the implicit challenge to his autonomy. "On Thursday, in fact," he heard himself say before he could think better of it. "Lady Mariselle has already accepted my invitation for afternoon tea."

He felt, rather than saw, Mariselle tense slightly beside him.

"Grandmother," Fin said as he appeared at Lady Amarind's side, "you're monopolizing the happy couple." He offered Mariselle a deep bow. "Lady Mariselle, you look lovely this evening."

"Thank you, my lord," Mariselle replied with a perfect curtsy. "Though I fear Lord Rowanwood's excessive floral tributes outshone me."

"Nonsense," Fin said. "I'm sure my good friend Evryn doesn't believe any bloom could possibly compare to your natural beauty."

"Absolutely," Evryn agreed. "My beloved shimmering dewdrop outshines all the flowers in Bloomhaven."

Mariselle summoned another pink flush to her cheeks. "You flatter me, my love."

"It isn't flattery if it's true," Evryn insisted, raising her hand to his lips once more.

Her expression froze into a mask of adoration that couldn't quite disguise the murderous gleam in her eyes. Under different circumstances, Evryn imagined her hand would have connected sharply with his face. He considered this another triumph in their unspoken contest.

Evryn lowered Mariselle's hand and turned back to the two elder ladies in time to see the meaningful glance the two exchanged. Lady Amarind inclined her head. "We mustn't monopolize you on such a special evening," she said, and the two women linked arms and turned away. Evryn had no doubt they were making a direct course to his grandmother to report the details of this uncomfortable encounter.

"Ah, I see Lord Emberdale," Fin said, gesturing across the ballroom. "If you'll excuse me, I promised him a word about the art auction. The two of you will be there, I presume? The night after tomorrow."

"Of course," Evryn replied smoothly, though he had forgotten all about it. He didn't often attend the annual art exhibition and auction hosted by the Emberdales. It ranked among the many formal occasions he typically abandoned in favor of the far more enticing freedom of racing through star-lit skies on Cobalt's back. Beside him, Mariselle nodded.

"Excellent." Fin stepped away, leaving the two of them alone once more, crystal glasses in hand. "I hope you're enjoying the evening, my precious cinnamon dumpling," Evryn said, his voice low but his eyes alight with triumph. "I certainly am."

"You've been insufferable," she replied through gritted teeth. "This performance has gone far beyond what was necessary."

"I disagree. The High Lady is delighted, society is convinced, and our charade remains intact. I'd call that a resounding success."

"You're deliberately trying to provoke me."

"I'm merely playing the role you assigned me," he replied innocently. "Is it my fault if I excel at it?"

Mariselle turned to face him fully, her expression transformed into one of such perfect adoration that anyone watching would have sworn she was utterly besotted. Only the dangerous glitter in her eyes betrayed the venomous thoughts behind her smile. "This isn't over, Rowanwood."

"Oh, I sincerely hope not, my little lavender teacake," he said, his smile widening. "We have an entire Season of such performances ahead of us. And I do hope you'll keep the flowers close by. They were enchanted *especially* for you."

Chapter Ten

The last thing Mariselle expected when she woke the following morning was to find herself nearly entombed beneath what could only be described as a botanical invasion of truly spectacular proportions.

She had gone to sleep the previous evening with Evryn's enchanted bouquets arranged around her bedchamber. The roses on her writing desk, the orchids adorning her vanity table, the purple blooms gracing the windowsill, and the melodic yellow flowers positioned on a small table in the far corner where their humming would provide the least disturbance to her slumber.

In the carriage on the way home, her mother had insisted the 'Rowanwood floral monstrosities' remain confined to Mariselle's chambers, expressing concern that they might somehow be designed to spy upon the Brightcrest household. Mariselle had thought this absurdly paranoid. Nevertheless, she had fully intended to dispose of the unwanted flora at the earliest opportunity, preferably by launching them from her window with enough force to knock out a gossip bird or two. Spy-flowers or common blooms, she wanted no part of Evryn's theatrical declarations of affection cluttering her private space.

But then Tilly had swept into Mariselle's room after the family's return from Solstice Hall with a delighted gasp and proceeded to arrange the bouquets before Mariselle could stop her. She had watched, paralyzed, uncertain how to explain that she wished to unceremoniously evict these perfectly lovely flowers from the man she was supposedly infatuated with. So, against her better judgement, she had left them.

By dawn, the flowers had multiplied with such enthusiastic vigor that Mariselle had awakened to find herself buried beneath cascading blooms, their stems having stretched and twisted throughout the night to create what resembled a floral prison. The roses had spawned dozens of offspring, the orchids had produced trailing vines that draped from every available surface, while the purple blooms had apparently decided to colonize her entire floor. As for the melodious yellow flowers, their whereabouts remained a mystery, their gentle humming now lost somewhere within the wild labyrinth of plants.

Mariselle's indignant shrieks had brought Tilly rushing into the chamber, where it had taken an embarrassingly large amount of time for the poor maid to extricate her mistress from the floral prison. The subsequent task of removing the multiplied blooms from her chambers had required the assistance of three additional household staff and multiple enchanted wheelbarrows.

Lady Clemenbell had observed the proceedings from the hallway, her gaze radiating cold fury, while Mariselle affected an air of lighthearted amusement that felt brittle even to her own ears. "Such passionate devotion!" she'd exclaimed with a forced laugh. "How fortunate I am to have captured the heart of a suitor with such abundant enthusiasm."

The words tasted false on her tongue, but she clung to her pretense of delighted bemusement while silently entertaining fantasies of pushing both Evryn and his mounds of enchanted flora off the Elderbloom Park bridge and into the Silverflow River.

Now, hours later, Mariselle sat in the pristine tranquility of Windsong Cottage, her jaw still clenched with indignation as she waited for the architect of her morning's humiliation to make his inevitable appearance. She had already spent considerable time examining all the documents she'd pulled from the shelves two nights before with Petunia's help, separating the architectural plans and technical specifications relevant to Evryn's particular magical abilities into their own pile.

She'd begun to examine the dream magic materials as well, appreciating her grandfather's meticulous attention to detail. His careful record-keeping meant she could bypass his extensive experimentation and numerous failures, proceeding directly to the methods that had ultimately proven effective.

The sound of approaching footsteps drew her attention toward the front door. She straightened in her chair, smoothed her hands over her skirts, and arranged her features into an expression of stern disapproval. The door opened to reveal Evryn Rowanwood, looking pleased with himself as usual. His dark hair was windswept form riding, and his storm-gray eyes held that familiar glint of mischief that never failed to set her teeth on edge.

"Good evening, my enchanted puffling," he said with exaggerated warmth, sweeping into an elaborate bow. "I trust you slept well last night after the ball?"

Mariselle rose from her chair, crossing her arms over her chest as she fixed him with a withering stare. "I suppose you found that vastly amusing."

"You'll need to be more specific," he replied, his tone infuriatingly pleasant. He closed the door behind him and removed his riding gloves. "I find many things amusing."

"Your little botanical prank," she clarified, her patience fraying further. "I awoke to find myself nearly entombed beneath a veritable garden of your enchanted monstrosities! The wretched things multiplied like spring rabbits overnight. I required rescue from my own bedchamber!"

Evryn's eyebrows rose in apparent surprise, though the corner of his mouth twitched with barely suppressed mirth. "How extraordinary. It was my understanding that those particular varieties flourish in the presence of warmth and affection. I confess I expected them to wither entirely in such inhospitable surroundings as Brightcrest Manor."

"You knew precisely what would happen."

"I may have mentioned to the florist that I desired enchantments possessing particularly … vigorous properties." He shrugged, the picture of innocence, as he took a few casual steps toward her. "How was I to know they would prove quite so enthusiastic in their growth?"

"You are incorrigible," she hissed.

"Thank you," he replied with a small bow. "I do try."

"You—" Mariselle bit off the remainder of her retort, recognizing that rising to his bait would only provide him with further entertainment. There was also the fact that she still required his cooperation, despite his infuriating demeanor. It would serve no purpose to throttle him before he had fulfilled his part in restoring Dreamland. Afterward, perhaps.

"If you're quite finished congratulating yourself on your childish pranks," she said, turning back to the table and snatching up the pile of rolled-up scrolls and leather portfolios thick with architectural drawings, "we have actual work to accomplish this evening."

She thrust the documents into his hands with enough force that he had to take a step backward. "I was here two nights ago and spent most of the evening examining every document I could find. Those contain all the technical specifications for the lumyrite network infrastructure that powered the original Dreamland. The instructions for how each crystal formation must be shaped and positioned are detailed therein. I trust you'll find them comprehensible enough."

Evryn grasped for a wayward scroll that had begun its descent toward the floor, his expression shifting from amusement to something resembling dismay. "All of this is for me?"

"Indeed." Mariselle returned to her seat, reaching for another volume. "You'll need to conduct a thorough examination of what remains of the original structure, determine what can be salvaged, and calculate what must be created anew. One of those portfolios contains detailed inventories of the original lumyrite installations, so you'll have precise specifications for replacement components."

"You cannot possibly expect me to manage all of this independently," Evryn protested. "The scope of work here would require months, even with a full team of experienced craftsmen."

Mariselle looked up, eyebrows arched. "Your great-uncle managed it perfectly well. I fail to see why you should find it beyond your capabilities."

"Yes, but—"

"And how would you know the scope of work required when you have not yet looked at a single document?"

"Because ... I ..."

"Because?"

He glared at her. She arched one brow a fraction higher. He said nothing.

"You can work over there," she told him with a dismissive wave of her hand toward the sitting area, where a tea table stood between the armchairs and sofa. "I'm occupying the main table tonight."

Evryn grumbled something she couldn't make out as he strode toward the sitting area and unceremoniously deposited the stack of documents onto the low table. He settled into an armchair, unfurled the topmost portfolio, and began scrutinizing the intricate technical drawings with furrowed brows.

Meanwhile, Mariselle returned her attention to the leather-bound volume before her, a text she'd identified as containing her grandfather's successful endeavors rather than his theoretical musings. Unlike the earlier journals filled with abandoned hypotheses, this tome chronicled the practical applications that had yielded tangible results. Its opening pages meticulously outlined something called the 'dream core.'

She had never heard the term before discovering this cottage and its documents. According to what she'd read so far, the dream core was the key to Dreamland's operation —a magical focal point that anchored the dream realm to the physical world. It was also the part she would need to pour all her magic into—once she figured out exactly how to use her manifested ability, and once she determined the location of the original dream core.

If she couldn't find it, or if it no longer existed, she'd have to construct an entirely new one. Worse, she'd probably need to enlist Evryn's assistance in crafting it, since the darn thing appeared to be made largely of lumyrite. The latter prospect filled her with dread, as Evryn would undoubtedly contrive some unnecessarily convoluted arrangement that —

"These specifications call for enormous quantities of raw lumyrite," Evryn said, interrupting her thoughts. "Where precisely do you imagine I'm to acquire such materials for the deteriorated components that require replacement in the original Dreamland infrastructure?"

Mariselle looked up, genuinely puzzled by the question. "Your family owns lumyrite mines, Rowanwood. Surely you have access to whatever quantities you require."

"I cannot simply appropriate lumyrite for personal projects," he protested. "The mines operate as a business enterprise. Every crystal is accounted for, every allocation documented. I cannot merely wander into the vaults and help myself to whatever strikes my fancy."

"Then you shall have to devise a plan," Mariselle replied. "I have every confidence in your resourcefulness. After all, you've proven quite adept at creative solutions when it suits your purposes." She paused meaningfully before adding, "Have you not, E. S. Twist?"

The reminder of their arrangement had its intended effect. Evryn sighed, rolled his eyes, and returned his attention to the architectural drawings with resigned acceptance. "Very well. I'll determine what can be managed."

"Excellent."

Silence descended upon the cottage as they each immersed themselves in their respective studies. The occasional rustle of parchment and soft exhalation of concentration were the only sounds disturbing the evening tranquility. Mariselle traced her fingertip along the yellowed pages, following her grandfather's elegant script as it guided her through increasingly complex explanations of the dream core's purpose and function.

Her breath caught when she turned to a page containing a meticulously rendered illustration. There, depicted in exquisite detail, was the dream core itself—a perfect sphere crafted from both a dull silvery metal and translucent lumyrite crystal. Intricate patterns had been etched across its entire circumference, flowing designs she was yet to determine the meaning of. She scanned several more pages, searching for any mention of the core's physical location within the original structure, but found none.

With a sigh, she pushed her chair back and stood, then crossed the room behind Evryn's chair and stopped in front of the bookshelf. Her fingers traced along the spines of leather-bound volumes and weathered journals, pausing occasionally to pull one free and examine its contents before returning it to its place.

Near the bottom shelf, she discovered a wooden box with tarnished brass hinges. She lifted the lid carefully, revealing yellowed pages filled with what appeared to be scorekeeping records—columns of numbers beneath a series of initials: V, R, K, N, T. She frowned. Whatever this was, it had nothing to do with the dream core.

With a disappointed sigh, she replaced the lid and returned the box to its position. She continued her methodical investigation of the shelves, pulling out folios and rifling through loose papers. Frustration mounted as she realized the vital information she sought was likely contained in the documents she had so imperiously handed over to Evryn.

She returned to the table and sat. Yes, she was going to have to ask him. "I need those—"

"I'm going outside," Evryn announced at the same moment she began speaking.

She narrowed her eyes at him. "Why are you going outside?"

"To compare these diagrams with what remains of the structure," he replied, rising from his chair and gathering several of the architectural plans.

"That will have to wait," she countered. "We must first locate the dream core."

Evryn exhaled dramatically, his shoulders slumping in theatrical exasperation. "And what, pray tell, is a dream core?" he asked with profound disinterest.

"The magical focal point of the entire operation. It's—" She waved her hand dismissively. "Never mind the details. We need to find it."

"Well," Evryn drawled, "since my side of the project can apparently wait, do you suppose you might be able to locate this crucial object without my assistance? I could perhaps join you on some other evening when—"

Mariselle stood once more, her chair scraping against the floor. "Would you start taking this seriously? Have you forgotten that the contract won't release either of us until Dreamland has been properly restored?"

"Or," Evryn muttered, just loudly enough to ensure she would hear, "until you recognize the sheer lunacy of this entire endeavor and abandon it, whereupon we find a competent professional to remove these binding marks for us."

"That," she said sharply, "is not happening. Now bring those drawings over here and help me locate the dream core."

Evryn approached the table and laid the drawings before her with exaggerated care, smoothing nonexistent wrinkles from the parchment. "And what if this precious core no longer exists?"

"It should. According to what I've just read, it was designed to be virtually indestructible. A necessary precaution given its central importance to the entire enterprise."

She exhaled a long breath, releasing some of her frustration, and turned the book she'd been reading toward him so he could examine the illustration more closely. "This is what we're looking for. We need to locate and retrieve it before any other work can proceed. Everything else depends upon having a functional dream core."

Evryn studied the diagram with reluctant interest. "I believe I saw this somewhere," he murmured after several moments. "I think it was …" He reached for the scattered drawings, leafing through them in search of one in particular. He pulled one out and laid it atop the others, then bent low over the table and traced a finger toward the center of the design. "Ah, yes." He rotated the diagram to face Mariselle and tapped a spot with his index finger. "Does that look like it? At the very heart of the central pavilion."

Mariselle leaned over the drawing, narrowing her eyes until she could read the tiny label alongside the illustration nestled within the intricate lines of the blueprint. "Yes, that's it!" she exclaimed. She straightened, rolled up the diagram, and thrust it into Evryn's hands. "Come along. We have excavation work ahead of us."

"Very well," Evryn said with a long-suffering sigh. "Lead on, my industrious little badger."

Mariselle shot him a warning glare. "We are not in public, Rowanwood. Your nauseating endearments are unnecessary."

"Forgive me. Old habits."

"Oh, and bring that lantern," she added, pointing to the brass-framed lantern hanging on a hook behind the door. She grasped the handle and pulled the door open before stepping into the cool night air. Evryn followed, lantern in hand and the rolled-up diagram tucked beneath one arm. She reached past him to shut the door as his magic flared briefly, igniting the dull crystal at the lantern's center. Warm golden light bloomed, casting long shadows across the ground.

Mariselle turned and faced the darkened ruins, a shiver of anticipation coursing through her veins. "Come on," she said, unable to keep the excitement from her voice.

They left the cottage and made their way along the overgrown path that led toward Dreamland's ruins. In the darkness, the intricate silvery patterns of their matching marks glowed faintly. As they walked, Mariselle found herself struck once again by the melancholy beauty of the abandoned attraction. In daylight, the ruins possessed a romantic quality. Elegant decay softened by moss and climbing vines. But at night, with shadows pooling around the broken arches and what remained of the pavilion frame, the destruction seemed more profound.

"Just imagine what it once was," she said, her voice growing wistful. "A grand pavilion tent stretched across this frame, shimmering with magic. A flag flying from the highest point, visible from anywhere in town. That archway over there was the grand entrance, leading directly to the pavilion where rich curtains were drawn back like the opening to some magnificent stage, welcoming visitors inside. One day soon, Rowanwood, we shall see it restored to its former splendor."

"Perhaps," Evryn said, sounding entirely unconvinced, "though I still maintain this is folly." They picked their way over a cluster of nightveil orchids, almost invisible in the shadows with their near-black petals. "Even if we manage to locate this dream core, and even if we somehow acquire the necessary materials and complete the reconstruction, what makes you believe Dreamland will be a success second time around? The original closed under rather spectacular circumstances, as I recall."

"The original closed because a Rowanwood and a Brightcrest could not agree on how to run it, and that resulted in devastating failure. Your great-uncle wanted more recognition for himself instead of all the acclaim going to my grandfather for constructing such a magnificent wonder, so he began recklessly experimenting with dangerous lumyrite configurations that resulted in the destabilization of the entire operation."

Evryn stopped and turned to face her, his expression incredulous. "That isn't what happened. Your grandfather *deliberately* sabotaged the lumyrite network so that he could blame the Rowanwoods for Dreamland's failure and force my great-uncle Thaelan out. Krenshaw Brightcrest wanted Dreamland for himself. He was looking for alternative power solutions that *he* could control so he wouldn't have to share with a Rowanwood."

Indignation burned in Mariselle's veins. "What nonsense! It was the selfishness of Rowanwoods, always wanting to take recognition for themselves, that led to the dream space collapsing and my grandfather being caught in eternal slumber."

Evryn took a step closer, his gaze never leaving hers. "No, your grandfather was caught in eternal slumber because *he overused his own magic.*"

Mariselle flinched. It was true that her grandfather's condition—which had lasted for almost ten years before death had finally claimed him—had long served as a solemn warning within her family. A cautionary tale of the consequences awaiting those who pushed their dream magic beyond its natural limitations.

But in family accounts, he had always been portrayed as the hero. The man who had sacrificed himself in order to buy precious time for innocent visitors to escape Dreamland before he himself became eternally imprisoned within the dream realm. Never before had someone cruelly declared that her grandfather's decade-long imprisonment within his own dreams was entirely his own fault.

Mariselle's chest rose and fell with heavy breaths, but her voice remained remarkably steady as she said, "And he would not have had to overuse his magic if *your* ancestor hadn't destabilized the dream space and forced my grandfather to try and save it."

Evryn's eyes narrowed further. "Except that it was *your* ancestor who caused that destabilization, not mine."

Mariselle whirled away and continued along the path, hands fisted at her sides. This was ridiculous, arguing about transgressions from the past that neither of them had even been present for.

"Go home," she told Evryn, not bothering to look over her shoulder at him. "I shall find the dream core myself."

She strode forward, the only sounds her own footsteps crunching against fallen leaves and the occasional swish of her skirts against rough stone or low bushes. The remains of the pavilion frame and the broken archways surrounding it created strange shadows against the star-strewn sky. Darkness deepened around her as the warm glow of the lantern grew increasingly distant with every determined stride she took.

"Brightcrest!" Evryn shouted, his voice echoing oddly among the remains of the once-grand structure.

She ignored him, quickening her pace despite the low visibility. Without warning, her skirts caught on something, and she tugged them free with an impatient jerk. Three steps later, her foot landed on loose gravel, sliding unexpectedly and twisting at an unnatural angle. She stumbled as pain shot through her ankle, barely catching herself against a crumbling column.

"Brightcrest, don't be ridiculous." His voice was closer now, irritated and alarmed all at once. The lantern's glow grew stronger behind her. "How are you going to get the dream core back to the cottage by yourself?"

She pressed forward, ignoring the pain flaring up the side of her ankle and pretending not to hear Evryn.

"Mariselle!" he called, and it was only the use of her given name, which she was quite certain she'd never heard him utter before, that stopped her.

She turned slowly to face him. "What?"

Evryn stood before her, the lantern held aloft in one hand, casting dramatic shadows across his features. His jaw worked as if he were physically chewing on words he didn't want to release. A groan of what sounded like actual pain escaped him before he finally said, "I … apologize. For what I said about your grandfather."

Mariselle's eyebrows rose, genuine surprise replacing her anger. "It looked like that hurt."

"It did."

She rolled her eyes, then took a deep breath, forcing herself to be calm. "I …" Yes, this was indeed difficult to say. She tried again. "I … apologize as well. For blaming your great-uncle."

Evryn blinked. "Astounding."

"What?"

"I didn't know a Brightcrest was capable of apologizing."

"Believe me, I'm equally shocked to hear the words 'I apologize' leave the lips of a Rowanwood."

The mention of his lips inadvertently drew her gaze downward. The lantern's shifting light cast shadows that somehow rendered his mouth fuller than usual. Irritated with herself for noticing such a thing at all, she quickly averted her eyes.

Releasing a sharp exhale, she said, "Can we perhaps both acknowledge that neither of us knows the full story about what truly happened between our ancestors? Can we stop arguing about the past and instead focus on the present?"

Evryn was silent for a moment before giving a reluctant nod. "I suppose that would be the sensible approach." He paused, his gaze dropping to her feet and then back to her face. "Did you … hurt yourself?"

"I'm fine," she told him, the irritation creeping back into her voice. She ignored the stab of pain in her ankle as they started walking again. This wouldn't have happened if she'd been wearing her riding boots. But the original plan was for Petunia to accompany her this evening, and so she'd snuck out in a carriage instead of on her pegasus.

"You're limping," he pointed out as they passed beneath an ornate archway draped in tangled vines and pale blossoms.

"I'm fine," she repeated. "It's nothing a simple charm won't fix when we're back at the cottage."

He hesitated for a beat. Then another. "I could—"

"Spare me the fake gallantry, Rowanwood."

He sighed. "As you wish, my luminous pestilence."

She choked on a laugh that practically ambushed her with its unexpected force. She cleared her throat and swallowed. "Stop that."

He said nothing, but she could somehow *sense* the triumphant smirk radiating from him.

They passed beneath the skeletal remains of the pavilion's outer ring, its enormous framework still reaching toward the sky despite decades of neglect. Dull lumyrite crystals remained embedded in the tarnished metal at regular intervals, occasionally catching the moonlight. Broken columns jutted from the earth like ancient teeth, while luminous moss had claimed the shadowed crevices, painting the ruins with an ethereal blue-green glow.

Up ahead, the ground sloped downward in uneven tiers where time and weather had worn away what once must have been a grand, multi-leveled promenade. Evryn stepped forward and, without hesitation, jumped lightly down onto the lower level. His boots crunched against gravel and broken stone as he turned back to look up at her.

She stood at the edge, testing the crumbling ground with the toe of her shoe and wishing yet again that she had worn riding attire this evening. A gown and a twisted ankle were going to make this difficult. Nevertheless, determination was a quality Mariselle possessed in abundance, and she would find a way down, dress, ankle, and all, if only to prove she could.

"Need a hand, my daringly impractical skylark?" Evryn asked.

She glared at him with narrowed eyes. "No."

"Excellent. Then I shall stand here uselessly while you twist your other ankle attempting to dismount like a dramatic goat."

She stared at him.

He offered a winning smile.

Silence stretched between them.

She sighed, long and theatrical. "Fine."

"Was that the sound of you accepting help?" he asked, eyes gleaming. "Shall I have it engraved?"

"Just get on with it," she muttered. "And don't you dare drop me."

"I would never," he said solemnly. "Not without warning." He lowered the lantern to the ground, then stepped closer and lifted his arms. "Try not to enjoy this too much."

She gave him a look that could have curdled milk, but didn't comment. His hands settled around her waist, and she braced hers against his shoulders. His firm, broad, and annoyingly steady shoulders.

He lifted her down with infuriating ease, the muscles beneath her palms flexing with the motion, and she was convinced he was lowering her excruciatingly slowly just to ensure maximum awkwardness for her—and to give himself the satisfaction of watching her squirm.

"See?" he said as he placed her gently on the ground, hands still warm at her waist. "No goat theatrics required."

She stepped hastily away from him, her ankle throbbing dully. "If anyone's performing, it's you. I merely participated under protest."

He grinned. "You wound me."

"Tempting."

She bent to retrieve the lantern and stepped past him.

They climbed carefully over fallen debris—Mariselle's skirts catching yet again on rough edges and tangled vegetation—and came to a halt at the edge of a circular platform. They had reached what appeared to be the remains of Dreamland's central area, a circular space where several of the larger pavilion structures had once stood, with a depression in the ground at the very center.

"I confess I remain somewhat confused as to *what*, exactly, this place once was," Evryn admitted, raising the lantern and surveying their surroundings. "That was the main entrance, correct?" He gestured toward the largest archway, its structure still intact despite the years of abandonment. "And those appear to have been administrative rooms of some sort." His hand swept toward several small adjoining structures. "But everything else is merely … empty space. A rather large amount of it."

"Yes," Mariselle replied, her tone suggesting this should be obvious. "The principal wonder of Dreamland was that it contained an actual fragment of the dream realm anchored within our physical world. Dream architects crafted ever-changing landscapes and experiences within this space, but none of them required physical form in the conventional sense."

"So visitors would enter beneath that archway," Evryn clarified, pointing again, "and then simply wander through what appeared to be empty air?"

"Yes, though to them, it felt entirely substantial. They experienced wonders beyond imagination, all manifested through dream magic." She regarded him with mild surprise. "Has your family never spoken to you about Dreamland?"

"Not if they can help it," he muttered.

"Well, you shall soon get to experience it for yourself."

Evryn made a noncommittal sound that Mariselle decided to ignore. His doubt changed nothing. Dreamland would be returned to its former glory, with or without his enthusiasm.

They ascended the shallow steps onto the large circular platform, their footsteps echoing slightly against the ancient stone.

"There," Evryn said, pointing toward the sunken area. "According to the diagram, the dream core was positioned directly at the center."

They approached the depression, which proved to be deeper than it had initially appeared. Years of leaves and debris had accumulated in the hollow. Mariselle knelt at the edge, brushing away layers of decomposed organic matter with her hands.

Evryn set the lantern down, unrolled the diagram beside it, and bent over the parchment. Mariselle glanced up, finding him studying the plans with one hand holding the edges flat while the other raised the lantern for better illumination.

"Interesting," he murmured as she returned to scooping up handfuls of dirt and leaves. "It appears this entire central area is supposed to have a power grid beneath it. A complex network of lumyrite veins that once powered the entire venue." He straightened, surveying the circular platform beneath their feet. "And it seems ..." He turned slowly, examining their surroundings with newfound attention. "Well, this whole circular slab appears to be intact. No visible breakage. Not even significant cracking. I wonder if that means the lumyrite network beneath remains intact as well."

"I could do with some assistance here," Mariselle said, trying to keep the irritation from her voice. She should have been pleased—she *was* pleased— that he finally seemed to be showing some level of interest in his portion of the project, but their focus right now was meant to be on locating the dream core.

"Why not use magic for this?" Evryn asked as he knelt on the opposite side of the depression. "We'll be here until dawn otherwise."

Mariselle sat back with a huff, annoyed that this hadn't occurred to her. "Very well. Could you assist me with that?" She couldn't quite bring herself to add the word 'please' to the end of her request. It was difficult enough asking a Rowanwood for help.

Before she could begin to draw on her own power, Evryn extended one palm toward the accumulated debris. The soil began to shift and move, layers of dirt and decomposed leaves rising into the air in neat, organized piles that settled themselves at the edges of the depression. As more material was cleared away, the outline of etched metalwork began to emerge from beneath decades of accumulated debris.

"Oh," Mariselle breathed, her irritation forgotten in the face of what they were uncovering. "Oh, look at that."

The metal surface that emerged was covered in intricate markings—flowing patterns exactly like those detailed in the illustrations Mariselle had discovered in her grandfather's notes. As more earth cleared away, it became apparent that they had found not just any metal surface, but the upper portion of a large spherical object partially buried in the ground.

"Is that—?" Evryn began.

"The dream core," Mariselle whispered, her heart racing wildly and her voice filled with wonder. "It's here. It's actually here."

The sphere was larger than the illustration had suggested, its surface a combination of etched silver metal and embedded lumyrite crystal that caught the moonlight in hypnotic patterns. Mariselle could barely contain the thrill coursing through her veins, threatening to burst from her chest in an undignified squeal of pure elation.

"Isn't it the most incredible thing you've ever laid eyes on?" she whispered.

When Evryn didn't respond, she looked up and found him watching her with an odd expression.

"What?"

He shook his head, settling back on his heels as he surveyed their discovery. "How do you propose we extract something of this size?"

"I believe, my dearest betrothed, that we shall have to attempt something no Rowanwood and Brightcrest have managed in over fifty years." She met Evryn's gaze over the dream core, her lips quirking up in challenge. "Work together."

Chapter Eleven

THE MOST SENSIBLE COURSE OF ACTION WOULD HAVE BEEN TO AVOID his grandmother entirely until the charade with Mariselle had reached its inevitable conclusion. Yet here Evryn was, approaching The Charmed Leaf Tea House the morning after helping Mariselle locate Dreamland's dream core. He had, after all, stupidly declared that Mariselle would be joining him at the tea house on Thursday afternoon—which was now *tomorrow* afternoon—and his grandmother needed to be warned.

The air carried the mingled scents of lavender and freshly turned soil as Evryn strode along the path that wound around the side of the building toward the back garden, where gnomes and garden pixies argued amongst the rows of herbs and flowers. His mind still lingered on the previous night's expedition. The memory of Mariselle's face when they'd uncovered the dream core—that moment of pure, unguarded wonder—had stayed with him. It was so at odds with her usual cold demeanor that for a heartbeat, he'd almost found her … bearable.

But the notion of actually restoring Dreamland remained utterly preposterous. Even if the lumyrite network remained intact beneath the ground, and even if Evryn managed to acquire and shape all the necessary lumyrite to replace the damaged parts, there still remained the fact that Mariselle was simply incapable of the complex magic required to bring Dreamland back to life.

Evryn had caught sight of a list of the various dream magic wielders who had been involved in the operation of the original attraction in one of Mariselle's open volumes the night before. Dream architects, dream guides, portal weavers, boundary warders—whatever they might be. And what could Mariselle do? Extract dream essence. That was all.

Still, he wouldn't try to stop her. The sooner they reached the part of this absurd plan where she realized she couldn't 'have Dreamland,' the sooner the farce could end. Her inevitable failure would release them both from this ridiculous bond, not because the magical contract would allow it, but because she would have to acknowledge the impossibility of her goal.

At that point, she would finally allow him to find an expert in magical law who could figure out how to discreetly break the contract for them. Then they could announce that the soulbond did not appear to be strong enough to overcome years of animosity, and that it had faded away naturally, leaving them no longer engaged. Evryn could then return to his comfortably inconsequential existence.

He reached the back entrance to the tea house and slipped inside, finding the kitchen already bustling with activity. The familiar warmth and sweet-spiced air enveloped him immediately, soothing his growing apprehension. Despite not visiting as frequently as Jasvian, the tea house kitchen had always been a sanctuary of sorts. Memories flashed unbidden—himself as a small boy darting between tables, snatching pastries meant for paying customers, his grandmother's voice calling after him in exasperation. She'd enchant a dustpan and brush to chase him through the kitchen and out into the gardens when his mischief threatened to disturb her patrons. He'd shriek with laughter as he ran, the brush bristles tickling his ankles while kitchen pixies cackled from their perches atop shelves.

His smile faded as the memory dissolved, leaving him to wonder when exactly that carefree part of his childhood had slipped away. The distance between himself and his grandmother had grown so gradually he couldn't pinpoint its origin. Was it around about the time of his manifestation, as he began testing his independence and chafing against family expectations? Or perhaps when his father died, which had happened shortly after Evryn's ability had revealed itself, grief shrouding the household during a time that should have been spent celebrating new magic. He hated to admit it, but he envied the close relationship Jasvian shared with their grandmother. His brother had always been the favored one, his tempest-calming abilities essential to the family business in a way that Evryn's magic never would be.

"Lord Evryn!" a bright voice called from across the kitchen. Looking up, he spotted Miss Lucie Fields, the young human serving girl who worked for his grandmother, at the large central worktable. An apron was secured around her waist, and a dusting of flour—or was it confectioner's sugar?—stood out against her light brown skin where it had settled across her right cheek.

A territorial line of sifted flour bisected the table's surface, an unspoken boundary that separated her domain from that of Orrit, the brownie who had been with The Charmed Leaf since the day the establishment opened. The small creature was currently hunched over his own workspace, tiny hands kneading scone dough with fierce concentration.

"The gossip birds were just chatting about you," Lucie informed Evryn.

"Ah, what delightful rumors are they spreading this morning?" he asked as he made his way toward her, navigating around a kitchen pixie that darted past with a silver spoon nearly as large as itself.

"They've been positively giddy about the engagement ball," she said, her hazel eyes crinkling at the corners as she grinned. "According to their dramatic reports, it was quite the spectacle."

"I dread to ask," Evryn said, plucking a candied cherry from a nearby bowl, "but exactly how embellished have their accounts become?"

"Hmm, let's see," Lucie said with a hint of mischief in her voice. She frowned down at the delicate chocolate shells taking shape beneath her careful hands. "Something about the soulbonded couple being scandalously familiar with one another. One bird insisted it witnessed Lord Rowanwood practically licking Lady Brightcrest's hand during an especially prolonged hand kiss. Another claimed you conjured flowers that whispered love poems so explicit that several elderly ladies nearly fainted."

"I can assure you, there was no hand licking. And the flowers merely hummed, though I'll admit they did occasionally emit sighs that might have been misinterpreted by those with vivid imaginations."

"How terribly boring," Lucie said with a laugh. "Nevertheless, my congratulations on finding someone who apparently inspires such devotion in you. It's rather unexpected, given the families involved, but I wish you every happiness with Lady Mariselle."

"Thank you," Evryn said, his smile slipping slightly as he remembered the charade and the real reason he was visiting the tea house this morning. "Those are rather impressive," he added, nodding toward the delicate chocolate confections and further delaying the inevitable confrontation that awaited him upstairs.

"Oh, thank you," Lucie said, her focus returning to her task. "Lady Rivenna is introducing a new tea service this week that includes enchanted chocolates. When consumed alongside particular tea blends, they enhance the flavor experience." Her fingers trailed through the air, shaping another piece.

Evryn watched, genuinely intrigued by the girl's skill. For a human working with magic, her control was remarkable. His gaze caught on the rose-gold ring adorning her right hand, a small lumyrite stone set at its center—the source of her magical amplification, no doubt. Humans required such aids to channel magic, possessing none of their own.

Behind Lucie, kitchen pixies darted about, polishing silver tea services and arranging cutlery with military precision. Hearth sprites tended the fires, their glowing forms pulsing with the perfect heat needed for each preparation. The controlled chaos of the pre-opening routine unfolded around them, a dance of magical beings and humans working in surprisingly harmonious tandem.

"Is my grandmother about?" Evryn asked finally, knowing he could delay no longer.

"I believe she's upstairs in the study with Lady Iris," Lucie replied.

"Thank you," Evryn said, squaring his shoulders as he headed for the door on the other side of the kitchen.

He stepped onto the polished wooden floor of the main part of the tea house, still empty of patrons at this early hour, and turned toward the staircase. The chairs remained neatly tucked beneath tables draped with freshly pressed cloths. Vines adorning the walls rustled slightly as he passed, one or two trailing fingers of greenery reaching out toward him as if in greeting before retreating back to their assigned positions.

The staircase loomed before him, each step taking him closer to what promised to be an uncomfortable confrontation. As he reached the top landing, voices drifted from the partially open door of the study. Iris's measured tones followed by his grandmother's sharper ones, both pitched with the unmistakable cadence of disagreement.

"… cannot simply dismiss what you've seen," Iris was saying, her voice more forceful than Evryn had ever heard it.

"Of course I can," his grandmother countered. "It's nonsense."

"And how do you know that?"

"Because what else could it possibly be?" Lady Rivenna demanded.

"Are you telling me that your interpretation of the leaves is incorrect?"

Evryn couldn't help raising his brows at the audacity of such a comment. His lips twitched in amusement. There were few who ever dared to suggest that his grandmother might be *incorrect* about anything.

"Of course not," Lady Rivenna responded. "The leaves themselves are wrong."

"And what about what *I've* seen?" Iris insisted. "You cannot dismiss—"

"What you have seen is nothing more than a possibility that will never come to pass," Lady Rivenna interrupted.

"Will you please stop cutting me off?" Iris said, a hint of exasperation bleeding through her typically composed demeanor. "You need to consider that even *your* machinations cannot stop something from happening if it's truly meant to be."

Evryn felt his lips curve into a delighted grin, despite his anxiety. Sweet, accommodating Iris—who had married into a family as formidable as the Rowanwoods and somehow managed to carve out her own place within it— was standing up to the intimidating matriarch herself. His estimation of his brother's wife rose several notches.

"I don't understand why you're defending this," his grandmother said, her voice tinged with genuine bewilderment. "The girl is truly awful."

Evryn could just make out the sound of Iris's sigh. "On that much we can agree. I certainly never imagined having Mariselle Brightcrest for a sister-in-law."

He froze, the realization washing over him like a bucket of ice water. They were discussing him and Mariselle. Whatever his grandmother had 'seen'—in tea leaves, presumably—pertained to his fraudulent engagement.

He shifted his weight, and the aged floorboard beneath his foot let out a betraying creak. The voices within the study fell instantly silent.

"Is someone there?" his grandmother called sharply. Footsteps moved toward the door.

Cursing inwardly, Evryn had no choice but to announce himself. "It's only me," he said, moving forward and pushing the door open fully. He stepped into the study with feigned nonchalance. "Good morning, Grandmother. Iris."

The study was warm and cozy with a large window allowing plenty of natural light in. These days, the space was commanded by two desks: the larger one, his brother's domain, positioned at an angle in one corner, while the smaller one, where Iris now worked as his grandmother's apprentice, stood before the window. Several comfortable chairs with plush cushions were arranged near the unlit fireplace. The walls held a modest but well-curated bookshelf, while carved wooden tables displayed fresh-cut flowers and delicately folded paper ornaments.

Lady Rivenna stood near the door, her silver hair arranged in its customary elegant knot, her posture rigid, while Iris leaned against her desk, arms crossed firmly over her chest. Her expression shifted from surprise to a carefully neutral smile.

"Evryn," she greeted him, lowering her arms and taking a step forward. "What a pleasant surprise."

"Is it?" his grandmother asked dryly. "I would have thought he'd continue avoiding me for at least another week."

Evryn attempted a casual shrug. "I've never been one for predictability."

"Indeed not," Lady Rivenna agreed, assessing him with her sharp gaze. "To what do we owe this unexpected visit? Or need I ask? I assume it has something to do with your ... situation."

The distaste with which she pronounced the final word made it clear exactly what 'situation' she was referring to. Evryn straightened his posture, summoning the determination that had propelled him here this morning.

"As a matter of fact, yes," he replied, plunging ahead before his courage could desert him. "I came to inform you that Lady Mariselle will be joining me for tea here tomorrow afternoon."

His grandmother's expression remained frozen for several heartbeats before she spoke, each word carefully enunciated. "She most certainly will not."

"Grandmother—"

"No Brightcrest has crossed the threshold of The Charmed Leaf in over fifty years," Lady Rivenna continued, "and I will not have that tradition broken for the sake of your inexplicable infatuation."

"With respect," Evryn countered, maintaining a calm he didn't entirely feel, "this is about more than tradition. Lady Mariselle is to be my—wife." He hesitated for only the briefest of moments this time over the word 'wife.' "She cannot remain perpetually excluded from a place so central to our family's life."

"Mariselle Brightcrest will never be your—" His grandmother squeezed her eyes shut, inhaled deeply, and groaned. "I cannot even utter the word," she finished, opening her eyes and fixing her piercing gaze on Evryn once more. "The answer is no. I will not have her here."

"It was not a request," Evryn said. "I've come as a courtesy to inform you of our plans, not to seek permission. Lady Mariselle will be joining me for tea tomorrow afternoon. If her presence is so distressing, perhaps you might find business to attend to elsewhere in the tea house during our visit."

His grandmother studied him for a long moment before approaching, stopping directly before him. The imperious mask she typically wore had slipped, revealing something Evryn rarely witnessed—raw emotion. For a startling instant, he thought he detected a sheen of tears in her eyes, but she blinked and it vanished so quickly he suspected he'd imagined it. When she spoke, her voice had lost its sharpness, replaced by an almost earnest quietness. "You are toying with things you do not understand."

"Then enlighten me," Evryn challenged. "Instead of making cryptic allusions, tell me exactly why this feud persists. It's clear there is more to it than we were brought up to believe. What did the Brightcrests do that was so unforgivable?"

His grandmother's expression shuttered. "It is not a matter for discussion."

"Convenient," Evryn remarked, his patience fraying. "You expect me to honor a grudge whose origins you refuse to explain."

"I expect you to trust that I have good reason for my objections!"

Once again, Evryn found himself wondering how this would play out if he were truly in love with Mariselle Brightcrest. If he truly intended to marry her, what would his grandmother do then? "Is your desire to maintain this ancient animosity truly of greater importance to you than my chance at happiness?" he asked quietly.

Lady Rivenna released a heavy sigh, and there was something almost desperate in her gaze. "Evryn, you will not find happiness with—"

"That is not what I asked," he said stiffly.

"Evryn—"

"If Lady Mariselle is not welcome here, then neither am I."

The declaration hung between them, absurdly dramatic considering the entire engagement was a charade destined to dissolve. Yet the words had tumbled from his lips with startling conviction, driven by some raw, unexamined need to test whether his grandmother valued an ancient feud above her relationship with him.

A heavy silence followed. Lady Rivenna stared at him, genuine surprise flickering across her features before hardening into something closer to hurt. "You would choose her over your family?"

"You would choose a *grudge* over your grandson?" Evryn countered immediately.

The two regarded each other for a long moment, neither willing to yield. Finally, with a long inhale through her nose, Lady Rivenna's shoulders stiffened further—if such a thing were possible.

"Three o'clock," she said, her voice clipped. "Mrs. Spindlewood will seat you near my private alcove—where I can keep an eye on both of you."

Without waiting for a response, she swept past him and out of the study.

Evryn's breath left him in a rush, the tension draining from his shoulders like water from a broken vessel. "Well," he murmured, "that went about as well as expected."

"Better than expected, I'd say," Iris offered with a gentle smile. "She agreed, after all."

"Under protest," Evryn pointed out, dropping into the nearest armchair. "And with clear intentions to make the experience as uncomfortable as possible."

"Your grandmother is …" Iris hesitated, visibly choosing her words with care. "Complex. Especially where the Brightcrests are concerned. I must confess I'm burning with curiosity about what she refuses to reveal." She perched on the edge of the chair across from Evryn, her brow furrowing thoughtfully. "Has Lady Mariselle offered any insights that might explain your grandmother's particular intensity on this matter?"

Evryn shook his head. "Her story differs somewhat from the one I was brought up with, though it's essentially just the opposing perspective of the same tale—each family blaming the other for Dreamland's failure rather than anything truly illuminating."

"Hmm." Iris stared passed him, apparently lost in thought for a moment.

Evryn studied his sister-in-law, recalling the conversation he'd overheard when he'd arrived. "What has my grandmother seen?"

Iris blinked and refocused on him, clearly startled by this abrupt subject change. "Excuse me?"

"The two of you were arguing about something when I arrived," Evryn said, deciding not to hide the fact that he'd overheard part of their conversation. "About something she'd seen. About something *you've* seen. Regarding Lady Mariselle and me. I assume the two of you were speaking of tea leaf reading. I know my grandmother still practices this ancient art."

Unease crossed Iris's features. "It … I … really can't say."

Evryn sat forward. "Even if I ask very nicely?"

She sighed. "You should ask your grandmother. It isn't my place to come between the two of you."

He slumped back in his chair. "I can imagine how well that conversation will go."

She gave him a sympathetic smile. "Yes. So can I." Her fingers twisted together in her lap, and she seemed to be searching for a safe topic to navigate away from dangerous waters. "Will you be at the art exhibition this evening?"

Oh. The Emberdales' art exhibition and auction. Evryn had forgotten about it entirely. "Uh, yes. Nothing quite like an evening of pretentious artistic analysis to follow a morning of family drama. I'm positively giddy with anticipation."

Iris laughed. "Indeed. Well, it shall be my first time attending. I'll see you there." She rose from her chair and moved toward the door, then hesitated at the threshold. Her hand rested on the doorframe as she turned back. "Do you truly love Lady Mariselle?"

The directness of the question caught Evryn off guard. He scrambled to assemble the practiced response he'd delivered countless times over the past days, but found the words sticking in his throat under Iris's sincere gaze.

"It's … complicated," he managed finally. "But the bond is real." That much was true, at least, even if the magical binding that tethered him to Mariselle was certainly not the romantic connection Iris believed him to be referencing.

"I see," she said, and Evryn had the disturbing sense that she *did* see. If not the full truth, then perhaps some of it. He shifted uncomfortably in the armchair, but Iris merely inclined her head in his direction and said, "I wish you a good day, Evryn. And try not to let your grandmother's resistance trouble you too deeply. I believe all will work out as it should."

She slipped from the room before he could formulate a response. After a moment, Evryn nodded to himself, finding peculiar comfort in her final words. Indeed, all would work out as it should—with Mariselle and himself eventually freed from their charade, the contract broken, and natural order restored. Rowanwoods and Brightcrests would return to their comfortable antipathy, precisely as they were meant to be.

Chapter Twelve

MARISELLE STOOD SLIGHTLY BEHIND HER MOTHER AND SISTER AS THEY glided through the entrance of the Emberdale Estate, her shoulders back and her expression perfectly composed, a small embroidered reticule clutched in one gloved hand. The Annual Enchanted Arts Exhibition & Auction was one of the most anticipated events of the Season, drawing most of Bloomhaven's elite society—which meant that even feuding families must endure each other's proximity for the sake of appearances.

Dusk sprites darted through the air, providing subtle ambient lighting, and crystal chimes suspended from the vaulted ceiling tinkled faintly. "How … enthusiastic the Emberdales are this year," Lady Clemenbell observed, her tone suggesting that enthusiasm was a rather vulgar quality. She cast a critical glance around the grand foyer, where multiple provocative displays of entwined figures had already drawn scandalized gasps from several matrons, who furiously fluttered their fans while simultaneously leaning closer for a better view. "Though perhaps they might have consulted someone with more refined aesthetic sensibilities for the arrangements."

"Indeed," Ellowa agreed, sniffing disdainfully. "Oh!" She jumped slightly as the nearest sculpture—a pair of nymphs—shifted fluidly before their eyes, the figures separating and becoming two winged feline creatures.

Mariselle kept her silence as she followed her mother and sister into the main gallery, though she wondered why the moving sculpture had surprised Ellowa. The invitation had quite clearly announced 'Transformative Sculptures: Magic in Motion' as this year's theme. One could hardly expect stationary art at an event specifically celebrating magical metamorphosis.

As they entered the main exhibition hall, Mariselle's gaze swept across the assembled guests, automatically seeking those to avoid. The Rowanwoods would be present, of course. The Emberdales maintained cordial relations with both families, positioning themselves as neutral territory within Bloomhaven's complex social landscape. Her mother and sister would no doubt keep their distance from the Rowanwoods, though Mariselle herself could hardly maintain her usual strategy of pretending they didn't exist. It would appear decidedly odd for the soulbonded bride-to-be to avoid her betrothed, especially after the gossip birds had broadcast across Bloomhaven how the enamored couple could scarcely keep their hands from one another at the High Lady's ball.

Across the gallery, pairs of ladies strolled arm-in-arm between the exhibits, their heads inclined toward one another in confidential conversation. Two sisters from the Windvalley family laughed softly as they gestured toward a sculpture of a pegasus whose marble mane moved inexplicably in an invisible breeze, while the Mosswood cousins pointed at an elaborate metal construction of hummingbirds, all joined at their wingtips, that morphed seamlessly into a collection of metal butterflies and then back again in an endless enchanted cycle.

Something in Mariselle's chest tightened at the sight of this easy camaraderie, the quiet intimacy of shared experience between young ladies who genuinely delighted in one another's company rather than merely tolerating each other's presence. She glanced at Ellowa, whose golden head was tilted critically as she examined an exceptionally tall stone statue of an elf. On rare occasions, Ellowa would draw Mariselle close like this, linking their arms as they moved through social gatherings, though typically only when she wished to share cutting observations about someone's appearance or behavior without being overheard. Still, perhaps tonight might be different. Perhaps they might actually discuss the art itself.

Tentatively, Mariselle shifted closer to her sister, her hand half-raised to touch Ellowa's elbow. But before she could complete the gesture, a dusk sprite drifted too near Ellowa's carefully arranged curls. Ellowa swatted sharply at the creature with a sound of disgust, the unexpected movement causing Mariselle to step back instinctively.

As she retreated, her gaze landed on a familiar figure across the room. Evryn Rowanwood stood with his mother near a sculpture of a golden stag, his expression unreadable as he watched Mariselle. How long had he been observing? Had he witnessed her pathetic attempt to win her sister's attention? Heat crawled up her neck, but she refused to show embarrassment. She lifted her chin, arranging her features into her most imperious expression before turning away, as though she'd merely happened to glance in his general direction and found nothing worth her continued attention.

The sight of him reminded her of the small gift nestled inside her reticule, a token she had carefully selected after much deliberation. A small smile curved her lips. She would find the right moment to present it to him, a carefully calculated gesture to further their charade.

"Mother," Ellowa murmured with sudden urgency, her voice dropping to that particular pitch she reserved for social emergencies, "I've just spotted Lady Lelianna Rowanwood and that insufferable peacock Mariselle has stupidly bound herself to across the room. Perhaps we should proceed to the east gallery? I'd hate for us to be forced into awkward pleasantries."

Mariselle looked over her shoulder and spotted Lady Lelianna saying something to Evryn while making subtle motions with her head toward the Brightcrests. Oh dear.

"Yes, quite right," Lady Clemenbell replied with a barely perceptible nod. "We shall remove ourselves immediately. Come along, girls." She gathered her skirts, already shifting her trajectory toward the adjoining room.

Mariselle trailed behind as they processed toward the east gallery, wondering idly if the Rowanwoods and Brightcrests would ever actually acknowledge each other's existence in public, or if they would continue this elaborate dance of avoidance until the end of days. It was almost comical how two families could occupy the same social spaces for generations without ever directly interacting.

"Lady Mariselle!"

Mariselle stopped at the sound of the familiar voice behind her. Turning, she found Evryn and his mother approaching, the former with a besotted smile that appeared strained at the corners, the latter with polite curiosity painted on her features.

"Mother," Mariselle began in an urgent whisper, turning back, "I don't believe I can avoid—"

But it was too late. Her mother and sister had already glided through the doorway into the next gallery, disappearing into the crowd with remarkable speed that belied their usual dignified pace. They had abandoned her without a backward glance.

Mariselle swallowed and straightened her spine, adopting the posture of serene confidence that had been drilled into her since childhood as she faced her so-called fiancé and his mother. It occurred to her in that moment that she had never once met Lady Lelianna Rowanwood face to face. This moment, awkward as it might be, was actually somewhat historic.

"Lady Mariselle," Lady Lelianna greeted her, offering a smile as she came to a stop. "I don't believe we've had the pleasure of being formally introduced, my dear. I've so been looking forward to meeting the young woman who has captured my Evryn's heart."

Mariselle curtseyed elegantly, her mind working rapidly to assess the situation. Lady Lelianna's smile seemed warm, but it was surely a careful performance. No Rowanwood could possibly be pleased about this match, just as no Brightcrest would ever truly accept a Rowanwood.

"Lady Rowanwood," she replied, her voice pitched to perfect politeness. "The pleasure is mine. Your son speaks of you with such devotion."

"Does he indeed?" Lady Lelianna's gaze shifted to Evryn. "How extraordinary. He does surprise me on occasion, though rarely in such flattering terms." Despite her teasing words, her eyes lingered on Evryn with such obvious affection that Mariselle felt an unexpected pang in her chest. It was the kind of look she had spent her entire life trying to coax from her own mother—warm, indulgent, and filled with genuine love that required no performance or achievement to earn.

"I admit I've heard precious little about you from him," Lady Lelianna continued, turning her attention back to Mariselle. "Do tell me more about this unexpected connection the two of you have formed."

"Mother," Evryn interjected, "perhaps we might discuss the exhibition rather than interrogating my betrothed?"

"Nonsense," Lady Lelianna replied. "There will be plenty of time for art appreciation. I'm simply becoming acquainted with the young lady who is to join our family." She turned back to Mariselle. "I must admit, we were all quite taken aback by the news. It has taken some … adjusting, given the nature of our families' bitter history. But in my quieter moments of reflection, I've been reminded that happiness often blooms in the most unexpected gardens. Who am I to question the ancient magic that has bound you together?"

"If only Grandmother shared your sentiment," Evryn muttered, just loud enough to be heard.

"My family has found the situation equally challenging," Mariselle replied, her practiced smile never wavering despite the strain. "They've spent decades nurturing their resentments, after all. But Lord Evryn and I are determined to honor what magic has ordained. The soulbond represents something beyond our petty family squabbles."

"Indeed," Lady Lelianna replied.

An awkward silence descended, punctuated only by the quiet murmurs of conversation around them. Mariselle found herself at a loss for words—a rare occurrence. The script for this particular social scenario simply didn't exist. What did one say to the mother of one's fake fiancé when decades of family animosity stood between them? Perhaps she should—

"Oh!" she exclaimed, her expression brightening with feigned excitement as she remembered the slim volume inside her reticule. "I nearly forgot! I have something for you, my love."

Evryn's eyes narrowed slightly, clearly suspicious of her sudden enthusiasm. "Do you indeed?"

"Yes." She reached into her reticule and withdrew the palm-sized leather-bound volume. "I saw it this morning in Thornberry's Rare Books and thought of you immediately. The shopkeeper assured me it contains the most romantic verses ever penned."

She extended the gift toward him, beaming with affected adoration. The book—*Devotional Poetry Collection: Sonnets for My Beloved*—appeared entirely innocuous. What Evryn didn't know was that she had spent the afternoon carefully modifying the contents.

"How thoughtful," Evryn said, warily accepting the gift. He lifted the cover to examine the first page, and Mariselle had to suppress a smile. The truly embarrassing poems didn't begin until page twenty-three.

"The shopkeeper said it's quite moving," she continued innocently. "I do hope you'll read it aloud to me sometime."

A nearby couple glanced their way, the woman sighing dreamily at this apparent display of spontaneous affection. The man nudged his companion and whispered something that caused her to blush.

"I shall treasure it," Evryn replied, closing the book and slipping it into his jacket pocket. His smile was filled with apparent tenderness, but his eyes met hers with unmistakable suspicion, a silent message that he didn't for one moment believe this to be a genuine gift.

Movement near the room's entrance caught Mariselle's attention, and she spotted Petunia being all but dragged into the gallery by her mother. Petunia's expression conveyed such profound ennui that Mariselle had to bite the inside of her cheek to keep from laughing.

"My dear cousin has just arrived," she said to Lady Lelianna, a note of genuine warmth creeping into her voice. "If you'll excuse me, I simply must greet her properly."

"Of course." Lady Lelianna replied. "It has been a pleasure to meet you, dear, and you simply must come to tea. At Rowanwood House. Tomorrow, perhaps? Or next week, if that would be more convenient. I shall send a formal invitation, of course."

Mariselle blinked, momentarily caught off guard. Tea? At Rowanwood House? This was venturing far beyond the public performance she'd anticipated. The charade was meant to be maintained at social gatherings, not intimate family settings. Though tea at Rowanwood House would at least provide Mariselle's mother with the 'intelligence-gathering' opportunity she'd been promised.

"That would be lovely," she heard herself say, the practiced social response emerging automatically. "Though I believe I'm having tea at The Charmed Leaf tomorrow afternoon with Lord Evryn."

"Oh, indeed! The Charmed Leaf!" Lady Lelianna gave her son a look filled with meaning. "How very interesting. Well, it shall have to be next week then, my dear."

"Yes, of course, my lady. Thank you. And I'm honored to have made your acquaintance."

Mariselle sank into a graceful curtsy as Lady Lelianna looped her arm through her son's and steered him away. Glancing up, she caught the unmistakable relief washing over Evryn's features as he allowed himself to be led away from her.

The feeling is mutual, she silently assured him.

She made her way across the gallery as Petunia was steered past Lord Jasvian and Lady Iris, who had apparently just arrived as well. Iris caught Mariselle's eye briefly, and Mariselle slowed, not wanting to endure the awkwardness of forced conversation with the half-fae woman. The memory of the encounter in the Thornharts' garden maze last Season still caused an uncomfortable tightness in her chest. But Iris merely regarded Mariselle with a carefully neutral expression before turning back to her husband.

"Cousin!" Mariselle called, reaching Petunia and her mother. "How lovely to see you both."

"Mariselle, dear," Lady Dawndale greeted her, her gaze immediately drifting past to scan the room for more important social connections. "You look well," she added, though her eyes never once settled on Mariselle's face.

"Thank you, Aunt. Might I borrow Petunia for a moment? I was hoping to show her a particularly fascinating piece in the west gallery."

Before Lady Dawndale could object, Petunia had already stepped forward, linking her arm through Mariselle's. "Do excuse us, Mother. I'm simply dying to see this extraordinary marvel."

They escaped toward the adjoining gallery, Petunia leaning a little on Mariselle's arm. "I must apologize for abandoning you last night," she said once they were safely out of earshot. "Mother insisted I help her select coordinating shawls for her summer wardrobe. A riveting three hours of my life watching her vacillate between 'blush pink' and 'dawn blush' as though the fate of the United Fae Isles hinged upon the distinction."

She sighed dramatically as they approached a bare-chested, larger-than-life fae male figure sculpted from silver-veined marble. The figure was posed mid-lunge, brandishing a glittering lumyrite sword as though frozen at the climax of some glorious myth.

"Then, to make matters worse," Petunia continued, "those darned gossip birds living outside my window kept me awake until all hours of the night, beside themselves with excitement over 'The Great Floral Exodus.' Something about mountains of flowers being carted out of Brightcrest Manor yesterday morning. I don't suppose you know anything about that particular horticultural phenomenon?"

Mariselle groaned. "My insufferable suitor. His wretched flowers multiplied overnight! I woke nearly suffocated beneath them. It took over an hour to clear them all away."

"How tragic for you, to be buried beneath tokens of devotion from your beloved."

"It wasn't devotion; it was sabotage," Mariselle insisted, though she couldn't help smiling at her cousin's teasing.

Her gaze traveled past Petunia and over the male sculpture. His arms bulged with improbably corded muscle as he held the sword aloft, and his torso was carved with such precision that each abdominal ridge caught the light. A cunning arrangement of sculpted leaves twined artistically over the lower part of his torso, doing its best to preserve his modesty—and failing by several strategic inches.

"Goodness," Mariselle said. "That's … quite something."

Petunia, who had been examining the sculpture as well, let out a dry hum of agreement. "Nothing says 'timeless artistic merit' like an impractically large weapon and a gratuitous display of torso." She folded her arms over her chest, her head tilting back as her gaze rose higher. "Ah, there it is. The noble anguish of a man who's just remembered he left his shirt in another realm."

A sound escaped Mariselle—something between a cough and a snort. She smacked a hand over her mouth.

"Or perhaps it's the eternal sorrow of realizing his sword is compensating for something," Petunia mused.

A strangled laugh burst from behind Mariselle's hand, which she tried in vain to smother, her shoulders shaking.

"In either case," Petunia added, "if one must swing about a lumyrite blade the size of a festival banner pole, one ought to at least wear breeches."

"Stop!" Mariselle hissed, eyes watering with mirth. "This is a *public* exhibition."

Petunia arched an eyebrow. "So is he."

Without warning, the sculpture shifted, stone muscles flexing as the sword swung in a wide, slow arc overhead. Both girls shrieked in alarm, stumbling backward and clutching each other before dissolving into full-bodied giggles. Mariselle grabbed Petunia's arm and pulled her behind a nearby sculpture of a benign-looking tree, its marble branches swaying gently as if stirred by an enchanted breeze. They peeked out from behind its trunk to observe the fae warrior from a safer distance.

The warrior had assumed a new pose of breathtaking arrogance, chin tilted at an angle that displayed his chiseled jawline to maximum effect, sword held casually at his side as though it weighed nothing at all. His gaze was fixed on some invisible horizon, his expression a perfect blend of noble suffering and smoldering intensity that suggested he alone carried the burden of understanding the universe's deepest mysteries.

"Is it just me," Mariselle said, "or does he look like he composes sonnets to his own reflection?"

Petunia snickered. "I daresay he's rehearsing a ballad to his upper arms."

"The upper arms are a bit much. Does one really need that many muscles to hoist a lumyrite blade?"

"Don't be absurd. Those are clearly conversational muscles."

Mariselle choked on another snort-laugh. "And what, pray tell, are conversational muscles?"

"Well, dear cousin," Petunia said, "they are, of course, muscles so unnecessarily prominent that they demand to be discussed in hushed tones behind a fan, ideally while someone's mother is scandalized and someone's aunt is intrigued but pretending not to be." She shifted her weight and winced slightly, reaching down to touch her ankle.

"What's wrong?" Mariselle asked immediately, her amusement fading to concern.

"It's nothing," Petunia said, straightening. "I tripped coming out of the house earlier and twisted my ankle. Simply my usual gracelessness on display."

"Did you not apply a healing charm in the carriage? Surely there was time before you arrived."

Petunia's expression tightened. "Mother wouldn't permit it. She said the discomfort would serve as a lesson in proper deportment."

"That's ridiculous!" Mariselle exclaimed, indignation flaring in her chest. "She would allow you to endure such unnecessary pain? What possible benefit could there be in your suffering? No, this won't do at all. I'm certain I have a remedy somewhere ..." She began rummaging through her reticule.

"Good stars, have you an entire apothecary's shop concealed within that dainty contrivance?" Petunia asked, leaning closer.

"It's enchanted, of course," Mariselle replied absently, still searching. "Extra space. All sorts of things. It's best to be prepared for any eventuality."

"You mean you like to be prepared to escape for a night of—"

"Shh!" Mariselle hissed, looking around momentarily before returning her attention to the contents of her reticule.

Her fingers closed around a small wrapped sweet, and she withdrew it triumphantly. "Here. It's an analgesic confection. It won't heal the sprain, of course, but it should relieve the pain for the evening. When you return home, your lady's maid can apply a proper healing charm."

Petunia accepted the sweet with a grateful nod. "Thank you, Mari." She popped it into her mouth, then winced and straightened suddenly. "Oh dear," she said around the sweet. "Mother has entered this gallery. She's almost certainly scanning the room for signs of my imminent disgrace. Oh, this is quite effective," she added, pointing to her mouth. "I feel it working already."

"Good," Mariselle said with a decisive nod. "We cannot have you limping about in pain all evening." She peered around the side of the sculpture and sighed as she spotted her aunt, whose expression suggested she had just come face to face with artistic depravity in physical form—though despite her look of scandalized horror, she did seem to be leaning closer for a better inspection of the fae warrior's glistening torso.

"I suppose I should find my mother as well," Mariselle said reluctantly. "Though I'd far rather spend the evening hiding with you and spinning elaborate tales about scandalously underdressed sculptures."

"Ah, well," Petunia said, "the Season is but newly begun. I daresay we'll find ample opportunities for hiding from both society and family."

Mariselle gave her cousin a warm smile. "However would I survive these dreadful affairs without you?"

"You wouldn't," Petunia said breezily. "You'd crumble under the combined force of your ghastly mother and sister and finally tell them exactly what you think of them. It would be unspeakably satisfying."

"Tunia!" Mariselle exclaimed, though her scolding was half-laugh, half-gasp.

"I jest, naturally. Well, perhaps only a little. But truly, Mari, you ought to try standing up to them. It would do wonders for you."

Mariselle shook her head, smile fading. "You know it wouldn't," she said quietly. "I'd pay for it afterward." She took a breath, straightening her spine and squaring her shoulders. "Now go, before that sculpture moves again and those modesty vines abandon all pretense. Your mother looks one gasp away from a dramatic swoon." She gave her cousin's hand a quick squeeze before Petunia stepped out from behind the marble tree and moved toward her mother.

Mariselle turned and circled the other side of the statue—and nearly collided with someone.

"Oh!" she exclaimed, stepping back hastily while the figure she'd almost walked into did the same. "I beg your pardon—"

The words died on her lips as she recognized Lady Iris. Instantly, Mariselle's posture stiffened, her chin lifting slightly as her walls came up. "Lady Iris," she said, her voice cooling to proper formality.

"Lady Mariselle," Iris replied with a polite nod. "Please excuse me. I didn't see you there."

Mariselle's eyes narrowed, her heart thudding faster. "Were you eavesdropping on us?"

"Not intentionally," Iris replied, her tone remaining even. "It's a public space, and I was merely admiring this particular piece." She gestured toward the marble tree. "I didn't realize until too late that you and your cousin were having a private conversation."

Mariselle's thoughts tumbled over themselves in sudden panic as she mentally retraced her conversation with Petunia. What exactly had they said? How much had Iris overheard? "I see," she said stiffly.

"Is …" Iris paused, then forged on. "Is Lady Petunia quite well?" she asked, a note of genuine concern in her voice. "She seemed to be in some discomfort."

"She's perfectly fine," Mariselle replied quickly, defensiveness coloring her tone. "It was merely a slight mishap. Nothing of consequence."

"Of course. Forgive me for prying."

Mariselle had already taken a step past Iris, eager to escape this increasingly uncomfortable encounter, but those words—*forgive me*—stopped her. Guilt churned inside her. It was she who should be seeking forgiveness after the cruel things she'd uttered last Season in the Thornhart maze. Though she had merely been following Ellowa's lead, fearing retribution if she didn't, the fact remained that she could have refused. She *should* have refused.

While Mariselle felt no qualms about directing disdain toward any Rowanwood—they had certainly earned her family's contempt with their condescension and their relentless campaign to exclude the Brightcrests from Bloomhaven's most coveted social circles—Iris was different. She hadn't been born into that pretentious, opportunistic family but had merely married into it. Poor judgment in selecting a husband hardly justified the cruel barbs Mariselle and Ellowa had flung at her that day in the maze—and at that point, Iris wasn't even involved with a Rowanwood yet, let alone married to one.

After a quick glance around to make sure her mother and Ellowa were nowhere in sight, Mariselle turned back. "Lady Iris, I …" She took a breath and forced herself to meet Iris's gaze. "About last Season. In the maze."

Iris's expression grew wary. "Yes?"

"What I said to you was …" Mariselle paused, struggling to find the right words. She wanted to blame Ellowa, to say that her sister had forced her to play along and that she'd had no choice. But there *had* been a choice, and Mariselle recognized the need to take responsibility for her own actions. "It was inexcusable. I should never have spoken to you that way. I'm truly sorry."

Iris stared at her, clearly taken aback. "Oh. Thank you for saying so."

The vulnerability of the moment was so foreign that Mariselle felt almost lightheaded, as though she'd stepped too close to the edge of a precipice. She blinked and gave her head a small shake.

"I believe the auction will be starting soon," Iris said, glancing over her shoulder toward the main gallery just as Lord Jasvian appeared in the doorway, clearly looking for her. Evryn appeared at his side, eyes narrowing when he spotted Iris and Mariselle standing together.

"Yes, of course," Mariselle said quickly, grateful for the shift back to safer, more formal territory. "We should probably join our families."

"Yes." Iris smiled tentatively. "The time for hiding has passed, unfortunately. Good evening, Lady Mariselle."

Iris turned and walked away, leaving Mariselle standing there, her thoughts suddenly racing in a dozen directions.

The time for hiding has passed.

Mariselle's mind darted further back, to her whispered conversation with Petunia. *I'd far rather spend the evening hiding with you … I daresay we'll find ample opportunities for hiding from both society and family.*

With a quiet groan, Mariselle allowed her eyes to slide closed for a moment. Iris had heard far more than she should have. Would she tell anyone? Or would the half-fae woman recognize, perhaps better than anyone, the difference between the masks society demanded and the truth that lurked beneath them? As Mariselle opened her eyes and set off in reluctant search of her own family, she wondered which was more terrifying—being exposed as a fraud, or being truly seen for exactly who she was.

Chapter Thirteen

Mariselle adjusted her gloves for the third time as the carriage approached The Charmed Leaf Tea House the following afternoon. Her stomach twisted into knots as she directed another nervous smile at Tilly, seated opposite her.

"I shall remain nearby, my lady," Tilly assured her. "Your mother was most insistent."

Of course she was. Lady Clemenbell had spent nearly an hour that morning delivering detailed instructions on what information Mariselle was to gather during this unprecedented visit to the Rowanwood establishment. "Note every magical enchantment," her mother had emphasized. "Pay particular attention to how they maintain such influence over Bloomhaven society. There must be some method beyond mere tea and gossip."

The carriage rolled to a stop, and Mariselle drew a steadying breath. She was about to become the first Brightcrest in living memory to step foot inside The Charmed Leaf. The notion sent a strange thrill through her, half trepidation, half rebellious excitement.

"I shall wait on those benches beneath the trees," Tilly said, gesturing to a pleasant seating area alongside the tea house as they descended from the carriage. "Should you require anything, simply send word."

Mariselle nodded, smoothing her pale blue gown as she approached the entrance. For years, she had passed this establishment, her mother invariably steering her to the opposite side of the street with a dismissive sniff. Now she stood before its welcoming facade, taking in details she'd never allowed herself to observe properly. The gentle curves of the architecture, the way trailing vines curled around the windows, the soft golden glow emanating from within.

The door opened as she approached, and her breath caught in her throat as she stepped inside. The interior was even more enchanting than rumor suggested. Warm wooden floors, tables draped with cream cloths, a delightful variety of tea cups and teapots. The walls were adorned with living vines whose golden-tinged leaves seemed to rustle with interest at her arrival. Floating faelights drifted near the ceiling in gentle patterns, several of them dipping lower as she entered, their glow intensifying slightly as if to better illuminate her.

The air carried a subtle symphony of scents—spiced tea, fresh-baked scones, delicate floral notes that shifted as she breathed them in. The very atmosphere hummed with magic, a tangible presence that seemed to assess her as she stood in the entryway.

"Lady Brightcrest," a voice called, breaking her reverie.

Only then did Mariselle become aware of the hush that had fallen over the room, the eyes turned toward her, the odd whisper here and there. The presence of a Brightcrest inside The Charmed Leaf was unprecedented, a spectacle so extraordinary that not a single member of Bloomhaven society present could fail to take note of it.

A slender fae woman approached, and Mariselle realized this was the woman who had just greeted her. "I am Mrs. Spindlewood, the tea house hostess," she continued. "Lady Iris informed us you would be joining Lord Evryn this afternoon. If you would follow me?"

Mariselle inclined her head in acknowledgment and followed the hostess through the main room, uncomfortably aware of the whispers that had resumed in her wake. She caught fragments—"a Brightcrest, can you imagine" and "never in all my years"—and held her chin a fraction higher. Let them gossip. She was here by invitation, after all. And what else did they expect now that she was supposedly engaged to a Rowanwood?

Mrs. Spindlewood led her to a table positioned near an alcove where a lush cascade of honeysuckle vines spilled from the ceiling, partially concealing the small private space beyond, where Mariselle could just make out a small round table and chair positioned beside a window.

"Lord Evryn sent word that he has been detained," Mrs. Spindlewood said, "but he should arrive shortly." She gestured toward a chair.

"Thank you," Mariselle said, then stopped as the chair scooted out from beneath the table and turned slightly, as if presenting its cushioned seat to her. Was that normal behavior in this establishment? Recovering quickly, she seated herself with as much dignity as she could muster.

"Your tea service shall commence momentarily," Mrs. Spindlewood continued. "The tea house itself will determine what blend is best for you."

Mariselle nodded. She had heard of this, the fact that The Charmed Leaf was enchanted to appear as if it possessed opinions regarding its patrons' tastes. She was curious to discover whether the establishment's magic would truly divine her preferences or if it might serve her something deliberately unsuitable. In her current state, with nerves fluttering wildly beneath her composed exterior, she scarcely knew what might soothe her own agitation.

As Mrs. Spindlewood departed, Mariselle felt a peculiar ticklish sensation on her shoulder. Turning slightly, she found a delicate tendril from one of the wall vines cautiously brushing its dainty leaves over her shoulder. She resisted the urge to flinch. The touch wasn't unpleasant, merely ... strange. Did the vines interact with all guests this way, or was she receiving special attention as a Brightcrest intruder?

Her gaze drifted across the room, searching for details she could later relay to her mother, though she doubted she would spot anything useful. If there *was* some scandalous secret at the heart of The Charmed Leaf's success, she doubted it would be on full display in the main room of the tea house.

A prickle of awareness crawled up her spine as her gaze traveled back to where it had begun, and—*Oh*. A shiver of apprehension darted up Mariselle's spine. For there in the private alcove, seated in solitary splendor on the chair that had previously been vacant, was Lady Rivenna Rowanwood.

Their eyes met across the intervening space, and Mariselle felt as though she'd been caught in the focused beam of a magnifying glass held to sunlight. Refusing to be intimidated, however, she lifted her chin a fraction higher, offering a polite smile that deliberately failed to reach her eyes. Lady Rivenna's only response was a slight narrowing of her gaze, as though Mariselle were a puzzle she found both tiresome and intriguing.

Neither woman looked away. The silent standoff continued, a wordless battle of wills conducted through the tea house air. Mariselle folded her hands primly in her lap, maintaining steady eye contact despite the thundering of her heart. She had been raised to hold her own in social warfare, after all.

Lady Rivenna's eyes narrowed further, genuine affront crossing her features when Mariselle refused to be the first to look away. The tea house itself seemed to grow still around them, as though holding its breath in anticipation.

After what felt like an eternity but could only have been a minute, Lady Rivenna rose with regal dignity and began approaching. Mariselle's heart leaped into her throat. It was one thing to maintain eye contact across the room; it was quite another to face Lady Rivenna Rowanwood directly. Every bit of proper upbringing insisted she show respect to this older woman, regardless of family animosity.

As Lady Rivenna reached her table, Mariselle stood and dipped into a respectful curtsy. "My lady," she murmured.

Without a word, Lady Rivenna settled herself elegantly into the chair opposite. Mariselle hesitated a moment, then reseated herself, awaiting whatever would come next.

For several heartbeats, Lady Rivenna simply studied her, continuing their silent assessment. Then, with deliberate slowness, she spoke. "Lady. Mariselle. Brightcrest." Each word fell between them like a stone dropped into still water.

"Yes, my lady," Mariselle replied, pleased that her voice emerged steady.

"I find myself in the unprecedented position of hosting a Brightcrest in my establishment," Lady Rivenna observed, her tone glacial. "A situation I never anticipated—nor desired."

"Your grandson extended the invitation," Mariselle said, matching the older woman's formal cadence. "I would not wish to disappoint him."

"No, I imagine you wouldn't." Lady Rivenna's gaze sharpened. "What manner of enchantment did you use?"

Mariselle blinked, feigning confusion. "I beg your pardon?"

"On my grandson," Lady Rivenna clarified. "What manner of magic did you employ to create this false connection between you?"

Heat flared in Mariselle's cheeks—half indignation, half terror that the truth might somehow be discerned. "I assure you, my lady, I employed no enchantment whatsoever. The mark that binds us formed of its own accord."

"Curious," Lady Rivenna replied, clearly unconvinced. "How extraordinary that such a phenomenon—so rare that many have lived entire lifetimes without encountering a single instance—should suddenly manifest between two people whose families have been bitter enemies for generations. A remarkable coincidence, wouldn't you agree?"

"Magic works in mysterious ways, does it not?" Mariselle said, her tone deliberately light.

"Do not offer me such vapid platitudes, child. I cannot yet discern the precise nature of your scheme, but I recognize artifice when I see it. Make no mistake, Lady Mariselle. Whatever this binding truly is, I will see it severed before I allow this absurdity to continue."

"Absurdity? You doubt our connection?" Mariselle asked, managing to sound wounded rather than alarmed.

"Yes," Lady Rivenna said bluntly. "Your connection is complete nonsense, a mockery of genuine bonds that offends anyone with even a modicum of sense."

"The High Lady seemed quite pleased by it," Mariselle countered in her politest voice. "But I'm sure you are not suggesting that the High Lady herself is lacking in sense."

An expression of absolute outrage flashed across Lady Rivenna's features, her lips pressing into a thin white line as she realized the trap Mariselle had so neatly laid. "You will not marry my grandson," she said. "There will be no Rowanwood-Brightcrest union. That is all there is to it." She rose from her seat with the same regal dignity that had accompanied her arrival. "Enjoy your tea."

With that, she departed, not toward her previous table but through a door that presumably led to the kitchen. Mariselle released a breath, her hands trembling slightly as she smoothed her skirts.

From her peripheral vision, she noted that Iris had quietly taken Lady Rivenna's vacated place in the private alcove, a notebook open before her. Unlike her formidable grandmother-in-law, Iris did not stare; instead, she bent over her notebook, quill moving across the page.

As she attempted to compose herself, a young woman approached her table—human, with soft brown skin and expressive eyes that widened fractionally in recognition. Mariselle placed her immediately: Lucie Fields, younger daughter of the dressmaker the Brightcrests steadfastly refused to patronize, whom she and Ellowa had publicly mocked on more than one occasion.

"Your tea, my lady," Lucie said, quickly averting her gaze as she set down a delicate silver tray bearing a porcelain teapot adorned with hand-painted butterflies and two matching cups. "The tea house has selected a rare duskmint-vanilla infusion for you. An unusual choice that happens to be among Lord Evryn's preferred blends. I believe you'll find it both calming and restorative."

"Oh, thank you." Guilt twisted in Mariselle's stomach as she recalled the cutting remarks she'd made at this girl's expense. Remarks that had drawn delighted laughter from Ellowa and her circle. She should apologize, as she had to Iris the night before.

But before she could muster a response, Lucie had already retreated, leaving Mariselle alone with the fragrant tea. She watched until Lucie disappeared beyond the door Lady Rivenna had vanished through, then turned her attention to the teapot. Her brows drew together in suspicion. Would Lady Rivenna stoop so low as to poison a guest in her own establishment? It seemed unlikely, yet Mariselle couldn't shake her wariness.

"Lady Mariselle," said a familiar voice, and Mariselle looked up to find Evryn standing beside her table, a strained smile stretching his lips. He made a show of bowing gallantly before taking the seat Lady Rivenna had vacated.

"I do apologize for my tardiness," he said in a low voice as he leaned closer, eyes flashing dangerously. "I was detained by an unexpected affliction I appear unable to free myself from. Perhaps you might enlighten me as to why I find myself incapable of maintaining a normal conversation without being overcome by—*Your golden hair, a cascade of light, sets my poor heart afire at night. I dream of braiding it into a rope, and swinging from it, shrieking with*—"

He clapped a hand over his mouth, his nostrils flaring with indignation as he inhaled sharply, eyes darting around the tea house as if to see whether anyone had overheard his mortifying outburst.

Mariselle stared, momentarily stunned, before a delighted laugh escaped her lips. She caught herself, cleared her throat, and reached for the teapot. "Is something the matter, my love? You are not usually so … effusive."

Evryn lowered his hand cautiously. "What have you done to me?" he demanded in a fierce whisper.

"I haven't the faintest idea what you mean," she replied, pouring tea into the first of the two cups. "Would you care for sugar?"

"Lady Mariselle," he growled, leaning even further forward, "if this is because of that ridiculous—*My darling muse, you radiant bean, the brightest sprout I've ever seen. Your smile, a sunrise on a trout*—Ugh!"

Mariselle nearly choked on her tea, hastily covering her mouth with a napkin as several nearby patrons turned to stare. Evryn's face flushed crimson, his expression wavering between murderous rage and acute mortification.

"You devious, conniving little—*Oh dearest heart, my sugared ham, my golden goose, my velvet clam. No poet's pen could ever convey—*"

He slapped a hand over his mouth once more as a matron at the next table sighed dreamily. Her companion pressed a hand to her heart. "How romantic. Young love is so refreshing."

An undignified snort of laughter escaped Mariselle as she raised her teacup to her lips once more.

Evryn clenched his jaw as he reached for his own cup, clearly struggling to maintain composure. "This is because of that absurd book of poems. What did you do to it?"

"I merely made a few artistic improvements," she replied innocently. "The original verses were terribly dull. I simply rewrote a few to give them the passionate flourish they so desperately needed and added a touch of enchantment to help you … remember them." She lowered her teacup and gave him her most dazzling smile.

"*You* wrote those dreadful verses?"

She placed a hand over her heart, her expression a perfect mask of wounded dignity. "I'm afraid my poetic talents cannot rival your own, my lord. Some of us must make do with merely adequate literary skills."

"And this enchantment," Evryn said through gritted teeth. "I trust it will fade with time?"

"Oh, eventually," Mariselle agreed vaguely. "Though strong emotions do seem to trigger it. Perhaps you should endeavor to remain calm."

Evryn set down his cup with exaggerated care. "I am the very soul of tranquility," he said, his voice tight with restraint. "Despite having just embarrassed myself in front of the entire—*I ache, I yearn, I hum and whine, each time I see your nose so f*—oh for goodness' sake."

Mariselle bit her lip in a vain attempt to suppress her laughter. "I quite liked the one about burning toast. I thought it was one of my better—"

"Don't. Do not even mention that blasted—*I burn like toast when you glance my way, crisped by the heat of your*—"

The rest of the verse became a mumbled groan as he covered his face with both hands.

"Yes, that one! Oh, darling, I do so love it when you recite poetry to me. It makes me—"

"Stop," he groaned, then lifted his teacup and drained half its contents in a single desperate swallow, as though he might drown the enchanted verses before they could force their way past his lips. Then he closed his eyes. When he opened them again, his expression had shifted from outrage to something closer to resigned amusement. "I suppose I deserve this after the flowers."

"Indeed you do," Mariselle agreed, surprised by his ready admission.

"Though I'm certain this is worse. My humiliation is far more public than yours."

Mariselle tilted her head, conceding the point with a slight nod. "Perhaps, though I believe waking up nearly suffocated beneath a mountain of enchanted flora is somewhat more alarming."

He frowned, genuine concern crossing his features. "You weren't actually in any danger, were you? The flowers weren't meant to—*My beloved pumpkin paste, your radiant face makes my heart race at frantic pace*—Oh good stars, Brightcrest," he muttered, dragging his marked palm over his face, "that is truly awful."

"Thank you," she said sweetly, remembering his words from the cottage several nights prior. "I do try. Now." She sat a little straighter, making sure to lower her voice as she said, "tell me when you are next able to meet."

"Early next week, I believe," he said, lowering his hand with a sigh. "My mother mentioned it this morning. She sent a formal invitation."

"Oh, no, I wasn't referring to anything public. But yes, I received your mother's invitation to tea and I've already accepted. What I meant was …" Mariselle lowered her voice further. "When are we next meeting about our … project?"

"Ah. Well, I had rather hoped we might ride this evening. Fin has been planning a most—"

"My enchanting poet," she interrupted with a pointed look, "as exhilarating as our nocturnal competitions may be, we have more pressing matters to attend to. Our endeavor requires immediate attention, unless you're particularly fond of our current arrangement."

He exhaled dramatically and drained his teacup before setting it down. "Well then. You'll be pleased to know that before I was afflicted with this verbal curse that makes me ever more determined to thwart your plans at every turn, I was investigating resources for the project."

Mariselle's interest immediately sharpened. "Oh?"

"I accessed the family vault at Rowanwood House," he said, voice even lower now. "There's a reasonable supply of lumyrite crystals that could potentially be used for our restoration efforts."

"How many?" she asked, leaning forward eagerly.

"Not nearly enough for a complete reconstruction, of course, but I noticed something interesting when we went in search of the dream core. The primary pavilion framework appears to contain most—possibly all—of the original lumyrite. Dulled with age and neglect, yes, but not destroyed."

"So we may not need to source a large amount?" Her voice lifted with cautious hope.

Evryn gave a noncommittal shrug. "Perhaps none at all. Which, upon further thought, isn't that surprising. Lumyrite is remarkably resilient, after all. The crystals themselves have remained sound while the metal supports that hold them have collapsed in several places. I think perhaps the lumyrite itself requires reshaping and reconnection rather than wholesale replacement."

A genuine smile curved Mariselle's lips. "That would simplify matters considerably."

"It would still require considerable skill," Evryn added. "The lumyrite shaping itself is easy enough for me, but repairing the foundational framework that houses the lumyrite presents a more complex challenge. And then there is still the matter of the lumyrite network embedded in the ground beneath the pavilion. We've yet to determine whether those underground veins remain intact."

"All the more reason for us to get started as soon as possible. I propose we meet at the cottage tonight."

"If you absolutely insist, my most treasured—*rutabaga of passion, turnip of desire, your eyes like fire*—" He clamped his mouth shut, face reddening once more.

"I'll take that as a yes," Mariselle said sweetly, just as motion caught her eye beyond Evryn's shoulder. She looked past him toward the private alcove and saw Iris's shoulders shaking with what appeared to be suppressed laughter, one hand to her mouth and her quill abandoned, though her notebook still lay open before her.

Panic flooded Mariselle like ice water in her veins. Could Iris possibly have … No, that was silly. She was far too distant from their table to have overheard anything. Even the elderly ladies sitting right beside them had misinterpreted the dreadful lines of poetry as charming declarations of young love, clearly hearing nothing of importance. Reassured, Mariselle reached for her teacup and lifted it to her lips, confident their secret remained secure.

Chapter Fourteen

THE MOMENT EVRYN STEPPED UP TO THE FRONT DOOR OF WINDSONG Cottage that night, he felt the headache that had been threatening all day settle firmly behind his eyes. The wretched poetry book's enchantment had faded somewhat, but still erupted at unpredictable intervals, particularly when his emotions ran high. And high they ran indeed at the prospect of another evening spent indulging Mariselle's impossible fantasy.

"Each heartbeat croons your name aloud, like a lovesick goat bleating far too pr—stop!" he hissed to himself as he reached for the door. He pushed it open with perhaps more force than necessary, and the sight that greeted him stopped him short.

Mariselle and another young woman—her cousin Petunia, if he recalled correctly—sat cross-legged on the rug in the sitting area, surrounded by a veritable sea of documents. Both had discarded their footwear, and Mariselle had somehow managed to arrange her skirts in a manner that would have caused any etiquette teacher to faint dead away. Evryn was reminded suddenly—and most oddly—of Rosavyn and her complete disregard for decorum and societal expectations.

Neither lady appeared to notice his entrance at first, absorbed as they were in a large architectural diagram of the dream core spread between them like an intricate map. Mariselle pointed to something while Petunia nodded, her auburn head bent close to her cousin's.

"… didn't realize initially that each lumyrite crystal will contain its own individual enchantment. Each will essentially become a separate piece of dream architecture. Collectively, they form the complete dreamscape."

"I see." Petunia tilted her head at an angle. "And the etched patterns …"

"For the wards. I must still do extensive reading on that part, as I've never—"

"What," Evryn interrupted loudly, "is she doing here?"

Both women's heads snapped up in unison, expressions shifting from startled to defensive in the space of a heartbeat. Petunia straightened, folding her arms across her chest. "Lord Rowanwood," she said coolly, making no move to rise from her undignified position on the floor. "Late, I see. My cousin did warn me that you have little respect for time."

"Well, your cousin did *not* warn me that we'd have company this evening," Evryn countered, turning his pointed gaze on Mariselle as he crossed to the large central table and dropped his riding gloves on the surface. "Is my understanding incorrect that this entire undertaking was meant to remain secret? Or is that requirement only applicable to me?"

"Petunia is entirely trustworthy," Mariselle replied, turning back to the document. "And more importantly, her magic is essential to Dreamland's operation."

"Of course it is," Evryn muttered, running a hand through his hair in frustration. "Another delusional Brightcrest with convenient magical abilities. How fortunate."

"As if I'm going to leave my dear cousin alone in your presence, Rowanwood," Petunia said.

"What about me?" Evryn retorted. "You don't think *I'm* the one in danger here, forced to endure her company unguarded?"

"Oh, for goodness' sake," Mariselle muttered, casually flicking her hand toward an armchair and sending a small cushion flying across the room at him.

Evryn ducked, narrowly avoiding the projectile. "You see?" he exclaimed. "I'm at risk of bodily harm!" He adopted a dramatically earnest tone. "Please, oh please, Lady Petunia, I implore you to chaperone your lunatic of a cousin every night in order to—"

This time it was Petunia who lobbed something across the room—a scroll clamp that bounced off his shoulder. "I don't know how you tolerate being in his presence for longer than a minute at a time," she muttered.

"With great difficulty," Mariselle replied, "and at no small cost to my sanity."

"And why," Evryn asked, tugging a chair back with an annoyed scrape, "are you sitting on the floor? Has it escaped your notice that there are numerous civilized seating options around the cottage?"

Mariselle didn't bother looking up. "Why should we not sit on the floor?"

Well. He supposed that was as good a reason as any.

With a resigned sigh, he sat and pulled his own pile of documents closer. "I don't recall seeing you here two nights ago, Lady Petunia," he remarked as he shuffled through the papers. "Will you be gracing us with your presence every evening?"

"It isn't as easy for me to slip away as it is for Mariselle," Petunia replied stiffly. "So there will be some nights when I'm unable to accompany her."

"Ah, so on those occasions, you've no qualms about abandoning your poor, helpless cousin to my dubious care?" Evryn asked, raising an eyebrow.

"Kindly do us all a favor and return to the task at hand, Rowanwood," Mariselle said, not bothering to look up.

Evryn opened his mouth to deliver a suitably cutting retort, but what emerged instead was, *Your elbow, love, a work of art, it bent and pierced my very heart. No joint on earth could so beguile—*" He clamped a hand over his mouth, his cheeks flaming as both women collapsed into peals of laughter.

"Oh, don't stop there," Petunia encouraged around her giggles. "Please, continue with your passionate declaration."

"It bends! It glints! It holds such style!" Mariselle recited, gasping for air between giggles as she clutched Petunia's arm. Petunia let out a most unladylike snort as the two of them doubled over, holding onto one another, entirely undone.

So utterly lacking in decorum were they that Evryn briefly wondered if he'd stumbled into some sort of bizarre alternate reality where Brightcrests behaved like actual people rather than porcelain automatons.

"That poetry book was positively inspired, Mari," Petunia said between residual giggles.

"It was rather brilliant, wasn't it?" Mariselle replied, trying—and failing—to smooth her expression into one of innocence.

"The most fun I've had in ages. We really ought to start on a second volume."

Ah. So Petunia had contributed to the atrocity. That explained a great deal.

Another thought suddenly struck Evryn as he took in their conspiratorial grins and unguarded ease. Had Mariselle told her cousin about his secret identity as E. S. Twist? The notion sent a fresh wave of panic through him. She'd promised not to reveal it to anyone, but what value did a Brightcrest's word truly hold?

He couldn't ask directly—if Petunia didn't know, he'd be revealing the very secret he was concerned about. Thinking quickly, he tore a corner off the nearest piece of parchment and scribbled a note, then tucked it into the front of a book and carried it over to where Mariselle sat.

"I believe this belongs on your pile, not mine, my precious pixie biscuit," he said, placing it beside her.

Mariselle frowned, picking up the book and opening it to look inside. While Petunia leaned over the diagram once more, Mariselle extracted Evryn's note and scanned its contents. Her expression darkened momentarily before she crumpled the paper in her fist and turned back to her work, pointedly ignoring him.

Frustrated and still uncertain, Evryn returned to his chair and attempted to focus on the documents before him. He had seen mention the other night, after they'd retrieved the dream core, of an enchantment that would allow him to determine the condition of the underground lumyrite network without the laborious process of excavation. He had no notion of how a spell like that might work, but it seemed the logical next step was to locate it and attempt this assessment.

He would do his part, certainly, to the extent of his ability. But he still harbored serious doubts as to whether this ambitious undertaking would actually succeed. There were glaring holes in the dream magic side of this operation—namely that neither girl possessed the sophisticated magical abilities their project required.

He listened to them now, picking up fragments of details about portal stability and threshold weaving and something to do with layered wards that would prevent nightmare entities from crossing into Dreamland. It all sounded ridiculously complex. Did they even know what they were talking about? Unlikely, considering that the most Mariselle was capable of was extracting dream essence. And as for Petunia's manifestation, he couldn't even recall what unremarkable ability she possessed. Certainly nothing spectacular enough to be memorable.

Still, despite his doubts, Evryn couldn't deny the surge of anticipation he had felt the other night as he'd stood on the central platform of the original pavilion, surrounded by what remained of Dreamland's lumyrite-inlaid structure rising around them like an elegant cage. His fingers almost itched to find the fractured pieces, to meld them back together, to sculpt and reshape crystal into forms of both beauty and function. It was his own unique magic that had stirred to life then, eager to be set free.

Probably not surprising, considering opportunities to truly exercise his abilities were rare. After his manifestation, he'd created countless ornamental pieces for Rowanwood House until every mantel and alcove boasted some lumyrite trinket or another, but once those spaces were filled, his talents had been largely relegated to curiosity status. He'd sought other outlets for his restless spirit then—first pegasus racing with its heart-stopping thrills, then writing with its subtler but no less potent satisfactions. Both pursuits he sorely missed, now that his time was consumed by tedious society events and this project that would no doubt amount to nothing.

He continued to leaf through leather-bound volumes and portfolios, searching for more information about the underground lumyrite network. But he found his attention repeatedly drawn to the two women on the floor. Their quiet chatter and occasional bursts of laughter proved distractingly incongruous with his mental image of Brightcrests as humorless, rigid aristocrats.

Mariselle, in particular, seemed transformed, her usual cold poise replaced by genuine animation as she explained something that sounded oddly as though it involved cotton candy and flamingos, her hands moving expressively through the air. This version of her—passionate, focused, almost radiant with enthusiasm—was entirely at odds with the calculating ice princess he'd known for years.

He found himself wanting to reach for a quill and one of his notebooks. Writing was how he made sense of contradictions like this—the gap between appearance and reality, the way people presented themselves versus who they truly were. It was his way of untangling complex emotions, of examining the subtle hypocrisies of society, and of capturing those rare, unguarded moments when someone's mask slipped to reveal the person beneath.

Who was Mariselle Brightcrest if not the cold, cruel adversary he's always believed her to be?

"I'm going to make some tea," she announced suddenly, rising from the floor. She stretched, arching her back slightly, and Evryn hastily returned his gaze to his documents.

As she padded on bare feet past the table, she discreetly placed a folded note beside his arm. He waited until she had disappeared into the kitchen before unfolding it, revealing a hastily scrawled message: *OF COURSE I didn't tell P. I gave my word, after all. Does that mean nothing to you?*

The indignation practically leaped from the page, and Evryn felt a twinge of guilt for his suspicion. Before he could examine the feeling further, Mariselle called from the kitchen, "Would you like tea, Rowanwood?"

"I'm not certain I trust anything in this cottage, even if it has been preserved for the last five decades," he called back.

"I brought my own tea blends from Brightcrest Manor," Mariselle replied.

"In that case, I certainly won't be partaking," he said, relieved to slip into their familiar pattern of antagonism. Who knew what dreadful concoctions Mariselle might brew.

"Your loss," she called back, but the rest of her words faded as Evryn's attention snapped to a particular page in the portfolio he'd been examining. There, in the margin beside a detailed diagram of the underground lumyrite network, were small, meticulous notes he'd come to recognize as his great-uncle's handwriting.

Lumyrite Echo Visualization, the heading read. Below it, concise instructions described an enchantment that would cause existing lumyrite in the ground to glow, causing a complementary glowing pattern above ground, effectively revealing the entire hidden network. Evryn could then compare this visible pattern to the original diagrams to determine what, if anything, had been damaged or lost.

He stood abruptly, rolling up both the plans that contained the drawing of the lumyrite network and the page he'd found the visualization spell on.

He tucked both beneath his arm as he announced, "I'm going to check something outside."

Petunia muttered something that sounded like, "Don't hurry back," and Mariselle didn't respond at all.

He slipped outside into the cool night air. The moon hung high overhead, bathing the ruins in silvery light as he strode toward them. He took a different path this evening, turning before the large cluster of nightveil orchids and walking beneath what had once been the grand entrance arch. Mariselle's description of the original Dreamland came to mind as he walked, and he tried to picture what it had once looked like.

He stepped onto the circular platform and moved toward the center where they had discovered the dream core. Reaching the circular depression, he knelt and unrolled the papers, spreading them flat on the stone surface. According to the spell instructions, he needed to position himself at the center of the network—precisely where the dream core had been—and then channel magic downward while reciting the incantation.

He closed his eyes, drawing a deep breath as he gathered his magic. This wasn't his manifested power, but rather the inherent magic that pulsed through the veins of all fae. The magic that made simple tasks like heating up a cooled cup of tea or tossing a cushion at someone else's head fairly easy. The familiar warmth began to build within him, that sensation like liquid sunlight flowing through his veins. He extended his hand over the hole, palm down, and began to murmur the words from Thaelan's notes.

Nothing happened at first. Then, gradually, a faint blue glow began to emanate from the earth beneath his palm. The light intensified, spreading outward in thin, glowing lines that traced complex patterns across the ground. The illumination continued to expand, revealing an intricate network that extended well beyond the pavilion area.

Evryn stood, watching in amazement as the entire lumyrite grid revealed itself. The blue light pulsed gently, forming complex geometric patterns. But from his current vantage point, he couldn't see the entire network clearly enough to compare it with the diagram. He needed a higher perspective. Good thing Cobalt was waiting nearby.

He stepped off the platform and picked his way across the ruins, passing moss-covered stones and more nightveil orchids, aiming for the trees where he'd left Cobalt. The trees he and Mariselle had raced through on the night of the Opening Ball, before all of this had begun.

"Where are you going?"

He stopped at the sound of Mariselle's voice, calling from somewhere behind him. Not accusatory but filled with genuine curiosity. Evryn turned to find her standing at the edge of the ruins, her eyes wide with wonder as she stared at the ground. "Is this ..." She gestured toward the illuminated patterns. "The lumyrite network?"

"Yes. I found the visualization spell in Thaelan Rowanwood's notes. I'm going to take Cobalt up for an aerial view to compare it with the original drawings." He turned and continued toward the trees.

"Oh!" He heard Mariselle hurrying after him. "I want to see too."

Of course she did.

Evryn reached his pegasus at the edge of the trees and began untethering the reins. "Is your mount nearby?" he asked, though he already knew the answer. She wasn't wearing riding gear. However she had arrived here tonight, it wasn't by pegasus.

"No, but yours is." She came to a stop beside him.

He paused, turning to face her with narrowed eyes. "We are not riding a pegasus together."

"Why ever not?" she asked, already moving past him toward Cobalt's side. "It shall be but a momentary ascent. Surely your beast can manage two riders for such a brief excursion."

"That isn't the point," Evryn protested, watching with growing alarm as she stroked Cobalt's neck. The traitorous creature nickered softly, apparently delighted by her attention.

"And what is the point?" she asked.

His mouth opened, then closed, then opened again. Was she being deliberately obtuse? The two of them would be pressed together on Cobalt's back, her body flush against his. The very thought made his stomach turn.

Still, he chose a different tack when he spoke out loud. "You're hardly dressed appropriately for—"

"So?" she said, brushing him off. "No one is here to observe us or enforce proper etiquette."

He sighed and spoke slowly, as if attempting to reason with a child. "How are you to sit astride a pegasus while wearing a *gown*?"

"It's a simple matter," she said, gathering her skirts. "I shall merely adjust my garments accordingly." She began hitching her skirts higher, revealing her ankles and then, horrifyingly, the curves of her calves.

Evryn averted his gaze, staring fixedly at a particularly fascinating bit of stone on the ground. "This is highly inappropriate," he muttered.

"Spare me your delicate sensibilities, Rowanwood," she replied, already bracing herself against Cobalt's side and beginning to hoist herself up. "I'm sure you've seen far more of a woman's form than this."

Now *that* was certainly not an appropriate topic for discussion. He refrained from commenting. Keeping his eyes down, he said, "I assume you don't need assistance with—"

"No, I do not need assistance. I am perfectly capable of mounting a pegasus. As you well know."

Yes, but not in a gown, he almost said out loud, then thought better of it.

He looked up once he was certain she'd mounted and caught a glimpse of bare skin far above her knee before he hastily looked away again, feeling his face grow warm. At least she'd been sensible enough to put her shoes back on before following him out here, though that did precious little to mitigate the impropriety of the situation.

With a resigned sigh, he mounted behind her, trying desperately to maintain some degree of space between them. The effort proved utterly futile. The moment he settled into position, they were pressed together from shoulder to knee, her back flush against his chest. He held himself rigid, arms extended awkwardly to grasp the reins on either side of her without actually touching her, like someone politely attempting not to hug a tree.

"What is wrong with you?" Mariselle asked with no small amount of impatience, leaning forward slightly and looking over her shoulder at him. "Have you forgotten how to ride?

"I assure you," he replied stiffly, "That is not the prob—"

His words cut off as Cobalt shifted beneath them, spreading his wings in preparation for takeoff. Evryn tensed immediately, arms tightening around Mariselle instinctively while his legs locked against hers to stay balanced. The contact sent an unexpected jolt through him, and he nearly pulled back again, but Cobalt chose that precise moment to launch skyward with a powerful downbeat of his wings.

The sudden acceleration forced Mariselle further back against his chest.

She said nothing, and he suspected—given her excitement about the glowing lumyrite network—that she hadn't even noticed. He, however, was suddenly finding the night air inexplicably warm and his cravat oddly constricting.

"Oh, isn't it beautiful!" she exclaimed, pointing downward.

Evryn focused on steering, keeping Cobalt just above the treetops, gliding in a wide, even circle over the ruins. "The diagram," he said, his voice sounding oddly strained to his own ears. "We need to compare it to what we're seeing."

"Yes, of course. Let me see it."

Of course she would insist on taking charge. Evryn fumbled with one hand to extract the rolled papers from inside his jacket, an awkward maneuver given their current position. He passed them to her.

"Hold onto me, would you?" she said. "I need two hands for this."

As though she'd asked him to pass the sugar, not compromise the last shreds of his dignity. He groaned inwardly, slipping one arm around her waist and anchoring her against him. Her warmth seeped through every layer of clothing. Her scent—vanilla?—tickled his nose. It was the most irritating thing in the world how perfectly she fit against him.

Cobalt continued gliding as Mariselle unrolled the diagram, holding it before them. Evryn leaned forward to see, his chin almost touching her shoulder. If she noticed this increased proximity, she gave no indication, her attention wholly focused on comparing the parchment to the glowing network below.

"It matches!" she exclaimed suddenly, a squeal of genuine excitement escaping her. "Do you see? The patterns are identical. Not a single break!"

Evryn felt a thrill race through him at her words. "That's ... good news," he managed, finding it difficult to form simple sentences while so acutely aware of every point of contact between them—shoulders, back, waist, legs. This was an affront to the natural order of things. No Rowanwood should be touching this much of a Brightcrest. Laws of propriety, physics, and common sense were being defied.

"Good news?" Mariselle twisted to look at him, her face mere inches from his, eyes bright with triumph. "It's extraordinary! This means you don't need to touch anything below ground. You can focus on repairing anything that's broken in the pavilion structure and reshaping or replacing lumyrite where necessary. That shouldn't take you too long, should it?"

Evryn found himself staring at her lips as she spoke, the way they curved with genuine enthusiasm, utterly different from her usual cold smirk. Yes, this was indeed a bizarre alternate reality. This much had been clear from the moment he'd walked into the cottage and found Mariselle and Petunia sitting on the floor.

"Rowanwood?" she prompted, and he realized he hadn't answered her.

"Uh, yes. I mean no. It shouldn't take too long."

"Excellent. Well, we should return to the cottage." She faced forward once more, to Evryn's great relief. "Petunia will be wondering what's become of us."

She rolled up the diagram and settled back slightly, shifting her position between his thighs, and—

No. For stars' sake, no. This ride needed to end. Now.

Chapter Fifteen

The enchanted carriage glided to a halt before Rowanwood House, its wheels barely touching the pebbled drive. "You haven't forgotten your mother's instructions, my lady?" Tilly said with a wry smile.

Mariselle rolled her eyes. "After she repeated them no less than seventeen times?" She shook her head. "Such a waste of breath. All her elaborate scheming and plotting, and it amounts to 'observe everything and report back the minutest detail.' As though I couldn't have determined that myself."

The truth was, spying for her mother ranked rather low on her list of priorities at present. Her thoughts were consumed by Dreamland. She and Evryn had spent several more evenings at Windsong Cottage, with Petunia joining them once. Her grandfather's instructions had proven remarkably effective—she'd made exceptional progress, successfully enchanting several crystals in the dream core.

Evryn had kept himself busy out on the ruins, having begun the reconstruction of the pavilion framework the night after they'd determined the underground lumyrite network was intact. She liked to tell herself his sudden burst of industry represented newfound dedication to their project, but the truth was far more obvious—it was simply his preferred method of avoiding her company. She had no complaints about the arrangement. The greater the distance between them, the less she had to endure his insufferable presence.

He showed precisely no interest in her particular magical abilities. Not once had he inquired about the true nature of her power or what she might actually be capable of. Sometimes she wondered if he still believed her manifestation was limited to the trivial display she'd performed at her debut last Season. But he could think what he wanted, she'd decided. She had complex magic to master, and precious little time to waste on proving that she was far more capable than he believed her to be.

Unfortunately, mastering dream magic would have to wait. Today she was forced to waste precious hours on tea at Rowanwood House, an obligation she'd been dreading since the invitation arrived. She wondered how many of Evryn's siblings would be present and whether they would be competing to outdo each other in haughty condescension.

Two footmen in crisp livery stepped forward from the front steps. One opened the door, while the other extended a gloved hand to help Mariselle descend the enchanted steps that had just shimmered into existence from thin air.

Rowanwood House rose before her, its warm honey-colored stone gleaming in the spring sunshine. Mariselle's heart fluttered traitorously in her chest as she and Tilly ascended the steps, her hands growing clammy within her fine silk gloves. Was she truly the first Brightcrest to cross this threshold? Or had there been a time—perhaps generations ago, in that shadowed era her family refused to discuss—when Brightcrests had moved freely through these halls, welcomed at Rowanwood gatherings like any other noble family?

One of the footmen swung open the polished double doors, and Mariselle drew a steadying breath before stepping inside, Tilly a reassuring presence at her back.

A butler appeared in the entryway, offering a dignified bow. "Lady Mariselle Brightcrest and maid, as expected," he announced. "Her Ladyship is in the drawing room. May I take your gloves, Lady Mariselle?"

She surrendered her gloves while her gaze traveled upward, taking in the graceful sweep of the staircase and the enchanted faelights that drifted near the ceiling, casting a warm glow despite the abundant natural light.

"If you please, miss," a housekeeper addressed Tilly politely, "you may wait below stairs with the others while Lady Mariselle takes tea."

Tilly glanced at Mariselle, who nodded her permission. The lady's maid curtseyed and followed the housekeeper down a discreet corridor, leaving Mariselle alone with the butler.

"If you would follow me, my lady," he intoned, leading her across the marble-tiled entrance hall.

As they proceeded, Mariselle found herself instinctively cataloging details for her mother. The enchantments were tasteful rather than ostentatious—a delicate shimmer over the windowpanes suggesting subtle weather wards, a faint golden sheen around the edges of portrait frames, preserving the artwork's color, and the occasional sparkle along the baseboards betraying a cleverly concealed draft-exclusion spell. Nothing extraordinary or particularly revelatory. Brightcrest Manor boasted far more impressive magical features, yet somehow felt ... colder.

She pushed the disloyal thought aside as they reached a set of double doors. The butler rapped lightly, then opened them. "Lady Mariselle Bright-crest, ma'am," he announced, stepping aside to allow her entry.

Mariselle squared her shoulders and glided into the drawing room, the picture of composure despite the anxious flutter in her stomach. The chamber was spacious and filled with light from the garden-facing windows. Comfortable seating was arranged around a low table upon which stood a pretty arrangement of folded paper flowers that moved subtly as if stirred by an enchanted breeze. Mariselle's gaze swept the space, taking note of its occupants—Evryn, his mother, and his younger twin siblings, Aurelise and Kazrian. A faint breath of relief passed through her. Thank the stars Rosavyn wasn't present.

Everyone rose from their seats in awkward unison. "Lady Mariselle," greeted Lady Lelianna with a strained smile. "How delightful that you could join us today."

"Thank you for the invitation, Lady Rowanwood," Mariselle replied, dipping into a graceful curtsy.

"It is quite the historic occasion, welcoming a Brightcrest into our home."

A suppressed snort drew Mariselle's attention toward one of the windows—and there on the window seat cushions lounged a young woman with dark hair and a distinctly unimpressed expression. Ah. So Rosavyn Rowanwood was indeed present. Wonderful.

"Rosavyn," Lady Lelianna said in a warning tone, and Mariselle's gaze bounced back to Evryn's mother. Though her smile remained in place, the look in her eyes could have frozen molten lava.

After a long beat, Rosavyn let out a dramatic sigh and unfolded herself from the cushions. "As you wish, Mother," she muttered as she moved to join her family with exaggerated slowness.

"Lovely," Lady Lelianna said, turning her gaze back to Mariselle, though her smile was no less strained. "These are my younger children, Kazrian and Aurelise." Kazrian bowed, fingers twitching restlessly at his sides as if he had too much energy and no way in which to release it, while Aurelise curtseyed, her eyes lowered. "And of course, you know——"

"My beloved moonpie," Evryn said, stepping forward and taking Mariselle's hand in his. He bent over it, his lips brushing lightly across the silvery pattern of the supposed 'soulbond' that swirled across her skin.

Over his shoulder, Mariselle caught sight of Rosavyn making exaggerated retching motions. Lady Lelianna's gaze snapped to her eldest daughter, and Rosavyn froze instantly beneath her mother's withering stare. The absurdity of the moment—this elaborate charade, Rosavyn's theatrics, the perfect tableau of family dysfunction—bubbled up unexpectedly in Mariselle's chest. She bit her lower lip hard to contain the wholly inappropriate laughter threatening to escape.

Lady Lelianna gestured toward the seating arrangement with forced brightness. "Please, let us all be seated. Tea will be served shortly."

Mariselle took her place on one of the sofas, carefully arranging her skirts as Evryn settled beside her—close enough that their proximity suggested intimacy, yet with sufficient space between them to maintain proper decorum. The air in the room felt thick with tension, every movement deliberate and measured. No one seemed to know where to look or what to say. The silence stretched uncomfortably until Evryn shifted, his hand disappearing into his coat pocket.

"I have something for you, my dearest," he announced. "A small token of affection." He withdrew a small velvet box and turned slightly to face her.

Oh good stars, what now? This was his retribution for the poetry gift, she had no doubt.

Evryn opened the box, revealing a delicate silver bracelet adorned with tiny blue stones that glinted like sunlight dancing on ocean waves.

"Oh, how exquisite!" Mariselle exclaimed, wanting nothing more than to knock the undoubtedly enchanted jewelry clear across the room. "You really shouldn't have."

"Nonsense," Evryn replied smoothly, mischief dancing in his eyes. "I thought of you the moment I saw it. The stones are a perfect Brightcrest blue, wouldn't you say? The exact color of your eyes." His own eyes danced with mischief as he said this, and Mariselle's suspicion increased another degree. "May I?" Evryn extended his hand, clearly intending to place the bracelet on her wrist.

Mariselle hesitated fractionally—she didn't want the unknown enchantment anywhere near her skin—but she could hardly refuse in the presence of his family. "Of course," she said, extending her left hand. Her muscles tensed involuntarily as the cool metal settled against her skin. A moment passed, then another. But nothing happened. Whatever enchantment lurked within the innocent-looking bracelet was clearly lying in wait, biding its time before revealing itself, much like the excruciatingly dreadful poetry she had forced upon Evryn.

As he fastened the clasp, all eyes dropped to her other hand, where the distinctive silvery pattern of the 'soulbond' gleamed against her skin. Mariselle resisted the urge to hide it within the folds of her skirts. Let them look. It was, after all, the entire reason for this awkward gathering.

"How lovely," she said, turning her wrist so that the bracelet's blue stones caught the light.

"We came across it in Vesper's Curiosities & Oddities yesterday," Aurelise offered tentatively, immediately confirming Mariselle's every suspicion. There was no way that something found in an oddities shop *didn't* possess some form of strange enchantment.

Evryn cleared his throat and sat a little straighter, directing a pointed gaze at his sister.

"Indeed, Aurelise expressed a desire to find something special for a friend's birthday celebration," he said smoothly. "I offered to accompany her. This particular piece caught my eye the moment I saw it." His gaze softened as it returned to Mariselle. "It seemed crafted specifically for you—as though the artisan had somehow glimpsed your very essence."

Mariselle pressed a hand to her heart, gazing adoringly at him while her eyes promised, *I will make you pay for whatever this latest trick is, you insufferable scoundrel.*

The drawing room doors opened, and a housekeeper entered carrying a polished silver tray. She set the tray down on the low table beside the paper flower arrangement before stepping back with a small curtsy. Lady Lelianna nodded her permission, and the woman began pouring steaming amber liquid into delicate teacups.

"I hope you'll forgive my less than complete family gathering," Lady Lelianna remarked, turning her attention back to Mariselle. "Lady Rivenna sends her deepest regrets. She was unable to tear herself away from The Charmed Leaf this afternoon."

"Please convey my understanding to Lady Rivenna," Mariselle replied, fully aware that the older woman regretted precisely nothing about missing this afternoon's gathering. Mariselle accepted a cup of tea with a gracious nod, relieved to be spared another confrontation with the Rowanwood matriarch.

An uncomfortable silence descended upon the room, broken only by the clink of silver against porcelain as spoons stirred tea, and the gentle tap of cups being returned to saucers. Each small sound seemed magnified by the tension.

Mariselle leaned forward slightly, desperately grasping for conversation. "Aurelise," she began, "were you successful in finding a suitable gift for your friend at the oddities shop? Besides serving as an excellent excuse for your brother to purchase jewelry, of course."

Aurelise's eyes widened slightly at being directly addressed, her teacup freezing halfway to her lips. After a moment, she carefully lowered it back to its saucer and offered a small smile.

"Unfortunately not," she replied, finding her voice. "Nothing seemed quite right for my friend. She has rather specific tastes. I did, however, discover the most intriguing enchanted box that Evryn was kind enough to purchase for me." Her face brightened with genuine enthusiasm. "It had the most curious inscription. What did it say exactly, Evryn? Something about … Oh yes. 'To the seeker of correspondence: Place your reply within and receive an answer that may change your path.'" Her eyes sparkled as she grinned. "Doesn't that sound intriguing?"

Lady Lelianna leaned forward with visible concern, her teacup making a sharp sound as she set it down. "That doesn't sound entirely appropriate, dear." She cast a questioning glance at Evryn, her brow furrowed. "You cannot know who might be on the other end of such correspondence. It could be someone quite unsuitable."

"Oh, I'm sure it's just a silly enchantment, Mother," Aurelise said. "Most likely there's no real person involved at all. I expect the magic will fizzle out quickly and the responses will cease. But I was curious nonetheless."

"There's no need to worry, Mother," Evryn said. "I spoke with the shop-keeper at length about the box's origins. He assured me it came from a most reputable source—a retired enchanter specializing in harmless novelties. The magic is self-contained and entirely benign."

Lady Lelianna's expression softened with visible relief. "Thank you, dear. I should have known you would have been thorough." She turned slightly toward Mariselle, lowering her voice in a confidential manner. "He's always been remarkably attentive to his siblings' needs. When they were younger, if he noticed any of them having a particularly difficult day, he would sneak down to the kitchens and convince the cook to prepare their favorite meal for dinner. Or he'd appear with just the right quip to make them laugh when they needed it most."

"Mother," Evryn interrupted with a pained expression, "is this the part of the tea where you share embarrassing childhood stories? Because I believe we had an agreement about that." He straightened his cuffs with exaggerated attention, clearly uncomfortable with being the subject of such fond remi-niscences.

"Hardly embarrassing," Lady Lelianna replied with a warm smile. "Merely illuminating." Her gaze slid back to Mariselle. "He's always been my most sensitive child, you know. Even as a little boy, he was the one who expressed his affection most readily. He gave the most wonderful hugs— would wrap his arms around my neck so tightly as if he never wanted to let go."

"Mother!" Evryn's face flushed crimson, and Mariselle had to bite her lip to contain her grin.

"Apologies, my dear, I can't help it." Lady Lelianna's eyes twinkled with mischief before she composed herself once more.

An awkward silence fell over the room as the conversation stuttered. Lady Lelianna cleared her throat delicately and returned her focus to Mariselle.

"Lady Mariselle, how are your ..." She appeared to grasp for words, her expression suggesting she was mentally weighing several possibilities—

prospects? ambitions? fashion sensibilities? "Parents?" she finished, then winced as though she immediately regretted it.

"They are quite well," Mariselle replied automatically. "Though rather … surprised by recent developments." This seemed a diplomatic way of describing her father's cold fury and her mother's calculating assessment of how to exploit the situation.

"I imagine so," Lady Lelianna said with a smile that conveyed perfect understanding. "This unexpected connection is quite astonishing for all involved."

"'Astonishing' is certainly one word for it," Rosavyn muttered into her teacup.

"Rosavyn," Lady Lelianna admonished gently.

"Forgive me, Mother," Rosavyn replied, not sounding remotely contrite. "I simply find it remarkable how my ordinarily courtship-averse brother has transformed into this lovesick shadow of himself. And all because of a—" She caught herself, but the word 'Brightcrest' hung unspoken in the air.

Mariselle took a measured sip of her tea, refusing to rise to the bait. It was hardly a surprise that Evryn's sister should dislike her. In addition to the long-standing animosity between their families, it appeared that Rosavyn was a good friend of Iris's, and she would no doubt have been aware that Mariselle had cruelly taunted her the previous Season.

"I understand the soulbond manifested during the Opening Ball at Solstice Hall," Kazrian interjected suddenly, leaning forward in his seat. "Was there a particular astronomical alignment that evening? I've been researching celestial convergences and their effects on spontaneous magical manifestations."

Mariselle blinked, caught off guard by the abrupt change in subject. "I … couldn't say," she replied. "I wasn't precisely observing the stars at the time."

"Of course not." Kazrian nodded. "You were focused on the immediate phenomenon. Could you perhaps tell me about—"

"Kazrian," Evryn sighed, "must you approach everything like a scientific inquiry? Even matters of the heart?"

"Especially matters of the heart!" Kazrian insisted. "The intersection of emotion and magic is woefully understudied. And when you factor in the possibility of some form of cosmic confluence—"

"I'm fairly certain it wasn't related to the alignment of Junivar with the fifth moon of Thackersberry," Rosavyn interrupted dryly.

"There is no fifth moon of Thackersberry," Kazrian replied with equal dryness.

"Snizzleberry?" she asked.

"Rosavyn."

"I could have sworn you were prattling on about some form of celestial *berry* at dinner last night."

"I believe it was a Bumbleberry," Evryn offered with a straight face.

"Ah, yes, that was it," Rosavyn said. "You gave us an entire speech about Professor Lumenwright's observations regarding the twenty-seventh moon of Winkleberry."

Poor Kazrian dragged a hand over his face, and Mariselle couldn't help herself. A most undignified snort of laughter escaped her before she could suppress it. The room fell silent, all eyes turning toward her in surprise. Rosavyn, in particular, stared as though Mariselle had suddenly sprouted wings.

"I beg your pardon," Mariselle said quickly, mortified by her lapse in decorum. "It's just—Thackersberry? Snizzleberry? These sound like names one might encounter in a children's nursery rhyme."

Rosavyn's lips twitched. "Indeed. 'The gnome from Thackersberry, whose nose was extraordinarily hairy,'" she improvised, her tone mockingly pompous. "'He sneezed with such might, he took sudden flight, and now orbits the sun quite contrary.'"

Mariselle's composure cracked entirely, genuine laughter bubbling up as she pictured the absurd image. "Can you imagine the professor's reaction? 'Most extraordinary! A gnome-shaped celestial body with unusual nasal properties!'"

Rosavyn's own laughter joined hers—a bright, unexpected sound that transformed her features from guarded hostility to unabashed amusement. For a brief, disorienting moment, Mariselle forgot she was supposed to be maintaining careful distance from these people. She lifted her teacup, hoping to compose her expression behind it.

"Charming, Rosavyn," Kazrian said with brotherly exasperation.

"Indeed," Evryn said to his sister. "I believe you'll find that you and Lady Mariselle share an appreciation for terrible poetry."

Mariselle choked on her tea. Evryn's hand moved immediately to her back, patting it a fraction too forcefully while giving her a look of mild concern. "Are you quite all right, dearest?"

"Perfectly fine," she said hoarsely. Her gaze darted back to Rosavyn, whose frozen expression suggested she'd just remembered precisely who she was laughing with and found the idea of having anything in common with a Brightcrest horrifying.

"I believe," Lady Lelianna interjected gently, though her eyes sparkled with barely suppressed mirth, "we have strayed rather far from polite tea conversation."

"Perhaps," Aurelise suggested after a pause, "we might discuss something more pleasant than Kazrian's theories? Lady Mariselle, do you have any particular interests or pastimes you enjoy?"

Mariselle hesitated. Her first instinct was to manufacture some appropriate feminine pursuit—embroidery, perhaps, or watercolors. But something about Aurelise's seemingly genuine interest made her pause. What could she safely reveal? Certainly not her nighttime pegasus rides, nor her illicit racing against their very own brother.

"I … enjoy sketching," she admitted finally, surprising herself with the honesty. "Though I'm absolutely dreadful at it."

Evryn glanced at her, brows arching slightly. He probably thought she was lying.

"I have journals filled with these terrible drawings," she continued, feeling oddly vulnerable. "I'm forever trying to capture scenes from my imagination, but they never come out right. It's quite embarrassing, actually."

The memory of Ellowa discovering one such journal flickered through her mind—her sister's mocking laughter as she flipped through the pages, pointing out every flaw, declaring that even a child could produce more skillful work.

"I doubt they're as bad as you claim," Aurelise said kindly. "Most artists are their own harshest critics."

"Oh, believe me, they're quite atrocious," Mariselle assured her with a self-deprecating smile. "But I continue to try. There are so many scenes in my head; I feel I must get them out somehow."

She straightened, startled at this second bout of honesty. What was wrong with her today?

"I understand completely," Aurelise replied. "I feel the same way about music. I practice for hours, yet my playing remains … well, Rosavyn once described it as 'what one might hear if an inebriated squirrel dashed across the keys.'"

"Aurelise!" Rosavyn protested. "That was when you were ten years old! Your playing is enchantingly lovely now, as are your original compositions."

Aurelise's cheeks flushed pink. "Do you really think so?"

"Of course. In fact, I'm convinced you're going to manifest some form of music-related magic."

Something twisted in Mariselle's chest as she watched this exchange. A sharp, unexpected ache. The easy affection between the sisters, the genuine support beneath the teasing, the clear regard they held for each other … it was utterly foreign to her experience with Ellowa.

"What about you, Lady Mariselle?" Kazrian asked, interrupting her thoughts. "Do you play any instruments? Or perhaps you sing?"

"I'm afraid not," she replied, composing her features carefully to hide the unexpected wave of emotion. "My sister Ellowa is the musical one in our family. I was always encouraged to focus on … other pursuits."

Like being invisible and never, ever disturbing the careful balance of the Brightcrest household with anything as inconvenient as authenticity.

"Well, it's true that Aurelise's playing is truly lovely," Lady Lelianna said, clearly sensing a lull in the conversation and attempting to steer it back on course. "Perhaps when you next visit, she might favor you with a performance."

Aurelise's eyes widened in alarm. "Oh no, Mother, I couldn't possibly subject Lady Mariselle to my—"

"I should like that very much," Mariselle said warmly. She offered Aurelise an encouraging smile. "I find music deeply inspiring. Certain melodies create entire worlds in my imagination, scenes and stories unfolding along with the music."

"Truly?" Aurelise leaned forward, her shyness momentarily forgotten. "That's exactly how it feels to me! Colors and patterns and landscapes, sometimes so vivid I lose track of time completely."

"Then you must play something for me next time," Mariselle urged, surprised to find that she hoped there *would* be a next time.

"I suppose I could," Aurelise conceded with a tentative smile.

"Just not that dreadful Snowflake piece written by that raven-haired composer who mistakes perpetual solemnity for artistic depth," Rosavyn interjected with a dramatic sigh.

Aurelise's head whipped toward her sister. "But you love that one! I heard you humming the opening section yesterday morning in the hallway."

"Only because you've forced me to hear it at least a hundred times," Rosavyn countered. "It's embedded itself in my mind like a musical parasite."

"Which is precisely what makes it an excellent composition," Aurelise countered triumphantly. "The hallmark of truly exceptional music is that it refuses to leave you, haunting your thoughts long after the last note has faded."

Rosavyn rolled her eyes. "Fine. The piece is tolerable. There. Are you satisfied?"

"From Rosavyn, 'tolerable' is practically a standing ovation," Kazrian explained to Mariselle with a conspiratorial grin.

"Rosavyn does hold rather exacting standards," Lady Lelianna observed, but her tone held no reproach, and the smile she directed at her daughter was almost teasing.

"I simply see no point in false praise," Rosavyn defended herself. "If everything is 'exquisite' or 'magnificent,' the words lose all meaning."

"There's a vast territory between false praise and soul-crushing criticism," Evryn pointed out.

"A territory you've clearly never explored," Rosavyn retorted. "Not when you described Lady Fawnwood's hat as 'the tragic aftermath of a ribbon factory explosion.'"

"To her face?" Mariselle gasped, then immediately regretted the outburst.

"Goodness, no," Evryn replied, looking horrified at the suggestion. "I do possess some small measure of tact. I merely whispered it to Rosavyn during Lady Whispermist's garden party two Seasons ago, and she laughed so suddenly she inhaled a mouthful of punch."

"Which then proceeded to exit through my nose in the most mortifying fashion imaginable," Rosavyn added, grimacing at the memory. "I've never forgiven him."

"She has, in fact, forgiven me," Evryn stage-whispered to Mariselle. "Though she'll never admit it."

"I most certainly have not," Rosavyn insisted. "Lady Whispermist still eyes me suspiciously whenever refreshments are served."

"The infamous punch incident," Lady Lelianna sighed. "I had nearly managed to forget."

As the siblings continued their good-natured bickering, Mariselle found herself simply … watching. There was a rhythm to their interactions, a familiar dance of teasing and defense, challenge and riposte. Yet beneath it all ran a current of what seemed to be genuine affection. Even Rosavyn's barbs lacked the cutting edge Mariselle associated with Ellowa's 'teasing.'

Lady Lelianna observed it all with the serene patience of a mother who had long since accepted her children's lively temperaments. Occasionally she would interject a gentle "Kazrian, really" or "Rosavyn, perhaps that's enough," but Mariselle could see she took genuine pleasure in their spirited exchanges.

Was this what family could be? This warm, chaotic, affectionate mess of contradictions?

A sharp pang of longing took her by surprise. The closest she'd ever come to this sort of easy companionship was with Petunia, and even that relationship required careful navigation around their parents' expectations and prejudices.

"… precisely my point," Rosavyn was saying. "The entire affair was an exercise in ostentatious misery. Children's parties should involve actual fun—games and sweets and perhaps a treasure hunt led by talking mice—not an endless parade of elaborate courses no child would ever willingly eat."

"Asparagus mousse," Aurelise recalled with a shudder. "Who serves asparagus mousse to a five year old?"

"Lady Whitewing, apparently," Kazrian replied. "Though to be fair, I don't believe anyone of any age should be subjected to asparagus in mousse form."

"Or any form," Mariselle found herself saying before she could stop the words.

"Yes!" Rosavyn exclaimed, turning to her with unexpected animation. "It's utterly vile, isn't it? This strange vegetable that everyone pretends to enjoy because it's considered sophisticated."

"And it's always arranged on the plate like it's meant to be admired instead of endured," Mariselle added, warming to the subject. "Society insists on serving it at every formal dinner as though it's some great delicacy instead of stringy green stalks that taste of bitter disappointment."

Rosavyn laughed. "Bitter disappointment! Yes, exactly! And it's always announced with such reverence—'tender young asparagus tips'—as if the adjectives somehow transform it into something desirable."

"As though youth and tenderness could redeem its fundamental nature," Mariselle agreed. "It's still asparagus."

"The elaborate conspiracy of asparagus appreciation," Rosavyn declared, her eyes alight with mirth. "An agreement among the elite to pretend that this objectively unpleasant vegetable is somehow the height of culinary sophistication."

They both dissolved into laughter, Mariselle allowing herself to once again conveniently 'forget' the years of family enmity that stood between them. It was only when she noticed Evryn watching her with bemusement and … something else she couldn't quite determine that she forced herself to straighten in her seat, pressing her lips together in a vain attempt to compose her features into something more befitting a Brightcrest in enemy territory.

"I beg your pardon," she said to Lady Lelianna, smoothing her skirts. "I didn't mean to speak so … freely."

"No need to apologize," Lady Lelianna assured her. "As you can see, my children express themselves without reservation. Though I do occasionally wish they would temper their candor with a modicum of decorum, particularly when we have guests." She directed a pointed gaze first at Rosavyn, then Evryn.

Evryn leaned toward Mariselle, his shoulder brushing against hers as he spoke in a mock whisper loud enough for everyone to hear. "Mother pretends to be horrified by some of our more inappropriate comments, but we've caught her laughing behind her napkin far too often to be fooled."

Lady Lelianna's lips pursed in exaggerated disapproval. She began to scold her son, but Mariselle was only vaguely aware of her words, distracted by Evryn's proximity and the way his breath ghosted across her cheek as he laughed.

She was reminded suddenly of the night they'd soared above the Dreamland ruins astride his pegasus, Evryn's arm encircling her waist, holding her firmly against him. At the time, she'd been entirely consumed by the glowing light of the lumyrite network illuminated across the ground below, by the thrill of discovering it perfectly intact. It wasn't until they'd begun their descent that she'd become aware of his nearness and how it wasn't entirely ... unpleasant. How she seemed to fit perfectly within the circle of his arm.

He drew back now, the moment of feigned intimacy having passed, and she shook her head a little, forcing her shoulders back. The bracelet slid down her arm, a reminder of his latest magical trick, no doubt designed to spring some mortifying surprise at the most inopportune moment.

The remainder of tea passed in more traditional conversation—the weather, upcoming social events, the latest ridiculous rumors the gossip birds were spreading. Yet something had shifted in the atmosphere. Rosavyn's hostile edge had softened, and Aurelise has warmed up considerably.

As the tea service was cleared away, Lady Lelianna turned to Mariselle with a warm smile. "You simply must join us again soon," she said. "Perhaps next week?"

"That's very kind," Mariselle replied. "I shall have to consult my calendar, but ... yes, I would enjoy that."

Evryn escorted her to the entrance hall, where Tilly had already been summoned from below stairs. As they waited for the butler to retrieve Mariselle's gloves, Evryn leaned slightly closer.

"You survived," he observed, his voice pitched for her ears alone. "And even managed to find common ground with Rosavyn, which I frankly thought impossible. I remain convinced that asparagus is perfectly acceptable, however. In fact, I rather like it."

"Your judgment is clearly impaired," Mariselle replied, though without real heat. "Though your family is ... not what I expected."

Something flickered in his eyes. He opened his mouth to say something, but before he could respond, the butler returned with her gloves, and the moment passed.

"I wonder how you'll fare when it's your turn to visit my family," Mariselle said, tugging her gloves on. "That should prove interesting."

Evryn's brows shot up. "My turn?"

She stifled a groan but kept her smile firmly in place, mindful of Tilly and the butler still close by. "My birthday dinner two weeks hence," she explained. "Mother will put on her usual show of organizing a simple family gathering, and it occurs to me now that it would look rather odd if my supposed beloved didn't attend."

"Your birthday?" Evryn blinked in surprise. "I had no idea."

"A formal invitation will be delivered soon," she said, then added in an overly bright and entirely fake tone, "Something to look forward to!"

The journey home passed in contemplative silence, with Tilly occasionally glancing at her mistress but seeming to understand that Mariselle needed the sanctuary of her own thoughts. She stared out the carriage window, her mind a tumult of conflicting emotions.

The Rowanwoods had been nothing like what she'd been raised to expect. There had been no coldly calculating plots, no obvious magical manipulations, no evidence of the heartless ambition her parents had always attributed to them. Instead, she'd witnessed warmth, genuine affection, and the kind of easy family dynamic she hadn't been aware was even possible.

Had it all been an elaborate performance for her benefit? She didn't think so. The siblings' interactions had felt too natural, too unguarded to be mere theater. And what would the point have been in a performance like that? No, it had to have been genuine.

The thought was mildly terrifying, for if the Rowanwoods were not as she had been taught, what else might be untrue?

A deep, aching sadness settled over her. Whether genuine or not, the Rowanwoods' family dynamic had shown her everything that was lacking in her own. The contrast between their easy affection and the cold formality of Brightcrest Manor had never been more stark.

And regardless of how enjoyable the afternoon had been, the fact remained: this was all temporary. She would never truly be part of their family. Once Dreamland was restored and the magical contract fulfilled, the charade would end. Evryn would return to his life, she to hers, and this brief glimpse of what family could be would fade into distant memory.

But she refused to surrender to such melancholy. Once Dreamland stood restored—her vision made manifest, her true abilities finally revealed—everything would change. Her parents would see her, truly see her, for perhaps the first time. She harbored no illusions that they would transform into the warm, affectionate family she'd glimpsed today; that fantasy was too far-fetched even for her dreamer's heart. But there would be respect where now there was only dismissal. Recognition where now there was only oversight. Things would be different. They would be *better.*

And that had always been the true purpose behind this desperate gamble.

Chapter Sixteen

Mariselle's first drowsy thought upon waking the following morning was that someone had apparently replaced her silk pillowcase with something that looked remarkably like the Brightcrest family banner—until she realized with mounting horror that the brilliant blue fabric cascading across her pillow was, in fact, attached to her head.

She shot upright, yanking a lock of hair before her eyes. The azure blue strand dangled between her fingers like a vivid declaration of magical mischief.

"Evryn Rowanwood," she hissed, her voice a venomous whisper. The bracelet. That wretched, beautiful, *enchanted* bracelet he had presented her with yesterday afternoon. She'd only worn it while at Rowanwood House and in the carriage ride home, but clearly that had been long enough.

Mariselle scrambled from her bed and flew to her vanity, where the looking glass confirmed her worst suspicions. Her hair—her glorious honey-gold hair that had been the envy of half the young ladies in Bloomhaven—now resembled the sky above a cerulean sea.

"Oh, my lady!" Tilly gasped as she entered with a tray bearing Mariselle's morning tea, nearly dropping it at the sight of her mistress. "Whatever has happened to your—"

"It appears," Mariselle said with deadly calm, "that my betrothed possesses a rather juvenile sense of humor."

"Your … do you mean Lord Rowanwood? But he is so devoted to you, my lady."

Mariselle silently cursed her careless tongue. There in a single unguarded moment, she'd nearly unraveled all her careful pretense. She composed her features into a mask of fond exasperation and released a tinkling laugh that she hoped disguised her momentary panic.

"Oh, forgive my temper, Tilly. What I meant is that this was an unfortunate accident. Lord Rowanwood presented me with the most exquisite silver bracelet yesterday, set with sapphires that match precisely this … unexpected hue. He acquired it at Vesper's Curiosities & Oddities." She sighed dramatically. "It seems even a man of his considerable magical knowledge can occasionally miss an enchantment hiding in plain sight. Rather endearing, really, that he was so eager to please me he didn't think to check for lingering spells."

Tilly approached cautiously. "Is it … all of it, my lady?"

Mariselle turned her head side to side, examining the damage. "Every last strand," she confirmed, running her fingers through the transformed locks that now shimmered blue instead of golden blonde.

"Shall I inform your mother?" Tilly asked, setting down the tray.

"And subject myself to her hysterical lamentations before I've even had my tea? I think not." Mariselle sank into her chair. "Tell her I'm indisposed. A headache, perhaps."

"Very good, my lady." Tilly bobbed a curtsy. "And what shall we do about …" She gestured vaguely toward Mariselle's head.

Mariselle tilted her head, studying her reflection. The blue was striking, almost a perfect match for her eyes. Evryn had been right about that. No doubt he'd meant to embarrass her with what was commonly known as a 'matron's enchantment.' The more venerable ladies of society often took to magically coloring their hair in their twilight years. Lady Whispermist's famous lavender coiffure had been the talk of Bloomhaven for nearly a decade, and there was the elder Lady Bridgemere, who had been sporting a vivid sunset coral for the last several Seasons.

Yet Mariselle couldn't help but recall those rare individuals blessed from birth with hair in shades that defied nature's ordinary palette. Unusual colors that marked them as touched by old magic. Individuals like the High Lady and her son, Prince Ryden.

"Remarkably," she mused, "I find I don't entirely hate it."

"It is rather … dramatic," Tilly offered.

"Precisely the word I would have chosen." Mariselle reached for the teapot. "My mother, however, will have several other choice words, none of which are suitable for polite company." She lifted the teapot lid and sniffed. "Is this the new blend? The duskmint-vanilla?"

The fragrance transported her instantly back to The Charmed Leaf, where she'd first savored its bewitching combination of cool mint and sweet vanilla. The taste had lingered in her memory afterward, prompting her to inquire if Tilly might locate some for her private collection.

"Indeed it is, my lady," Tilly replied with a hint of pride. "Not the easiest treasure to unearth, but I managed to find a supplier."

"How wonderful. Thank you, Tilly."

After Tilly departed, Mariselle cradled the delicate porcelain cup between her palms, savoring both the warmth and the fragrant steam as her mind turned over the morning's complications. The hair was a problem, certainly, but not her most pressing one. The Dreamland project waited for no one, not even victims of magical practical jokes. And after her mother's thinly veiled ultimatum the previous evening, Mariselle felt time slipping through her fingers. Lady Brightcrest had made it painfully clear: if Mariselle couldn't soon produce something of value to leverage against the Rowanwoods, her mother would accelerate her search for a practitioner willing to sever the soulbond.

But she was tantalizingly close to being able to attempt a test dreamscape. A simple one, nothing too elaborate, but enough to prove that all this work wasn't for nothing. She merely needed to enchant a few more of the dream core's crystals. An evening's work, perhaps several. That was all it would take before she could walk through Dreamland not merely in her mind, but with her own two feet.

Well, that wasn't *all* it would take. Evryn needed to finish reconstructing the lumyrite-embedded framework. And there was the matter of the protective wards. She was still determining precisely how to weave them. But the wards weren't strictly necessary for a brief experimental foray. A quick test wouldn't leave her in the dreamscape long enough for nightmare entities to attempt crossing over.

With no social obligations cluttering her evening calendar, tonight presented the perfect opportunity to advance their work. With any luck, Petunia and Evryn would be free too. She reached for the middle drawer of her vanity and withdrew her hand mirror, turning it this way and that as she examined its surface with a sigh. It appeared the restoration spell she'd applied days prior had not yet fully taken hold; faint lines still traced the path of each individual shard from when it had shattered. It seemed the enchantment required more time to mend completely.

With a small sigh, she returned the mirror to its velvet-lined compartment and closed the drawer with a gentle click, then reached past the side of her vanity and pulled the silver bell-cord that would summon one of the household pixies. Then she quickly penned a note to Petunia requesting her presence in the greenhouse as soon as possible. For Evryn, however, she crafted their customary coded message. A seemingly innocent lover's note that would appear to anyone else as mere sentimental drivel:

My dearest, the nightveil orchids we discussed remind me of your eyes when you smile. Perhaps I shall dream of them tonight. Yours in tender affection, M.

She had just finished when a faint tap at her door signaled the arrival of the pixie. She crossed the room and opened the door to find the tiny blue-tinged creature on the other side. The pixie froze mid-hover, its wings stuttering in shock as it registered her transformed appearance. It emitted a piercing chime of surprise that made Mariselle wince. She fixed it with a withering stare that brooked no comment on matters beyond its station.

"Please take this directly to Lady Petunia next door," she instructed the pixie, handing over the first note. "And place this one in the hollow stone by the front gate for the messenger pixie service to collect on their morning rounds. Thank you."

With the pixie gone, Mariselle dressed quickly, deciding not to wait for Tilly's return. She struggled with the buttons at the back of her day dress, then resorted to a minor fastening charm that coaxed them into place—an unladylike shortcut her mother would never have approved of. "Magic is no substitute for the proper dressing skills of one's lady's maid," she'd say. But Lady Clemenbell wasn't here right now.

Mariselle twisted her transformed blue locks into a serviceable chignon, securing it with two enchanted pins that immediately tightened and adjusted themselves to hold every strand in place. She examined her reflection with a critical eye, then cautiously opened her door and peered into the hallway.

Evasion was now the priority. Her mother and Ellowa would be taking their breakfast in the sunroom, no doubt dissecting the previous evening's gossip, and her father was probably already locked away in his study with his endless correspondence. That left the rarely used west lounge as her escape route—a chamber with worn velvet settees and bookshelves crammed with generations of eclectic reading material. Mariselle had always favored its cozy, comfortable disarray, but Lady Clemenbell had declared it 'hopelessly provincial' and 'unsuitable for anyone worth impressing' years ago.

Mariselle slipped through the corridors, pausing at corners and ducking behind elaborate crystal flower arrangements whenever a servant appeared. At last, she reached the west lounge, pushing open the heavy oak door with a sigh of relief. To her surprise, the usually dim chamber was flooded with morning light, the heavy velvet curtains pulled back and windows flung wide. The unexpected brightness momentarily dazzled her.

"Mariselle Brightcrest. How extraordinary that you should appear precisely when I was inquiring after your whereabouts."

Mariselle froze, one hand still on the doorknob. That voice—cultured, commanding, and utterly unmistakable—belonged to the one person in her family more formidable than her mother.

"Grandmother," she said, turning slowly to face the diminutive woman seated in a wingback chair beside the bookshelf. "What a ... delightful surprise."

Lady Nirella Brightcrest raised a single eyebrow. "Is it? I find it rather surprising that you've been in Bloomhaven for at least a fortnight and have yet to come and visit me. Particularly given the fact that you've apparently formed a *soulbond* with none other than a Rowanwood. Did you imagine I wouldn't wish to be informed that the decades-old feud between our families was being bridged by my own flesh and blood? Or perhaps you thought I was too decrepit to attend the engagement celebration of my own grand-daughter."

Mariselle's stomach dropped to somewhere in the vicinity of her silk slippers. "Grandmother, it—it all happened so quickly. The High Lady—it was less than a day's notice—and you so rarely attend social events these days—"

"And now," her grandmother continued, her gaze traveling upward, "you appear to have transformed yourself into some sort of exotic water nymph. How very innovative of you."

Despite herself, Mariselle felt her lips twitch. Her grandmother, whose hair had been a sophisticated shade of pearl pink for almost as long as Mariselle had known her, was hardly one to judge. "It was not entirely intentional, Grandmother."

"Few of life's most interesting developments are." Lady Nirella gestured imperiously to the chair opposite her own, her eyes never leaving Mariselle. Despite her age and the regal stiffness of her bearing, there was something in her gaze that still sparkled. Sharp, watchful, never missing a thing. "Sit. Explain yourself."

Mariselle hesitated, her blood turning to ice as a memory surfaced—the elegantly penned signature of Lady Nirella Brightcrest flowing across the bottom of that fateful contract she had discovered at Windsong Cottage. The elaborate charade of the 'soulbond' might fool society, might even deceive her parents and the High Lady, but her grandmother? If anyone could see through this fabricated connection to what the marking on Mariselle's hand truly represented, it would be the woman who had negotiated the original agreement with Valenrik Rowanwood.

Mariselle crossed the room on legs that felt suddenly wooden, her heart performing a frantic, uneven rhythm. Conflicting emotions warred within her—genuine pleasure at seeing her grandmother after so long, tangled with mounting dread. Unlike most of Bloomhaven's elite families who retreated to country estates when the Bloom Season ended, Lady Nirella maintained her residence at Bloomhaven's edge year-round, which meant Mariselle hadn't seen her since last Season.

She lowered herself into the indicated chair, forcing her breathing to remain steady. "I was going to call upon you," she said, arranging her skirts. "This weekend, in fact."

"Were you indeed?" Lady Nirella's tone suggested she found this claim about as credible as the existence of economical goblins. "How fortuitous that I've saved you the trouble."

Before Mariselle could formulate a suitably respectful retort, the door burst open and a harried-looking footman appeared.

"My lady, I've searched the morning room, the blue parlor, and—" He caught sight of Mariselle and stopped short. "Oh. Lady Mariselle. Your mother has been asking for you."

"How convenient that you've found her loitering in my presence," Lady Nirella remarked dryly. "You may inform Lady Clemenbell that her daughter is attending me."

The footman bowed and retreated, but not quickly enough to escape Lady Clemenbell herself, who swept into the room like an agitated thundercloud.

"Mariselle! I've had half the household looking everywhere for—" Her mother's voice cut off abruptly as she registered her daughter's appearance. Her face drained of color. "WHAT HAVE YOU DONE TO YOUR HAIR?"

Mariselle winced at the volume. "Good morning, Mother."

Lady Clemenbell advanced, circling Mariselle as if inspecting an offensive sculpture. "Is this—are you—" She appeared to be having difficulty forming complete sentences. "Blue! Your hair is *blue*!"

"How remarkably observant," Lady Nirella murmured.

"I believe," Mariselle said with admirable composure, "that it may be the result of the bracelet Lord Evryn gifted me yesterday. A simple enchantment gone awry, perhaps. He found it at that charming little curiosities shop and most likely didn't realize it contained a spell of some sort."

Lady Clemenbell clutched dramatically at her chest. "Vesper's Curiosities & Oddities? Well of *course* it contained a spell! That Rowanwood boy has done this deliberately! This is an outrage! What will people say?"

"They will say," Lady Nirella interjected coolly, "that the young Lord Rowanwood has a surprisingly whimsical sense of humor, and that my granddaughter carries off an unusual hair color with remarkable elegance. Now, Clemenbell, I require a private audience with Mariselle regarding matters that do not concern you."

Lady Clemenbell drew herself up like an offended peacock. "Mother Brightcrest, with all due respect, anything concerning my daughter most certainly does concern me."

"Does it?" Lady Nirella tilted her head. "How fascinating that you've only just remembered this fact, when you've spent years devoting all your attention to Ellowa." She gave a dismissive wave of her hand and turned away from Mariselle's mother. "I shall ring when we've concluded our discussion."

Mariselle bit the inside of her cheek to keep from smirking as her mother's face flushed. Lady Clemenbell opened her mouth, closed it, then turned on her heel and stormed out, her magic slamming the door with enough force to rattle the ornaments on the mantelpiece.

"You shouldn't provoke her so," Mariselle said, though she couldn't keep the appreciation from her voice. "She'll be impossible for days now."

"Your mother has been impossible since the day she married into this family," Lady Nirella replied dismissively. "Now, show me your hand."

Mariselle hesitated only briefly before extending her right hand. It wasn't as though she could refuse. She bit her lip as her eyes traced over the glimmering silver lines of the fake 'soulbond.' How furious would her grandmother be when she realized what it truly signified?

Lady Nirella took Mariselle's hand in her own and leaned over it, examining the mark with such intensity that Mariselle half expected it to begin smoking under the scrutiny.

"Hmm," Lady Nirella said finally. Then she reached toward the small side table, her gloved fingers closing around a leather volume whose presence Mariselle had missed until this moment. She opened the book to a marked page and held it beside Mariselle's hand. The illustration depicted what appeared to be an identical mark, rendered in meticulous detail.

Mariselle's stomach plummeted. The charade was over. Whatever differences existed between a genuine soulbond mark and the contract mark on Mariselle's hand, her grandmother would discover them now. She felt lightheaded with panic, her carefully constructed plans dissolving around her.

A wild impulse seized her—to confess everything, to pour out the truth about the cottage, about accidentally agreeing to the contract, about her hopes and plans for Dreamland. If anyone might understand her fascination with the abandoned attraction, it would be the woman who had experienced it at the height of its splendor. Her grandmother, who had shared tantalizing fragments of Dreamland's wonders throughout Mariselle's childhood, painting pictures with words of a place where imagination became reality.

She opened her mouth, on the verge of revealing everything, when her grandmother snapped the book shut and pronounced, "It does indeed appear to be a true soulbond. How extraordinarily inconvenient."

Mariselle hesitated. Closed her mouth. Relief flooded through her, followed by the reminder that she needed to maintain the pretense of being helplessly, desperately enamored with Evryn Rowanwood. "Inconvenient?" she repeated, feigning indignation. "But Grandmother, I love—"

"Stop." Lady Nirella set the book aside and took both of Mariselle's hands in hers. "My dear, you do not *love* him," she said gently, her eyes filled with a compassion that Mariselle rarely witnessed in her family. "What you're experiencing is old magic interfering with your heart's natural inclinations, placing emotions within you that were never truly yours to begin with."

Unlike her parents' hysterical objections, her grandmother's calm rationality created a space where Mariselle felt she might actually be heard rather than merely lectured at. The absence of histrionics was almost startling after her mother's near perpetual state of crisis.

"Would it really be so bad, Grandmother? To marry a Rowanwood?"

Lady Nirella was silent for a long moment, her gaze distant as though she were seeing beyond the confines of the room, perhaps into the past itself. "Yes," she said, refocusing on Mariselle. "It would be."

Her quiet declaration carried the weight of absolute conviction, yet Mariselle remained confused. The more she interacted with the Rowanwoods, the more this ancient animosity seemed like a relic that had outlived its purpose.

"What really happened, Grandmother?" she asked, her voice quiet but earnest. "All those years ago. What could possibly justify maintaining this feud for generations?"

Lady Nirella's face became as still as carved marble. "I won't speak of it." Something in her expression—a fleeting shadow of old pain—made Mariselle fall silent.

"The bond must be broken," her grandmother continued after a moment. "And it *can* be broken, despite what romantic nonsense is written in those novels you think I don't know you read." She squeezed Mariselle's hands, a small smile finding its way onto her lips. "One day, my dear, you will thank me. When you are free to marry someone you truly love. Someone worthy of the remarkable young woman you've become."

The tenderness in her grandmother's voice brought a lump to Mariselle's throat. "I've missed you," she said suddenly, impulsively pulling her hands free of her grandmother's grip and throwing her arms around the older woman.

Lady Nirella hesitated for only a moment before wrapping Mariselle in a tight hug. "You should visit more often, dear," she said, her voice slightly gruff. "I've missed you too."

She released Mariselle and straightened her shoulders. "Now, I suppose I had better go and speak with your mother." A sigh escaped her, heavy with the weariness of one who had survived countless familial storms and now faced yet another with resigned fortitude. "It seems, for once, that we are in agreement over something."

Chapter Seventeen

THE RIDICULOUS PAGEANTRY OF THE BLOOM SEASON HAD PROVIDED Evryn with enough satirical material to fill a dozen notebooks, not just the one currently balanced on his knee as he lounged in the window seat of Windsong Cottage almost two weeks after the surprisingly enjoyable tea with Mariselle at Rowanwood House.

A gentle breeze through the open window stirred the trailing vines that adorned its frame, their leaves tickling his ear and momentarily drawing his attention from the page. He shifted his position slightly and turned a few pages back to the start of his notes, crossed out the title *The Bloom Season*, and replaced it with *The Relentless Parade of Vanity*. That suited his purposes far better.

He lifted his quill as his eyes drifted from the notebook to Mariselle sitting cross-legged on the cottage floor, dressed in her riding gear, that startling blue braid tumbling carelessly over one shoulder. Her hands hovered above the dream core, fingertips occasionally twitching as if playing an invisible instrument. Her face was a portrait of fierce concentration, brows drawn together, lower lip caught between her teeth.

He found his gaze lingering on that blue hair more often than he cared to admit. It had been at least ten days since his bracelet's enchantment had activated, transforming her golden locks to that vibrant azure, and her hair showed no signs yet of returning to its original shade. Surprisingly, she hadn't seemed particularly bothered by it. Even more surprisingly, Evryn had found he rather liked it. It suited her somehow—bright and unexpected, like the flashes of genuine passion he'd glimpsed beneath her carefully maintained facade.

Evryn dragged his attention back to his notebook with more effort than should have been necessary. The society matrons' desperate machinations to secure matches for their daughters provided particularly fertile ground for mockery. He cast his mind further back, to the evening of that ridiculous art auction, where Lady Whitewing's strategic deployment of her niece's décolletage had been nothing short of tactical warfare.

He scribbled another observation, his quill scratching satisfyingly across the parchment. The work was a welcome distraction from the bone-deep exhaustion that had settled into his limbs over the past ten days or so. Multiple nights of painstaking magical labor, reconstructing the broken sections of the original Dreamland frame, melding fragmented lumyrite back together until his fingers cramped and his eyes burned.

Mariselle had been noticeably frustrated by the amount of time it had taken him—longer than she'd estimated apparently—but he'd finally completed the task earlier this evening. He'd confirmed there were no remaining breaks in the structure by using the same incantation he'd employed to visualize the underground lumyrite network. The ride on Cobalt had been blissfully solitary—Mariselle too engrossed in her precious dream core to request joining him, thank the stars. Without the distraction of her pressed against him, he'd been able to focus entirely on the task at hand.

And what a sight it had been. The lumyrite pattern of the completed frame stretching out below him, glowing with ethereal brilliance against the shadowy ground. Fully intact now, the skeletal structure hummed with potential.

Of course, it still looked nothing like what he imagined the original Dreamland had once been. There was no covering on the frame, after all. Mariselle had mentioned a grand tent of some sort. Had she given a moment's thought to where this magical tent would come from? Who would manufacture it? What it would cost? Probably not. She'd been consumed with the dream core, hunched over it night after night—sometimes with her cousin's assistance, sometimes on her own—imbuing it with who knew what kind of potentially catastrophic magic.

But Evryn's part was done. The frame had been restored. His obligation fulfilled. Earlier this evening, he'd asked—quite reasonably, he thought—if he could leave. There was still time to join his friends for the evening race through Westhollow Woods. He'd overheard Crispin boasting to Fin while at the Rowanwood Masquerade the other night—a most welcome respite from Mariselle and her Dreamland schemes—about some new modifications to his saddle that would supposedly give him an edge. Evryn had been looking forward to witnessing the inevitable humiliation when those modifications failed spectacularly.

But Mariselle had said no. With infuriating casualness, she'd informed him that she needed his help with 'something' when she was done. What that 'something' might be, she hadn't deigned to specify. So here he remained, prisoner to her whims yet again.

He'd turned to writing instead. Perhaps it was foolish, considering he was in the presence of the very woman who had stolen his previous manuscript and was currently blackmailing him with it. But she already knew his secret. Already possessed ample evidence against him. What further damage could be done if she glimpsed this latest work?

And he was tired, dammit. Tired and irritable and in desperate need of the particular comfort that only came from the scratch of quill on parchment, from the satisfaction of crafting perfect phrases. So he wrote, his characters coming to life on the page.

"Yes!"

Evryn started at Mariselle's sudden exclamation of triumph, his grip tightening involuntarily around his quill. She had sprung to her feet, hands raised above her head in a most unladylike display of exuberance.

"Has something momentous occurred?" he inquired dryly. The dream core on the floor appeared entirely unchanged to his eye, yet Mariselle beamed at it as though it had performed some remarkable feat.

"Oh, I wish you were Petunia!" she exclaimed wistfully, clasping her hands beneath her chin.

Evryn wasn't entirely certain how to respond to that statement. Was he meant to feel slighted at being an inadequate substitute for her cousin?

"My most sincere apologies for failing to be your beloved cousin," he remarked. "If you'll recall, I did request permission to leave earlier this evening."

"Don't be silly," Mariselle said, dropping back to her knees beside the dream core. "You're not going anywhere yet. I still need you. I merely meant that Petunia would properly appreciate the significance of what I've just accomplished."

He almost made a snide comment about whether it involved dream essence extraction, the paltry magic she'd displayed at her debut, but thought better of it. Their verbal sparring had become almost comfortable in its predictability, but that particular barb felt unnecessarily cruel.

And there was also … *I still need you.*

The offhand comment stuck in his head, though he knew, of course, that she hadn't meant it in any significant sense. Perhaps because it wasn't something anyone ever said to him. He wasn't *needed.* Not the way his older brother was.

He shook himself from his thoughts, and turned back to his notebook. Mariselle was focused on the dream core again, and he found it easy to lose himself in his writing once more.

At some point, she rose from the floor and wandered past, though her movements barely registered. Absorbed in his notes, Evryn continued refining a character loosely based on Rosavyn—one he intended to use as a vehicle to critique the relentless societal pressure placed on young fae to manifest. Rosavyn managed to maintain her carefree attitude, her eyes sparkling with delight when Kazrian and Aurelise—two years younger than her—showed the first stirrings of their abilities, but Evryn hadn't missed the way her smile grew more strained each time someone commented on her lack of manifestation.

After another few minutes, the unmistakable clink of porcelain from the kitchen caught his attention. Mariselle was making tea. He glanced up briefly, then returned to his writing, determined to finish his thought before the interruption fully derailed his concentration.

Then a crash and the sound of shattering porcelain startled him. He sat forward abruptly, his notebook sliding from his knee to the floor with a soft thud.

"Is everything all right?" he called out, already half-rising from his seat.

Mariselle responded immediately. "Yes, everything's fine. Nothing more than a moment of clumsiness."

Evryn hesitated, one hand still braced against the window frame. "Do you need—"

"No, I do not need assistance, Rowanwood," she cut him off, though her voice still held a trace of its earlier glee rather than any real irritation. "I'm perfectly capable of cleaning up a few broken teacups."

He reached for his notebook and sat back with a sigh. Stars forbid he should dare offer a lady assistance. He resumed his writing. He was busy with a paragraph about how society's obsession with magical manifestation created a cruel paradox—those who needed the most support received the least, abandoned to their 'failure' just when compassion was most needed—when Mariselle appeared at his side.

"Have you seen these before?" she asked, presenting two teacups. "I accidentally knocked over the tray with the cups I usually use and had to reach higher than normal for replacements. I found these."

Evryn leaned a little closer to look. Each teacup was exquisitely crafted, with delicate floral patterns in soft blues and greens curling around the rim. But what caught his attention were the names painted on the sides in elegant gold script, nestled artfully among the painted leaves: *Rik* on one, *Venna* on the other.

"They're part of a set," Mariselle continued. "There are others in the kitchen labeled *Thaelen*, *Kren*, and *Rella*."

Evryn frowned as he took one of the cups from her hand to examine it more closely. "Who are Rik and Venna?"

Mariselle gave him a look that said, *Are you being intentionally dim?* "Your grandparents? Valenrik and Rivenna?"

A loud snort escaped Evryn. He handed the teacup back to Mariselle. "You cannot be serious. Do you think there's a single person in the entire United Fae Isles who could get away with calling my grandmother *Venna*?"

"Well, when you put it that way," Mariselle said, "no, I can't imagine that. But who else could it be? And Kren and Rella are obviously Krenshaw and Nirella. My grandparents. And have you ever heard of someone named Sera? Her teacup is in the kitchen too."

Evryn shook his head.

Mariselle studied the delicate teacups with a thoughtful expression. "What do you think this means?"

With his mind still lingering on the half-written passage in his notebook, Evryn struggled to formulate a sensible answer. "I …" He shrugged. "I don't know. Probably nothing of consequence."

"Nothing of consequence? Our grandparents had personalized teacups hidden away in this cottage like some sort of … clandestine tea society," Mariselle exclaimed, her eyes wide with scandalized delight. She turned the cups in her hands, examining them from every angle as though they might reveal additional secrets. "Not just any teacups. Ones with … *diminutive* forms of their names. *Familiar* names. You don't think they were …" Her voice lowered conspiratorially, hovering between fascination and horror.

Evryn raised an eyebrow, immediately understanding her implication. "Friends? Impossible," he scoffed, though the evidence in her hands suggested otherwise.

"Then how do you explain this?"

Evryn inhaled deeply, searching his mind for an answer that made sense. 'They were friends' was not only improbable, it was as likely as discovering gossip birds had taken a vow of silence.

"We know Krenshaw Brightcrest and Thaelan Rowanwood were business associates. We know they often worked here at the cottage. I also know that Thaelan and his older brother, my grandfather, were considered to be close. I suppose it's not entirely beyond imagination that they might all have shared tea here occasionally, along with their wives—in a strictly professional capacity, of course."

"I suppose," Mariselle said, though she sounded unconvinced.

After another moment's pause, she turned and headed back to the kitchen, where the light clinking of porcelain and the gentle splash of water indicated she was preparing tea. Evryn tried to refocus on his writing, but the words refused to flow. Instead, his mind kept circling back to those teacups. His grandmother being called 'Venna' by anyone, let alone Brightcrests, seemed utterly inconceivable.

The quiet sounds of Mariselle's movements in the kitchen filled the cottage. A few minutes later, she emerged, a steaming cup in her hand. She rounded the table and stopped beside the window seat. "I made you some tea," she said, then smiled and turned the cup so he could see the label. "In the *Rik* teacup."

Evryn eyed the steaming liquid warily. She'd offered him tea before, and he'd invariably declined, knowing better than to accept anything from those deceptively delicate hands. But tonight, an oddly familiar aroma wafted from the cup. Something comforting. Something he actually enjoyed.

"What is it?" he asked, making no move to take it.

"An infusion of duskmint and vanilla. Apparently you like it?"

His eyes narrowed further. How did she know his preferred tea? And more importantly, why would she trouble herself to prepare it? The blue-haired menace before him did nothing without purpose, without calculation.

"Why would you go to the trouble of brewing the tea I like?"

She rolled her eyes with dramatic flair. "Because *I* like it. I thought you might want some too." When he still made no move to accept the cup, she let out an exasperated sigh. "Oh, for goodness' sake."

She lifted the cup to her own lips and took a deliberate sip before returning it to its saucer and extending it toward him once more. "See? Perfectly safe."

He regarded the cup with even greater revulsion now. The thought of putting his lips where hers had just been caused an inexplicable heat to crawl up his neck. Absolutely not.

Reading his expression with irritating accuracy, she rolled her eyes again and rotated the teacup on its saucer. "There. So that your perfect lips do not have to be *tainted* by touching the same part of the cup my lips have touched."

Despite himself, Evryn felt one eyebrow arch upward as he finally took the cup from her. "You think my lips are perfect?"

Without missing a beat, she replied, "I think your lips are perpetually formed into a self-satisfied smirk that must be exhausting to maintain. Perhaps the tea will help you relax that particular muscle group."

Evryn found that his lips were indeed curved into a smirk, and he couldn't help laughing quietly as she crossed back to the kitchen. He took a cautious sip of the tea—which was, infuriatingly, brewed exactly as he preferred—and placed it on the window sill within easy reach.

He returned to his writing, Mariselle returned to her dream core. He sipped the tea and followed his thoughts across the page. After some time, he noticed the quill moving more sluggishly, his usually precise handwriting becoming increasingly erratic. An unnatural heaviness settled over him, as if the very air had thickened.

How long had he been writing? Minutes? Hours? The words before him blurred, dancing across the page. His eyelids grew impossibly heavy, each blink lasting longer than the one before.

With dawning horror, realization cut through the fog clouding his mind. The tea. She'd put something in the tea. How could he have been so foolish?

"You … you *poisoned* me," he slurred, the notebook sliding from his suddenly weak fingers. His limbs felt weighted with lead, his head too heavy to hold upright.

The last thing he saw as his eyes slid shut was Mariselle leaning closer, her blue hair gleaming in the faelight as she blew him a kiss.

"Sweet dreams, Rowanwood," she whispered, her voice following him down into darkness. "See you on the other side."

Chapter Eighteen

Consciousness returned to Evryn in fragments—disjointed sensations that refused to coalesce into coherence. His limbs felt impossibly heavy, his thoughts scattered like dandelion seeds in a breeze. He struggled to focus, to anchor himself against the disorienting fog that enveloped his mind.

"Goodness, you're heavy. I can barely move you, even with magic."

Mariselle's voice floated to him from somewhere both near and impossibly distant. He tried to respond, but his tongue seemed unable to follow his commands.

Without warning, the world shifted, and Evryn found himself dropping through space. A startled grunt escaped him as he landed with a solid thud on something that yielded ever so slightly beneath his weight. Something that rustled as he moved and scratched lightly against his palms and the exposed skin at his nape.

Music drifted around him, a lilting melody that rose and fell in spellbinding patterns. Tinkling notes cascaded like water over stones, while a deeper, rhythmic undercurrent pulsed with clockwork steadiness. It reminded him of childhood visits to traveling fairs, of whirling rides and colored lights, of laughter and wonder, of that enchanted ballerina music box Rosavyn had cherished as a child.

With considerable effort, Evryn forced his eyes open fully and struggled to sit upright, rubbing vigorously at his face. The world gradually sharpened into focus. A world that appeared … pink and blue? He blinked again. Pearl pink grass and the azure blue of Mariselle's hair. She was kneeling beside him, her face turned away, her mess of a blue braid far too close to his face.

He immediately leaned back, putting some distance between the two of them. "You drugged me!" he accused, his voice still slurred at the edges.

She turned to look at him, an amused smile on her lips. "Such dramatics. It was merely a mild sleeping draught."

"Merely a—you really did drug me!" Indignation and disbelief warred in his voice.

"If Petunia were here, she could have taken you across the threshold while you were awake—that's her manifested magical ability, in case you haven't been paying attention, and a vital ability for the operation of Dreamland. But she was unable to join us this evening, and I simply couldn't endure another night of waiting, so I had to make you fall asleep first. Though waking you up this side has proved considerably challenging, which is precisely why we need Petunia's magic."

Evryn stared at her incredulously, his mind still reeling from the sheer audacity of her actions. "You might have simply *explained* your intentions instead of resorting to tea steeped with sleeping draught."

"Would you have drunk it?" Her eyebrow arched, challenge evident in her expression.

Evryn conceded the point with a reluctant grimace. Of course he wouldn't have willingly consumed anything that would render him unconscious in a Brightcrest's presence.

"You're utterly mad," he muttered, still struggling to fully orient himself. "Where did you cart me off to anyway?"

A laugh escaped her, bright and genuine. "You still haven't realized, have you?"

Evryn looked up, only now beginning to comprehend his surroundings. A few paces away, enormous tree-like structures towered impossibly high, their trunks a soft lavender that darkened to deep purple at the base. But these were no ordinary trees. Their canopies consisted of what appeared to be massive plumes of spun sugar in varying shades of pink, their lavender branches bearing glistening golden apples.

"What in all the stars …"

He started to swivel around, but before he could complete the motion, Mariselle cried out, "Oh wait!" and scrambled behind him. "Don't look yet," she said as her hands came down over his eyes.

He tensed immediately. "What are you—"

"Close your eyes," she whispered, her breath warm against his ear in a way that sent a shiver dancing through him. "And count to three."

The sudden intimacy caught him entirely off-guard—her fingers pressed lightly against his eyelids, the unexpected proximity of her body, her breath a whispered caress against his ear. A peculiar warmth unfurled in his chest, spreading outward until his skin seemed to tingle with heightened awareness.

The music around them began to shift, its tempo increasing, its melody growing more complex. The rhythm pulsed with a new urgency, building toward some unseen crescendo as Mariselle's voice counted softly near his ear.

"One … two … three—"

She pulled her hands away, and as the music swelled to its triumphant peak, Evryn opened his eyes to a world beyond anything he could have imagined.

The sky above them had transformed into swirls of cotton candy pink and lavender blue. Beneath their feet, the ground had become a mosaic of polished candy-colored stones that sparkled with each step. Flamingoes dressed in rainbow tutus promenaded along a stream of flowing silver that tinkled like wind chimes as it passed. Kites shaped like butterflies and dragons drifted lazily upward.

And at the center of this otherworldly space rotated a magnificent carousel, its platform inlaid with swirling patterns of mother-of-pearl and opal that shifted colors with each revolution. But unlike any carousel Evryn had ever seen, the carved creatures that adorned it—crystalline horses with flowing manes, iridescent sea serpents, and phoenix-like birds with rainbow plumage—were not fixed in place.

As he watched, a shimmering horse detached itself from its golden pole and stepped gracefully off the revolving platform. It trotted a few paces before spreading previously hidden wings and soaring into the star-filled space above, leaving a trail of luminescent particles in its wake.

Golden pathways branched out from the central carousel, leading to floating islands where fountains sprayed not water but liquid light in ever-changing colors. Gardens of impossible flowers bloomed and transformed before his eyes—roses that opened to reveal miniature galaxies at their centers, and vines that twisted themselves into animated shapes that danced with each other when they met.

The air itself seemed alive, carrying not just music but also ephemeral scents—vanilla one moment, cinnamon the next, then something that somehow evoked the memory of a childhood game he'd once loved.

He was vaguely aware of Mariselle moving to stand beside him. Her voice softened to a whisper filled with wonder. "Look what we created."

He stared in awe, utterly transfixed by the impossible spectacle before him.

Look what we created.

A warmth bloomed in his chest, expanding outward like ripples in a pond, a feeling so intense and unfamiliar that he couldn't begin to name it. It was something primal and profound—pride and wonder and astonishment all tangled together with something else he dared not examine too closely.

Mariselle looked up at him, her joy so unfiltered, so achingly lovely, and something in his chest … stuttered. He looked away, hoping the feeling would drift past, but it settled over him instead, quiet and certain and resolute.

Oh dear.

"This is Dreamland?" he murmured, feeling a little unsteady, his awe now entwined with the quiet thrum of something he was trying very hard not to feel. "We're inside Dreamland?"

"We are," she said proudly. "A piece of the dream realm brought into physical reality. It can be anything, not only this, but this is what I chose to build tonight. Oh, and look at this!"

She stepped away from him, arms spread wide as if about to begin a performance. The music shifted again, adopting a slow, hypnotic rhythm that seemed to pulse through Evryn's veins. Mariselle lifted one hand and gripped the imaginary brim of a hat, and as she slid her hand across this non-existent brim, it began to take form before his very eyes.

Not only that, but her entire outfit began to change, her practical riding gear transforming as the magic rippled downward from her hand. The plain fabric of her jacket lengthened and deepened in color, becoming a magnificent coat of deep amethyst, embellished with pink satin accents and gold embroidery. The coat's tails flared dramatically, partly forming a skirt that swirled around her legs as she moved. A fitted pink and gold corset cinched her waist, and atop her head sat a tall, angled hat of midnight violet with a single rose-gold feather arching elegantly from the side.

Evryn's thoughts scattered at the sight of her. Whatever treacherous thing had stirred in his chest earlier was now joined by a sudden, vivid awareness of her body—the confident set of her shoulders, the playful gleam in her eyes, the way the fantastical costume accentuated curves that, while more obvious in her riding gear than in a dress, he had studiously avoided noticing before.

Heat flared low and sharp, catching him off guard. He swallowed hard and tried valiantly to remember how breathing worked.

Mariselle danced away from him, twirled, and called out, "Welcome, one and all, to Dreamland, the Enchanted Carnival of Slumbering Wonders!" She removed her hat and tossed it into the air, where it spun rapidly, growing larger until it burst into a kaleidoscope of stained-glass butterflies. They scattered in all directions, their wings glittering in the cotton candy light.

She laughed, spun around again, and sashayed back to Evryn's side with a mischievous twist to her lips. "Terribly theatrical, isn't it?" she said, eyes sparkling with mirth. "My mother would suffer an immediate apoplexy if she saw me prancing about in such attire. Can you imagine? She'd probably lock me in my chambers for a month. No, this little performance is purely for my own amusement. And yours, I suppose," she added with another lilting laugh, seemingly unaware of the effect her current appearance was having on him.

She twirled once more, her figure briefly enveloped in a ripple of iridescent light. When the shimmer faded, her carnival attire had vanished, replaced by her familiar riding gear, the startling blue braid once again tumbling carelessly over one shoulder.

And at that moment, watching her manipulate her own appearance, her words struck him again: *This is what I chose to build tonight.* Suddenly he realized what should have been obvious from the start: "You're an architect. A dream architect."

"Of course," she said, looking around. "How else did you think I planned to accomplish something like this?"

"I ..." He bit back the admission that he had never truly believed she could accomplish anything of substance. It had become suddenly and dramatically clear how wrong he'd been. "Why didn't you tell me?"

She shrugged. "You didn't seem interested. And I suppose I assumed you would guess. None of this would be possible otherwise."

"But your debut … this isn't what you presented. Your display was …"

She arched a brow. "Weak? Uninteresting?"

"To be honest, yes. I don't understand why your family would hide an ability so … impressive."

A shadow flickered across her features, and she glanced away without answering. Evryn's eyes widened with realization. "Wait. Your family is unaware as well?"

She nodded. "Only Petunia knows."

"Why?"

Mariselle turned away slightly, her fingers idly tracing patterns in the air that left faint luminescent trails. "It's a rare manifestation. A *valuable* manifestation. And in my family, valuable things tend to become … assets. Managed. Directed. Rarely by the one to whom they belong. I suppose I wanted the chance to shape it myself first—to prove I could. To have something that was mine before they decided what it ought to be. Perhaps then, I might have some say in the direction of my future."

Evryn watched her quietly, turning her words over in his mind, each one revealing more than she perhaps intended, and yet still not quite enough.

They both looked up as a magnificent flower-shaped hot air balloon drifted overhead, its gossamer silk panels shimmering with pastel hues. Each petal displayed a living scene—children riding silver foxes, airborne dancers, and teacups floating on candyfloss waves. Music spiraled down around them as the enormous bloom began to open, its petals peeling back in elegant succession to reveal inner layers of light and glittering particles. With a luminous flourish, the flower fully unfurled, scattering stardust-like petals across the sky in a breathtaking display of color and light.

Mariselle's laughter filled the air again. "Isn't it truly spectacular?" She grasped his hand and squeezed, then let go, seemingly without noticing what she'd done. "Come, I want to show you more." She stepped away, and Evryn stared at his open hand, half expecting to see some trace of the warmth she'd left behind.

He found himself following her, drawn by her evident delight in this world of her creation. She moved with the confident grace of someone in their natural element, occasionally gesturing to bring new wonders into being

—a shower of glittering stars that fell around them before transforming into tiny singing birds, a bridge made of rainbow light that arched over a stream of flowing silver.

"We can actually do this," he said faintly, reaching out to touch one of the crystal blooms. It chimed more loudly at his touch, and the galaxy within spun faster. "Dreamland can be *real* again."

Her smile contained a trace of bemusement this time. "Of course we can. I never doubted it."

"But—wait. How are we—is the dream core not still sitting in Windsong Cottage?"

"No, I moved it back to its original position at the center of the pavilion."

He stopped. "On your own?"

"Indeed, on my own. With magic. It was heavy, yes—as were you, I'll have you know—but I managed." She placed her hands on her hips, both brows arching. "I happen to be capable of a great many things, Rowanwood."

"Yes, I'm beginning to realize that," he answered quietly

As they wandered deeper into the dreamscape, Evryn's gaze was drawn upward to where the impossible sky gave way to shifting clouds. Dark shapes moved there, undulating and coalescing like shadows of ink dropped in water.

"What might those be?" he asked, gesturing toward the roiling shadows.

Mariselle followed his gaze. "Oh. Nightmare entities, I imagine."

"Nightmare entities?" He repeated, his tone carrying distinctly more alarm than hers.

"There's no need to be concerned about them. I've constructed simple protective boundaries for now. While I've yet to perfect the art of weaving wards complex enough to permanently protect Dreamland, these modest defenses should keep such entities at bay during our brief visit."

He turned back to her. "I recall you mentioning wards while working on the dream core with your cousin. Is this a skill related to your dream architect abilities?"

"No. Dream warding constitutes its own distinct magic. You may have heard of this type of ability in relation to the production of Dream-Bright Elixir? It's an essential part of keeping nightmares at bay."

"Ah." Evryn had, of course, never paid the slightest attention to what might be contained within Dream-Bright Elixir. He angled his head then. "So you've manifested two distinct magical abilities?"

"I …" She trailed off, her expression becoming guarded, gaze drifting away from his scrutiny.

"Wait." He stepped closer, lowering his voice despite there being no one else to hear them. "More than two?"

A playful smile curved her lips as she met his eyes again. "Do you suppose I shall reveal all my secrets to you in a single night, Rowanwood?" The teasing lilt in her voice did nothing to mask the very real wall she'd erected between them.

"You're already privy to my greatest secret," he reminded her. "I could hardly share any of yours without risking you divulging mine in return."

Her expression shifted, caution giving way to consideration. "That is indeed true. Perhaps I shall consider sharing them." She glanced over her shoulder, her smile fading. "But for the present …"

The light dimmed perceptibly, as though a cloud had drifted across an unseen sun. Evryn followed her gaze and noticed with growing unease that the shadowy shapes appeared darker and somehow … closer. The music that had surrounded them since their arrival took on a discordant note, the once-pleasant melody twisting into something vaguely unsettling.

"I believe it would be best for us to return to the waking world," Mariselle said. "I can't say how long my simple wards might hold."

"Indeed," Evryn said, then looked around at the vast dreamscape stretching in all directions. "Did you build an exit into this fantastical realm?"

"If Dreamland were operating with all magical systems properly integrated and functioning, then yes, there would be an exit, and a dream guide with threshold magic—someone like Petunia—would be stationed there to escort you out. But in the absence of that particular magic, you must be asleep in order to cross the boundary between the dream realm and the waking world."

Evryn let out a humorless laugh. "I do hope you've brought additional portions of that tea you drugged me with. I find it difficult to imagine falling asleep naturally with shadows known as *nightmare entities* circling above."

Mariselle gave him a smile that was somehow both apologetic and amused. "The process is actually far simpler than that."

"What do you mean?"

"I can simply ..." She hesitated, meeting his eyes. "Induce a state of slumber."

Evryn stared at her. "And it did not occur to you to employ this method at the cottage instead of brewing tea laced with a sleeping draught?"

"Well," she said, giving him a pointed sort of look, "I did not imagine you would willingly permit me to touch you."

Her words echoed with unintended weight, and Evryn was aware of a flush creeping up his neck. He cleared his throat. "In that case, yes, I suppose the sleeping draught made more sense."

"But now there is no other way, so ..." She lowered herself to the ground and sat cross-legged before reaching tentatively toward him, the patterns on her hand glimmering faintly. "May I?"

Evryn hesitated, then sat across from her and took her hand. The contact was innocent enough, but the markings seemed to pulse with warmth where they aligned, as though recognizing each other. Evryn felt a peculiar tingling sensation spreading up his arm, across his chest, and finally enveloping his mind in a gentle, insistent fog.

"Is this another dream-magic related ability?" he managed to ask, his words already beginning to slur as his eyelids grew heavy.

She gave a small nod. "Indeed it is. My father's cousin possesses this particular type of magic." She hesitated, then added, "It appears I've manifested quite the collection of dream-related abilities."

The world began to blur around the edges, colors bleeding into one another, the music fading to a distant hum. Evryn felt himself swaying.

"You have proven," he murmured as darkness began to claim the edges of his vision, "to be entirely unlike what I had always presumed to know about you."

And then he tumbled into the depths of sleep.

Chapter Nineteen

THE BRIDGEMERE HOUSE grand salon hummed with conversation and the occasional burst of laughter, all illuminated by the soft glow of crystal orbs hovering near the ornately carved ceiling. Mariselle stood near a refreshment table, absently adjusting her sheer lace gloves and enjoying the distance from her family, who had occupied themselves elsewhere in the room. The evening's musicale had drawn quite the assembly of Bloomhaven's elite, all eager to witness the newly renovated music room and the magical instruments the Bridgemeres had commissioned at considerable expense.

Her thoughts, however, remained firmly anchored in the impossible landscape she had crafted the night before. The memory of Dreamland—of standing within her own creation as it flourished around her—still sent shivers of delight cascading through her whenever she recalled it. Even now, as she nodded politely to Lady Fawnwood's elaborate description of her daughter's latest magical accomplishment, Mariselle's mind kept drifting back to cotton candy skies and stained-glass butterflies.

"Ah, there she is—my glitter-dusted bonbon!" a familiar voice called, interrupting her reverie.

Mariselle turned to find Evryn approaching, his sister Aurelise at his side. An unexpected flutter stirred in her chest at the sight of him—so different now from how she'd left him in the early hours of this morning, slumped in peaceful oblivion on the sofa at Windsong Cottage.

She'd exhausted her remaining magic transporting his sleeping form out of Dreamland and across the ruins, and perhaps had lingered a moment longer than propriety allowed, studying him in unguarded repose. Without his perpetual mask of rakish nonchalance, his features had softened, lips parted, dark lashes resting against his cheeks as his eyes moved in dreams. This was not the Evryn Rowanwood she thought she'd always known.

She'd been struck by the same realization when stealing glances at him earlier that night at the window seat, quill moving across parchment with focused intensity. There was a depth to Evryn Rowanwood that he deliberately concealed from the world.

She had wondered then, standing there while he slept, what dreams occupied his sleeping mind. If she'd listened closely, she would have heard the whispers.

But she'd left before that could happen.

And now here he was, theatrical facade firmly back in place, all practiced charm and exaggerated gallantry. Glitter-dusted bonbon indeed. His latest ridiculous pet name was no doubt a reference to the gown she'd chosen this evening—a glittering creation of twilight amethyst silk and subtle pink detailing that caught the light with every movement—though she preferred to think of it as a reference to the colors of her fantastical Dreamland outfit rather than a sugary confection.

"My beloved velvet-voiced vexation," she greeted, extending her hand to him.

Evryn blinked once. Then—slowly, deliberately—arched a single brow, the corner of his mouth curling in what could only be described as a dangerous smile. "Oh," he said softly as he captured her fingers and bowed low over her hand. "We're playing along now, are we?" He brushed a kiss over her hand, where the glimmering soulbond mark was faintly visible through the sheer fabric of her glove.

"Of course," she said sweetly. "It's only fair I begin addressing you with the reverence you so clearly believe you deserve, my well-dressed pest."

An unguarded snort of laughter escaped Evryn as he straightened, his eyes darting to hers and his fingers tightening briefly around her hand. But he composed himself quickly, smoothing his expression into one of polished charm.

"In that case, I should inform you that you look particularly enchanting tonight, my ravishing orchestrator of chaos and corsetry."

Mariselle pressed her lips together but failed to hide her amusement at the increasingly ridiculous endearments. "I'm writing that last one down."

"I'll inscribe it on your calling card, if you like."

A giggle tugged Mariselle's attention sideways, and she was reminded of Aurelise's presence. The younger girl watched Mariselle and Evryn's exchange with puzzled interest, as though she couldn't fathom this particular type of affection.

"Miss Aurelise," Mariselle said warmly, turning toward her. "How lovely to see you this evening."

Aurelise dipped into a graceful curtsy, though her fingers nervously twisted the fabric of her gown. "Good evening, Lady Mariselle."

"I understand you'll be performing tonight?" Mariselle said.

Aurelise's eyes widened in what looked suspiciously like panic. "Yes. The Bridgemeres extended the invitation, and Mother insisted. She believes my abilities are sufficient for such an occasion, and I'm truly honored to have been asked. Though I confess, I'm rather anxious about the performance. I can't help but worry about disappointing such distinguished company and embarrassing my family."

"You'll be magnificent," Mariselle assured her, reaching for Aurelise's hand and giving it a small squeeze. "Your family has nothing but praise for your abilities."

"And you needn't worry about impressing everyone," Evryn told her, his tone gentler than Mariselle typically heard him use with anyone else. "Simply play as you do at home, when you believe no one is listening."

Mariselle observed this softer version of Evryn with quiet fascination, remembering the comments his mother had made during tea at Rowanwood House.

My most sensitive child. Remarkably attentive to his siblings' needs.

Evryn had clearly found the comments exceedingly embarrassing, but Mariselle was beginning to see the truth of them now. The discovery was both unsettling and strangely satisfying—like finding an unexpected piece that completed a puzzle she hadn't realized was unfinished.

"Thank you, brother," Aurelise murmured, giving Evryn a grateful smile.

From across the room, Mariselle spotted Rosavyn engaged in animated conversation with Kazrian and their mother. "I should rejoin them," Aurelise said, noticing Mariselle's gaze. "She only permitted Kazrian and me to attend because she promised Lady Bridgemere we would both be on our absolute best behavior."

"And because she's convinced your magical manifestation could occur any day now and that it will be something music-related," Evryn added. "She believes exposure to accomplished musicians can only nurture your latent abilities." His voice softened further, meant for his sister's ears alone. "Though I did remind her that constantly watching for signs puts unnecessary pressure on you. Your magic will reveal itself when it's ready, not when it's convenient for Mother's social calendar."

Aurelise flushed slightly. "It's nothing so exciting as all that. I have no notion of what sort of magic I might manifest. I simply enjoy playing, that's all."

"Of course," Mariselle agreed smoothly, recognizing the girl's discomfort. "Though from what I've been told, your talent speaks for itself, magical or otherwise."

After Aurelise departed to rejoin her family, Evryn offered Mariselle his arm. "Shall we mingle, my honey-glazed orchid? Or would you prefer to scandalize society by sharing a private waltz on the terrace where anyone might glimpse us beneath the moonlight, quite unaccompanied and therefore deliciously improper?"

"That does sound like delightful fun." Mariselle accepted his arm, aware of several pairs of eyes tracking their movement.

As they made their way through the crowded salon, Mariselle caught fragments of conversation. Gossip about an ill-considered match, speculation about who might be invited to Lady Rivenna's Annual Tea Leaf Reading, and of course, whispers about Mariselle's still-shocking blue hair.

"—unintentional, so I've heard—"

"—something to do with the overzealous affections of her betrothed?"

"—quite becoming, in its way, though one wonders what her mother—"

"Have you recovered yet from your first trip into Dreamland?" she asked in a low tone, turning her attention away from the gossip.

"Dreamland, perhaps. Seeing you in that theatrically scandalous outfit— now that I may never recover from."

A burst of laughter surprised her, even as she felt her face flush. It had seemed entirely natural, once she was inside Dreamland, to transform her ordinary garments into the spectacularly flamboyant carnival-like attire she'd only ever imagined. But out here, in the waking realm, she was mildly horrified to discover she'd been so swept up in the moment that she'd revealed that part to Evryn.

"It was magnificent," he said, his voice pitched low, genuine. "All of it. Every single moment."

She stopped and looked up at him. "Do you—"

"Lady Mariselle!" a shrill voice called out, startling her. She looked around and found Lady Locklear approaching, her daughter Cordelina trailing behind. "I simply must hear about your experience at the Blackbriar garden party last week. I heard the most fascinating gossip regarding their son's abrupt and unexpected return to Bloomhaven that very morning."

"I'm afraid I observed nothing particularly noteworthy," Mariselle replied smoothly.

This was not entirely true. Lord Hadrian Blackbriar had indeed made quite the entrance, but Mariselle had been too absorbed in memorizing a particular enchantment for Dreamland's dream core to pay much attention. Besides, she had no intention of feeding Bloomhaven's insatiable appetite for gossip, especially when she herself had become one of its favorite courses.

"Really?" Lady Locklear's expression fell. "How disappointing."

"Indeed," Mariselle agreed, eager to change the subject. She caught sight of Cordelina sending furtive glances toward Kazrian, who appeared oblivious to her attention. "Your daughter looks lovely this evening, Lady Locklear."

The older woman immediately brightened. "Yes, doesn't she? The shade was specially enchanted to complement her coloring."

As Lady Locklear launched into an extensive monologue about the gown's creation, Mariselle felt Evryn's hand settle at the small of her back, a gesture that would appear affectionate to observers. The warmth of his palm radiated through the fabric of her gown, steadying and somehow intimate despite its theatrical purpose. All part of their charade, of course, but Mariselle found herself gravitating toward that warmth, her body shifting subtly into his touch like a flower seeking sunlight.

She would have to be careful not to act this way at tomorrow night's birthday dinner. Such casual intimacy would be unthinkable. Her parents might reluctantly tolerate this engagement for appearances—and for whatever secrets they hoped she might extract from the Rowanwoods—but they would not stand for this sort of impropriety in their own home. It would likely push them over the edge, causing them to do everything in their power to break the 'soulbond' immediately.

The mere thought of the impending family dinner sent a cold ripple of apprehension through her, dulling the pleasant warmth of Evryn's touch. Though at least her grandmother would be present tomorrow night to stand like an immovable wall between her and her parents. Mariselle's gaze swept across the crowded salon, instinctively searching for the familiar stern profiles of her parents. Even now, they might be watching.

Finding no sign of them among the guests, she allowed herself a small exhalation of relief and angled herself a little more toward Evryn. He leaned close, his breath tickling her ear as he murmured, "I believe we're being summoned to the music room." He nodded toward Lady Bridgemere, who was gesturing elegantly for her guests to proceed through the adjoining doors.

"Oh thank the stars," Mariselle whispered back, relieved at the timely interruption. "If I had to hear one more word about the precise shade of seafoam green …"

"My sincerest apologies, Lady Locklear," Evryn interrupted with a charming smile, "but I'm afraid I must steal my fiancée away. Lady Bridgemere is beckoning us to the music room."

"Of course, of course," Lady Locklear simpered, casting a speculative glance between them. "You two are simply inseparable these days, aren't you? Such a dramatic change from your previous interactions."

"Dramatic indeed," Evryn replied, his smile never wavering. "Never a dull moment when a Brightcrest and a Rowanwood are in the same room."

Mariselle allowed him to guide her away, aware of his hand still resting against her back. "That woman is determined to extract some scandalous tidbit from us," she muttered once they were out of earshot.

"The entire Bloom Season runs on scandal and speculation," Evryn replied dryly. "Without it, I suspect half of Bloomhaven would expire from sheer boredom."

The Bridgemeres' music room proved to be a marvel of magical acoustics.

The domed ceiling was inlaid with intricate patterns that caught and amplified sound waves—if one were to believe Lady Bridgemere's effusive dissertation on the subject, delivered with the passionate intensity of someone who had personally invented sound itself—while the walls were paneled in rare imported resonance wood. Cushioned settees, elegant armchairs, and small clusters of stools had been arranged to provide optimal viewing of the raised performance area, where a magnificent piano crafted from pale luminescent wood took center stage.

Evryn guided Mariselle toward a pair of armchairs positioned to one side of the room. The space gradually filled with Bloomhaven's elite, the low hum of conversation creating a pleasant backdrop as everyone settled into their seats. Mariselle caught sight of several matrons casting curious glances in their direction, their heads bent together in whispered conversation.

"We remain the subject of considerable speculation," she observed.

"Would you expect anything less?" Evryn asked, his expression amused. "I expect our 'soulbond' shall provide fodder for gossip for years to come."

"Months," Mariselle corrected, keeping her voice low. "Once we've completed our project, we can announce the dissolving of our engagement."

Something flickered across Evryn's features—too quickly for her to interpret—before his usual mask of casual charm returned. "Of course. How could I forget our temporary arrangement?"

Before she could respond, Lady Bridgemere stepped onto the raised platform. "Honored guests," she began, "welcome to our humble home. Tonight, we are delighted to share our newly renovated music room and the exceptional talents of several distinguished performers."

The first few performances proved pleasant if unremarkable. A young lord performed a competent but uninspired rendition of a popular ballad on the celestial stringed bow, followed by twin sisters whose harmonized singing was technically accurate but lacked genuine emotion. Then came one of the younger Bridgemere sons, whose violin playing was so painfully off-key that Mariselle had to press her lips together firmly to suppress her reaction.

She felt rather than saw Evryn's shoulders shaking with silent laughter beside her. When she dared a glance in his direction, she found him studiously examining the floor, though the corners of his mouth twitched tellingly.

"Stop it," she whispered, fighting her own amusement. "It's dreadfully impolite."

"I'm merely appreciating his … unique interpretation," Evryn whispered back, still not looking at her.

"His unique attempt to murder that poor composition, you mean."

A snort of laughter escaped him, quickly disguised as a cough. Several heads turned in their direction, and Mariselle adopted an expression of concerned attention as she patted Evryn's arm solicitously.

"Perhaps some water, my love?" she suggested, loud enough to be overheard.

"I'll be fine, my precious pearl," he replied, matching her volume. "Simply overcome by the moving performance."

When the Bridgemere boy finally concluded his assault on musical sensibilities, Mariselle joined in the polite applause with perhaps more enthusiasm than warranted, relieved the ordeal had ended.

Evryn leaned in until his lips nearly brushed her ear. "I'm beginning to think we should reconsider Aurelise's participation tonight. Far from beneficial exposure, this display might actively corrupt her musical sensibilities."

A quiet laugh bubbled up from Mariselle's throat before she could contain it as she inclined her head in agreement. In that moment of conspiracy, she almost forgot they were meant to be pretending.

A subtle shift in the atmosphere drew her attention toward the entrance, where a ripple of whispers and movement indicated the arrival of someone significant. Mariselle turned to look, her breath catching slightly as she recognized the newcomers—the High Lady herself, accompanied by Prince Ryden.

She moved through the room with effortless grace, acknowledging greetings with regal nods as she made her way toward the seat that had evidently been reserved for her near the front. Her son followed in her wake, his posture relaxed yet somehow still managing to convey the proper deference to his mother's position.

"I wouldn't have thought the High Lady would be interested in attending a private musicale," Marisela said under her breath.

"Nor I," Evryn replied. "Though it's clear she was invited, and I supposed she does occasionally grace certain events with her presence if she finds them of interest."

As the High Lady seated herself, Ryden continued a few steps further, coming to a halt beside Evryn's chair.

"Rowanwood," he greeted quietly, his tone casual. "Mind if I join you?"

"Your Highness," Evryn replied with a slight nod. "Not at all."

The prince dropped into the empty chair on Evryn's other side, stretching out his long legs with a sigh. "Mother insisted I accompany her tonight," he explained in a low voice. "Apparently, my continued absence from 'appropriate social engagements' has become concerning."

"How fortunate for us all," Evryn remarked.

"Lady Brightcrest," the prince acknowledged, leaning forward slightly to catch her eye. "You're looking well. The blue hair is an interesting choice. I approve, of course." He gestured to his own midnight-toned hair.

"Thank you, Your Highness. It's a cleverly disguised enchantment that reduces wind resistance during high-speed flight," she added without missing a beat. "I look forward to putting it to use during our next race."

"Ah, yes, we've missed your presence in our nocturnal adventures," Ryden said with a roguish grin. "Particularly the delightful spectacle of Rowanwood's wounded pride whenever you best him."

"It was only three times," Evryn muttered. "Hardly worth mentioning."

"Four," Mariselle corrected sweetly. "And once the whirlwind of wedding preparations subsides, I intend to make it five. Savor your temporary reprieve, gentlemen."

Lady Bridgemere had returned to the platform, hands clasped dramatically at her breast as she gushed about the unprecedented honor of the High Lady's attendance. Mariselle settled back in her chair, half listening as the conversation between Evryn and the prince continued in hushed tones beside her.

"Speaking of wedding preparations," Ryden continued, "are they progressing to your satisfaction? Mother keeps asking for details, as if I'm somehow privy to your intimate affairs."

"Everything is proceeding splendidly," Evryn replied.

Ryden leaned back in his chair with a sigh. "Count yourself fortunate, then. At least you no longer have to concern yourself with finding a wife."

"Still being pressured to make a match?" Evryn asked quietly as movement on the other side of the room signaled the next musician was coming forward.

"Increasingly so," Ryden replied, his voice dropping to a murmur. "Mother has hinted that this may be my last Season of freedom before she presents me with an ultimatum. 'Choose someone suitable, or I shall choose for you,' I imagine she'll say."

There was genuine frustration in his voice, his mask of irreverence slipping in the presence of his close friend. Mariselle's gaze slid back to him with curiosity just as he tilted his head and added, "Is that your sister, Rowanwood?"

Mariselle faced forward as Aurelise stepped onto the platform, her hands clasped tightly before her as she approached the magnificent piano.

"Our next performer," Lady Bridgemere announced, "is Miss Aurelise Rowanwood, whose musical gifts have been the delight of private gatherings for some time. Tonight, we are honored that she has agreed to share her talent with us."

A polite smattering of applause followed as Aurelise seated herself at the piano, her back straight, her shoulders tense. Mariselle caught the slight tremor in her hands as she positioned them above the keys, hesitating a moment too long. Just as the silence began to stretch uncomfortably, Aurelise closed her eyes, took a deep breath, and began to play. The first notes were hesitant, almost tentative, and for a moment Mariselle feared she might falter.

But then, as if some internal threshold had been crossed, Aurelise's entire demeanor transformed. Her shoulders relaxed, her expression softened, and her fingers began to move across the keys with fluid grace. The melody that emerged was hauntingly beautiful—complex and layered in a way that suggested far more experience than a girl of seventeen should possess.

As the music swelled, Mariselle became aware of a subtle shimmer in the air around Aurelise, like heat rising from sun-warmed stone. She watched, captivated, the music washing over her in waves that seemed to resonate with something deep within her own magic. There was power here, nascent but undeniable.

She glanced at Lady Lelianna across the room and recognized the look of pride on the woman's face—and was struck by a deep and profound sense of sadness. Even if her own mother had known the full extent of Mariselle's abilities, Lady Clemenbell's eyes would never have held that fierce maternal pride.

A slight movement drew Mariselle's attention, and she refocused on Evryn and Ryden. The latter was leaning forward slightly in his seat, his usual mask of casual indifference completely absent. Gone was the affected boredom, the deliberate nonchalance, the studied disregard for propriety. In their place was raw, unguarded appreciation, a vulnerability she suspected few had ever glimpsed.

She smiled to herself as she turned her gaze back to the subtle shimmer dancing in the air around Aurelise. It seemed they were all affected by the enchantment of her magic.

The final notes of the piece lingered in the air, sustained by the room's magical acoustics before slowly fading into silence. For a moment, no one moved or spoke, the entire assembly held in thrall by what they had witnessed. Then applause erupted, more enthusiastic than for any previous performer.

Aurelise opened her eyes, looking momentarily startled to find herself before an audience. A shy smile curved her lips as she rose and curtseyed deeply, her cheeks flushed with pleasure.

"She's extraordinary," Mariselle said as the applause died down, leaning closer to Evryn, her hand on his arm.

"Isn't she?" he answered, pride evident in his voice as he reached over and placed his hand on hers. He squeezed lightly and then left his hand there, in a way that seemed entirely natural.

Or at least, it had felt entirely natural—until she noticed it. And then, quite suddenly, it was all she could notice. The gentle pressure of his palm against hers, the warmth of it seeping through her glove, the slow, absent-minded path his thumb traced across her skin. Was it intentional? Was someone watching? Was this still part of the performance? The questions tangled with a rush of sensation that made it difficult to think, to be anything other than acutely aware of him.

It was maddening. This was entirely unnecessary to their performance. She really should move her hand. But instead, she left it precisely where it was and forced her attention back to the stage as the next musician took his place.

She drew a measured breath, schooling her features into polite interest as the opening notes of the next piece filled the room. This peculiar flutter in her chest was nothing more than the discomfort of prolonged contact with a

Rowanwood. A perfectly natural aversion, heightened by the artifice of their charade. That was all. It would fade, just as the silver mark binding them would fade once they had fulfilled the terms of the contract.

She simply needed to remember what truly mattered: Dreamland, her family's legacy, and finally earning the love and recognition she had craved for so long.

Chapter Twenty

THE BRIGHTCREST DINING ROOM WAS A STUDY IN COLD ELEGANCE, ALL sharp angles and glacial perfection, much like the family who occupied it. Evryn sat amid the splendor, acutely aware that he was witnessing what might well be the most uncomfortable dinner in all of fae history.

The contrast to the previous evening was jarring, like stepping from sunlight directly into shadow. The atmosphere the night before had become remarkably—and unintentionally—intimate, with the warm lighting of the chamber, the beauty of the music, and the inexplicable fact that Evryn's hand had somehow ended up resting upon Mariselle's. By the time he'd become aware of it, his thumb was already tracing patterns across her gloved skin, and removing his hand would have only called more attention to its placement. So he had left it there, and Mariselle hadn't pulled away, not seeming to mind. If anything, she'd leaned in closer as the evening progressed.

But now, the Mariselle sitting across the dining table from him seemed an entirely different person—remote and untouchable, meeting his gaze only briefly and with cool detachment, as though the previous night's closeness had never occurred.

What a contradiction she was.

For the past few nights, since stepping into Dreamland for the first time, Evryn had begun attempting to decode the puzzle that was Mariselle Brightcrest. Ink flowed across his notebook as he'd scribbled late into the night, documenting his observations since the start of the Season. Eventually, a portrait had begun to emerge on the page that bore little resemblance to the cold rival he'd believed he knew.

He'd written of her at the art auction, that fleeting moment when he'd seen her reach for her sister's arm with what appeared to be an instinctive need for connection, only to be rudely rebuffed. He'd noted her hushed conversation with Iris, in which—according to what he'd heard later from Jasvian—Mariselle had actually apologized for whatever had occurred in the Thornhart maze last Season.

His quill had traced the gradual softening of her demeanor during tea at Rowanwood House, how her shoulders had lowered by increments, her laughter becoming bolder, as though she'd momentarily forgotten the enmity between their families. Even more telling had been his account of her with Petunia, the easy, unguarded affection between cousins, their interactions unmarred by calculation or restraint.

But nothing had flowed from his quill with such vivid detail as her transformation in Dreamland—that moment of pure, unabashed joy as she'd twirled beneath an impossible sky, her laughter as bright and uncomplicated as a child's.

He'd reviewed these writings, searching for any evidence of the haughty Brightcrest ice princess. Instead, his observations had revealed someone completely different. Someone with unexpected depths, hidden vulnerabilities, and a warmth he never imagined she possessed.

But here was the ice princess now, across from him at the Brightcrest family table, encased once more in that flawless armor of frigid propriety. Straight-backed and distant, her expression a masterpiece of detached politeness, she was every inch the Mariselle he'd thought he'd known—the one his writings had so thoroughly contradicted.

Evryn grabbed his glass of amberberry wine and swirled it. The evening stretched ahead like an endless path of slippery ice, and he found himself missing the warmth of Dreamland's cotton-candy skies and Mariselle's genuine smile.

His arrival earlier had been an exquisite exercise in barely concealed hostility. Each Brightcrest had greeted him with the precise minimum of courtesy required, their smiles never reaching eyes that scrutinized him with the cold calculation of appraisers assessing damaged goods.

Lord Brightcrest's handshake had been just firm enough to avoid insult while communicating volumes of distaste, while Lady Clemenbell's curtsy was so shallow it bordered on impertinence, and Mariselle's sister Ellowa hadn't bothered to disguise her contempt at all. Only Mariselle's cousin Petunia had offered anything resembling genuine warmth—a fleeting, sympathetic glance that spoke of her own outsider status within this glacial dynasty.

As the evening progressed and wine flowed more freely, their hostility had crystallized into a practiced performance. A carefully choreographed dance of praise for some and indifference toward others.

"Tell me, Ellowa," Lord Brightcrest said, his voice carrying across the table, "how progresses your enchanted embroidery for the High Lady's Solstice exhibition? Mistress Moonleaf mentioned your silverthread technique was quite revolutionary."

Ellowa preened, setting down her fork with deliberate grace. "Quite well, Father. The Royal Artisans Guild has requested I demonstrate my method at their next gathering, once the Bloom Season is over."

"As we expected," Lady Clemenbell nodded, her smile beatific. "Your artistic sensibilities have always been impeccable."

Evryn took another sip of wine, his gaze drifting briefly to Mariselle. Not a single word of acknowledgment had been directed her way. She cut her food with precision, each movement displaying flawless etiquette, her expression unchanged as though she'd long ago grown accustomed to being rendered invisible at her own family table.

He wondered what they might say if they knew of some of her more unorthodox accomplishments. "Outperforms even the most skilled riders atop a pegasus," he imagined Lord Brightcrest announcing with grudging pride. "Can dash at top speed through moonlit forests with the grace and swiftness of a woodland spirit," Lady Clemenbell might add, perhaps while dabbing away a tear of maternal joy. "Possesses the delicate touch of a master thief, having liberated manuscripts from beneath a writer's nose without detection," Ellowa could declare with a hint of admiration.

My little blue-haired thief, Evryn thought, the phrase floated unbidden through his mind. He smiled into his wine glass. That was one he hadn't used before. It suited her, though—this woman who had somehow stolen into his thoughts with the same stealth she'd employed in borrowing his writings.

And her laugh—stars, her laugh in Dreamland. He'd been completely mesmerized by it, that sound of pure, unrestrained joy. It was quite possibly the best laugh that had ever existed, bold and genuine in a way that made everything else fade into insignificance.

He glanced up and found Mariselle watching him with a slight furrow between her brows, most likely questioning why he was smiling at whatever inane thing her parents had just said.

He cleared his throat and wiped his expression clean. "Lord Dawndale," he ventured, turning to Petunia's father, "I understand your trading house has developed new protective containers for transporting delicate magical artifacts. Are these innovations applicable to other sensitive cargo?"

Lord Dawndale barely glanced up from his plate. "Possibly," he replied, the single word hanging in the air for a moment before he returned his attention to his meal, effectively closing the conversation before it had begun.

An awkward silence descended, broken only by the delicate clink of silverware against fine porcelain.

"Oh!" Lady Dawndale exclaimed suddenly, as though remembering a particularly vexing thought. "You simply cannot imagine the nightmare we're enduring next door. An absolute infestation of gossip birds has taken up residence in our garden. Wretched creatures, squawking the most inappropriate observations at all hours."

"They're merely repeating what they hear, Mother," Petunia interjected mildly.

"That's precisely the problem," Lady Dawndale huffed. "I had every intention of mixing a proper deterrent potion to be rid of them, but Petunia" —she cast an exasperated glance at her daughter—"actually advocated for the pests. Said they add 'character' to the garden, of all things!"

Evryn suppressed a smile. What an entertaining turn of events. He'd overheard Petunia complaining about those 'feathered menaces' outside her window while working on the dream core with Mariselle, and now she was protecting the darned things. But of course she was. Mariselle's dry-witted cousin would naturally find kinship with those feathered truth-tellers, both of them refusing to soften reality with comfortable lies. In a family that traded in veiled insults and pristine facades, both Petunia and the birds were unwelcome disruptors of the carefully maintained illusion.

"Speaking of gossip and its circulation," Lady Brightcrest said, her tone deceptively light as she turned her gaze toward Evryn. "Your grandmother's tea house has quite mastered the art, hasn't it? Fascinating how information flows so efficiently through certain channels. The Charmed Leaf has become quite the sensation over the years. One wonders what … special methods the Rowanwoods might employ to achieve such remarkable popularity."

"Mother," Mariselle murmured, the warning clear in her tone.

"It's merely conversation, dear," Lady Brightcrest replied without looking at her daughter. "Surely Lord Rowanwood doesn't mind sharing a few trade secrets with his future family?"

"If there are any trade secrets to share, Lady Brightcrest, I fear I am woefully uninformed of them," Evryn replied politely.

"Ah, I see." Lady Brightcrest returned to her meal with evident displeasure, neatly slicing her asparagus spears into precise sections.

Evryn pressed his lips together, recalling Mariselle's comment about stringy green stalks tasting of bitter disappointment. Now was not the appropriate time to laugh out loud.

"I must say, Lord Rowanwood," Lady Brightcrest continued after chewing thoughtfully on a sliver of asparagus, "you've been most tolerant of our daughter's limitations." Her smile was brittle as she gestured toward Mariselle with her fork. "Not every gentleman would be so understanding."

Evryn had to pause for a moment in his attempt to mask his incredulity. Was Mariselle's own mother truly speaking of her this way? "Tolerant is hardly the word I would choose, Lady Brightcrest," he replied.

"Oh?" Lord Brightcrest's eyebrow arched. "What word would you choose, then?"

Confused. Fascinated. Increasingly enchanted. None of which he could admit out loud. "Fortunate," he said instead, reaching for his wine glass once more. "Exceedingly fortunate that the soulbond chose the two of us."

Across the table, Mariselle's fork paused halfway to her lips, her eyes flicking up to meet his for the briefest moment before returning to her plate.

"How diplomatic," drawled Ellowa, twirling her wine glass between slender fingers. "Though I wonder if you'll feel the same once you've spent a winter with her. Mari does tend to grow rather tedious with prolonged exposure."

Petunia, seated beside Mariselle, set her knife down with slightly more force than necessary.

"I'm sure Lord Rowanwood has already discovered Mariselle's shortcomings," Lady Brightcrest added, as if discussing the weather rather than eviscerating her daughter's character before company. "She was never quite as quick to master the social graces as Ellowa. We've tried, of course, but one must accept that some plants simply won't flourish no matter how carefully tended."

"Mother," Mariselle said, lowering her fork and directing a polished smile at Lady Brightcrest, "perhaps we might discuss something else? I've been meaning to enquire about the plans for—"

"Of course not, dear," Lady Brightcrest interrupted. "Lord Rowanwood is to be your husband. He ought to know precisely what he's getting."

The silence that followed Lady Brightcrest's pronouncement stretched like a taut wire. Evryn's grip tightened on his wine glass as he absorbed the casual cruelty of her words. Around the table, the other family members seemed perfectly content with this assessment, as though discussing Mariselle's perceived deficiencies was nothing out of the ordinary.

"Indeed," Lord Brightcrest added, dabbing at his mouth with a pristine napkin. "We do apologize, Lord Rowanwood, for the rather unfortunate circumstances. Had the soulbond not appeared, I'm certain your affections would have naturally gravitated toward someone more suitable."

Ellowa's laugh tinkled. "Poor Mari. At least the soulbond ensures you won't have a choice in the matter, Lord Rowanwood. Otherwise, I fear she'd have remained quite permanently unattached."

Evryn glanced at Petunia as something cold settled in his chest. Petunia's knuckles had gone white around her fork, though she kept her gaze fixed resolutely on her plate. Even she, who clearly cared for Mariselle, remained silent in the face of this systematic dismantling.

"Of course, we've done our best with her," Lady Clemenbell continued, gesturing toward Mariselle as though she were an unsatisfactory piece of furniture. "But some deficiencies simply cannot be corrected through proper guidance. Her artistic pursuits, for instance. Hardly the sort of accomplishments that benefit a family of our standing."

Hardly the sort of—Evryn almost blurted out that she'd created an entire wonderland from nothing but her imagination. But that was Mariselle's secret to reveal, not his.

Across the table, he watched as her lips pressed into a thin line and she inhaled deeply through her nose. Her eyes took on a glassy quality as she stared through her plate rather than at it, retreating somewhere deep within herself.

Lord Dawndale cleared his throat diplomatically. "Perhaps we might speak of more pleasant matters? The weather has been quite—"

"Nonsense," Lady Clemenbell waved him off. "Lord Rowanwood is to be family. Better he understand precisely what sort of burden the soulbond has saddled him with. At least he'll be aware of how low to keep his expectations."

The remark struck Evryn with the force of a clenched fist wrapped in silk. This wasn't merely family teasing or gentle correction. This was an artfully delivered gutting, wrapped in the veneer of parental concern. And Mariselle didn't flinch. She merely sat there, spine straight, like someone who knew better than to bleed where her parents could see.

And all of a sudden, there it was. The truth presenting itself plainly for the first time: The mask Evryn had mistaken for years as Brightcrest arrogance was in fact a shield, painstakingly crafted to deflect the constant barrage of familial disappointment. She hadn't built walls to keep others out, but to keep herself intact within the very place that should have nurtured her.

"Well," Lady Brightcrest continued airily, "at least she's learned not to argue when corrected. That's some improvement, I suppose."

"A blessing indeed," Lord Brightcrest agreed. "Nothing quite so unattractive as a woman who cannot accept criticism gracefully."

Something inside Evryn snapped.

"I'm afraid I must disagree," he said, his voice cutting through the conversation.

The table fell silent. Every eye turned to him, and he could feel the sudden tension crackling in the air.

"I beg your pardon?" Lady Brightcrest's eyebrows rose in delicate surprise.

Evryn set down his wine glass with deliberate care and leaned back in his chair, his gaze sweeping the assembled faces before settling on Mariselle's parents. "I said I disagree. With your assessment of Lady Mariselle. And I feel compelled to correct what appears to be a fundamental misunderstanding."

Lord Brightcrest's brow drew lower. "I assure you, Lord Rowanwood, there is no misunderstanding. We are merely being forthright about our daughter's limitations and—"

"With all due respect, Lord Brightcrest," Evryn continued, his tone remaining pleasant even as his eyes hardened, "there is indeed a grave misunderstanding if you believe that I consider myself in any way tolerant of Lady Mariselle's 'limitations,' as you put it. One cannot tolerate that which does not exist."

Lord Brightcrest blinked. "I beg your pardon?"

"What I mean to say," Evryn elaborated, "is that Lady Mariselle possesses no limitations of which I am aware. Quite the contrary."

He turned to meet Mariselle's wide-eyed gaze directly.

"In my observation, Lady Mariselle possesses an intellect that is nothing short of extraordinary and quite possibly one of the most vibrant imaginations I've ever encountered. And beneath her carefully maintained reserve lies a remarkable warmth and optimism that is nothing short of magnetic. I find myself captivated by the genuine light she carries within her, carefully hidden though it may be from those who don't care enough to look."

A hushed stillness fell over the table as he continued, his voice gathering quiet strength.

"Beyond these traits, she has shown herself to be possessed of remarkably sharp wit and resourcefulness. She observes and understands the subtleties of social dynamics with a perception I've rarely encountered." A pointed glance around the table. "A skill I imagine has been honed through considerable practice."

Lady Brightcrest's mouth had thinned to a tight line.

"As for her magical capabilities," Evryn continued, warming to his subject, "I can only assume that if she has ever appeared anything less than exceptional, it was by deliberate choice rather than any inherent deficiency."

Mariselle's face had gone perfectly still, her eyes never leaving his.

"I am continually impressed by her creativity and her determination in the face of discouragement. She is, without a doubt, the best thing the Brightcrest family has ever produced—though clearly by happy accident rather than through any nurturing influence from her family—far superior to anyone or anything else in this room."

A fork clattered against fine porcelain. Ellowa's mouth had fallen open.

"And I," Evryn concluded, holding Mariselle's gaze across the table, "am singularly privileged to soon call her my wife."

Complete silence reigned. Evryn could hear the crystal chandelier tinkling overhead as a breeze drifted through the open terrace doors.

Mariselle's face, previously so disciplined and controlled, now betrayed a storm of emotion. Her lips parted slightly, her breath coming in quick, shallow intervals. Her facade—that perfect, polished mask of composure—had fractured, revealing something raw and vulnerable beneath. And in her gaze, as it held his with an intensity that seemed to strip away all pretense between them, Evryn saw a question burning so fiercely it almost spoke aloud: Did he truly mean those words, or was this merely another performance?

"Well," Lord Dawndale said, breaking the uncomfortable silence with forced joviality, "it appears the soulbond has had quite the effect on young Rowanwood. Most … passionate."

The conversation awkwardly resumed, though the atmosphere remained charged. Evryn noticed how Lord and Lady Brightcrest exchanged terse glances, how Ellowa stabbed at her food with renewed vigor, and how Mariselle seemed unable to look directly at him, her cheeks flushed.

After the main courses had been cleared, a footman approached and murmured something to Lady Brightcrest, who brightened immediately.

"Ah, excellent," she declared. "The Starlace Soufflé will soon be served. We shall take dessert on the terrace."

As the party rose and began to migrate toward the open doors, Evryn found himself falling into step beside Petunia. "Starlace Soufflé?" he inquired quietly. "Is that a Brightcrest specialty?"

Petunia gave him a sideways glance, her expression sardonic. "It's an enchanted dessert," she explained in low tones. "Rather showy—rises only when it's exposed to cool starlight. Traditionally served outdoors because the warmth of the faelights makes it wilt like an offended debutante."

"Ah." Evryn nodded. "A birthday tradition for Lady Mariselle, I take it?"

Petunia's lips quirked. "It's Ellowa's favorite, actually. Mariselle prefers simple blushberry tart. But I don't believe anyone bothered to ask her preference."

Of course they hadn't. Evryn suppressed a surge of indignation as they stepped onto the balcony, where servants were arranging chairs in a semicircle, facing outward toward the gardens.

The family spread out around the edges of the terrace, and Evryn found himself awkwardly positioned beside Lord Brightcrest and Lord Dawndale, who were discussing the art auction from two weeks prior and expressing their mutual horror at the exorbitant sum bid for "that shockingly improper sculpture of the nearly nude fae warrior." He shifted discreetly to one side, increasing the distance between himself and the two men. Though he doubted they would make an attempt to draw him into their conversation.

Looking around, he spotted Mariselle approaching her mother, who was directing one of the servants to reposition several chairs to her satisfaction. Mariselle leaned close to ask Lady Brightcrest something, her hand resting on her mother's arm. Lady Brightcrest flinched and twisted just enough to dislodge her daughter's hand, her gaze narrowing as she offered a reply through gritted teeth.

Mariselle stepped back, wrapping her arms around herself, her expression settling into that familiar mask of poised indifference. But Evryn had seen beneath it now, had glimpsed the yearning that lay behind her practiced composure.

And frankly, he'd had quite enough of this appalling spectacle.

He crossed the terrace in several long strides. Without hesitation, he slid an arm around Mariselle's back, drawing her closer to his side.

"Darling," he said, dipping his head so his words brushed against the shell of her ear, the picture of improper familiarity, "you seem cold. Shall we step inside for a moment?"

Lady Brightcrest's eyes flared wide, fixed on Evryn's arm around her daughter. Her eyes snapped to his, and he met her outraged stare with cool composure.

Then, quite deliberately, he lifted his free hand and trailed his knuckles from the curve of Mariselle's shoulder down the length of her arm. When he reached her hand, he slid his fingers between hers and laced them together with casual intimacy.

His expression didn't change, but the glint in his eyes said it clearly: *Do go on. I dare you.*

Lady Brightcrest drew herself up with all the imperious hauteur her modest stature could muster and inhaled sharply. "You will not—"

But Evryn was already turning Mariselle away from Lady Brightcrest, guiding her toward the doors. Inside—within view of the terrace, though blessedly out of earshot—he guided her toward a corner of the dining room where an arrangement of moonlilies and twilight roses spilled from an urn atop a low side table.

"Thank you," Mariselle said before he could speak, her voice light and airy, a practiced social laugh escaping her lips. "It was becoming a touch cold outside." She smoothed an invisible wrinkle from her sleeve before her gaze traveled to somewhere over his shoulder.

Evryn studied her face, noting the careful way she avoided meeting his eyes. "Are you all right?"

"Of course," she replied with a bemused smile, finally glancing at him. "Why wouldn't I be?"

He blinked, momentarily stunned. Was she truly going to stand there and pretend that the evening's cruelty was so commonplace it didn't warrant acknowledgment? He curled his fingers at his side to keep from reaching out for her again. The urge to touch her, to offer comfort, was becoming increasingly difficult to resist.

"Everything that happened at dinner," he said slowly.

Mariselle waved a dismissive hand, another light laugh escaping her. "Oh, that was nothing. I've survived far worse, believe me."

The casual way she said it, the matter-of-fact acceptance in her voice, made something twist inside him. He watched as she straightened her shoulders almost imperceptibly, her chin lifting a fraction higher in what he now recognized as a defensive posture.

"I should thank you," she added, still not quite meeting his gaze, "for your defense of me at the dinner table. You played your part admirably."

Played his part. As though every word hadn't been absolutely sincere.

"My grandmother was supposed to attend this evening," she continued, smoothly changing the subject. "But it seems my mother conveniently 'forgot' to send the invitation and only informed me of this tonight." A small, rueful smile curved her lips. "They would have been a little … different in her presence."

"I'm sorry," Evryn said quietly.

"Oh, no, I'm the one who should apologize for subjecting you to that dreadful ordeal. I've grown accustomed to the barbs and slights, but you …" She shook her head, giving him a look of playful sympathy. "Well, I don't suppose you've ever had to endure anything quite so unpleasant at Rowanwood House. You may have to take a few drops of Dream-Bright Elixir tonight to ward off the nightmares."

Evryn couldn't bring himself to match her attempt at levity. Though he was intimately familiar with using humor to dance away from anything serious—had built his entire social persona around never allowing a sincere moment to linger too long—there was something profoundly wrong about allowing her to minimize what he'd witnessed.

"Mariselle …" he said quietly, his voice trailing off as he struggled to find the right words, unwilling to simply let the moment pass yet uncertain how to navigate these unfamiliar emotional waters.

Then he remembered the folded slip of parchment he'd tucked into his waistcoat pocket earlier, the delicate gift wrapped carefully inside. For a moment, he hesitated, suddenly and oddly shy about the gesture. Up until this moment, he hadn't been entirely certain he would give it to her.

He'd woken that morning with fragments of the previous night's musicale still playing through his mind. He'd dreamed of how they'd sat side by side, his hand over hers, though in his dream, she hadn't been wearing a glove. Instead, he'd been able to trace his finger over the gleaming silver patterns of the marking on her skin.

In the dream, those delicate lines had felt warm beneath his touch, almost alive with magic. She'd turned her hand over and laced her fingers through his, palm to palm. He'd looked up then, startled by the intimacy of the gesture, wanting to see her face—but the moment of startled awareness had shattered the dream, waking him and leaving him strangely curious about what expression he might have found in her eyes.

After waking, his thoughts had circled inevitably to the evening ahead— her birthday dinner. The realization that he should give her a gift had struck him with unexpected force. The thought had immediately conjured memories of their various mischievous gifts—the embarrassing poetry book, the bracelet that had turned her hair that remarkable shade of blue—but this time felt different. This time, he wanted to offer something genuine, something unmarked by their usual need to maintain the upper hand. A gift that might actually mean something to her.

In a moment of inspiration, he'd risen from his bed and crossed to the writing desk positioned near his window. He'd taken the piece of lumyrite he'd been using as a paperweight and let it soften in his palms, his manifested ability glowing faintly beneath his skin.

Now, standing in the Brightcrest dining room with the distant sounds of conversation drifting from the terrace, Evryn withdrew the parchment envelope and extended it toward her. "I almost forgot. I have something for you. A small token."

Mariselle regarded the slim envelope with a considerable degree of suspicion, her blue eyes narrowing as she made no move to accept it.

"I promise you," Evryn said, unable to suppress a small smile at her wariness, "this gift is entirely genuine. No colorful hair enchantments or multiplying flowers this time."

"Forgive me if I find your assurances less than completely reassuring," she replied dryly, though after another moment's hesitation, she reached out and took the slip of parchment. "You have something of a reputation for magical mischief."

"Only when the occasion calls for it," he murmured, watching as she loosened the parchment folds and let the gift slide into her hand, where it caught the light with a quiet gleam.

Her quiet intake of breath was barely audible, but he caught it nonetheless. On her palm lay a delicate hairpin, its tip adorned with a tiny pegasus no larger than her thumbnail, exquisitely sculpted from faceted lumyrite. The stone shimmered with opalescent light, catching the glow of nearby faelights and scattering it in soft prismatic sparks, as though the creature might take flight at any moment.

"Oh, it's beautiful," Mariselle whispered, lifting the pin with careful fingers and turning it to examine the tiny creation from all angles. "Wait." She looked up at him. "This is lumyrite. Did you fashion this?"

He nodded. "May I?" he asked softly, stepping closer, one hand rising hesitantly.

She nodded wordlessly, still gazing at the delicate pegasus. He took it from her, and she turned her head slightly to the side. As he carefully gathered a section of her azure hair, the intimacy of the gesture struck him unexpectedly—this quiet moment, away from the performance and pretense. He slid the pin into place, taking his time as he adjusted a wayward strand of hair, ensuring the delicate creature was displayed to its best advantage.

"Perfect," he murmured, his voice rougher than he'd intended as he stepped back.

She looked at him with her head still slightly tilted, a slow, sly smile curving one corner of her lips, and for the first time that evening, Evryn saw a genuine spark of mischief light her eyes. "Please tell me it's going to neigh loudly every time my mother tries to say something to me. That would be absolute perfection."

He broke into a grin. "I *knew* I forgot something. Truly, I'm disappointed in myself."

"Perhaps there's still time to—"

"Mari!" Ellowa's voice rang out, cutting Mariselle off. "Lord Rowanwood! The dessert is about to be served!"

Mariselle's smile faded, and as they turned back toward the terrace, Evryn leaned closer and murmured, "If you'd like, I could perform the neighing myself every time your mother opens her mouth."

A laugh escaped her—bright, irrepressible, bubbling past her lips before she clamped a hand over her mouth. "Oh, I *dare* you," she whispered.

"Don't tempt me. I've been told I do an impeccable stallion impression."

Mariselle nearly doubled over, clutching his arm as laughter shook her shoulders. "Of course you do," she managed between gasping breaths.

And Evryn found himself thinking he'd gladly make a complete spectacle of himself—even in front of Mariselle's awful family—if it meant hearing that laugh again.

Chapter Twenty-One

Mariselle swayed gently in her wicker hanging chair, its soft creaking a familiar lullaby that matched the rhythm of the waves. She sat on the wraparound porch of the seaside cottage, her bare feet curled beneath her, the cushions molding perfectly to her form as they had countless nights before. This was her favorite dreamscape, the private realm she had crafted long ago, where she was safe and untouched by the waking world.

The evening's humiliations—every cutting remark her parents had made —began to dissolve, fading into the warm hush of the sea breeze like ink in water. Each gentle arc of the hanging chair seemed to rock away another sharp-edged memory.

The first stars had begun to emerge, brighter here than they ever appeared in the waking world. The constellation she had named Courage—a formation that existed nowhere on any astronomer's chart—winked into existence directly above the cottage.

Beyond the balustrade with its delicate turned spindles, the silver-rose sand captured the last blush of an eternal sunset. The twilight cast a soft glow over the sea, just enough to reveal the gentle ripples that lapped against the shore. Ripples that beckoned with quiet promise, as if they too longed to soothe and cradle. Later, perhaps, she would wander down and wade into those dream-warmed waters, letting them lift her, hold her, dissolve the weight of everything until she floated, untethered and unburdened. But for now, the rhythmic swaying of her chair and the sound of waves kissing the shore were healing enough.

Mariselle closed her eyes and drew a deep breath, filling her lungs with air that tasted of salt and possibilities. Her mind drifted inevitably to Evryn and his unexpected defense of her at dinner. She could hardly believe he'd dared to speak to her parents like that. She had frozen in that moment, her carefully composed mask of poised indifference crumbling away, her breath heightened, every part of her suddenly, acutely awake. She'd been unable to tear her gaze from his storm-gray eyes as they held hers with unwavering certainty. He'd spoken with such conviction, such startling intensity, that for several heartbeats she'd almost believed he meant every word.

And I am singularly privileged to soon call her my wife.

It was absurd, of course, this flutter in her chest whenever she recalled his words. As if she truly desired to marry a Rowanwood. What a preposterous notion. It was merely the novelty of being defended, of someone standing between her and her family's callous comments. Nothing more than gratitude magnified by the heightened emotions of the moment.

Darling.

Darling, you seem cold.

For goodness' sake, she needed to stop replaying his words in her head. His voice, deep and velvet-smooth and so unlike the theatrical charm he usually wielded when society was watching. And the way he'd trailed his knuckles all the way down her arm and interlaced his fingers between hers. It sent a shiver through her just thinking about it.

And then that exquisite pegasus hairpin. She reached up to touch it now, her finger finding the delicate pointed tips of its lumyrite wings. She was still half convinced it was going to reveal some dreadfully embarrassing enchantment. And yet … he'd seemed sincere when he'd said it was a genuine gift. And he'd crafted it himself. Especially for her. That knowledge stirred something warm and dangerous in her chest, something she refused to examine too closely for fear of what she might discover.

She rose from the hanging chair and crossed the weathered porch to the steps, her bare feet silent against the wood. With merely a thought, she could transform her attire—conjure a flowing nightdress, an elaborate ballgown, her riding ensemble. Such details hardly mattered in this dream realm, and tonight she remained in the evening gown she'd worn at dinner. Yet one element never varied in this dreamscape: her bare feet. There was something profoundly comforting about the sensation of her toes sinking into the cool, yielding sand.

The lowest step creaked softly as she came to a stop. She stood there, letting the gentle rhythm of the waves soothe her tumultuous thoughts, the shoreline stretching infinitely in both directions.

"Mariselle?"

She yelped, her hand flying immediately to her chest, her heart instantly racing as she whipped around toward the source of the familiar voice. But her foot missed the edge of the step, and she toppled unceremoniously onto the sand in an undignified heap of skirts and flailing limbs.

"Mariselle!" he called again, concern in his voice this time. She scrambled to her feet, hearing the urgent crunch of his footsteps as he ran toward her across the sand, the sound impossibly real in this place where no one else had ever set foot.

Evryn.

Evryn was here.

In her dream.

"Are you all right?" he asked, slowing to a halt just before her.

"What—what are you—how did you—" She hastily brushed strands of blue hair out of her face, her gaze darting around as if she might find an explanation somewhere. She struggled to compose herself, to find her usual poise. "What are you doing here?"

His brows knit faintly, but the corners of his mouth curved upward in unmistakable amusement. "I don't believe I've ever seen you flustered before. It's rather endearing."

"Evryn!" She choked on his name, immediately correcting herself. "Rowanwood!"

"Where are we, by the way?" he added, looking around, seemingly oblivious to how completely *wrong* this was. "I presume you drugged me again and pulled me into Dreamland? Though I could have sworn I fell asleep in my own bed this evening and not at Windsong Cottage."

Mariselle blinked, words catching in her throat, flames heating her face. She shut her eyes and pressed her fingers to her temples. "Oh, this is not good," she muttered. She was *dream sharing*. That must be what this was. How in all the realms had she allowed such an intimacy to occur?

"Is everything all right?" Evryn took a step closer.

She lowered her hands, took a deep breath, and tried not to feel supremely awkward as she said, "You are, ah … in my dream."

His brows rose as if in polite query. "Your dream?"

"My dream. Not Dreamland. *My dream.*"

His eyes narrowed a touch. "This feels considerably more real than a dream."

"Yes, well, that's—I believe that's—I mean to say … yes. I think that's how it works."

He watched her for a moment longer, then let out a quiet laugh, warm and disbelieving. "I've really never seen you like this before."

"Because you're in my dream!" she burst out, unable to quite meet his eyes. "And it's terribly awkward!"

"Why?"

Did she truly need to explain this? Had he never encountered the concept of dream sharing? That phenomenon where trust forged a pathway between two sleeping minds, possible only when one of the two possessed some form of dream magic. It was considered terribly intimate, and as she'd reminded Petunia not long ago, the experience was rumored to be quite … pleasurable. Though at present, she felt herself slowly perishing from mortification, which was decidedly *un*pleasant. Perhaps this wasn't dream sharing after all.

"Because it means that I … I've … let my guard down. I … allowed you in. Somehow. Without knowing it." She cringed internally at her sheer lack of eloquence. Her face was surely the color of a tomato by now.

Evryn watched her a while longer, his expression softening. "Should I leave?" he asked. "I don't want to upset you further."

Gracious, that voice again. Like warm honey poured over her senses, settling somewhere deep within her chest and unraveling all her defenses.

"It's … well … no. I don't mind. Having you here, that is." The admission felt like stepping off a ledge, exhilarating and terrifying at once. She pressed both hands to her midriff, shoulders drawn back as she attempted to reclaim some semblance of dignity. "You merely … startled me."

"My apologies. I'm not sure how I ended up here. Or why I appear to be in my riding gear," he added, looking down at himself with a frown. "And if I *were* to leave, I don't quite know how I'd accomplish that."

"I don't know either," Mariselle admitted. "This hasn't happened before."

His gaze captured hers once more, and stars above, was it the enchanted twilight of her dreamscape that rendered his eyes so mesmerizing? She couldn't look away.

The silence between them stretched, filled only by the gentle percussion of waves against the shore and the distant call of dream-birds that existed nowhere in the waking world. The stars above them seemed to pulse with each heartbeat.

"Did you create all of this?" he asked eventually, his gaze sweeping over the cottage, the shore, the endless twilight sky.

Relief washed over her as his attention shifted away, freeing her from that magnetic gaze and offering safer conversational ground. She drew a deep breath, salt air filling her lungs. "Yes. When I manifested, soon after I turned eighteen, my dreams became far more vivid. More real." She turned slowly, surveying her creation. "I discovered I could control them, could fill them with anything I desired. That was when I realized I possess dream architect magic."

She faced the cottage and began ascending the steps, her fingers trailing along the weathered railing. "This is my favorite dreamscape. I modeled it after a seaside cottage where my siblings and I stayed with my grandmother one summer in our youth—the year my parents chose to enjoy Bloomhaven and the Bloom Season unburdened by 'tagalongs.' Here, twilight never yields to darkness, the stars shine with impossible brilliance, the moon hangs larger in the sky, and everything feels … safe. I dance barefoot on the sand or wade into the water or simply sway for hours in the hanging chair, listening to the sound of the ocean."

She forced herself to stop talking before she accidentally spilled her entire soul to him. That was the way it was with dream sharing, so she'd heard. Something about existing together within the realm of one's deepest thoughts made truth flow like water between cupped hands. The intimacy of sharing one's innermost self created a vulnerability both terrifying and exquisite.

"It's beautiful," Evryn said.

"Thank you." She settled at the edge of the porch, bare feet resting on the top step, knees drawn toward her chest and palms smoothing the fabric of her gown.

After a moment's hesitation, Evryn climbed the steps and sat beside her. "So you can craft dream landscapes. You possess an ability relating to dream wards. You can induce sleep with a mere touch." He leaned back on his hands. "What else can you do?"

"What makes you think I can do anything more than that?" she asked lightly.

"I'm starting to suspect there's always more when it comes to you, Mariselle Brightcrest."

She allowed herself a small smile as his words sent a pleasant shiver through her. "All right then. You're correct. There is one other ability I've manifested. I can …" She hesitated, biting her lip, but the urge to share more of herself with him was overwhelming. She turned her head and met his gaze hesitantly. "I can hear dreams."

"Hear dreams?" he repeated. "What do you mean by that?"

She reached down, her fingertips creating delicate swirls in the scattered sand that had found its way onto the wooden porch. "At night, when all is still and quiet, I hear the dreams of those sleeping nearby like overlapping whispers. It was so dreadfully overwhelming when the ability first manifested. I keep a dream-chime above my bed now. My parents believe it's merely one of those silly charms that's meant to induce pleasant melodies in dreams, but I managed to enchant it with a ward that keeps most of the whispers at bay."

Evryn straightened, his expression shifting from curiosity to something more guarded, a flash of vulnerability crossing his features. "Did you—after we were in Dreamland and you left me asleep in the cottage—"

"Oh, no, I would never," she assured him. "I left before I could hear anything. Well, I'll admit I was tempted to stay a little longer and listen, but I didn't."

He nodded slowly, turning his face toward the sea, expression thoughtful once more.

"What sorts of things do you dream about?" Mariselle asked. "When you're not inadvertently trespassing in my dreamscape, that is."

He shifted beside her, suddenly looking awkward. "Oh, a wide variety of things," he said vaguely.

Her smile widened at his evident discomfort. "What are you hiding?"

"Nothing." But the denial came too quickly, and the faint color in his cheeks belied his words.

"You know, in dreams, it's exceedingly difficult to lie convincingly," she told him, leaning sideways to bump him lightly with her shoulder. "The truth hovers on the edge of our tongues, waiting to spill free."

"Yes, I can tell." He rubbed his jaw, glancing at her with a sidelong look that mingled sheepish embarrassment with unmistakable warmth. "Your dreamscape appears most eager to draw a confession from me that I'm not quite ready to make."

She laughed. "Very well then. I'll allow you your secrets. I know it's different when one can't control their own dreams. Tell me about your writing instead," she continued. "When did E. S. Twist first put quill to parchment? What inspired you to begin? Before discovering your manuscript, I never would have imagined you harbored such talent."

"Ah, talent is it? I seem to recall you referring to my writing as 'thinly veiled allegorical drivel.'"

She rolled her eyes. "I may have been a touch hasty in my initial assessment."

"*May* have been?" This time it was he who leaned over and bumped his shoulder playfully against hers. "Very well. It began as simple journaling," he admitted, his gaze drifting toward the horizon. "A way to ..." He rubbed one hand along the back of his neck. "Well, to process my frustrations at being perpetually overshadowed by my older brother's far more significant magic."

"More significant?" Mariselle's brows arched in genuine astonishment. "Evryn, you reconstructed the physical parts of Dreamland. All that lumyrite shaping ... it was no small feat, and was something only you could accomplish. Dreamland's resurrection would have been impossible without your particular gifts."

His gaze lingered on her face with an expression she couldn't quite decipher. "I find I rather enjoy the sound of my name on your lips," he said softly, then immediately appeared startled by his own admission. "Well, that declaration was entirely unplanned." He looked pointedly up at the starstrewn sky, as if addressing it directly. "You really are determined to embarrass me, dreamscape."

She laughed, a delicate flush spreading across her cheeks. "I believe you may be missing the more significant revelation here—that neither you nor your magic are in any way inconsequential."

Evryn drew in a deep breath, hand rising to rub awkwardly along his jaw again. "Well, be that as it may. I continued writing, but my daily observations began to transform into something else. Characters started emerging from the people around me. Fictional scenarios, invented settings." He paused, a small, wry smile tugging at his lips. "I spent months during the quiet season working up the courage to submit my first story to the literary section of the Gilded Gazette. But then they accepted one. And then a second and a third. And I finally felt as though …" He shrugged. "As though I'd achieved something of my own."

Mariselle nodded, watching him, understanding what he meant. "And why E. S. Twist?" she asked, curiosity warming her voice. "There must be a story behind the name."

"It's silly," he demurred, shaking his head. "Ridiculous, really."

"Tell me. I promise not to laugh."

Evryn hesitated, then sighed in surrender. "E for Evryn, obviously. S for Secondson." A self-deprecating smile crossed his face. "And Twist … for twisting the truth into fiction. Taking what I observe and transforming it into something new." He glanced at her, vulnerability plain in his eyes. "I told you it was ridiculous."

"I like it."

"Flattery, Lady Brightcrest?" His lips curved into a smile. "I shall endeavor not to let it go straight to my head."

"*Lady* Brightcrest?" she repeated with a laugh. "I see you are actively resisting the dreamscape's invitation to openness."

Evryn's smile deepened, genuine warmth replacing his earlier guardedness as he leaned toward her, closing the distance between them by inches. They fell quiet then, the silence stretching between them, delicate and charged with possibility, neither willing to look away.

"Mariselle," he said softly, and a shiver danced down her spine, because she rather liked the sound of her name on his lips too. "I am … perplexed."

"Oh?"

"By what I witnessed earlier this evening."

"Ah." She withdrew slightly, the gentle warmth that had enveloped them moments ago retreating like the tide, leaving her exposed to the chill memory of her family's cutting remarks.

"You present yourself to the world with such fierce independence and unwavering confidence, yet in your family's presence, those qualities seem to vanish entirely. Why do you not assert yourself with them as you do with others? With *me?* Why do you endure such treatment from them when you would permit it from no one else?"

She turned away, her gaze finding refuge in the endless horizon where sea met sky. Her fingers curled around the edge of the step. "It's … complicated." She inhaled deeply, then let her shoulders fall. "And extraordinarily simple, I suppose. I merely … want them to love me. To value me. And they've never wanted a daughter with … spirit."

The admission hung in the air between them, raw and honest in a way that would have been impossible in the waking world.

"That's why restoring Dreamland means so much to me," she continued. "If I can accomplish something of such magnitude, something that brings glory to the Brightcrest name, they'll finally see me differently. Once they witness what I'm truly capable of creating, they won't speak to me as they did tonight. My achievements will demand the respect they've always withheld."

"Mariselle," he said gently. "Your true worth isn't measured by your accomplishments. It exists simply in who you are."

She turned to look at him, pressing her lips together and blinking away the tears that threatened. There was a slight tremor in her voice when she said, "Is that so, Evryn Secondson Twist?"

Something in Evryn's expression shifted, recognition dawning in his eyes as her words mirrored his own counsel back to him. He drew back slightly, his gaze sliding away from hers, a small frown puckering his brow. "I suppose that's … something to consider."

After another moment's pause, she said, "Perhaps we should divert ourselves from this particular line of conversation. It seems to have grown rather more intimate than either of us anticipated."

"Might I say one thing more?" he asked.

She nodded.

"I suspect Dreamland isn't solely about proving yourself to your family. I've witnessed how you come alive when working on it. The way your eyes light with genuine passion. When we stepped into that realm, your entire being radiated joy. It wasn't the expression of someone merely seeking approval. That was the face of an artist in love with her creation for its own sake."

A smile bloomed across her face, warmth spreading through her chest at his words. They rang true in a way she couldn't deny. No language could fully capture the exhilaration she'd felt wandering through Dreamland.

"May I share another thought?" he asked, leaning forward slightly. "An idea."

Her lips curved into a wry smile. "Are you truly asking permission, or merely preparing to tell me regardless of my answer?"

His eyes crinkled at the corners, a flash of appreciative humor crossing his features. "Dreamland is magnificent as it is, but I've been thinking … what if it could be more than a collection of wondrous scenes?"

She tilted her head. "What do you mean?"

"What if visitors experience a story rather than merely scenes? With themselves the characters? There could be several, and visitors could choose the narrative they like best. Or perhaps a different story for each day of the week. Something of that nature."

Mariselle watched his face brighten, his voice warm with enthusiasm. "I like that," she said. "Do you have any ideas?"

"I've had several brewing. Though I'd like to hear yours as well, if you have some."

"I need to contemplate the possibilities, but I'm genuinely enchanted by the concept,"she replied. "I've already begun crafting more intricate environments and experiences, so narrative would be a natural evolution—a way to thread those moments into something cohesive and meaningful."

"Excellent. While you think on it, I have another question."

A smile tugged her lips. "Of course you do."

"How easy is it for you to create dream versions of Cobalt and Cinder within this realm?And if they were to materialize here, might we actually ride them?" His eyes brightened with unmistakable longing. "I find myself rather missing our nocturnal flights. It's been some time since we raced beneath the stars."

A grin spread across Mariselle's face as anticipation coursed through her veins—that familiar, exhilarating promise of stars rushing past and the unmatched freedom that only flight could offer.

"Consider it done," she said, standing and looking out across the beach, where two magnificent pegasi had just descended from the twilight sky, their hooves sending up a glittering spray of seawater as they landed gracefully in the shallow surf.

"Prepare yourself, Rowanwood," she said as her evening gown shimmered and rippled, restructuring itself into her riding attire. "For you're about to taste defeat at my hands once again."

Chapter Twenty-Two

LAUGHTER ROSE ABOVE THE HUM OF CONVERSATION FILLING The Charmed Leaf Tea House the following night, warm and uninhibited in a way that sparked something in Evryn's chest. His gaze settled on the source: Kazrian, Aurelise and Rosavyn on the other side of the table, and Mariselle, sitting beside him. Kazrian was currently recounting some tale that appeared to require dramatic hand gestures, while Rosavyn—who had managed to maintain her cold attitude toward Mariselle for approximately three minutes before giving in to laughter—leaned forward occasionally to embellish on the details of the tale, and Aurelise kept dissolving into giggles.

It had been a last-minute decision this morning to extend an invitation to Mariselle for his grandmother's tea leaf reading, an annual event at which Lady Rivenna performed a somewhat theatrical divination of tea leaves for an intimate gathering of select company.

When Mariselle had first arrived, stepping gracefully through the doorway in a gown several shades darker than her still very blue hair, their eyes had met across the crowded tea house. In that singular moment, something intangible yet profound had passed between them—a silent acknowledgment of boundaries crossed during their shared dream the night before.

But then she'd joined his family at their table, and the moment had dissolved, leaving them to resume their elaborate performance as a soul-bonded couple and the subject of Bloomhaven gossip.

The evening's entertainment had proceeded, with his grandmother presenting each guest with a specially prepared teacup before guiding them through the precise ritual of tea leaf reading. She'd moved from person to person with dramatic flourish, examining the patterns left behind and pronouncing fortunes with grand certainty. The room had filled with laughter and delight throughout the performance, everyone understanding it was merely elegant entertainment. The enchanted cups, designed to reveal distinctive patterns, were all part of the orchestrated spectacle.

His grandmother had navigated the room like a queen in her court, utterly in her element and visibly relishing every moment, while pointedly ignoring the presence of a Brightcrest in her hallowed tea house.

Evryn had to admit that he'd barely paid attention to the evening's theatrics. His mind had been elsewhere, drifting between the unexpected warmth he felt seeing his younger siblings accept Mariselle into their circle, and the persistent memories of the previous night, when he had somehow found himself inside Mariselle's dream.

Dream sharing.

The term had surfaced in his mind the moment she'd explained what was happening. He'd heard her brother Alaryn Brightcrest mention it once, describing it as some sort of intimate joining of minds, possible when at least one of a pair of people possessed any sort of dream-related magic.

Indeed, Evryn had felt a connection to her unlike anything he'd experienced before. The walls between them had fallen away, and he'd wanted nothing more than to lay bare his very soul to her. She had revealed parts of herself, too—the real Mariselle beneath the cold Brightcrest exterior. There had been something genuine between them, a connection that had felt profound and real.

But now, in the jarring lucidity of the waking world, doubt crept in. How much of that connection had been real, and how much had been the effect of dream sharing itself? Perhaps the intimacy he'd felt was merely the nature of the experience, nothing more. The thought left an unexpected hollow feeling in his chest.

Across the table, his mother leaned in to contribute to the animated conversation between Kazrian, Rosavyn and Aurelise, her eyes alight with merriment. Jasvian, seated on Evryn's other side, remained apart from their lively exchange, though his face was notably free of its habitual stern expression. Like Evryn, he seemed content merely to observe the proceedings with quiet interest.

Throughout the evening, Evryn had not failed to notice how his brother occasionally lifted his gaze to seek out Iris—who was attending their grandmother this evening—until his eyes landed on her. The two had already exchanged multiple soft glances and secret smiles. There was a time when Evryn might have regarded such sentiments with inward derision, but now … Well. Now he found himself possessed of altogether different feelings on the matter.

Evryn turned, intending to draw his brother into conversation, only to start slightly upon discovering that Jasvian had been regarding him with a thoughtful expression.

"Your affection for her is real," Jasvian said.

Evryn blinked, taken aback by this sudden declaration.

"For Lady Mariselle," Jasvian confirmed, as if there might be someone else present whom Evryn had so-called 'real affection' for. Evryn was about to protest before remembering that he was supposed to be maintaining the pretense of utter adoration for her.

Mariselle chose that moment to turn her head in their direction, perhaps because she'd heard her name. She smiled, a brief question in her gaze, before returning her attention to the other side of the table.

Jasvian gestured with his head toward a quieter corner of the main floor, near the stairs that led to the tea house's upper level. "Walk with me?"

Evryn hesitated for a moment, wondering if perhaps he should remain with Mariselle, but she appeared perfectly at ease in the company of his family. He nodded, and the two of them stood.

"They seem to be getting along rather well," Jasvian said as they crossed the room, apparently having had the same thought Evryn had just had.

"Much to Grandmother's chagrin, I'm sure," Evryn replied.

A small laugh escaped Jasvian. "She'll survive the shock."

"Will she?" Evryn asked, his tone light though the question was in earnest. "I have my doubts."

"I believe she will. Lady Mariselle is … not exactly what any of us believed her to be. I suspect even Grandmother might soften given some time in her presence."

But therein lay the difficulty—getting Grandmother to remain in Mariselle's presence for longer than it took to execute a dismissive sniff.

They reached the corner and came to a stop. "I confess I'm rather surprised myself by the way this has all turned out," Jasvian said. "When you first announced your supposed magical binding to Mariselle Brightcrest, something felt distinctly … off. As though you were performing a role rather than experiencing it. It was as if you were trying to convince *yourself* of the connection as much as you were trying to persuade us."

"Oh, but I *do* give such a convincing performance," Evryn said, automatically conjuring his usual armor of theatrical charm. "You should've seen the reviews. There was rapturous applause and one particularly enthusiastic pigeon threw a flower."

Jasvian regarded him with exasperation. "Evryn. Is it impossible for you to engage sincerely when the conversation turns to something of actual significance? This is your future we're speaking of. Your happiness."

Evryn spread his arms and gave an exaggerated bow. "Do I not look the very picture of happiness? Positively radiant, if I do say so myself."

Jasvian stepped a little closer, his eyes narrowing. Not in irritation, but in quiet scrutiny. The kind that made Evryn feel, uncomfortably, as though he were being read like one of his own manuscripts.

"Yes," Jasvian said softly. "That's what I mean. You *do* look like the picture of happiness. Because of a Brightcrest. Which—frankly—borders on unbelievable."

Evryn's smile dimmed. He inhaled slowly and took a step back, lowering himself to sit on one of the worn steps that led up to the study, elbows resting on his knees. He stared at the floorboards for a moment, gathering his thoughts.

He wished he could speak the truth. He wished he could explain that this was all an act, that Jasvian has never had anything to worry about, that it would soon be over. And he wished he could somehow express the deeper truth that lay beneath the facade—that he might not *want* it to be over.

He looked up at his brother. "Are you still opposed to this marriage?"

Jasvian was silent for a beat, the sounds of conversation and clinking teacups drifting behind them. Then, with a wry smile, he said, "Surprisingly, no. Not anymore. I've been …" He looked up, past Evryn, and Evryn followed his gaze until it landed on Iris. "I've been made aware of some things recently. And now …" He exhaled and focused on Evryn once more. "And now, seeing the way you look at Lady Mariselle, I don't find I have it in me to object any longer."

Evryn arched a brow. *"Things?"* he repeated. "Would you deign to share some of this older-brother wisdom?"

Jasvian shifted, looking uncomfortable for a moment. "It doesn't matter."

Evryn chose not to press the matter. He suspected these 'things' his brother spoke of were the kind of earnest revelations about love and destiny that struck otherwise sensible people once they'd locked eyes with their soul-mate and lost all capacity for logic.

"My point," Jasvian continued, "is that you have my support. I'll stand with you, if necessary, against Grandmother."

Evryn stared at his brother, momentarily speechless. Of all the responses he'd anticipated to bringing Mariselle to the tea house, unconditional support from Jasvian had not been among them.

"Thank you," he managed after a moment. "That's … unexpectedly generous."

"Is it?" Jasvian gave him a faintly bemused look. "Evryn, you're my brother. Do you think I want anything less than the best that life can possibly give you? I've been lucky enough to find a love that has transformed my existence into something infinitely more meaningful than I'd ever imagined possible. Why should you not have the same? Why should your happiness be diminished simply because of the family name attached to the one who brings it to you?"

A curious tightness constricted Evryn's throat. Was that the way Mariselle made him feel? It had begun to feel that way while sitting beside her on a dream porch overlooking a dream ocean, her shoulder lightly bumping his as they'd spoken more freely than they'd ever spoken before. But he wondered again if that was only the intimacy of dream sharing.

He released a small breath of a laugh, standing and meeting his brother's gaze. "I think perhaps you should be having this conversation with Grandmother."

"Oh, I intend to," Jasvian assured him. He gripped Evryn's shoulder in solidarity before they turned back toward the gathering.

"Evryn, dear," his mother said, approaching him before he reached the table. "Could you find Kazrian? I believe he wandered into the kitchen, but he's been gone rather longer than fetching a pastry should require."

"Of course," Evryn replied, glancing past his mother and noting that Kazrian was indeed gone from the table. Rosavyn had excused herself as well and appeared to be assisting Iris with extinguishing a small blaze that had erupted among the enchanted paper decor that fluttered near the ceiling. Undoubtedly the work of the mischievous hearth sprites he could see scampering across the tea house floor toward the kitchen.

Aurelise and Mariselle now sat closer together, their heads bent in conversation, occasionally breaking into shared laughter. The sight sent a warm current through him, settling somewhere beneath his ribs.

The tea house kitchen was quieter this evening than when Evryn had visited early in the morning almost three weeks prior. Several kitchen pixies were busy washing used teacups and plates, while one had apparently worked itself to exhaustion already and now lay fast asleep on the central worktable, tiny limbs splayed as it snored quietly. Kazrian, however, was nowhere to be seen.

Evryn frowned, moving deeper into the kitchen's domain. He noticed the pantry door stood a jar, and as he approached, he heard the unmistakable sound of muffled laughter—Kazrian's distinctive chuckle followed by a softer, more melodic laugh that took him a moment to place.

Pushing the door open wider, Evryn discovered his brother and Lucie Fields seated on the floor of the pantry, their backs against shelves of tea canisters.

"—absolutely cannot be true," Lucie was saying, her cheeks flushed and her eyes bright with amusement.

"I swear," Kazrian insisted. "It was quite a sight to behold."

They both dissolved into laughter again before noticing Evryn standing in the doorway. Their expressions shifted immediately to identical looks of guilty surprise. Lucie was on her feet in an instant, Kazrian following a moment later.

"Evryn!" he exclaimed, a bit too loudly. "We were just, ah—"

"Discussing the inventory," Lucie supplied quickly, her hands twisting together.

"The inventory of … wine?" Evryn inquired mildly, eyes landing on an open amber-hued bottle with a slender neck, partially concealed behind Kazrian's boot.

Kazrian cleared his throat. "Quality control. Very important aspect of … inventory."

Evryn suppressed a smile, thinking of his own recent lapses in propriety. "I see."

"Please don't tell Lady Rivenna," Lucie said, her expression growing more concerned. "I was only taking a short break, and Kazrian poked his head in here looking for, um …"

"That starwhisper chamomile blend Mother likes so much," Kazrian supplied.

"Right. That." Lucie nodded vigorously. "And we got to talking—*only* talking, I swear—and … I … um …"

"I'm hardly one to judge anyone's questionable behavior," Evryn said, backing out of the doorway. "Continue with your … quality control."

Relief washed over both their faces, followed by surprised gratitude.

"Mother was looking for you," Evryn added to Kazrian. "I'll tell her you're …assisting with kitchen matters."

"Much appreciated," Kazrian replied.

"But perhaps don't spend too long in here. She'll likely come looking for you herself at some point."

"Noted."

Returning to the main room, he found Mariselle was now gone from the Rowanwoods' table as well. His eyes scanned the room for her, and a sudden pang of alarm tightened his chest when he spotted her on the far side—cornered by his grandmother.

Mariselle should have remained at the Rowanwoods' table where it was safe.

Instead, she'd noticed the dancing flames that Rosavyn and Iris were attempting to subdue near the ceiling and had risen instinctively to offer her assistance. The blaze was modest in size, but her natural inclination to help had overridden her better judgment.

Once the mischievous fire had been properly extinguished, rather than returning directly to the relative sanctuary of her seat, Mariselle found herself drawn toward the opposite side of the tea house, captivated by its enchanting decor.

A suspended silver teapot captured her attention, elegantly enchanted to display the time in luminescent numerals that rippled across its burnished surface. She circled it with quiet appreciation, admiring how the craftsmanship revealed itself differently from each angle. So thoroughly absorbed was she in this examination that when she finally turned away, she nearly collided with Lady Rivenna's imposing figure

"Lady Mariselle Brightcrest," the Rowanwood matriarch said, her voice cool as winter frost yet carefully modulated to avoid drawing attention. "You have remarkable audacity, returning to my establishment."

Mariselle's stomach tightened, but she dropped into a brief, perfectly executed curtsy before straightening and lifting her chin slightly. "Lady Rowanwood. Good evening."

"Was your previous visit not sufficient?" Lady Rivenna's eyes narrowed. "I believe I made my sentiments regarding your presence here quite clear then."

"You did," Mariselle acknowledged, maintaining her composure despite the flutter of nerves in her chest.

"Yet here you stand," Lady Rivenna continued, "in my tea house once more. The question that presents itself, rather insistently, is *why*."

Around them, the evening continued in pleasant ignorance of their tense exchange—laughter from a nearby table, the delicate melody of porcelain against porcelain, the faint rustle of leaves as they moved against the walls.

"I was invited," Mariselle said simply, exactly as she'd said during her first visit. "By your grandson."

"Most likely because you enchanted him to do so," Lady Rivenna muttered. Then her voice took on a sharper edge. "What precisely do you want, Lady Mariselle? What is your aim in inserting yourself into my family's affairs?"

"Tonight? I merely wished to witness your renowned tea leaf reading event firsthand, having heard such remarkable accounts of the event."

Lady Rivenna leaned closer, her voice becoming an icy hiss. *"What. Do you. Want?"*

"I want to be you!" The words burst from Mariselle before she could contain them, startling them both equally.

Lady Rivenna blinked, momentarily robbed of her usual poise. "What?"

Mariselle felt heat rising to her cheeks. "That is—I want to be *like* you," she amended hastily, the words tumbling out in an uncharacteristic rush. "You've built something remarkable here. This tea house. Your place in society. The respect you command. Everyone in Bloomhaven speaks your name with reverence."

Lady Rivenna regarded her with an expression Mariselle couldn't quite decipher—suspicion mingled with something that might almost have been surprise. "You wish to emulate *me*?" she asked finally, studying Mariselle's face as though searching for signs of deception. "A Brightcrest, admiring a Rowanwood?"

"I admire achievement," Mariselle replied, steadier now. "And strength. And the ability to create something lasting, something that brings joy to others. Why wouldn't I admire that? Why wouldn't I aspire to achieve something similar one day?"

Lady Rivenna gave her a look that suggested she thought Mariselle entirely incapable of achieving anything close to the legacy she had so meticulously crafted over decades of dedication and sacrifice. After several more moments' pause, she drew herself up. "Well. That is ... unexpected. Though I remain unconvinced of your sincerity."

"That's fair," Mariselle conceded. "Regardless, the tea leaf reading was excellent fun. I've never experienced anything quite like it. Fascinating, truly. Thank you." She offered another polite curtsy.

Lady Rivenna merely watched her, eyes narrowed, saying nothing.

Mariselle turned, exhaling a shuddery breath, and found Evryn heading toward her. She met him halfway to the Rowanwoods' table.

"Are you all right?" he asked, his eyes darting briefly over her shoulder. "I saw you with my grandmother and feared the worst."

Mariselle laughed softly, the tension in her shoulders beginning to ease. "I believe I may have just shocked Lady Rivenna Rowanwood," she admitted. "And not entirely in a bad way."

"Oh?" A slow, approving smile spread across Evryn's face. He moved to stand beside her, sliding a hand around her waist until it settled at her lower back. He drew her closer than was strictly proper, and as the two of them headed back toward the Rowanwoods' table, he leaned close and murmured, "Now there is a story I should very much like to hear."

Chapter Twenty-Three

Evryn tucked his riding cap and gloves into Cobalt's saddlebag, then ran a hand through his hair, attempting to restore some semblance of artful disarray. His boots crunched softly over the ground as he made his way past the quiet remains of Dreamland toward Windsong Cottage, telling himself how silly it was to be here at all. Dreamland's lumyrite structure was intact now. There wasn't anything left that required his particular abilities.

It was her. He knew it. Some undeniable magnetic pull toward Mariselle Brightcrest had drawn him here tonight, like a dusk sprite to a flame.

The previous evening at the tea house had left him … unsettled. He'd found himself gravitating toward her as the night progressed, leaning closer during conversation, seeking excuses to touch her hand or brush against her shoulder, until his mother had begun directing pointed glances of disapproval his way.

Even after returning home, sleep had eluded him entirely. He'd tossed restlessly among his bedsheets, mind filled with her laugh, her quick wit, the subtle vanilla scent that clung to her hair. Some small, foolish part of him had hoped he might find himself in her dreamscape again, but dawn had arrived without any such encounter.

He'd risen from bed with the disquieting realization that he missed her—

that in the span of mere weeks, Mariselle Brightcrest had somehow become the axis around which his thoughts revolved.

Now, hours later, he walked past the remains of the outer Dreamland ruins, where luminous moss clung stubbornly to the stone. While the essential lumyrite structure that powered Dreamland had been completely restored, the site's exterior still showed signs of decay—crumbling columns and half-fallen archways.

He reached the path that traced through the cottage garden and followed it until he stood before the front door. He pushed it open, stepped through, and was immediately hit with the sound of laughter—bright, breathless, and utterly unrestrained.

Mariselle.

The sound spilled from the sitting area like sunlight through an open window, and for a moment, Evryn could do nothing but stand still and listen, the sound weaving through him like a spell, disarming and golden.

He closed the door, taking in the scene before him. Mariselle and Petunia were sprawled comfortably on the floor, surrounded by books and papers in various states of disarray, with the dream core sitting to one side. Petunia held a plate of half-eaten jam tarts, while Mariselle sat cross-legged, hugging a cushion to her chest, her skirts arranged with a complete disregard for propriety that would have scandalized half of Bloomhaven. Her hair was still blue, Evryn noted, and she was bent forward over the cushion, gasping with laughter.

She looked up, cheeks flushed, eyes dancing. "Oh, Evryn! Petunia loves your idea about adding narrative experiences to Dreamland. She has some additions." She immediately dissolved into laughter again, barely managing to get out, "Tell him, Tunia."

Evryn did not miss the fact that she'd called him *Evryn* and not *Rowanwood*, possibly for the first time ever in the waking world, but he did his best to focus on her cousin.

Petunia appeared composed as ever, but there was a dangerous sparkle in her eye. "Right," she said crisply. "So we begin with a historical romp involving scandalous laundry thefts."

Evryn blinked. "Pardon?"

"Visitors must infiltrate a floating manor staffed entirely by ghostly footmen in cravats made of cobwebs," she explained. "Their mission is to recover a set of monogrammed petticoats that once belonged to the Grand Duchess of Silkenwhim, who, incidentally, haunts the laundry room and sings aggressively off-key opera when provoked."

Mariselle was doubled over now, shoulders shaking with laughter.

"And," Petunia continued, entirely unbothered, "the escape route involves leaping from a window onto a floating picnic blanket made of bubbles, flown by a flamingo in a waistcoat."

"Of course it does," Evryn said.

"Oh, and then," Petunia said with a businesslike nod, "we pivot to interpretive kettle dancing."

"I'm afraid to ask."

"As you should be. Guests are assigned an enchanted kettle that whistles a different tune according to the color of their clothing. They must perform a synchronized dance routine in the Valley of Echoes, where each misstep is punished by a gust of floral confetti and very judgmental squirrels. The glittery pink sort."

"Highly judgmental," Mariselle wheezed. "They wag their tiny paws."

"And finally," Petunia concluded, "the grand finale: guests must outwit a sentient wig."

Evryn raised both eyebrows.

"A bewitched bouffant," Petunia said, "crafted from starspun threads and the regrets of debutantes past. It has opinions about social hierarchy. Guests must either flatter it with elaborate compliments or duel it in the Glittering Grove using parasols and riddles."

Mariselle collapsed backward onto the rug with a gasp. "I cannot—I'm *crying*, Tunia."

Evryn watched her, an incredulous smile spreading across his face. Mariselle, completely unguarded, breathless and radiant and entirely improper. And standing in the middle of the room, he realized—utterly, quietly, undoubtedly—that he was in love with her.

Petunia looked up at him. "We're taking Dreamland very seriously."

"Clearly," he said, voice a little rough. "I cannot wait to see what the wig has to say about my fashion choices."

"Oh, it loathes your boots," Petunia informed him. "But it might forgive you if you bow deeply enough and recite a limerick about its tragic past as a garden hedge."

Mariselle made a strangled noise into her sleeve. She was practically rolling on the floor now.

Evryn tore his gaze away, directing it firmly at the far wall. He cleared his throat and tugged slightly at the collar of his riding gear. Perhaps he ought to have stayed home. Mariselle's presence was proving far more tempting than he'd anticipated.

Petunia squinted up at him as she lowered the plate of jam tarts to the floor beside her. "What brings you here, Rowanwood? Tired of being adored on all sides, were you? Did you come in search of someone to insult you properly?"

Evryn raised a brow. "Naturally. I knew I could rely on Windsong Cottage for the warmest barbs."

"We reserve our finest scorn for our favorites."

"I'm honored, truly." He cast a glance at the papers, sketches, and half-empty teacups strewn across the floor. "I thought perhaps you might require help. Some charming, insightful genius to lend his talents to the cause."

Petunia snorted. "Ah, yes, because what this operation truly lacks is ego."

Mariselle, who had finally stopped laughing, pushed herself upright with a fond shake of her head. "Since you're here, Rowanwood" —ah, he was *Rowanwood* once again, not *Evryn*— "you may as well be useful. I believe we need to do some reorganization. We've managed to scatter papers and scrolls and diagrams and notebooks everywhere."

"We thrive in creative catastrophe," Petunia said breezily, brushing crumbs from her lap. "It's where all the best ideas live."

"Well, I can certainly be of assistance," Evryn said. Especially if it meant unintentionally (intentionally) brushing Mariselle's hand with his while they accidentally (intentionally) reached for the same book.

"Oh!" Mariselle exclaimed. "We discovered something rather interesting earlier. I accidentally knocked down one of Lady Eugenia's journals from the top shelf, and while leafing through it before replacing it, I noticed margin notes written in a hand entirely different from her own."

"Am I supposed to know who Lady Eugenia is?" Evryn enquired.

"Yes!" Mariselle looked faintly annoyed. "I'm quite sure I told you. She was the botanist who lived here before my grandfather ended up with this cottage. But that's beside the point. The margin notes were written by my grandmother. She signed her initials beneath all of them."

"Your *grandmother*? Why would she be writing in a botanist's journal?"

"It seems she took an interest in Lady Eugenia's research. But again, Evryn, you appear to be missing the point."

Evryn again. He was delightfully distracted by this. "And the point is …"

"She spent time here. Long enough to peruse the journals. Long enough to take an interest and make notes."

Evryn frowned. "I suppose that *might* be considered … interesting."

"Exactly," Mariselle said as she turned back to the papers scattered before her and began gathering them. "I intend to ask her about it when I next see her. And the teacups with the names painted on the sides."

After that, time passed in pleasant disorder. They gathered and stacked books, sorted diagrams, collected the wide variety of self-inking quills that had somehow migrated to the most curious and unlikely corners of the cottage, and debated whether to do anything about the fact that the rug now bore permanent impressions from the patterns on the dream core. And all the while, Evryn did his best to remain within a scandalously close radius of Mariselle—though her cousin, whether by accident or sheer diabolical instinct, had an exasperating knack for inserting herself directly between them at every opportunity.

Eventually, Petunia groaned and flopped back against the edge of the sofa. "Alas," she said, "I must depart."

Mariselle looked up from where she was sorting notebooks and documents into two separate piles: those relating to dream architecture and those that involved warding. "Already?"

"I told you about the gossip birds, did I not?" Petunia said, pushing herself up from the floor. "They've taken to starting up their nonsense at almost precisely midnight every night. Their squawking wakes half the house, and then Mother storms into my room in a fury and leans out the window to shriek back at them." She sighed. "It goes without saying that I need to be safely tucked into bed before this pleasant nightly occurrence."

"Oh, I was hoping to continue working on the wards tonight," Mariselle said, unable to keep the disappointment from her voice.

"Lady Petunia can take your carriage now, and I can escort you home later," Evryn offered smoothly. "If you'd like to stay here longer, that is."

"The two of you on one pegasus?" Petunia raised an eyebrow. "I think not, Rowanwood."

Evryn, watching Mariselle from the corner of his eye, noticed the way her eyes widened slightly and her lips pressed together. She bent over her books as though they had suddenly become the most fascinating thing in the world. Ah. She hadn't told Petunia they'd already shared a saddle.

He turned back to Petunia with perfect solemnity. "You're right. Much too improper. I shall fetch a carriage immediately. That way, Lady Mariselle and I can be thoroughly inappropriate behind velvet curtains instead."

Mariselle made a sound that was somewhere between a snort and a gasp. Petunia rolled her eyes. "Very well. Mari hasn't voiced any recent objections to your company, so I shall presume she does not fear for her virtue or her life. I suppose I may entrust her safe conveyance to you."

Evryn gave a grave nod. "Your faith moves me to tears, Lady Petunia."

From the direction of the floor, Mariselle muttered something that included the word 'insufferable,' though it was accompanied by a laugh.

Once Petunia was gone, quiet slowly settled over the cottage. Mariselle had opened one of the warding books and was seemingly absorbed in its contents, and Evryn took a few moments to simply watch her.

She had composed herself somewhat, sitting slightly more elegantly than before, though the evening's mirth still lingered in the gentle flush across her cheeks. The pegasus hairpin he'd crafted for her birthday gleamed softly in her hair, nestled alongside two longer pins whose subtle enchantment emitted a faint shimmer as they valiantly attempted to maintain order among her rebellious locks. Their magic was fighting a losing battle, however, as plenty of wayward strands had already escaped to frame her face.

Without a word, he lowered himself to Petunia's vacated spot on the floor, right beside Mariselle. "Tell me about the warding," he said, looking for an excuse to engage her. "What do the different patterns on the dream core mean?"

"Oh!" She looked up, her face brightening. "It's fascinating, actually." She launched into an elaborate explanation of the metallic patterns etched into the dream core, but Evryn absorbed precisely none of it. He found himself instead captivated by the animation in her features, the way her eyes lit up, how her hands sketched intricate patterns in the air as she spoke, punctuating her thoughts with graceful gestures.

"And … what remains to be done before Dreamland is ready to reveal to your family?" he asked when she'd finished. His gaze traced over her long lashes, her Brightcrest-blue eyes, the perfect curve of her mouth.

"We've made considerable progress," she said, looking over at the dream core. "I'll continue refining the scenes, adding depth and complexity—incorporating your storytelling elements. Not Petunia's absurd suggestions, of course." Her lips quirked in amusement. "She and I discovered that several crystals need to be imbued with her particular magic, allowing guests to cross the threshold between waking and the dream realm without her physical presence. Not strictly a necessity, but once the attraction is operating at a larger scale, it stands to reason that her constant attendance would prove impractical. And then there is the warding, of course. It's advancing well, though I still have more work to do in that regard."

She tucked a strand of hair behind her ear. "As for the exterior—the pavilion or tent that once sheltered the lumyrite framework—that's purely aesthetic. I don't believe we need to concern ourselves with that before the initial reveal. Once my family experiences Dreamland from within, they'll understand its value immediately. The outer appearance can be addressed later. So, in a few days, perhaps a week, we'll have a fully functional version of Dreamland." Her tone was calm, businesslike, though she wouldn't meet his eyes now. "Even if the outer aesthetics aren't complete, it should be enough to present to my family. Enough to fulfill the contract."

Evryn nodded slowly. "I see."

"And once the contract is satisfied," she went on, her voice carefully neutral, "and the marking on our hands fades, we can announce that the soulbond seems to have disappeared. That it could not withstand the years of animosity between our families. That we no longer intend to marry."

The words landed sharp and clean, like a blade pressed to the space between his ribs.

I am singularly privileged to soon call her my wife.

Evryn wanted that. Oh, stars, it hit him square in the chest again just how much he wanted that. And he was almost entirely convinced she wanted it too.

Setting aside the sudden tightness in his chest, as though invisible hands had reached in and gently squeezed his heart, he schooled his features into a rakish half-smile. "Pity," he said lightly, tilting his head as he watched her. "I must admit, I rather thought you'd have fallen for me by now."

Her eyes snapped to his. She blinked once, then burst into laughter. Bright, loud, and utterly amused. "You cannot be serious."

He made a show of placing a hand on his chest. "You wound me. Have you not heard of the famed Evryn Rowanwood charm?"

"I've heard tales," she said, struggling to contain her laughter. "None of them impressive."

He leaned a little closer. "Are you telling me you don't believe I could seduce you?"

"A Rowanwood seduce a Brightcrest? Ha!" Laughter danced in her eyes. "I should like to see you try."

"Oh? Would you now?" The quiet note in his voice shifted the air. Warm. Low. Dangerous.

She recognized the trap a moment too late—but she was Mariselle Brightcrest, and he knew she would never back down from a provocation. Exactly as he'd expected, she folded her arms, spine straightening, a challenge in her gaze. "Go on, then. Convince me."

Evryn turned fully toward her, slow and deliberate, never breaking her gaze. "I must warn you," he murmured, reaching out his hand, palm up. "Once I begin, I do not stop until I'm entirely victorious."

Another laugh escaped her, but there was a vulnerability in her gaze as she placed her hand lightly in his. "If your grand seduction begins with such staggering self-regard," she remarked, "I remain decidedly underwhelmed thus far."

"Oh, darling, I promise to thoroughly impress you before this game is through."

He caught the flare in her eyes before he lowered his gaze to her hand. Her palm sat lightly atop his, and with his other hand he began tracing the silvery patterns of the contract mark, following the spiraling path toward her wrist. He turned her hand slowly, then brought it to his mouth.

He kissed the inside of her wrist. Soft. Lingering. A whisper of heat against the fragile flutter beneath her skin. He heard the quiet inhale of her breath, but she didn't pull away. "Tell me when to stop," he murmured in a low tone, lips grazing over her skin.

Another kiss. Just below the first. Then another, further up, along the delicate inner curve of her forearm. Still no protest, and Evryn's breath hitched faintly, the weight of restraint coiling tighter in his chest. He'd imagined this, dreamed it, but the reality of her skin beneath his mouth was far more exquisite than anything his mind had conjured.

His thumb brushed over the curve of her wrist, while his lips traveled higher. He pressed a kiss to the crook of her elbow. Her breathing had shifted, uneven now, shallow, and he drew back just enough to look at her. Lips parted, eyes closed, lashes casting delicate shadows across her skin.

He lifted her hand once more, uncurling her fingers and pressing his lips to her palm. "You're not telling me to stop," he said against her skin, his voice huskier now, rough around the edges. "Should I take that to mean you're unaffected?"

She opened her eyes slowly. They were darker now, pupils blown wide. "Naturally," she answered, though the breathy tremor in her voice betrayed her.

He smiled against her palm, gaze still holding hers. "I don't think you're being entirely honest, Lady Mariselle."

"And I—" Her voice broke on the word. She swallowed. "I think you place far too much confidence in your abilities."

His smile stretched wider. Oh how he adored this game. He lowered her hand, though his thumb still traced lazy circles across the staccato of her pulse. His other hand slipped to the small of her back, splayed possessively against the curve of her spine as he drew her closer, until there was no more air between them, only shared breath and molten awareness.

Her chest rose and fell faster now, lips parted, and the dimming faelight had turned her skin to gold. Her lashes fluttered—half-lowered, dazed.

"Nothing?" Evryn asked, his voice a low, rough rumble as he lowered his lips to the bare skin between her neck and shoulder.

She exhaled a shuddering breath. "Nothing. I have yet to see … evidence of this … legendary Rowanwood charm. You'll have to try harder."

He let out a quiet laugh, low and unsteady against her shoulder. "Oh, darling," he whispered, the words threading between them like silk, "I can definitely do that."

His fingers rose to the delicate twists at the back of her head and felt for the pins that anchored the arrangement of her hair. He slowly eased one free, then the other. A cascade of soft blue curls slipped loose, tumbling over her shoulders. He dropped the pins onto the sofa behind her, leaving the tiny pegasus secured within the waterfall of waves that now framed her face.

"Have I mentioned," he murmured, reaching up to gently slide his fingers through her hair, "how exquisite you look in blue?"

Her eyelids wavered and closed again, a tremulous breath escaping her parted lips like a secret surrendered to the night.

He slowly swept her hair aside in a languid motion with one hand, while his other gently tilted her head just enough to bare the curve of her throat to him once more. "Tell me," he whispered again, brushing a kiss against the pulse point at her throat, "when to stop."

But she didn't say a word.

And he didn't stop.

His fingers slipped into the silken waves at the nape of her neck, tightening ever so slightly as his lips began a slow, deliberate trail upward. His other hand traced from the curve of her shoulder down the length of her arm, fingers gliding over silk and skin until he found her hand and laced his fingers through hers. She tightened her grip—fierce, unyielding—as though this were the only thing tethering her to the world while the rest of her threatened to unravel.

With each kiss, he felt her breath catch. He traced the line of her jaw, each press of his lips against her skin drawing increasingly ragged breaths from her the closer he moved to her mouth.

"Stop," she breathed suddenly on a sharp exhale.

She tugged her hand free and pushed him away, scrambling past him and standing. Her cheeks were flushed, her hair disheveled. "I believe," she said, attempting to smooth her wrinkled skirts and adjust her bodice while determinedly avoiding his gaze, "you've made your point. This game is over. I should return home before the hour grows any later."

"Mariselle," he began, rising to his feet, apology already forming on his lips. "I'm—"

"I bid you goodnight," she interrupted, already moving toward the door.

"Wait," he protested, following after her. "How do you propose to return home?"

She paused at the door, still not looking at him. "Cobalt is rather fond of me. I'm sure he won't object to bearing me home. I shall send him back for you once I arrive."

And before Evryn could say another word, she was gone, the door banging shut in his face.

Chapter Twenty-Four

MARISELLE SLIPPED THROUGH HER BEDROOM WINDOW, HER movements as silent as she could manage despite the thundering of her heart. The cool night air clung to her skin as she carefully closed the glass pane behind her, fingers trembling so fiercely she nearly fumbled the latch.

She pressed her back against the wall, waiting for her pulse to settle, for her breath to even out, for the heat in her cheeks to subside. None of these things happened.

Her bedchamber was dark and empty. No Tilly waiting with a raised eyebrow and a knowing smile, ready to help her out of her gown and into a nightdress. Mariselle had insisted her lady's maid not wait up for her these past weeks, as her visits to Windsong Cottage stretched later and later into the night. Instead, Tilly would artfully arrange pillows beneath the coverlet to create the illusion of a sleeping form before ensuring her parents had retired to their chambers and then seeking her own bed, leaving Mariselle free to slip in unnoticed.

She had never been more grateful for the solitude than tonight.

With unsteady steps, she crossed to the vanity and sank onto the cushioned stool, finally confronting her reflection in the silvered glass. A stranger stared back at her—cheeks flushed, hair tumbling in wild disarray over her shoulders. The tiny pegasus hairpin gleamed amid the waves, the only remaining anchor from her earlier, more composed self.

I promise to thoroughly impress you before this game is through.

It hadn't been merely a game though. She'd known that from the moment Evryn had first pressed his lips to her skin. His voice echoed in her mind, low and rough with desire, his words a whisper against her throat. Her fingers rose unbidden to the spot where his lips had brushed, where she could still feel the ghost of his touch.

Tell me when to stop.

But she hadn't wanted him to stop. That was the terrifying truth of it. If panic hadn't overtaken her at the last moment, she would have let him continue. Would have pulled him closer. Would have surrendered completely to whatever lay between them.

She reached up and gently touched the pegasus hairpin, the delicate lumyrite wings cool beneath her fingertips. The gift he'd crafted with his own hands. For her.

"This is madness," she whispered to her reflection. If she truly cared for him—if he truly cared for *her*—what did that mean for them? For this farce that was soon meant to come to a close?

Oh, darling …

A hundred ridiculous pet names, but *darling* … That was the one that was real. That was the one that slipped past her defenses and melted something inside her. And his voice—deep and quiet and ruinously husky. It had the power to undo her entirely.

She needed to speak to someone, needed to make sense of the chaos in her mind before it consumed her. Without another thought, she crossed to her bedside table and withdrew the small silver hand mirror.

"Petunia," she whispered, pressing her palm flat against the glass.

The mirror's surface rippled like disturbed water, then went dark. Mariselle waited, counting her heartbeats. When nothing happened, she pressed her palm to the glass again and began pacing the length of her room.

"Petunia," she repeated, more insistent this time. "Wake up, Tunia, please. It's urgent."

The mirror remained dark for several more moments before flickering to life, revealing Petunia's face, half-obscured by tangled hair and one cheek squashed against a lace-trimmed pillow. Her eyes blinked blearily. "Mari?"

she mumbled. "Whaswrong? Someone better be dead for you to have woken me at this hour."

"Tunia, I think …" Mariselle stopped pacing, her gaze focusing somewhere beyond the mirror, seeing again the liquid heat in Evryn's gaze. "I think …"

Petunia rolled onto her back and moaned sleepily. "Could we perhaps continue this discussion at a more civilized hour when you've determined precisely what it is that you *think*?"

Mariselle refocused on her cousin and took a breath. "I think I love him."

Petunia blinked, sleep clearing from her expression. "Who?"

"Evryn."

Petunia pushed herself up in a flurry of tangled hair. "You cannot be serious."

"I'm entirely serious."

"Oh, Mari, no!" She threw herself back onto her pillows with a groan. "I *knew* I should not have left the two of you alone there tonight. I could tell something was different."

"I don't know what to do," Mariselle moaned, resuming her pacing. "We're supposed to end this entire charade soon, but now … now I cannot stop thinking of him, and I want to be near him all the time, and I want to say things that will make him *smile*, and when he touches me, even just the slightest—"

"Stop." Petunia held up a hand. "You've clearly lost your mind. I suppose the kiss of the Rowanwood plague does that to a person."

Mariselle gave her cousin a rueful smile. "There was no kiss. There was *almost* a kiss—and my entire body almost ignited in the process—but I left before anything more could happen."

"Oh, thank goodness. Perhaps you still possess some sense."

"But what am I to do? Our families … well, mine at least is determined that a Rowanwood-Brightcrest union shall never take place."

"Mari …" Petunia sighed, shifted against her pillows, and tucked her hair behind one ear. "You need to be sensible about this. Is it even real? I don't want to hurt you by pointing this out, but Evryn is likely leading you on. He has a reputation, remember? This is probably nothing more than a game to him. He's spent years perfecting the art of charming women into losing their composure. You're just another conquest."

Mariselle slowly shook her head. "I don't believe that's true. I might have agreed with you a few weeks ago, but now ..." She sighed dreamily as she lowered herself to the edge of her bed. "You haven't seen how he is when we're alone. How different he is. So ... attentive, thoughtful, sincere. Especially in my dream. You know how difficult it is to be anything but honest in a shared dreamscape."

Petunia shoved herself upright again, eyes widening in complete horror. "Mariselle Brightcrest! You *dream shared* with him?"

"It wasn't intentional!"

"That's even worse!" Petunia gasped. "It happened when you didn't even *intend* it to? It's ... it's ... that means you didn't even realize how much you've allowed yourself to trust him. Mari, you must have dropped your guard entirely with him."

"Is that so bad?" Mariselle asked in a small voice.

"Yes! He's a Rowanwood! You need to stop and think rationally about all of this instead of gallivanting through your subconscious with the enemy."

"But he's not the enemy anymore," Mariselle whispered. "He truly isn't. And after spending some time with his family, I don't believe any of them are."

Petunia groaned dramatically and flopped back onto her pillows, one arm flung across her forehead. "You're hopeless."

Mariselle sighed, a soft, dreamy sound, and mirrored her cousin's action, falling back onto her own bed with one hand over her heart. "I know."

"Completely, utterly, beyond all reasonable salvation," Petunia continued.

"Mmm," Mariselle hummed in absent agreement, her gaze fixed on nothing as she held the mirror loosely at her side while replaying the feeling of Evryn's fingers threading through her hair.

"You're not going to get over this, are you?"

Mariselle rolled onto her stomach and propped herself up on one elbow as she gazed into the mirror. "I don't think one can just *get over* love, Tunia," Mariselle replied softly.

"Your parents shall expire on the spot when you tell them you wish to go through with this," Petunia pointed out. "Their melodrama will echo through the ages."

"Perhaps they'll come around," Mariselle suggested, though her voice lacked conviction. "Once they see Dreamland, once they understand what Evryn and I have accomplished together …"

She stared past the mirror, reliving the sensation of his fingers sliding between hers. Remembering how tightly she'd held onto him, how his touch made her feel secure and safe in a way she'd rarely known.

Anticipation tightened inside her. "Oh, Tunia, I don't know how I am to last until I can see him again tomorrow. The time feels as though it's stretching endlessly before me."

"Tragic indeed. I shall alert the gossip birds to spread the news: Lady slowly perishes of impatience."

Mariselle ignored her. "And when I *do* see him, what then? What am I to say? Oh, Tunia, it's the most maddening conundrum. I long to be near him, and yet I haven't the faintest idea what I'll say once I am."

Petunia threw an arm over her eyes and yawned. "You could ask him about his conversational muscles," she mumbled.

"Petunia! That isn't remotely helpful."

"Why? He's clearly the sort to possess conversational muscles."

"No, dear cousin, he possesses muscles that are very much made for lifting things." Mariselle's skin flushed at the memory of Evryn helping her down over the Dreamland ruins, his shoulders broad and firm beneath her hands. "I know because I have … ah … been lifted."

Petunia lowered her arm, brows shooting upward.

"Over the Dreamland ruins!" Mariselle added hastily, her face burning.

"Yes, that definitely sounded like what you meant."

"Petunia Dawndale!"

"Mariselle Brightcrest!"

Mariselle started laughing. "What now? Are we simply stating each other's names until—"

She froze, a sound reaching her ears from somewhere outside her room. Footsteps. Muffled voices.

"Oh no," she whispered, then flattened her palm on the mirror's surface before shoving it beneath her pillow. She scrambled off her bed in the same instant her bedroom door burst open, revealing her father standing in the doorway, still fully dressed despite the late hour. Behind him loomed her mother, wrapped in a silk dressing gown, her face a mask of cold fury.

"I told you I heard voices," Lady Brightcrest said, her gaze sweeping the room. "And look, here she stands! Still in her evening gown and looking entirely … compromised."

"Where is he?" Mariselle's father growled. "Where are you hiding him?"

Mariselle took a step forward, confusion giving way to understanding as her mother barged past her father and stalked toward the wardrobe, flinging it open with such force that the doors banged against the wall.

"Mother, there's no one—"

"Do not lie to us," Lady Brightcrest snapped, striding past Mariselle toward the dressing screen. "I know that Rowanwood boy was in here. I heard voices. He—oh!" Her gaze landed on the cleverly arranged pillows beneath the bedcovers. She marched triumphantly past Mariselle and tore the coverlet back—

Then spun back to Mariselle. "What is this?" she demanded as the disturbed pillows settled.

"Look at yourself," Lord Brightcrest said in a cold voice. "Your hair is a mess, your gown is wrinkled, and your bed is arranged to give the false impression of a sleeping form. You have clearly been out this evening. *Unchaperoned.*"

"Father, it isn't what—"

"Do not insult our intelligence," he said, his voice dangerously quiet. "Where were you? With him?"

Mariselle exhaled slowly. She supposed there was no point in denying it. Her appearance along with the pillow arrangement was evidence enough that she had snuck out. "Yes. But nothing—"

She broke off. She'd been about to assure them that nothing of an improper nature had occurred, but that wasn't precisely true. If it had been any other night, then perhaps yes. But tonight? Tonight had been very different.

Her father, however, wasn't about to give her a moment more to come up with an explanation. "This is beyond acceptable behavior!" her father exploded, his face flushing dark with rage. "Sneaking out to rendezvous with a young man, unchaperoned, at this hour? Have you lost all sense of propriety? Of dignity? Was anyone witness to this shameful display? Any of those damned birds? Do you understand what this would do to your reputation— to our family name—if even a whisper of this reached society's ears? The Brightcrest legacy would be tarnished for generations!"

"N-no, Father, there was no one else present. The family name will—"

"Thank the stars for small mercies. Now. I met with that Lord Hemenlock this evening," he continued, his tone clipped. "The lord with the disjuncture manifestation. He believes a soulbond should be no different from other enchantments he's broken. The procedure will take place the day after tomorrow."

The world seemed to tilt beneath Mariselle's feet. "What?"

"You have utterly failed in the one useful task we assigned you—to extract any information that might give us leverage over the Rowanwoods," her father said with cold dismissal. "Your inability to perform even this simple duty only confirms our judgment. It's time we sever this abominable connection to that family."

"But I love him!" Mariselle blurted out.

And unlike the first time she'd uttered those words to her parents in this very room, she now meant them wholly and entirely.

Her father's expression shifted from anger to disgust. Before she could react, he advanced, hand shooting out, fingers closing around her wrist in a grip so tight she gasped. "Love?" he spat the word. "I told you never to utter that word again in regard to a *Rowanwood*."

His grip tightened further, sending a pulse of pain up her arm. Mariselle whimpered, trying to pull away, but he held fast, his fingers digging into the delicate bones of her wrist.

"Do you understand me?"

"Father, you're—"

"I said *do you understand me?*"

"Let go of me!" she shouted, shoving hard against his chest with her free hand as some spark of defiance that usually sputtered and died in her parents' presence ignited like a flame.

He released her wrist, the look on his face suggesting it was more from shock than from the force of her push. For a moment, they stared at each other, mutual disbelief hanging in the air between them.

Then his hand came up, fast and merciless, the crack of the slap echoing in the quiet room. The force of the blow sent her stumbling backward, the edge of her bed catching her behind the knees. She collapsed onto the mattress, her palm rising to her stinging cheek, tears aching behind her eyes.

"Dear," her mother murmured, and Mariselle saw enough through her fingers to know that her mother was placing a restraining hand on her father's arm—though whether out of concern for Mariselle or fear that servants might hear, it was impossible to tell.

Lord Brightcrest shook his wife off, breathing hard, pointing a trembling finger at Mariselle. "You will remain in this room until further notice. Your mother and I will personally escort you to the procedure the day after tomorrow. The only time you will leave this house is when you're accompanied by one or both of us. Your bedchamber will be enchanted to prevent your departure. You have proven yourself untrustworthy, and I will not have the Brightcrest name dragged through the mud because my daughter cannot control herself around a Rowanwood."

The finality in his voice sent a chill through her. This was truly happening. They were going to break the bond, separate her from Evryn, lock her away like a shameful secret.

As the two of them turned and made for the door, she sat up, one hand still covering her throbbing cheek. "It's not a soulbond," she blurted out, desperation overtaking caution. "There is no soulbond. There never was."

Her parents turned back to her, twin expressions of shock on their faces.

"What did you say?" her mother whispered.

The words tumbled out in a desperate rush. "There is no soulbond. It's a marking that relates to a magical contract. A contract drawn up by Grandmother and Valenrik Rowanwood years ago. An agreement to restore Dreamland."

"Dreamland?" her father barked. "This is about *Dreamland?*"

"Evryn and I accidentally triggered the contract when we came across it at Windsong Cottage. And it seemed like it might actually be possible to fulfill. He possesses the lumyrite shaping ability, and I possess the magic necessary for dream architecture, so we decided to go ahead. We made up the entire soulbond story so we could work on the restoration project in secret without having to answer questions about what the magical marking related to," she continued, her voice growing strength as her parents simply stared, mouths agape. "It looks almost precisely like a soulbond, so the story came naturally. And Father, we're so close. So close to restoring it to what it once was. Dreamland will be *ours!* It will rival the influence of The Charmed Leaf. It will bring prestige to our family—"

"You lied to us," her mother said, her voice hollow with disbelief. "To society. To everyone."

"I had to," Mariselle insisted. "I knew you wouldn't listen until I had something tangible to show you. But Dreamland is *extraordinary*. If you could only see it for yourselves—"

"You lied about your *magic?*" her mother hissed.

"I—"

"Are you saying you possess *architect abilities?*" her father asked, his voice low and dangerous.

"Yes," she answered quietly. Her cheek was beginning to throb harder now, the pain radiating outward across her face.

He took a step closer, his finger raised to point directly at her once more. "Know this, Mariselle. It matters not how wondrous Dreamland could be if you actually had the first notion of what to do with the power you have *lied* to us about. What matters is that the Brightcrests will never, *ever* undertake any venture that relies on cooperation with a Rowanwood."

"But—"

"As for these abilities you've been hiding from us," he continued, "we will find a way to put them to proper use. And this changes nothing regarding that detestable marking on your hand. Whether a soulbond or a contract mark, it will be removed two days hence."

They moved toward the door. Her mother stepped out first, while her father paused and looked back. "The possession of dream architect magic is perhaps the singular aspect of your existence not entirely steeped in disappointment. It's a shame you chose to reveal it to us this way. Nevertheless, we shall find a suitable purpose for it."

The door closed behind them with a decisive click. Footsteps. Murmurs. Then the distinctive hum of enchantments being woven into the wood, the walls—spells to keep her trapped within.

Mariselle sat frozen on her bed, pain pulsing in steady waves from both her wrist and her cheek. The enormity of what had just occurred washed over her. She had revealed the truth about everything—and it had not mattered. It meant nothing to them. *She* still meant nothing to them.

Well, they seemed to prize the discovery of her dream architect abilities, but it was painfully clear they viewed the magic as deserving a worthier vessel than herself—as if even this extraordinary gift was somehow diminished by its connection to her. It was perhaps fortunate she hadn't mentioned the various other abilities she'd manifested.

Mariselle squeezed her eyes shut, allowing tears to fall, and finally accepted that nothing she ever did would make a difference to her family.

With a shaking hand, she reached up to find the pegasus hairpin still nestled in her hair. It was likely only the intricate tangle of her curls that had kept the pin anchored in place as the wind had swept through her hair during Cobalt's flight home—though the pegasus had flown unusually slowly, as if sensing his passenger wasn't properly attired for his usual racing speeds.

She gently pulled the pin free from her hair, placed it on the palm of her marked hand, and wrapped her fingers loosely around it. And then, still in her wrinkled gown, she curled onto her side atop the bedcovers and wept until exhaustion finally claimed her.

Chapter Twenty-Five

THE DREAM WAS DISJOINTED IN A WAY THAT MADE MARISELLE'S familiar twilight dreamscape waver like a mirage in desert heat. The waves crashed too loudly against the shore, then fell utterly silent before roaring again. The colors of twilight shifted unnaturally, bleeding from ink-dark purple to blinding silver in violent pulses, as though the very sky were a wounded thing gasping for breath.

Her parents' words echoed in her mind.

You have utterly failed …

You have proven yourself untrustworthy …

… entirely steeped in disappointment.

The tears that had soaked her pillow in the waking world seemed to have followed her here, making the dreamscape blur and distort as she staggered toward the crashing waves and collapsed onto the sand. It had happened before, this intrusion of waking sorrow into her private sanctuary when her heart was too heavy with profound distress to allow peaceful slumber.

"You ran away from me."

The voice behind her sent a jolt through her body. She turned to find Evryn standing there, a teasing smile playing on his lips, though a certain hesitation seemed to hold him back.

"Evryn," she whispered, relief washing through her so strongly it made her dizzy. "You're here."

His smile faltered slightly. "What did you say?" His voice sounded distant, as though he were speaking from underwater.

"I said—" But the dreamscape rippled violently, the beach beneath them seeming to dissolve for a moment before reforming. When it stabilized, Evryn stood a few paces closer, his playful expression replaced with concern.

"Mariselle? What's wrong?" He reached for her, took her hand, pulled her to her feet—but the world tilted, and when it righted itself once more, there was distance between them again.

"My parents," she began, the words feeling thick in her throat. "They discovered—" The sound disappeared from her own ears, though her lips continued moving. She could see confusion spreading across Evryn's features.

"I can't hear you," he said, frustration evident in his voice. "Something's different tonight."

The edges of the dreamscape shimmered and blurred, the ocean fading to translucence before solidifying once more. Evryn's form flickered like a candle flame in a breeze.

"You're upset," he said, moving toward her once more. "I'm so sorry, Mariselle. What happened in the cottage earlier … if I'd known it would make you so upset, I would never have—"

She shook her head vigorously, hoping to make him understand, even if he couldn't hear her words. "It's not that. It's not you. It's my parents. They —" She tried to explain, but the sound seemed to be swallowed by the very air around them. Tears of frustration welled in her eyes. "They know every-thing, and now they've locked me away," she managed, though she couldn't tell if the words reached him.

Evryn's expression grew more troubled as he watched her lips move. He stepped closer, only to have the dreamscape fragment around them, sending him further from her when it reformed.

Mariselle wrapped her arms around herself as her tears fell faster, the salt-sting of them a cruel mockery of her beloved ocean. Even her sanctuary had betrayed her now, fracturing into pieces that reflected her shattered state, leaving her adrift and more utterly alone than she had ever felt before. She sobbed, and the stars above winked in and out of existence. The waves froze mid-crash before surging forward again.

Evryn moved toward her with careful, deliberate steps, as though walking on ice that might crack beneath him. He reached out, touched her shoulder, and she felt the warmth of his hand through the fabric of her sleeve.

This time, the dream did not fragment.

He pulled her gently into his arms, one hand pressed firmly against her back while the other cradled the back of her head, fingers threading through her hair as he guided her tear-streaked face to rest against his shoulder. The contact sent a shudder of relief through her entire body.

She sensed him saying something, murmuring against her hair, but his words disappeared into the wind that gusted one moment and fell utterly still the next. She pressed her face against his shoulder, breathing in the scent of him. The dreamscape around them steadied slightly, the violent shifts slowing to a gentler undulation.

After what could have been moments or hours, he pulled back slightly to look at her face. "Remove your slippers," he said, his voice surprisingly clear.

"What?"

He gestured toward her feet, which she realized were still clad in delicate evening slippers. "You told me you like to dance barefoot in the sand."

Something within her longed to smile, but the night's wounds were still too fresh. She slipped her feet free, feeling the cool sand beneath them, grounding her. The dreamscape steadied further.

Evryn's hands found her waist, drawing her close again. Her head rested against his shoulder. He began to move, a slow, gentle sway that bore no resemblance to the structured dances of ballrooms. If anything, it was more an embrace set in motion than a dance, but she followed his lead, feeling her heartbeat gradually slow to match the rhythm of their movement.

The cool sand shifted between her toes with each step, while the ocean's gentle hush created a soothing cadence that matched their unhurried movements. The stars above regained their brilliance. The cottage solidified completely.

"Are you all right?" Evryn's voice was quiet but not distant.

She nodded, her cheek brushing against his shoulder. "Thank you," she whispered. The dreamscape's newfound peace felt too fragile to disturb with louder words, and her spirit—though steadying beneath his touch—remained like a bird with crumpled wings, needing stillness to heal.

"You asked me before," he said quietly, "what I dream of." He paused, drawing back slightly so he could look down into her eyes. The world around them held perfectly still, as if the dream was holding its breath. "I dream of this."

His hands rose to cup her face, his thumbs brushing gently against her cheeks. Then he leaned forward and brought his mouth to—

Mariselle blinked awake, a gasp in her throat and the phantom touch of an almost-kiss on her lips.

Chapter Twenty-Six

MARISELLE PACED THE PERIMETER OF HER BEDCHAMBER. SEVEN STEPS along the wall with the window. Turn. Twelve steps past her wardrobe. Turn. Seven steps toward the dressing screen. She stopped and forced herself to take a steadying breath, eyes closed for a moment. It had been barely a day, and already she felt as though she may lose her mind.

She paused at the window once more, pressing her fingertips against the pane. The enchantments her father had woven hummed against her skin, an unpleasant vibration.

She turned away, continuing her circuit. As she passed the vanity, she caught sight of the small silver hand mirror and wondered if Evryn had received the message Petunia had sent him this morning.

Her cousin had been nearly frantic with worry after their abruptly terminated conversation the night before. They'd spoken as soon as they were both awake that morning. Well, after Mariselle had stared at the canopy above her bed for a not insignificant amount of time, replaying the sensation of *almost* having been dream-kissed. She had then told herself that it was the least of her concerns at that moment, and had reached for the hand mirror.

She'd explained to Petunia about her parents discovering her absence, that they knew all about the Dreamland plans—and didn't appear to care—and that they intended to remove the contract mark tomorrow. She'd been careful

269

to omit certain details—like her father's hand striking her face, or his fingers crushing her wrist with enough force to leave a ring of mottled purple beneath her skin.

"I'll send word to Evryn," Petunia had promised after Mariselle requested she dispatch a note with the earliest available messenger pixie. "Though I shan't be able to assist you at the cottage this evening. Mother has invited Lord What's-His-Name with the one yellow eye to dinner. The gentleman who's been hinting about seeking a 'youthful companion' since his last wife expired. Mother is convinced he intends to offer for me this very evening, despite my assuring her that I would sooner court a toad."

Now, as dusk deepened outside her window, Mariselle paused to examine her appearance in the mirror above her vanity. The bruise on her cheek had darkened overnight to a dark blueish purple, stark against her pale skin. She'd spent a considerable amount of time that morning carefully applying layers of powder and cream to conceal it. With similar care, she'd wrapped a delicate silk ribbon around her wrist, securing it with a bow that appeared decorative but served to hide the worst of the bruising there.

She would have preferred a simple healing charm, but she'd realized with dismay that morning that her reticule—with its magically expanded interior containing a variety of useful potions and charms—had been left behind at Windsong Cottage in her haste to flee Evryn's seduction attempt.

At the thought of Evryn, her mind immediately conjured the almost-kiss from her dream. The way his hands had cradled her face, how he'd leaned in, his lips just a breath away from hers before she'd awakened with a start. She pressed her fingers to her mouth, then immediately dropped her hand, frustrated with herself.

"Focus," she whispered. She couldn't afford to be distracted now.

Somewhere in between staring at her canopy and reaching for her mirror to speak to Petunia, Mariselle had felt her determination solidify, her resolve crystallizing into an unshakable plan. The contract between the Brightcrests and Rowanwoods had been clear: restore Dreamland to functional capacity. They were so close now. So tantalizingly close. But what would happen if her parents succeeded in removing the contract mark tomorrow? Would it somehow undo all their work? Unravel the delicate magic she'd already woven into the dream core? She couldn't risk it. She had to finish tonight.

A soft knock at her door broke through her thoughts. She stilled. Dinner. This was the moment she'd been waiting for.

"Enter," she called, smoothing her skirts and positioning herself beside her bed, the perfect picture of resigned captivity.

The door opened to reveal not Tilly, as she'd hoped, but one of the younger kitchen maids she wasn't well acquainted with, carrying a tray. Behind her stood Hadley, one of her father's most trusted footmen, his expression impassive as he supervised the delivery of her meal.

Mariselle's heart sank. She'd feared her parents might have dismissed Tilly upon discovering the ruse with the pillows, suspecting her lady's maid of aiding in her nightly escapes. The absence of her most loyal ally within the household confirmed those suspicions.

"Your dinner, Lady Mariselle," the maid said, bobbing a curtsy as she entered.

Mariselle smiled, a practiced curve of her lips that didn't reach her eyes. "Thank you."

The young woman approached, balancing the tray carefully. Hadley remained in the doorway, ever vigilant. He'd been guarding her room since her parents left for dinner at the Silverthorns earlier.

Now. It had to be now.

As the maid drew near, Mariselle stepped forward as if to take the tray, deliberately moving too quickly and causing the maid to startle. The tray tilted, a glass tumbler wobbling precariously.

"Oh! I'm so sorry, my lady—"

"No, no, it was my fault entirely," Mariselle said, reaching out to steady the tray with one hand while her other hand brushed against the young woman's bare wrist.

The effect was immediate. The woman's eyes widened in surprise, then glazed over, her muscles going slack as sleep overcame her. The tray began to tip, and Mariselle caught it swiftly as the young woman slumped forward against the edge of the bed and then slid to the floor.

"So sorry," she whispered, directing an apologetic look at the woman's sleeping form as she hastened to set the tray down on the bed.

"What's going on?" Hadley called, alarm sharpening his voice as he stepped into the room. "Lady Mariselle, what's—"

"Oh!" Mariselle gasped, pressing a hand to her chest in convincing distress. "Hadley, please! I don't know what happened—she just collapsed!"

The footman rushed forward, concern etched across his features. He knelt beside the unconscious maid, checking her pulse, entirely focused on the young woman's still form as Mariselle made a show of leaning over him while pressing her palm to the exposed skin at his neck. For several moments, nothing happened, but then Hadley's movements became sluggish, his head beginning to droop as his expression shifted from concern to vague confusion.

He swayed on his feet, and Mariselle caught him awkwardly as he fell, bracing herself against the edge of the bed and groaning with the effort of lowering his considerable weight to the floor.

She straightened, breathing hard, looking between the two of them with a twinge of guilt. They would sleep deeply for several hours and wake with nothing more than mild confusion about how they'd come to doze off at their posts.

Moving quickly now, Mariselle slid her enchanted mirror out from beneath her pillows—she planned to speak to Petunia later—hurried past the two sleeping forms, and paused in her doorway. After glancing both ways down the hall, she closed her bedroom door behind her and set off.

Mariselle's parents had taken an enchanted carriage out to dinner, but fortunately the Brightcrests owned more than one. It was a simple matter, as it had been numerous times before, to slip past the main stables where the horses and pegasi were kept alongside the conventional carriages. The grooms were invariably occupied with the evening feed at this hour, and the night watchman had the regrettable habit of dozing in the small anteroom by the tack room.

The adjoining carriage house, with its blessedly whisper-quiet hinges, housed the family's collection of enchanted conveyances. Mariselle had perfected the cloaking spell for the carriage over the past weeks, and within minutes, she was seated comfortably within the now-invisible vehicle as it glided silently away from Brightcrest Manor, responding to her whispered destination without hesitation.

When at last it arrived at the furthest accessible point near Dreamland, Mariselle flung open the door without waiting for the carriage to come to a complete stop, her mirror still clutched in one hand. Her slippered feet hit the ground with a soft thud, and she gathered her skirts, uncaring of the brambles that caught at the delicate fabric as she hurried along the winding path toward Windsong Cottage.

"Please let me have enough time," she whispered, the words a desperate prayer carried away by the evening breeze. She quickened her already hurried pace, pulse thrumming with urgency as she reached the door and pushed it open.

The faelights brightened as she stepped inside, illuminating the cottage almost exactly as she'd left it the night before. It appeared Evryn had done some further tidying of the space after she'd fled, but her books, notes and diagrams were all precisely as she'd left them.

For a moment, she was consumed by the memory of sitting cross-legged on the floor mere inches from Evryn, his fingers tracing the spiraling patterns on her arm and along her wrist, his lips pressed to the sensitive hollow of her neck, the whisper of his breath against her skin.

Darling …

The way his hands had slid through her hair, freeing it from its pins. Something deep within her had begun to unravel as he'd—

With a sharp intake of breath, Mariselle forced the memories away, pressing a fist to her brow. She couldn't afford such distractions. Not now, when she needed to focus her efforts on the dream core. Not ever, since her parents had made it abundantly clear that she would never marry a Rowanwood.

She stifled the sob that rose in the back of her throat, threatening to choke her, as she placed the hand mirror on the large oak table and moved to the sideboard. She opened the drawer she'd placed the contract into that first night. Dreamland would never be hers, but she could at least finish it. She could fulfill the terms of the contract and release both herself and Evryn from its magical obligations before her parents' forced severance potentially damaged the delicate work they'd accomplished.

Then Evryn could steward Dreamland into its new era—she trusted his vision and his understanding of what the realm needed to flourish. He did not possess dream magic, but he could search the isles and find another dream architect to work with. The thought made tears well in her eyes again.

She blinked them away and raised the parchment to the light, her eyes moving methodically over each line, reminding herself of the exact requirements that must be met before the contract would consider their obligation fulfilled.

The heirs bound by this mark shall combine their magics to restore Dreamland to its former glory. She continued reading. *The binding mark shall remain until such time as Dreamland stands ready to welcome visitors once more …*

Well. That was somewhat vague. In its current state, Dreamland might already be considered prepared to welcome visitors. She and Evryn had been inside. Did they not count? She bit her lip and scanned the terms once more. It was likely the wards, she decided. They needed to be properly completed. After all, Dreamland could not be considered 'ready' if it was not entirely safe.

She crossed to the sitting area, kicked her slippers off, and sat on the rug. Drawing her knees up to her chest and closing her eyes, she mentally reviewed what needed to be done. She'd transferred the magic for multiple completed core scenes, but the transitions between them needed refinement. The narrative structure Evryn had suggested remained only half-integrated. And the wards, of course. The protective dream magic that hummed through her veins but still needed to be transferred via complex spells into the swirling patterns etched across the dream core's surface. The part that was the furthest from being complete.

Finish the scenes and narrative first, she told herself. *Then return to the warding spells.*

She tucked her hair behind her ears, shifted across the floor until she sat beside the dream core, and began. The work required absolute concentration, steady hands, and a clarity of vision that left no room for distraction.

Which was precisely what she needed—to lose herself in the work, to forget everything else. Her father's cold fury and her mother's disappointment and the way Evryn looked at her with that teasing sparkle in his eyes. To forget the throbbing pain in her wrist and the ghost of almost-kisses on her lips.

Time blurred as she worked, the cottage quiet save for the rustle of papers, the occasional scratch of her quill as she added to her notes, and her own measured breathing. The crystals embedded in the dream core pulsed brighter with each new addition, responding to her magic, absorbing her vision.

The effort drained her with each passing minute, a bone-deep weariness seeping into her limbs. She had already poured so much of herself into this work over endless nights, her magic bleeding into the dream core until it sometimes felt as though parts of her essence lived within the crystals themselves. Reality began to blur at the edges of her vision, wisps of half-formed dreams whispering enticingly to her, offering the sweet oblivion of sleep. She blinked firmly, turning her wrist this way and that, allowing the sharp pain to clear the fog from her mind.

"Mariselle?"

She startled, her quill jerking across the page and leaving a jagged streak of ink, and looked up to find Evryn closing the front door behind him, loosening the collar of his riding jacket. His hair was windblown, his riding gear slightly disheveled, as though he'd come in haste.

"You're here," she said, relief flooding through her. She couldn't recall entirely *why* she'd requested he come. He couldn't help with the dream core's magic, and she'd made it clear to herself that she could not afford to be distracted by any lingering romantic notions or dangerous seduction games between them. No, she had simply … needed him. His steadying presence. And now that he was here, all she wanted to do was fall into his arms.

Which could not happen.

"Of course I'm here." He crossed the room toward her, concern evident in his eyes as they swept over her face. "I would have come sooner, but Petunia's message only reached me this evening. I had thought, after last night … after the way you left … that you might not want me here." He crouched down, though he took care to keep a respectable amount of distance between them. "I'm so sorry. I didn't mean to upset you with that silly game of—"

"My parents know everything," she interrupted.

He paused, eyes widening. "What?"

"They discovered my absence last night. They were … displeased." She steadfastly avoided Evryn's gaze as she continued. "I ended up telling them everything. About Dreamland, the contract, the false story regarding the soulbond. I didn't mention your manuscript, of course. Which reminds me …"

She rose and returned to the sideboard on the other side of the room, where she opened the drawer beside the one that housed the contract and removed the rumpled collection of pages that had been the catalyst for this entire endeavor.

"I should have returned this to you some time ago. I'm sorry." She held the manuscript out to him.

After a moment, he slowly reached for it, a small frown pulling at his brow and his eyes seeming to focus somewhere beyond the pages, as though he'd barely registered what she was handing him. His eyes slid up to meet hers.

"Mariselle, what happened last night?" His gaze was too keen now, too searching, as though he'd already guessed more than she wished him to know.

She took a breath and focused on her hands. The ribbon she'd tied around her wrist that morning was still there, though looser now. She needed to redo it when Evryn wasn't looking. "As I said, my parents were … displeased to discover that I'd been out unchaperoned with … with you." She swallowed. "They have arranged to have the contract mark removed tomorrow. Someone with a 'disjuncture' manifestation, I believe it is. And they … they've confined me to my bedchamber. With enchantments."

"*What?*"

"Though clearly I determined a way to sneak out, or I wouldn't be here," she continued, stepping past him and returning to the sitting area. He followed her.

"Mariselle, stop, please. Look at me."

"I cannot *stop*, Evryn," she insisted, something desperate in her voice now. She turned to face him, though she still couldn't meet his eyes. "Tomorrow, the connection between the two of us and the contract will be prematurely severed. If we haven't yet fulfilled the contract terms, what will happen? Will all my work on the dream core be undone?"

"I … don't know."

"Precisely! We do not know! And that is why I cannot stop. I must finish this. I must …"

The edges of her vision wavered briefly, a fleeting moment of lightheadedness that made her instinctively reach for the nearest armchair to steady herself. It passed, but not before Evryn noticed the subtle motion, his gaze missing nothing as he took a step closer.

"Mariselle—"

"I'm fine," she interrupted automatically.

"Your hands are shaking," he said, concern deepening in his eyes.

"I am merely … agitated. Because I need to continue with my work, and you're insisting I stop and … what? Talk?"

"I'm insisting you stop because you appear to have driven yourself beyond all reasonable limits. How much magic have you given the dream core tonight?"

"Not nearly enough," she muttered.

"Mariselle, this is serious." He advanced another few steps. "You need to slow down. However important you think Dreamland is, it's not worth your—"

"Of course you would say that!" she shouted, tears of frustration burning behind her eyes now, fear and desperation making her lash out. "Of course you would have no notion of how important it is to me! You already have *everything* you could possibly want! A family that loves you unconditionally, writing that fulfills you, freedom to go wherever and do whatever!"

He was already shaking his head before she'd finished. "I don't have everything," he said quietly, his gaze holding hers. He moved until he stood right before her. "I don't have *you.*"

His words pierced through her defenses and something deep within her broke open, releasing a flood of longing and grief and the impossible hope she'd held onto for so long. Tears spilled down her cheeks as she shook her head.

"Don't say things like that," she whispered shakily, swiping at her cheek with one hand. "You know it isn't possible. It's never been possible. Not with our families—"

"My family *likes* you, Mariselle. We can—"

"*My* family will never allow it! Your family is wonderful and warm and I wish I could call them my own brothers and sisters. I wish I could …" She sucked in another shuddering breath. *I wish I could have you,* she wanted to say.

Instead she dragged the backs of her hands across her tear-streaked cheeks. "This is all I have, Evryn," she choked out on a sob. "My magic. And even that my parents intend to harness for their own gain now that they've discovered what I can do. Please just let me finish this. I need to finish this. Before they take everything else from me."

Her words fell into an oddly strained silence, because Evryn had gone perfectly still, his gaze no longer holding hers, focused instead on something else on her face. "What is that?" he asked, his voice low with quietly restrained horror.

And Mariselle froze. Because she knew precisely what he had just seen.

"It's—nothing," she stammered, her hand rising to cover her cheek, where her tears must have dissolved the carefully applied cosmetics.

But Evryn's gaze shifted again, widening with further horror as it landed on her wrist where the loose ribbon had slid aside, revealing the dark circle of bruises that marked the delicate skin beneath. "Mariselle—"

"It's nothing," she repeated, firmer this time, lowering her hand and lifting her chin.

But Evryn's bright, unyielding gaze caught hold of hers, and his voice held an intensity she had not heard before when he said, "What happened last night?"

Her pulse thundered in her ears and a strange rushing sound had begun to fill the corners of her mind. She blinked the odd sensation away. "Evryn, none of that is important now. I need you to help me ..." She trailed off as the world blurred alarmingly at the edges again.

"Mariselle?" There was an unmistakable edge of fear in his voice now.

The cottage swam before her eyes, reality growing thin and permeable. Whispers called out to her, enticing and seductive, promising rest and escape. She felt cool sand beneath her feet, saw twilight-tinted waves crash over the large oak table.

Then the room tilted sharply.

She heard Evryn call her name, felt his arms around her, and then nothing at all as the dream realm claimed her.

Chapter Twenty-Seven

"Mariselle!"

Evryn lunged forward, catching her as she crumpled, her body suddenly boneless in his arms. Fear stole his breath, turned his blood to ice. "Mariselle?" His voice emerged as a ragged whisper. "Wake up. Please wake up."

But her face remained slack, her breathing slow.

Panic surged through him, cold and paralyzing. She had pushed herself too far, poured too much of her magic into the dream core. He'd seen the signs, had tried to make her stop, but she had been so desperate, so determined—

He gathered her closer and stepped around the sofa. The cottage's small bedroom lay just beyond the main sitting area, a space he'd barely glimpsed during their many sessions here. He shouldered the door open, revealing a modest chamber with a single bed draped in faded linens, a nightstand, and a simple wardrobe. All perfectly preserved exactly as the rest of the cottage had been.

He placed Mariselle gently on the bed, careful to position her head on the pillow. Her blue hair was stark and vivid against the pallor of her skin.

"Please," he whispered, his fingers finding the pulse at her throat. It fluttered beneath his touch, present, but unsteady. "Please wake up. Please wake up."

But she didn't stir.

This was more than ordinary exhaustion. He knew it with a certainty that hollowed him out. This was the kind of exhaustion brought on by extreme magic use. What he didn't know was the true extent of how bad it was. Had she pushed herself too far? Was she forever trapped now in the dream realm, the way her grandfather had been?

The thought filled him with such paralyzing fear that for several moments he could barely breathe. He forced himself to suck in a gasp of breath as he lurched away from the bedside. He tugged at his hair, his breath ragged, words tumbling from his lips in an endless succession of *no* and *please* and *somebody help her.*

But this was utterly useless. Of course nobody would help her if all Evryn did was stand at her bedside and plead for it. He had to send for someone. But who? And how?

He was in the kitchen before his mind could form a coherent plan, frantically searching for a dusk sprite or a kitchen pixie—any magical creature that might carry a message. But Windsong Cottage, long abandoned until their recent project, housed no such helpful beings.

He could go himself, of course. Cobalt's wings would carry him through the night faster than any carriage. But he couldn't leave Mariselle alone. What if something happened to her while he—

"Mari?" A familiar voice, female and concerned, called from somewhere in the main room. "Mariselle, are you there?"

Evryn's head snapped up, relief flooding through him so intensely his knees nearly buckled. "Petunia!"

He rushed back into the main room, expecting to see Mariselle's cousin at the door. But it was closed, the entrance standing empty, the cottage silent save for—

"Hello? Mari, are you there?"

The voice seemed to come, oddly enough, from the large table Evryn so often worked at. Atop its polished surface lay a small silver hand mirror he hadn't previously noticed, its surface rippling like disturbed water. Evryn approached cautiously, then nearly sagged with relief as Petunia's face appeared in the glass.

He had never seen the mirror before, but this was clearly how Mariselle and her cousin communicated. "Rowanwood?" Petunia's eyes widened in surprise as Evryn picked up the mirror and peered into it. "Where's Mariselle?"

"She's—" His voice cracked, and he cleared his throat. "She's unconscious. I don't know what happened. She was working on the dream core, and I think she used too much magic. She seemed exhausted and then she simply … collapsed. I can't wake her."

Petunia's expression shifted from confusion to alarm. "How long has she been like this?"

"I—I don't know." He began pacing again, the mirror held up before him. "Ten minutes? Twenty? It feels like hours." He raked a hand through his hair. "I don't know what to do. She needs help. Someone who understands dream magic, or—or overuse of magic or—something!"

"Um, okay, I …" It was disquieting to see the normally unshakeable Petunia so uncertain and flustered. Something about it added to Evryn's heightened sense of panic. "Our grandmother!" she said suddenly. "I'll send word at once. Or—should I go myself?" She dragged a hand over her face. "I can find a way to—No, a kitchen pixie would be better. They're incredibly speedy when properly motivated."

"Yes, okay, thank you."

Petunia's face swung out of view before Evryn could say another word, and the mirror went momentarily dark before revealing a glossy surface and his own haggard reflection. He placed it on the table and hurriedly returned to Mariselle's side.

Lady Nirella was a good suggestion, he told himself. She would undoubtedly have tried every possible solution to bring Mariselle's grandfather back after he fell into his dream state. She would know something that could help.

What he tried *not* to think of was the fact that she lived on the far side of Bloomhaven.

Evryn dragged the room's only chair to the bedside. He took Mariselle's hand in his—her hand that bore shimmering silver patterns and no bruising —and traced his thumb over her knuckles. "Please wake up," he whispered again. "I love you. I need you. The world would be a darker place without your bold laugh and your determined spirit and your gloriously vivid imagination." He clenched his jaw and blinked back tears. "Please. Just wake up."

She remained still, her chest rising and falling in slow rhythm.

"Your grandmother is coming," he continued. "She'll know what to do."

Time stretched, elastic and merciless. Evryn paced. He held her hand. He spoke to her. He stood at the wall, his brow and fists pressed to the floral wallpaper, eyes scrunched shut as he screamed silently, never having felt more useless in his life.

But as the minutes ticked by with no change, desperation clawed at him with increasing ferocity. Where was Lady Nirella? Had Petunia's message reached her? What if she arrived too late?

He found himself on his feet yet again, pacing the small room, unable to contain the restless energy of fear. Every few circuits, he would return to Mariselle's side, checking her pulse, her breathing, before resuming his agitated movement.

The night deepened outside the cottage windows, and Evryn's control began to fracture. His mask of barely maintained composure splintered with each passing moment. He found himself in the main room again, his gaze falling on the window seat where he'd once sat peacefully writing, what felt like a lifetime ago.

He crossed to it, bracing his hands against the windowsill, staring out at the darkness. Tangled vines framed the view, their golden edges shimmering faintly. "Help me," he whispered, his voice breaking on the words. "Help me, help me, help me. I can't lose her." His forehead pressed against the cool glass as tears finally escaped, trailing down his cheeks. "Please, I can't lose her."

The admission tore from him with raw honesty. He knew he loved her, but he felt it now with a certainty that eclipsed all other truths he'd ever known, as essential to his being as breath or heartbeat. She was fire and steel and tender vulnerability intertwined in a singular spirit, and the thought of that brilliant light being extinguished was unbearable.

He pushed away from the window, wiping roughly at his face with his sleeve. Breaking down would not help Mariselle.

So he returned to her side.

And time passed.

He could not say how long it had been when he heard the sound of approaching footsteps outside the cottage. His heart lurched, hope surging through him so violently it was almost painful.

Finally. Lady Nirella had arrived.

Evryn launched out of the chair and back into the main room. He crossed it with long strides, wrenching the door open before the visitor could knock.

"Thank the stars you're—"

But the words died in his throat.

For standing on the threshold, her silver hair gleaming in the moonlight, was not Mariselle's grandmother, but his own.

Chapter Twenty-Eight

"WHAT ... HOW DID YOU ..." EVRYN'S WORDS DISSOLVED INTO stunned silence as he stared at his grandmother's face. Her usually immaculate appearance was notably disheveled—silver hair hastily gathered into a loose braid that hung over one shoulder, and her voluminous plum-colored cloak covering what could only be a nightdress beneath. She must have left home in great haste.

His mind struggled to reconcile her unexpected presence with the desperate hope he'd been clinging to for Lady Nirella's arrival. At the same time, a childlike sense of relief washed over him. His grandmother had always been the immovable pillar of their family, the one who could mend any situation with a sharp word or a decisive action. Perhaps she could fix this too.

Lady Rivenna remained on the threshold, her gaze drifting past Evryn with a peculiar hesitancy, an almost reverent disbelief, as though she couldn't quite accept that she was standing at this particular doorway. When she finally looked at him, her expression remained distracted, distant.

"You ... called," she said simply.

"What?"

"Never mind." The familiar briskness returned to her manner as she stepped past him into the cottage, her posture straightening with resolve. "What has happened, my boy? I sensed you're in great distress."

Evryn blinked, momentarily bewildered by this revelation as he shut the door and faced her. "But … how?"

The question hung between them for only a moment before Evryn's mind leaped back to what truly mattered: Mariselle. Lying unconscious. Each passing moment potentially pulling her deeper into the dream realm.

"It's Mariselle," he said, his voice breaking slightly. "She's—"

"Are the two of you *alone* here?" his grandmother demanded, her voice rising sharply.

"That is beside the point!" Evryn shouted, the strain of the night's events cracking through his veneer of composure. "She is unconscious! She has exhausted her magic, and I can't wake her!"

Without waiting for his grandmother's response, he turned and strode toward the bedroom. Lady Rivenna followed, and as Evryn swiveled in the doorway to look back at her, he caught her keen eyes sweeping over the window seat, the table, the scattered notes and books, the dream core sitting on the rug.

An image of the teacups with painted names on the side came to mind, and he had to remind himself that this was not the first time his grandmother was visiting this cottage. In fact, it was entirely possible she was more familiar with this space than he was.

Rivenna paused beside him in the doorway, her breath catching as she took in Mariselle's still form on the bed.

"What happened?" she asked, her voice quieter now.

"She's been enchanting the dream core. Pouring all her magic into it. She's an architect, Grandmother. A dream architect. Capable of incredible magic." He couldn't help the pride that slipped into his voice as he said this. "But she pushed herself too far this evening, and she collapsed, and now—"

The cottage door swung open behind them, cutting off Evryn's explanation. He turned to see Lady Nirella Brightcrest striding into the cottage, pearl pink hair tumbling from what had clearly been a hasty arrangement, now coming loose from its pins in the same sort of disarray as Lady Rivenna's.

The room went utterly still.

The two grandmothers locked eyes across the space, and something unspoken charged the air between them. Decades of bitterness crystallized in that single shared glance, rendering the space between them both vast and fragile, like too-thin ice over deep water.

"What," Lady Nirella said, her voice dangerously soft, "is going on here?"

Though she stood barely tall enough to reach Evryn's shoulder, Lady Nirella emanated the same formidable presence as his grandmother, her spine iron-straight, her chin lifted in challenge.

"I received an urgent message from my granddaughter Petunia," she continued. "Something about Mariselle being in danger and to come to Windsong Cottage immediately." Her sharp gaze shifted to Evryn. "I assumed I would find Petunia here—not you, Lord Rowanwood. This appears to be the height of impropriety. I hope—"

Her words cut off as her attention caught on the dream core sitting on the rug. Her eyes widened as they traveled over the scattered papers, the open books, the detailed diagrams.

"The contract," she murmured, a note of disbelief in her voice. Her gaze flashed back to Evryn's, then down to his hand where silvery patterns shimmered faintly, and then back up to his face. "The two of you agreed to the contract. This, then, is the true matter at hand."

Lady Rivenna stepped forward. "What contract?"

"The true matter at hand," Evryn said, anxiety welling up inside him again, "is that Mariselle has pushed herself far beyond the boundaries of magical safety, pouring far too much of her power into that dream core. She collapsed, and I cannot wake her. I—I am afraid that what happened to her grandfather has happened to her."

Lady Nirella strode forward and brushed past them both, directing a loaded look at Rivenna as she said, "What happened to Krenshaw was entirely different." She hurried to Mariselle's side and took her hand. "You both need to leave," she continued without looking up. "I will handle this."

"No." Evryn's response was immediate and uncompromising. "I will not leave her side."

Lady Nirella straightened, her expression transforming into one of such profound affront that one might have thought Evryn had suggested something truly scandalous rather than simply refusing to leave. "You cannot remain here, Lord Rowanwood. It is entirely improper."

"What is *improper*," Evryn said through gritted teeth, barely able to contain his fury now, "is how you have allowed your granddaughter to be treated by her own family. Do you have any notion of what has been happening in that house?"

"Evryn!" his grandmother hissed, her tone carrying a clear warning that even now, even in these extraordinary circumstances, he was expected to address his elders with respect.

"How *dare* you speak to me like that," Lady Nirella said, clearly having the same thoughts as Lady Rivenna. "Mariselle's parents may be firm, they may be somewhat … cold. But there is nothing *improper* going on."

Evryn held her gaze, his voice low with suppressed anger when he said, "So you are aware of the bruises then?"

Lady Nirella went perfectly still, as though someone had replaced her with a statue carved from ice. When she finally spoke, her voice emerged with such glacial coldness that frost might have formed on the windowpanes. *"The what?"*

Evryn gestured toward Mariselle, as if to say, *See for yourself.*

Lady Nirella turned and looked again at her granddaughter. "That … that is …"

"Not from when she collapsed earlier," Evryn said quietly. "That is from whatever happened last night while she was at home."

Lady Nirella's shoulders visibly tightened beneath her traveling cloak, and she drew a deep breath that seemed to physically pain her as it filled her lungs.

"Now please accept that I am not leaving this cottage," Evryn continued, "and focus your energies on finding a solution that will bring Lady Mariselle back to us, rather than wasting precious moments on propriety that does not matter in the least in the face of her condition."

"Very well," Lady Nirella said. "You may remain here—in the other room —while I attend to her recovery. And do not despair," she added in a tone that was a fraction gentler. "Her condition, while grave, bears little resemblance to what befell her grandfather. What you witness now is the consequence of magical depletion, a serious matter to be certain, but not the irreversible entrapment that claimed Krenshaw's mind." She cut another glance at Rivenna when she said this.

"Oh thank the stars," Evryn breathed, pressing a shaking hand to his brow.

"If I recall correctly, this cottage houses Lady Eugenia Glendell's complete collection of journals, and within those pages, I am confident we shall discover the precise treatment required to restore her."

"If I may," Lady Rivenna said stiffly. "I believe I remember which of the journals might contain something of use."

Lady Nirella's head snapped up. "I have no intention of allowing you anywhere near my granddaughter's recovery. Your assistance is neither required nor welcome."

"Are you *quite* serious?" Evryn exploded, frustration and fear finally reaching their breaking point. "Will you truly allow ancient grievances to dictate your actions when Mariselle's consciousness hangs in the balance? Can you not set aside your pride and mutual antipathy for a single evening and *work together to help her?*"

His shout reverberated through the small room, leaving a ringing silence in its wake. The two grandmothers stared at him, identical expressions of shock on their faces.

Lady Nirella was the first to recover. "Very well," she said, the words clearly costing her. She looked at Lady Rivenna with obvious reluctance. "Which journal are you referring to?"

"If you would be so gracious as to permit me a few moments at the bookshelf," Lady Rivenna replied, every syllable dripping with condescension, "I'm sure I can locate it without difficulty. I … may have employed one of the remedies myself. Years ago, after excessive magical expenditure, when I was —" She paused, her expression flickering with something unreadable, as though the words carried a weight only she and Nirella could fully comprehend. "When I was first working on the many enchantments that would ultimately be woven into The Charmed Leaf Tea House."

Lady Nirella regarded her warily for a moment before giving a curt nod. "Show me. Please," she added, the word emerging from her lips with such evident strain that Evryn was reminded of the first time he'd forced himself to utter the words 'I apologize' to Mariselle. That was the first night they had begun their work here together. How long ago it seemed now.

The two women moved toward the door, an uneasy—and most likely temporary—truce forming between them as they stepped into the main part of the cottage.

Evryn crossed the room to Mariselle's side, lowered himself to the edge of the chair, and took her hand. His thumb traced over the swirling patterns that marked her skin, and he lifted her hand to his lips, pressing a gentle kiss against the side of her wrist. The mark that had begun as their elaborate deception had transformed into something that felt genuine and significant, a visible symbol of the very real bond that now existed between them.

Beyond the bedroom, the cottage filled with the soft murmur of voices as the grandmothers searched through Lady Eugenia's journals, their years of animosity temporarily set aside in service to something more important.

Chapter Twenty-Nine

Mariselle drifted toward consciousness on a gentle current, the familiar weight of dreams gradually lifting as morning light painted gold across her eyelids and awareness filtered in. She registered sensations one by one—the softness of worn cotton beneath her cheek, the distant chirping of birds, and most curiously, the steady rhythm of someone else's breathing very close to her own.

She opened her eyes slowly, the world resolving itself in gentle increments, and found herself looking at Evryn's sleeping face mere inches from hers. His features were softened, and he had one arm curled beneath his head while the other lay outstretched toward her on the coverlet. For one disorienting moment, she couldn't reconcile where they were or how they'd come to be lying so close together, but a single startling thought filled her mind with perfect clarity—that she would happily wake to this sight every morning for the remainder of her days.

And then she remembered.

Her parents. Being confined to Brightcrest Manor. Pouring so much of herself into the dream core. Shouting at Evryn. The room tilting in a frightening and dizzying way.

Her heart pattered faster for several moments, clouds attempting to gather at the edges of her mind, but she surrendered to the sweet haziness of leftover sleep, comforted by the simple fact that Evryn was near.

After another minute or so, he stirred. His eyelids fluttered open drowsily, blinking several times as though filtering reality from dreams, until his gaze finally landed on her. Their eyes met.

"You're awake," he breathed, the words escaping him like a prayer he hadn't dared offer aloud.

"I am." A small, tired smile tugged at her lips. "You're lying beside me."

His mouth curved. "Astute as ever."

She would have teased him, but her voice caught on the next breath. There was something raw in his gaze as it traveled her face. Something that made her pulse stutter.

Softly, almost reverently, he reached toward her and brushed a strand of hair away from her temple. "Darling," he murmured, the word barely more than air, "your hair is golden again."

"Oh." She managed a faint smile. "I'm sorry. I know you preferred the blue."

Evryn let out a shaky breath, his expression twisting in a way that made her chest ache. "It does not matter to me what color your hair is," he said, emotion thick in his voice. "I love you regardless. If I am granted nothing else in this life but the chance to show you, every single day, how utterly, unconditionally, and completely you are loved for exactly who you are, then I will count myself the most fortunate man in all the realms. You, Mariselle Brightcrest, are treasured beyond measure."

Her breath caught as his words settled into places within her heart that had always stood empty. Tears gathered, silver and bright, and she pressed her trembling lips together.

Utterly and unconditionally.

Treasured beyond measure.

And then her mind caught on another three words: *Every single day.*

"Evryn Rowanwood," she managed to whisper. "Are you asking me to marry you?"

An uncharacteristic vulnerability wavered in his eyes. "Yes."

Her smile stretched wider despite the lump in her throat.

"Don't worry, this isn't the official moment," he added. "I have a whole production planned. You know how I excel at performance."

"Oh, I have no doubt. Will it involve magically multiplying floral arrangements?"

"Of course. At least a dozen varieties."

"And dreadful poetry?"

"The very worst. I know how much it delights you."

She let out a quiet laugh, and the sound seemed to soften something in him. He reached for her hand, his fingers entwining with hers as if it was the most natural thing in the world. "I mean it," he said, his voice dropping to a husky timbre that sent warmth cascading through her veins. "I fully intend to go down on one knee, and I am fully prepared to do it right now, no flowers, no poetry, no pageantry—"

"No." She reached for his sleeve, fingers curling to stop him as he began to shift. "I find I rather like you exactly where you are. Lying right here beside me."

He stilled, then leaned in a fraction closer, the ghost of a smile on his lips. "Mariselle Brightcrest," he said in a low and scandalized tone, "how delightfully improper of you."

"It's what we're known for, isn't it?" she murmured, voice hushed.

They lay there for a long moment, breathing in the hush that had settled between them, hearts thrumming in time, fingers tracing slow, gentle patterns across each other's palms.

"You scared me," Evryn whispered, eyes never leaving hers. "You terrified me. No, you very nearly unmade me. I thought I might never see your beautiful smile again or hear your laugh."

She shook her head, bit her lip, trying not to give in to the emotion that threatened to overwhelm her. "I'm so sorry. I should not have pushed myself that far. I couldn't see how close I was to the edge until I was already falling. I was so desperate to finish. Desperate to …" She shrugged, her shoulder pressing into the mattress. "I wanted to achieve something of my own before my family takes possession of my magic."

And speaking of her family …

"Evryn," she whispered, her heart sinking as the terrible confrontation with her parents surfaced in her mind. Had she really allowed the dreamy haze of sleep to lull her into thinking that any of this could be possible? "My family will never—"

"Your family will not be a problem."

"Evryn, unless the very foundations of the earth have shifted beneath our feet since yesterday, nothing has changed to suggest that my parents might—"

"Mariselle?"

The voice came from the next room, and Evryn scrambled off the bed so fast, Mariselle could have sworn it had caught fire beneath him. He knocked the chair over, caught it, righted it, then almost stumbled into the wall.

Mariselle sat up. "Was that … my grandmother?"

Before Evryn could answer, Lady Nirella Brightcrest herself appeared in the doorway, draped in a traveling cloak over what appeared to be a night-gown. Her hair—which Mariselle had never seen in anything but an impeccable arrangement—tumbled in disarray around her shoulders. Despite this unprecedented state of dishevelment, she carried herself with the same rigid posture she might display at a formal reception at Solstice Hall.

Her sharp eyes took in the scene—Mariselle sitting up on the bed, Evryn standing awkwardly by the wall as though he'd been magnetically propelled there—and her lips betrayed the faintest of quirks.

"I see Lord Rowanwood possesses the reflexes of a startled hare," she remarked dryly. "How fortunate, as it spares me the effort of reminding him about proper distances between unmarried young people."

"Grandmother," Mariselle breathed, still struggling to reconcile this version of Lady Nirella with the immaculate figure she'd known all her life. "What are you doing here? How did you—"

"I received an urgent message last night regarding your condition," Lady Nirella replied, moving into the room. "Though I'm relieved to see you've recovered." Her gaze slid to Evryn, who appeared to be attempting to blend into the wall. "No doubt thanks to the remedy that Venna—" She caught herself with a loud cough and immediately forged on. "That Lady Rivenna and I prepared."

"Lady Rivenna?" Mariselle echoed, feeling as though she'd awakened in an entirely different reality than the one she'd left.

"Yes," her grandmother confirmed, her tone suggesting this was merely a minor inconvenience rather than an earth-shattering development. "She is presently asleep on the window seat, while I managed a few hours on the sofa. Not the most comfortable arrangements, but needs must when dealing with magical exhaustion."

Mariselle swung her legs over the edge of the bed. "I don't understand. How did you both—"

"It seems you and Lord Rowanwood agreed to fulfill the Dreamland restoration contract," Lady Nirella cut in. "A fact I might have appreciated knowing before discovering you unconscious from magical depletion. I believe it is time for the two of us to return home—*my* home, not Brightcrest Manor—where we may discuss the implications of this in private."

Mariselle's head spun with everything that was happening. Her limbs were still heavy from sleep, her mind still trying to reconcile the presence of both grandmothers in this cottage, and her heart still processing a proposal. Evryn Rowanwood wanted to marry her! And now she was simply expected to … leave?

"Would someone kindly explain what this mysterious contract is that everyone except myself seems so intimately acquainted with?" Lady Rivenna's irritated voice carried from beyond Nirella. As Mariselle peered around her grandmother, she spied Lady Rivenna standing in the adjacent room, similarly disheveled, with arms crossed firmly over her chest. She wondered briefly if this was the first time the formidable proprietress of The Charmed Leaf was *not* the first to be privy to the machinations occurring within her own family circle.

"Let me explain," Evryn said with a sigh, walking out of the room.

After a brief hesitation, Lady Nirella inclined her head, signaling that she and Mariselle should follow.

"Lady Mariselle and I discovered this cottage during one of our—" Evryn paused, clearing his throat, "—nighttime excursions."

Both grandmothers' eyebrows shot up in perfect synchronization.

"We were racing each other on pegasi," he clarified hastily.

At this, they looked even more horrified.

"I suppose that explains the unconventional choice of attire," Lady Nirella muttered, eyeing Evryn's riding gear with distaste.

"In any case, we found ourselves here, at Windsong Cottage. When our hands touched the door—Mariselle's was cut, mine scraped—the door opened, and we discovered a contract inside. A binding magical agreement stipulating that Dreamland would remain sealed until heirs of both families willingly consented to its restoration. The contract clearly stated that the signatories' blood would activate it when freely given alongside a sworn oath."

"And you both … what? Accidentally swore an oath?" Lady Rivenna asked incredulously.

"Uh, yes. In the heat of argument. As one does."

Lady Rivenna shook her head, muttering something that included the word 'fools.'

"This contract," Evryn added with a pointed look at Mariselle's grandmother, "was signed by Nirella Brightcrest and Valenrik Rowanwood."

At the mention of these two names, Lady Rivenna's gaze shot instantly to Lady Nirella, her eyes filling with betrayal. "You drew up this contract with my husband, and neither of you ever bothered to mention it me?"

"You and I were not exactly speaking to one another, were we?" Lady Nirella said primly.

"I cannot imagine what Rik's excuse was," Lady Rivenna muttered, directing her look of betrayal at the oak table now.

"I always wondered if he told you about it," Mariselle's grandmother said softly. "If it's any consolation, I don't think either of us believed that any Brightcrest and Rowanwood heir would ever agree to it." Her gaze shifted back to Mariselle then. "And I should note that we did not specify the exact nature of the binding mark. Curious that it should take the particular pattern it took."

"Indeed." Lady Rivenna crossed her arms and directed her gaze at her grandson. "So this 'soulbond' the two of you claimed to have suddenly developed—this 'love' you apparently have for one another—is all a complete lie?"

"No!" Mariselle and Evryn blurted out at the same time, their eyes immediately finding one another across the room.

"Well, it was at first," Mariselle corrected. "But … things have changed."

Evryn gave her a small smile. "Things have most certainly changed."

Lady Rivenna groaned with dramatic distaste. Then she rolled her shoulders, straightened, and very firmly said, "Evryn, it is time we left."

Mariselle watched as Evryn faced his grandmother and very simply said, "No."

Lady Rivenna blinked, then fixed him with a glare that could have silenced an entire flock of gossip birds. "Evryn."

"More than five decades, Grandmother. More than *fifty years*." Evryn's gaze slid to Lady Nirella, then back to his grandmother. "Have you not hated each other for long enough?"

Lady Nirella drew herself up. "You do not know what you speak of—"

"Then tell us!" he roared, throwing his hands up. "All these cryptic statements, these vague allusions. We are the ones who bear the weight of your hatred. A feud whose origins remain shrouded in secrecy while its poison continues to shape our lives!"

Lady Nirella huffed. "Now is not the time. Mariselle is still recovering, and we—"

"I'm perfectly fine, Grandmother," Mariselle said quietly, "and I shall remain here until this matter is thoroughly resolved."

"You will do no such thing," her grandmother told her. "You and I—"

"I LOVE HER!" Evryn burst out. "Do neither of you understand that?" He turned his desperate gaze toward Lady Rivenna. "Grandmother, *I love her*. She and I *will* have a future together, and we would very much like it if both our families could be part of that future."

Silence descended. Mariselle's heart thrummed as Evryn's words rang in her ears.

I love her.

She and I will *have a future together.*

But the two grandmothers stood rigid, their gazes fixed on anything but each other, the weight of decades pressing down upon all of them like a physical force.

"You were friends," Mariselle said quietly, and the look that shot instantly between her grandmother and Lady Rivenna told her that her guess was right. "Close friends," she added. "That's why there is so much hurt here. The deepest wounds can only be inflicted by those we hold dear."

Another silence fell as the two grandmothers regarded each other, something unspoken passing between them.

"Perhaps," Lady Nirella said carefully, "it is time certain truths were told."

Lady Rivenna's expression remained impassive, but she gave a single, terse nod. "Very well."

Chapter Thirty

MARISELLE WATCHED AS RIVENNA MOVED TOWARD THE WINDOW SEAT, her hands clasped tightly in front of her, while her own grandmother settled on the edge of the sofa, arms crossed defensively over her chest. The tension between them was almost tangible, a delicate spiderweb stretching across the room, decades of hurt and anger woven into its threads.

Mariselle looked at Evryn, her heart suddenly pounding oddly in her chest. He inclined his head toward the armchairs, and she moved to sit beside him.

"Where do we begin?" Rivenna asked quietly.

"With Seravine," Nirella replied, her voice sharp with old pain. "It all began with her."

"Sera," Mariselle murmured. "The teacup labels," she added in a whisper to Evryn. He nodded.

"Lady Seravine Bluebell," Rivenna said without turning from the window. "She was a childhood friend of mine. The Bloom Season had just begun and I … I invited her to Bloomhaven. Her first Season here." Her shoulders sagged slightly, and there was something in that small gesture that spoke of decades of guilt.

"Krenshaw and your Great-Uncle Thaelan had built Dreamland into something magnificent," Nirella continued, nodding at Evryn when she mentioned Thaelan. "It all began in this little cottage, and even though it had grown into so much more, we still met here regularly. Krenshaw and I, Rivenna and Valenrik—newly married—and Thaelan. We were close."

"And then … Seravine," Rivenna sighed. She turned away from the window and joined them in the sitting area, settling into a seat across from Nirella.

"Thaelan was immediately captivated by her," Nirella continued. "Do you remember how he would craft tiny lumyrite sculptures of whatever caught her eye during their walks?"

Rivenna nodded, a ghost of a smile crossing her lips before it disappeared. Mariselle's mind immediately conjured an image of the tiny lumyrite pegasus Evryn had fashioned for her. The realization that he had unknowingly echoed his great-uncle's romantic gesture sent a strange shiver through her, as though their present was somehow echoing the past.

"He courted her earnestly," Nirella continued. "Showed her all of Dreamland's wonders. He was so hopeful. But Krenshaw … my *husband* …"

Mariselle watched as her grandmother bit her lip, a sheen of tears forming across her eyes. The sight was so foreign, so utterly at odds with the composed, formidable figure Mariselle knew, that she felt momentarily unmoored.

"Krenshaw and Nirella were married," Rivenna continued, her tone careful, as if she were treading on glass that might splinter. "They had two children. From the outside their life appeared perfect. But …"

Rivenna trailed off, her eyes on Nirella, and it seemed to Mariselle that she was giving Nirella the space to continue. This was her part of the story, after all. Nirella inhaled deeply before continuing. "Our marriage had grown distant," she said stiffly, "and Seravine began a dangerous game."

Mariselle felt her heart begin to race faster. She could sense where this was leading, and it filled her with dread.

"She encouraged Thaelan's affections while secretly … pursuing Krenshaw."

"She manipulated them both," Rivenna said, bitterness evident in her tone. "Using their friendship against them."

Evryn leaned forward. "What happened?"

"Thaelan discovered them," Nirella said simply. "He followed Seravine one evening and witnessed … an intimate exchange between her and Krenshaw in a private corner of Dreamland."

Mariselle's breath caught. "Oh."

"The betrayal destroyed him," Rivenna said quietly. "Rik and I both watched it happen. Not just Seravine's duplicity, but the violation of trust from his closest friend. Thaelan and Krenshaw had been so close—best friends, business partners."

"There was a confrontation," Nirella continued, "one evening when the six of us ended up in a private space inside Dreamland together. Thaelan confronted Krenshaw with what he had discovered. They argued—violently. Seravine tried to intervene, to explain away what Thaelan had seen, but her words only made everything worse."

"They fought," Mariselle said quietly, understanding beginning to dawn.

"With magic," Lady Nirella confirmed. "Within the dream space itself. It was … catastrophic." Her voice shook slightly. "Krenshaw used magic that was only meant to incapacitate, but instead it created a rift that pulled Thaelan into the raw dream realm."

"It killed him instantly," Rivenna whispered. Her gaze lifted and settled on Nirella with cold finality. "Krenshaw Brightcrest killed Thaelan Rowanwood."

"It was an accident!" Nirella cried, emotion thick in her voice. "And he tried to save Thaelan! He tried to pull him back but only succeeded in partially pulling himself into the dream realm instead."

Mariselle raised a shaking hand to her lips. "Is that … is that how Grandfather ended up trapped in slumber? And that's … that's what truly caused Dreamland's magic to fail?"

Her grandmother nodded, her gaze still fixed on Lady Rivenna. "And none of it would have happened if Seravine Bluebell had never been invited to Bloomhaven."

"*You* encouraged the duel that night!" Rivenna hissed.

"I did not! And if I had—what of it? Everything had already spun wildly out of control by then!"

"Stop," Evryn said, his voice cutting through their rising anger. "Let me understand this clearly," he continued. "This decades-long feud, this poison that has infected both our families for generations, stems from a tragic accident involving a woman who isn't even present. Have either of you directed even a fraction of this animosity toward the person who actually stood at the center of this conflict?"

The answer hung in the silence that followed, as clear and damning as if they had spoken it aloud. Decades of blame had flowed between these two women, yet none had been reserved for the one who had sparked the tragedy.

"She left," Rivenna finally said. "The very next day. Without a word to any of us."

"You could have supported each other through your grief," Mariselle said quietly, "instead of distancing yourselves from each other."

"If there was any distancing to be done, *she* mastered the art of it," Rivenna said, directing a tilt of her head toward Mariselle's grandmother.

"How dare you suggest I withdrew without cause!" Nirella exclaimed, her voice rising with decades of pent-up anguish. "You had *everything*—your husband, your tea house, your standing in society, which only continued to grow! While I was left with nothing but ruins and a husband lost to the dream realm!"

"But … why did that keep you from coming to me?" Rivenna asked, brows pulling together. "I wanted to reach out to you. You were the one who made it all but impossible!"

"*I* made it impossible? *Your family* was the first to start spreading rumors about the entire incident that were entirely untrue."

"My—" Rivenna looked outraged. "It was the *Brightcrests* who first—"

"Please!" Mariselle interrupted, loudly enough to be heard over the two of them. "You have already missed out on more than fifty years' worth of friendship. If you were truly once friends, if you truly both wished to bridge the gap that began to grow between you after this tragedy, then perhaps now is the time to stop fighting."

The two grandmothers fell silent, their gazes locked across the space between them. Something shifted in that shared look—a softening around the edges where decades of rigid animosity had calcified. Nirella's chin trembled almost imperceptibly, while Rivenna's fingers twisted together in her lap. Neither spoke, but tears gathered in both their eyes as they watched each other.

There was recognition in that silence, a mutual acknowledgment that beneath the layers of hurt and blame, something of their former connection remained. Weathered and scarred, but not entirely destroyed.

"Perhaps, Rella," Rivenna said quietly, "your granddaughter is right. Perhaps it is time we stop passing down our pain."

Nirella took in a shuddering breath before nodding slowly. "Perhaps it is time to let our grandchildren build something better than what we destroyed. And perhaps … perhaps it is time to admit that I have missed you."

A soft, tremulous inhale broke the quiet, and Mariselle watched in astonishment as a single tear traced its way down Rivenna's cheek. She was convinced this was the only room in all the United Fae Isles to ever have witnessed such vulnerability from the indomitable woman.

And then, in a moment that would have sent shockwaves through all of Bloomhaven society and caused an epidemic of disoriented gossip birds to plummet from the sky in collective astonishment, Rivenna Rowanwood and Nirella Brightcrest rose from their seats, crossed the small space between them, and embraced.

Mariselle and Evryn embraced too, of course, which was followed by both grandmothers clearing their throats in perfect unison and informing them with renewed authority that while certain ancient grudges might be laid to rest, propriety certainly had not been.

Lady Nirella added pointedly that she expected to see at least a full arm's length of space between them at all times until proper vows had been exchanged. At that, Mariselle had pressed her lips together to suppress her smile and taken an exaggeratedly large side-step away from Evryn, who promptly measured the distance with his hand as if to verify its adequacy.

And then, before anyone could enjoy the moment too much, the Brightcrests had arrived.

Evryn had been at the door the instant they realized exactly who was approaching the cottage—thanks to Mariselle's mother shrieking her name while she and Lord Brightcrest were still some distance from the building. But Mariselle had caught Evryn's arm and given him a pleading look, stopping him before he could charge outside and do something ridiculously heroic like challenge her father to a duel (though there was a part of Mariselle that would have enjoyed witnessing this; Evryn, undoubtedly, would have won).

Now Mariselle stood outside Windsong Cottage, her grandmother at her side who, despite her disheveled appearance, still managed to project such formidable authority that even the morning breeze seemed to hesitate before disturbing the folds of her traveling cloak.

Lord and Lady Brightcrest picked their way through the brambles with visible distaste. Their enchanted carriage waited in the distance, gleaming in the morning light. As they approached the edge of the clearing where the cottage's garden path began, they paused, taking in the scene before them with evident displeasure.

"Mother," Lord Brightcrest acknowledged Lady Nirella with a stiff nod before his gaze settled on Mariselle. "I see you've managed to escape your confinement. How predictable." His tone carried the same cold dismissal she'd grown accustomed to, but for the first time, Mariselle felt it glance off her rather than pierce through.

"We've come to collect our daughter," Lady Clemenbell announced, chin lifted as though she were addressing servants rather than family. "The procedure to remove that … mark … is scheduled for this afternoon."

Lady Nirella stepped forward. "My granddaughter will not be accompanying you anywhere."

"I beg your pardon?" Lord Brightcrest's brows shot up. "She is our daughter, and she—"

"She is a woman who has been subjected to unconscionable treatment under your care," Lady Nirella cut in, her voice dropping to a dangerous pitch, and Mariselle realized that Evryn must have told her grandmother what he guessed had happened. "A fact that will be addressed separately. For now, understand this: Mariselle's affairs no longer concern you. She will be residing with me from this day forward."

A bright, unexpected warmth bloomed inside Mariselle's chest at these words—the first she'd heard of such an arrangement. The prospect of living with her grandmother suddenly seemed like the most wonderful gift, a sanctuary she hadn't dared hope for. Well, perhaps not quite as wonderful as waking beside Evryn every morning would be, but that particular joy would have to wait until proper vows had been exchanged and the grandmothers' strict rules about 'arm's length' no longer applied.

Lady Brightcrest gave a dismissive laugh. "This is absurd. You cannot simply—"

"Of course I can," Lady Nirella replied, ice coating each syllable. "I may have failed in my duty to protect her before now, but that ends today."

Lord Brightcrest's jaw worked from side to side, muscles tensing beneath his skin as he visibly struggled to maintain his composure. "Do you understand what a disappointment you're inheriting? This sudden claim of dream architect abilities—how convenient that she waited until now to reveal this magic. And even if it were true, she lacks the discipline to harness such power properly." His gaze flicked contemptuously to the side, toward where Dreamland lay, its skeletal structure fully restored. "This childish fantasy will collapse like a house of cards the moment anyone with actual discernment examines it. She simply doesn't possess the capability."

Indignation burned through Mariselle's veins. She took a step forward and stood beside her grandmother. "I've been inside, Father. I most certainly do possess the capability to bring this so-called 'childish fantasy' back to life."

Her father made a dismissive sound, and Mariselle's grandmother shook her head. "How embarrassing it must be to have so vastly underestimated your own daughter. It seems you have not the faintest idea what she's capable of."

"I am entirely—"

"I will not be returning to Brightcrest Manor," Mariselle interrupted firmly, meeting her father's gaze directly.

His face darkened with rage. "You ungrateful—"

"Enough!" Lady Nirella's voice cracked like thunder. "One more word against my granddaughter, and I shall ensure that every social door in Bloomhaven closes to you both for the remainder of the Season." She swept her gaze between them. "I may have spent decades avoiding certain social circles, but I now find myself in the renewed friendship of someone whose whisper can determine whether you receive invitations or polite regrets for the remainder of your lives."

Something shifted in Lord Brightcrest's expression. A flicker of calculation replacing the anger. "This discussion is not over," he said finally, though the fight had gone out of his voice.

"On the contrary," Mariselle replied, feeling a strength she'd never known in the presence of her parents. "It is very much over."

She watched as her parents retreated, her mother casting one last contemptuous glance over her shoulder before they disappeared into their carriage. As the conveyance pulled away, Mariselle breathed in deeply, and it felt as though invisible bindings had been loosened from her chest after years of gradual tightening.

Her grandmother's hand found hers, squeezing gently. "You stood your ground admirably," she said, a note of pride warming her voice. "Now, I should very much like to hear what you've managed so far with this Dreamland restoration project. I find myself quite excited at the prospect of experiencing its wonders again."

Mariselle faced her grandmother as a grin spread across her lips. "Truly? You'll help us?"

"My dear, was I not the Brightcrest who signed the original contract?" Light sparkled in her grandmother's eyes as she smiled. "If anyone has hope of Dreamland one day being restored to its former glory, it is surely I."

Evryn turned away from the window, forcibly tamping down the surge of protective rage that demanded he march outside and deliver to Lord Brightcrest the same treatment he'd inflicted upon Mariselle. Instead, he faced his grandmother, reminding himself that Mariselle stood with Lady Nirella now —an unyielding guardian whose steel had only just begun to reveal itself.

Lady Rivenna sat motionless in the armchair, her hands resting lightly on its worn upholstery. The commanding woman who typically filled any space with her authoritative presence seemed momentarily diminished, her gaze fixed on some invisible point, her thoughts clearly adrift in the currents of long-buried memories.

"How did you know to come?" Evryn asked her.

Lady Rivenna looked up, her expression clearing as she focused on Evryn. She gave him a small smile before her gaze swept to the window seat that overlooked the cottage garden. "There is a connection between this cottage and The Charmed Leaf." She rose and moved to the window, her fingers tracing the edge of a vine that curled along the sill, its leaves rimmed with a delicate border of gold.

"Do you see these?" she asked. "The very same vines now cover the walls of The Charmed Leaf, though they've grown considerably since their humble beginnings. Nirella gifted the first cutting to me shortly after Valenrik and I were married. She had developed quite the fascination with Lady Eugenia's botanical journals and the remarkable specimens cultivated here." Her fingers continued their gentle exploration of the vine. Then she turned to face him.

"When you called out in distress last night, it wasn't precisely me who heard you. It was the tea house. It seems the vines maintained their connection to their origin—a fact I was not aware of until last night when the tea house, sensing your desperation, alerted me to your need for help with such urgency that I departed without a second thought."

Evryn momentarily set aside the unsettling notion that The Charmed Leaf possessed some form of consciousness capable of 'alerting' its proprietress—a matter to be pondered at a later time. Instead, his attention caught on the words *without a second thought.*

The phrase settled inside him with unexpected weight. All his life, he'd positioned himself as the redundant second son, the amusing but inconsequential spare heir, forever orbiting the periphery of his grandmother's regard while Jasvian stood firmly at its center. He'd built an elaborate fortress of nonchalance around this belief, fortifying it with each perceived slight, each unintended oversight.

Yet here was his grandmother, her hair in disarray, her nightgown still visible beneath her hastily donned cloak, having abandoned all sense of propriety and decorum upon discovering his distress. She hadn't paused to weigh his importance against other considerations or to question whether his troubles warranted her immediate attention.

She had simply come.

"There is something else I must confess, Evryn," Lady Rivenna said, turning away from the vines and lowering herself onto the cushions of the window seat. "I saw this coming."

Evryn blinked. "What, Mariselle's collapse?" At the stern look from his grandmother, he hastily corrected himself. "*Lady* Mariselle."

His grandmother's gaze grew distant once more, traveling across the room. "No. I saw ..." She sighed. "A reconciliation. Of significant proportions. The specifics were hazy to me, but the moment you made your announcement about that supposed 'soulbond' and your engagement to Lady Mariselle, I knew. Iris knew it too. In fact, what she saw was a lot clearer than what I saw."

Evryn found himself nodding slowly. "I recall the two of you exchanging a loaded look the moment I announced the engagement. I presume you've taught her your tea leaf reading ways."

A small smile quirked his grandmother's lips. "I have, though she has her own methods of seeing … possibilities."

"Yet you still refused to support the match the moment you heard about it," Evryn pointed out. "Why?"

"Nothing is written in stone, my dear boy," she replied, her tone suggesting he'd missed something elementary despite never having been invited to decipher so much as a single tea leaf in his life. "What I glimpse are merely possibilities—doorways that may open before a person's path. And I could not bear the thought of our family being joined to the Brightcrests after all this time, so I was determined you would choose a different door.

"Besides, I believed Lady Mariselle to be cut from the same cloth as her parents—selfish, manipulative, cold. She seemed the worst possible match for someone with your warmth and spirit." His grandmother's expression softened. "Beyond that, the idea of ancient magic forcing you into a union—even had it been with someone other than a Brightcrest—was something I did not feel comfortable supporting. Love should come from choice, not compulsion."

She smiled then, a smile that was genuine and warm, and rose from the window seat. She crossed to where Evryn stood, took his hands in hers, and gave them a firm squeeze. "It brings me comfort to know that what exists between the two of you now has blossomed from your own hearts, not from any magic that would bind you against your will. And I must say," she added with a spark of mischief dancing in her eyes, "I'm beginning to think I rather like Lady Mariselle."

Chapter Thirty-One

MARISELLE RETURNED TO THE COTTAGE WITH LADY NIRELLA, AND THE moment the grandmothers disappeared into the kitchen with promises of a 'proper tea, not whatever passes for refreshment in this abandoned cottage,' Evryn caught her eye with a meaningful glance toward the garden door.

"Sneak outside with me?" he whispered to her, stacking several books with exaggerated care while Lady Rivenna's voice drifted from the kitchen.

Mariselle bit her lip to suppress a smile, dutifully rearranging papers until the clink of cups and saucers suggested their grandmothers were thoroughly occupied. With a quick nod from Evryn, they slipped out the garden door and into the dappled sunlight that filtered through the canopy of trees surrounding Windsong Cottage.

They paused for a moment just outside, breathing in the sweet tangle of honeysuckle and wild roses that perfumed the morning air. In the distance, Dreamland stood waiting, no longer a ruin but a monument to possibility.

Freedom. That was what it smelled like, Mariselle thought. Freedom and possibility.

Evryn reached for her hand, his fingers sliding between hers with the easy familiarity of puzzle pieces finding their match.

A bubble of awed laughter suddenly burst from her lips. "They embraced!

Evryn, they *embraced!* They admitted they *missed* one another! If I hadn't witnessed it with my own eyes, I'd never have believed it possible."

"I'm half convinced I never actually woke up this morning," he replied, shaking his head in wonderment. "Perhaps I'm still asleep."

"And my grandmother wants to help with Dreamland," Mariselle added, her smile growing impossibly wider. "She wants us to succeed. She's proud of what we've accomplished."

Evryn squeezed her hand. "Of course she is. I'm beginning to think your grandmother is remarkably similar to mine—rigid as granite on the outside, but underneath, she's essentially a spun-sugar cloud with feelings."

Mariselle's laughter rang out louder at that, and Evryn's grin stretched wider. He tugged gently on her hand. "Come. I want to show you something."

He led her along a narrow path between flowering bushes, his hand warm in hers. They passed a small tree laden with clusters of glossy crimson berries that gleamed like jewels. "Oh, I'm positively famished!" Mariselle exclaimed, reaching out and snagging one as they strolled by.

She had already popped it into her mouth when Evryn turned, his expression shifting quickly from surprise to concern. "Did you just—Mariselle, what if those are poisonous!"

She rolled her eyes, chewed, and swallowed. "They're perfectly safe, you ridiculous man. Though I thank you for your concern. I realize you have precisely zero interest in things of a botanical nature, but I've actually had a look at some of Lady Eugenia's journals. These are laughing rubies. They cause a slight tingling sensation on the tongue that feels like effervescence."

Evryn's eyebrow arched slowly upward, one corner of his mouth lifting in a way that sent heat crawling up her neck. "Effervescence on the tongue? Is that so?"

"It is," she replied, trying to pretend she was entirely unbothered by that look of his. "Would you like to try one?"

"I absolutely would like to try one," he said, his smoldering gaze never leaving hers.

"Of the berries," she clarified with a laugh, then turned and grabbed another one.

She brought it to his mouth, then paused, the air suddenly becoming charged between them. Her heart pattered faster. His eyes held hers as she gently placed the berry between his lips, and she found herself unable to resist tracing the pad of her finger along the soft curve of his lower lip. The slight catch in his breath—a barely audible hitch that revealed his composure wasn't nearly as steady as he pretended—sent a thrill through her.

But then, predictably, his lips curved into that insufferable, irresistible grin. "You just wanted to touch my mouth."

Well, it was true, so why deny it? "Astute as ever," she said with a half smile, echoing his earlier words. She reached for his hand again and added, "Now, what was it you wanted to show me?"

They continued a short distance along the path until they reached a small clearing among the trees. At their feet lay a patch of pale sand. Evryn pointed to it.

"You want to show me … sand?" Mariselle asking, one brow arching.

"Yes. I spotted it from the window."

"How extraordinary," she replied with exaggerated wonder. "I've never before witnessed such remarkable … grains. Is it possible they're enchanted? Perhaps they whisper secrets if one listens closely enough?"

He rolled his eyes, bent closer to her ear, and whispered in that low, honey-warm voice that sent a shiver through her, "Dance with me, darling. You're already barefoot."

Ah. And suddenly the sand made sense.

Evryn's hands found her waist as hers settled naturally on his shoulders, and their bodies drew together with the quiet certainty of two pieces finding their match. His thumb traced a whisper-soft circle at her side as they began to sway, their feet pressing gentle impressions into the sand. As in her dreamscape, this wasn't dancing in any formal sense. It was simply being together in motion, their foreheads nearly touching, breath mingling in the narrow space between them.

His eyes never left hers, as though memorizing each fleck of color in her irises. The world beyond their small circle of sand ceased to exist, contracted to the singular point where they held each other, moving as one.

"Are you preparing to get down on one knee, Evryn Rowanwood?" Mariselle whispered.

His lips stretched up on one side. "I am. How can you tell?"

"I believe I hear the distant whisper of terrible poetry gathering in the air around us, preparing to assault my ears at any moment."

He smiled, shook his head with fond exasperation, and then slowly lowered himself to one knee before her, his eyes never once breaking from hers, as though afraid she might disappear if he looked away even for a moment.

"Mariselle Brightcrest," he said, his voice steady despite the vulnerability in his eyes, "I want to be the one who makes you feel cherished beyond words each day that passes, the one who is there to catch you when you fall. I want to kiss away your tears when you cry and laugh improperly loudly with you when you're happy." He grinned, eyes shining. "The kind of laughter that makes stuffy lords and ladies turn and stare."

She let out a sniffle-laugh, tears of joy gathering in her eyes.

"I want to walk beside you through the landscapes of your dreams, and more than anything, I want to love you, exactly as you are, for as long as you'll let me." He took a breath. "Would you do me the extraordinary honor of becoming my wife?"

Mariselle was quite certain she had never been happier in her life.

In a rush of movement she wasn't fully conscious of initiating, she found herself on her knees in the sand before him, as though her body refused to maintain even that small distance between them. "Yes," she answered, tears brimming in her eyes as she looped her arms around his neck.

His laughter vibrated against her skin as he pressed his face into her neck, though the slight tremor in his voice revealed he was just as overwhelmed as she was. "You're not supposed to kneel too, you impossible woman."

"Well, what did I tell you earlier about liking you right beside me?"

He drew back just enough to smile down at her, one hand rising to gently cradle her face, his thumb tracing the delicate curve beneath her lower lip. "I believe, my dainty destroyer of sanity, it was something scandalous involving a bed."

She snorted. "Dainty destroyer of sanity?"

He rose, pulling her up with him before looping his arms around her waist and lifting her effortlessly. Her feet dangled above the sand, his face tilted up to hers as their eyes met in a moment of suspended delight. "Ambrosial chaos nugget?"

"Oh no."

"Resplendent bog truffle?"

She laughed, bright and bold and unrestrained.

He lowered her gently to the ground. "When you laugh like that, darling," he said huskily, bringing his lips to her neck, "you are my undoing."

"Then I shall make it my life's purpose to laugh every day," she promised. "To undo you repeatedly and thoroughly."

She turned her head just as he lifted his, and finally, *finally* their lips met.

It was not tentative or careful. It was the culmination of every stolen glance across the cottage, every teasing exchange in crowded ballrooms, every maddening brush of fingers and withheld desire. It was a breathless, dizzying surrender—like tumbling off the edge of something vast and wondrous and terrifying, and finding that she did not care at all about the fall.

A quiet gasp caught at the back of her throat as his hand tangled and tightened in her hair, his other hand drawing her firmly against him. And in his embrace, she found herself truly held for perhaps the first time. Secure, safe, beloved in a way she had never dared to imagine possible.

Next in the series ...

Don't miss the third book in this delightfully whimsical series!

Once upon a time, in a land not so far away, a young science graduate named Rachel found that the real world wasn't a place she wanted to inhabit all the time. So she decided to escape into the magical realms that had occupied her mind since childhood.

Armed with a vivid imagination, Rachel spends her days conjuring up fantastical worlds filled with adventure, romance, and plot twists, where readers can escape the real world along with her.

Rachel lives in Cape Town, South Africa, with her husband, two little wildlings, and three fur-babies.